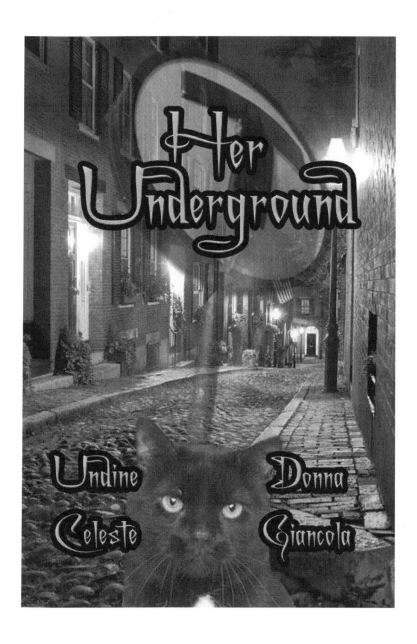

Her Underground

Undine Celeste

Donna Giancola

HER UNDERGROUND

∞

An eco-friendly mystery

Undine Celeste & Donna M. Giancola

Editor in Chief: Nik Morton

Cover Art:
Select-O-Grafix, LLC. www.selectografix.com

Publisher's Note:

This is a work of fiction. All names, characters,
places, and events are the work of the author's imagination.

Any resemblance to real persons, places, or events
is coincidental.

Solstice Publishing - www.solsticepublishing.com

And the formula of the Eleusinian mysteries is as follows:

> *"I fasted;*
> *I drank the draught;*
> *I took from the chest;*
> *having done my task,*
> *I placed in the basket,*
> *and from the basket into the chest."*

Beautiful sights indeed, and fit for a goddess!

~Clement of Alexandria, 3rd century

Prologue

In the beginning there was the Goddess; infinitely vast, holding all things in herself. She was, is and will always be the Creatrix of everything that was, is and will ever be. One day, the Goddess spun a spiral moving within her and out of this spiral gave birth to luminous spirit and physical matter. Their names are countless, but her children have come to be known as god, the father, and mother earth, or the spirit plane and the physical plane. The Goddess then looked upon her children with such happiness and explained that without love nothing perfect would come, that the art and craft of creation is one that must have pure and perfect love. Thus with perfect and pure love came the first children deities of Heaven and Earth: north, east, south and west, also known as earth, air, fire and water. Upon the land as it was, they made the first of trees. The tree grew high and its roots grew low and it was luminous and physical. The tree itself has been known by many names, but has come to be known as the world tree or the tree of life and knowledge. Once they completed their task, they looked into the Goddess and asked if what they created was good. She replied, 'Everything within me is as I am.'

ELEUSIS, GREECE, 585 B.C.E., THURSDAY

The women stood in a close circle inside Demeter's temple. The altar fire made of cedar and yew logs lit the backdrop of the cave walls. The opening stood towards the east as the harvest moon rose high in the night sky, illuminating the secret ceremony below. Hand in hand, heart to heart, all stood ready for the magical rite, each knowing what they did now they did for future generations. It was true. The time had come. The ways of the Mother Goddess were coming to an end. War and violence were taking over the earth. What in modern times was referred to as the "golden age" of Greece had not fully matured, and yet, some could read the signs that foretold the tale of the changes to come. It was both the beginning and the beginning of the end, and even though this next cycle would last thousands of years, it was doomed to self-destruction and obliteration of the earth …unless these women did what they came here to do.

For centuries, high priestesses had been coming to this sacred mountain spur in Eleusis. Ceremony after ceremony had been performed in this underground cave situated high above the Aegean Sea. They came to celebrate life's mysteries, to thank the Goddess for the harvest, to transform and receive her power. But tonight, the celebration was of a different kind. They poured the libation and gave offerings of barley and wheat. They stood sky-clad as the night air blew through the fire, their skin reflecting the amber glow. Their faces revealed little emotion, but their eyes shone brightly with tears of joy, laughter, and sorrow too. This was not a sacrifice but an offering of hope and courage to protect the earth. They placed the ring in the fire. The ground shook. They began their incantation.

"We were, are and always will be as she is! Breath for breath, life for life, around and around the cycle is bound."

Stones and rocks fell from overhead. The ground shook under their feet. The earth trembled and shook their hearts. The cave opening began to collapse, imploding upon itself. The women stood still, holding fast, never breaking the connection and knowing that their strength was in each other. The earth closed in around them, embracing them in darkness. This was not the tomb of their death. This, they created, was to become the portal for life.

Historians would not treat them kindly, but that's their misinterpretation, intentional or otherwise. The rites of the Eleusian mysteries celebrated illumination and enlightenment in a living metaphor, as with the spark of a flame in the dark of night or with a jolt of ecstatic splendor which later would be called "shameful" and "licentious." But they were not ashamed, nor even fearful. They invested no energy in dark negativity. Joy and love are true reflections of divinity, so they drank the draught and filled their baskets, preparing for the next cycle to come. Those women dared to feel the living pulse of the cosmic spiral.

Today, Demeter's temple still remains on the top of Mount Eleusis. Standing silent, it appears a mere tourist destination, but ancient magic never wanes. If you pay attention, you can still feel it.

Chapter One

THE BIG DIG

BOSTON, MASSACHUSETTS, 2010 C.E., MONDAY

"Your honor!" Alex protested along with the sound of the gavel, reminding her that she was in contempt if she continued.

"These families should not have to put up with a public transportation station encroaching onto their sacred lands!" But the judge disagreed and his decision was final.

She had never lost a case before. Now, while riding a crowded train back into downtown Boston, she had a headache and was trying to make sense of the senseless outcome. It was her last ditch attempt to keep the tribe's sacred land sacred. It didn't work. She hated that she had to patronize the same transportation agency that just bested her in court, but it was the only way she could be sure to get to her class on time.

Bam-bang! The deafening sound rocked the train, pulling Alex out of her thoughts of defeat.

I should be used to this by now, she scolded herself.. No one else seemed disturbed. For more than five years, the perpetual pounding of the Big Dig had vibrated the city with sounds of construction workers digging deeper into the earth. But Alex still hadn't gotten used to it and each plunderous sound reminded her of the arrogant ideologies espoused in court that morning by her opposing counsel. She shuddered to think that such a disruptive scale of construction was now sure to invade the sanctity of an Indian reservation. Sitting alone in a train full of strangers, she couldn't help but glimpse certain parallels between the judge's disregard for tribal tradition and the gutting of the earth underneath her. Her own observations made her uncomfortable. Alex had always been quite conservative, torn between her upper class breeding and her humanitarian ideals. She mustered her concentration and thought instead about today's lecture.

Dr. Alexandra Martin was a law professor at Suffolk University Law School for as long as the Big Dig had been pounding. She enjoyed the leisure and academic freedom her career afforded, while still enabling her to provide pro bono representation for some of the local tribes around New England. The benefits Alex attained from being the daughter of two renowned Harvard scholars were accompanied by an internalized voice tending towards tradition, duty and sacrifice. She inherited her mother's poise and her father's lean, angular body. His emotional distance, however, imprinted a yearning for approval that often prevented her from hearing and following her otherwise keen intuition.

Today's lecture will be on Property Rights and International Law, she thought. Realigning her posture against the stiff plastic seat, she drew the connections she hoped her students would make between land, law and government. She wondered whether this particular group of students would make the same mistakes the judge made this morning, or appreciate that indigenous people's property and knowledge have been stolen again and again, throughout history, in the name of law, religion and progress.

The Big Dig rumbled again, bam-bang! For a moment Alex lost her balance on the edge of the seat and reached out to grip the passenger bar in front of her, knocking another passenger with her elbow. He didn't seem to notice.

The Big Dig was known as the largest urban works project of its kind. Attempting to alleviate the above ground congestion, it rerouted traffic underground so that overpasses became underpasses, bridges became tunnels, and what was above ground was now below, or soon would be.

Like everyone else, Alexandra Martin knew that the sound of the digging and the banging was the inevitable side-effect of progress. Each boom-bang held the promise of better days to come. But the chaos caused by the transition had stamped itself upon the unconsciousness of residents, commuters and tourists alike. The Big Dig had literally become the pulse of the city and lately, it had been stirring in Alex a creepy, anxious kind of angst that she, on principle, preferred to ignore. Given her own peculiarities and her chosen field's emphasis on Cartesian logic and quantifiable rationality, she was well equipped to dismiss the subtler energies that were accelerating within her.

Bam Bang!!!

That last thunderous sound was catastrophic: one hundred twenty feet below the surface of the city, workers blasting new tunnels through the earth just discovered that the earth blasts back!

One man now lay dead. He was not struck by the tumbling boulders or ricocheting shrapnel, but by the thrust of the blast as the explosion, which was calculated for solid rock, reverberated through a hollow, cave-like ventricle and ruptured a vital source of energy more powerful than the dynamite used to violate it.

The earth seemed to collapse as other construction workers bolted from the danger, scrambling upward, back toward the light of the surface.

* * * *

"What in the world are they doing down there?" Mayor Marino's voice was barely audible over the sound of a flock of geese flying past his closed office window.

"This project can't handle any more incompetence. I've promised the people accountability and I expect the same from those damn consulting engineers! They're certainly getting paid enough for it. The media isn't going to sleep on this kind of story!" He looked into the blank face staring back at him, the unfortunate deliverer of bad news.

"Weren't there tests?" Getting no response the Mayor tried again, "didn't anybody conduct any tests?"

"Sir?" It was John Doherty's job to know when Marino had vented enough frustration. As the liaison between the Mayor and the Governor for the Big Dig project, he dealt only with the problems, rarely the solutions. Having the Mayor's attention, he continued, "Of course, there were lots of tests, but the seismic imaging didn't reveal any substantial hollows in this area. We used the most state-of-the-art geophysical technologies but even they aren't designed to reveal fractures and voids of this size, only much larger anomalies. Besides, the Washington Street area is one of the few built on solid ground and some hollows were to be expected. But this? This is a surprise to everyone sir."

"Really?" the Mayor turned and looked out his office window. "What the hell's wrong with those geese today?" Throws of geese kept streaming past city hall. He charged, "John, I want to know everything about that chamber that can be known."

"So far," John replied, "it appears to be an ancient temple, more than just a naturally occurring cove. The governor has already been contacted and there are both state and federal regulations that direct protocol for this kind of discovery. It will slow down this phase of the project, sir."

"Tell me something I don't know."

Marino's salt and peppered hair fell against the line of his Italian temples as he thought about the situation suspiciously and searched for patterns of meaning that might imply it was a hoax or some form of terrorist activity.

A commotion outside the window then drew their attention. Marino stepped to the large square window and looked down over City Hall Plaza. A hefty flock of geese was stalking around the entrance doors, bullying the people who were trying to enter City Hall. Women screamed shrill cries as the geese opened their wings to their widest expanse and honked them back from the main doors.

"What is going on down there?" Marino asked rhetorically. John joined him at the window.

"Perhaps they want to file a complaint about their city?" He couldn't help adding with his laughter, "Did they have an appointment with you Mr. Mayor?"

Both men laughed, but they were keenly aware that this was one of the most bizarre scenes they had ever witnessed through those windows. As they watched, two uniformed men appeared on the scene, having come out of the building from a doorway outside their view. One of them was holding a metal floor sign and placed it at a safe distance from the circle of geese. The other man waived his arms, guiding the people away from the flock and rerouting them to another entrance. Order seemed to have been restored.

Marino turned his gaze to John Doherty and resumed, "Get a hold of the president at Harvard and ask if they can get their archeologists on board."

"Sir, it's customary to use state and federal resources for these finds."

"The governor can use whoever he wants to officially, but I want Richard Lyons involved, I can trust him. Besides, if we wait for the feds, it will take too long. I've got to start coming up with an alternative route to get this last phase of the project finished."

Marino paused a moment, then added, "Get me the latest engineer's report, ASAP. But otherwise, I want to keep knowledge of this quiet ...for as long as we can. Thank you John."

Doherty picked up his notebook and jotted down some notes as he walked out the door.

* * * *

The vibratory residue of the last explosive sound still tingled the nerve endings throughout Alex's body. She had never been more grateful to arrive at her destination. The doors opened alongside the platform. Rumbling and crackling sounds still audibly surrounded the station.

Frenzied herds of trench coats, concerned about the loud noises and erratic flickering of lights, rushed past Alex as she moved slowly. She focused on where she was going, determined to avoid being swept by the mob down one of the many stairways leading from the train's platform. She felt unusually alone in the crowd of other bewildered commuters but she cut through the masses gracefully and made her way, exiting the turnstiles.

As she felt her way to the right tunnel, she became acutely aware of the dank cold and the history of her stone surroundings. The light trembled upon the dark granite boulders worn dull from weathered years and carved out in the shapes of stairs, walls, and ceilings. Now she could see the top of the stairwell and felt the blistery wind. The echoes of briefcases and high heels bouncing from the stone mimicked the boom-bang that she still felt in the pit of her stomach.

She refused to give it a second thought, but people rushed past. Alex was careful not to make eye contact. She stepped aside into the alcove of a double-sized doorway and took a moment to wrap her pink scarf tightly around her neck and to find her shearling trimmed gloves, preparing for the outside frost.

Breathing deeply, she glanced to her right and peered through the doors of the original Filene's Basement. What lay behind the cold steely grates were the remnants of the last great bargain shopping in downtown Boston. She pulled on her gloves and mounted the final set of stairs, hopeful to leave her growing anxiety under the surface, shielded from natural light. The cold wind pushed against her as she emerged into the dim haze of a February morning.

As she turned the busy corner onto Tremont Street, she was slapped by another gust of wind and the sounds of the homeless street prophets demanding money as they handed out a newspaper called "Spare Change." It cost a dollar.

"Got any change?" the tallest guy with the beard asked her as she approached. His grating voice rapped at her rapidly fraying nerves. His mere size threatened aggression but Bostonians rarely responded. Hardy from their environmental trials and driven by a strict Puritan work ethic, most everyone hurried off to work. Alex followed suit.

The law school building lay adjacent to one of the nation's oldest public green spaces, the Boston Commons, and she was grateful for the building's proximity and protective facade. When she walked through the main doors she was met by a gush of warm air from the overhead heaters and a cold acknowledgement from the security guard behind the bullet proof window. Faces of staunch judges and slick deans hung from the lavish structure's ornate inner walls. Long marble pillars rose three stories into the air and held up a clear glass dome at the top of the building. The architecture created an overall feel of opulence, omnipotence and sound judgment, all of which fit well with her sensibilities. The heels of her boots echoed familiarly from the Italian marble flooring of the lofty foyer and she headed off to class, sure that the disruptions of her morning had finally come to a close.

Richard Lyons sat with a few other senior faculty members, deciding in this more discreet setting, the pending outcome of a younger female colleagues' application for tenure. It was customary and even expected for this select group of gentlemen to gather at the Harvard Club after their early morning classes to streamline politics and policy in this fashion. Aside from the heavy leather furniture and herringbone jackets, the fraternal nature of their meetings would aptly remind one of an ancient Roman bath.

A uniformed runner interrupted the discussion by passing a small, folded slip of paper to Richard, who was seated in the far corner. The other men exchanged glances, acknowledging their mutual understanding as Richard read privately the message that was intended only for him. He then stood to leave.

These men formed the subcommittee for which there was no official committee. Here they would meet regularly to update each other with information, forming a seamless, far-reaching web to act as the eyes, ears and, when necessary, the strong arm of their cause. Knowing where one may be reached enabled a rapid flow of information.

Richard walked away from the table and exited the front room of the gathering hall, through a series of tall doorways. He passed through the inner billiard lounge and then the ceremony courtyard. He followed a route lined by ornate mahogany paneling until it took a sharp bend that revealed a stairwell passageway. Descending, he adjusted his collar and wondered what this summons would entail. The instructions were brief, as was customary. But the signature indicated something big was going on. Paul hadn't personally called him to the Vault in many years.

Two doors stood closed at the bottom of the passage. Richard approached the one on the left. In pace with his step, the detailed brass knob turned and the door opened to reveal a tall muscular figure ready to greet him. He remained silent but gestured Richard on.

Richard could see the doorway to the Vault further inside. It was arched, reminding him of the protocols of power that described and preserved everything Richard had ever known and appreciated. He passed through and walked into the Vault's anteroom. A crisp white alabaster bust of Plato sat atop the centerpiece of a large table and his hollowed-out eyes seemed to follow Richard as he moved.

Paul Schroder, Harvard's President, was in the back archives when Richard entered.

"Welcome, Richard," Paul's voice could be heard from the back row, "take a seat." The shape of Paul's familiar figure emerged from behind one of the five long rows of shelves that made up this great archive, referred to as "the Vault" by those who knew of its existence.

Paul was a large and imposing man. He stood six feet, four inches tall with a thick crop of silver hair and rich blue eyes. Dressed in a classic navy suit he came up the central aisle in an easy stride to join Richard at the table in the anteroom.

The five areas of the Vault were organized to represent the five great patriarchal traditions, Chinese, Christian, Greek, Islamic and Judaic. The corridors met together at the edge of the anteroom furnished with a large examination table and five armchairs. Each hallway contained the sum total of humanity's wisdom and cultural traditions. Artifacts, scrolls and documents extending across all time, place and history were warehoused in this massive space, most of which were believed to be lost, destroyed, forgotten, or otherwise made non-existent.

Richard watched Paul's demeanor change as he took one of the seats and passed a sealed manila folder across the table to him.

"This may not be anything. But while it is in our own backyard, so to speak, it must be dealt with. I've heard from both your old friend, Al, as well as our other friends from abroad."

Richard was instantly intrigued and asked, "What would prompt the Mayor to seek the assistance of this organization? I can't imagine what similar concerns Al might have with our friends abroad."

"It seems there has been a discovery, here in Boston." Paul answered, "From what I've heard it has some familiar and peculiar qualities to it. We need to know what we are dealing with. Like I said, it's probably nothing. Could be just an old Indian site, but we need to be sure."

"What kind of site do you think this is, Paul?"

"It could be like the others."

"No," he protested, "it's simply not possible."

"Some of our friends have concerns."

"Based on what? There's no logical way. We're on the wrong continent."

"So we thought. But the symbols are there. Let me correct myself, I have verification that at least some of the symbols are there. Don't get yourself too worried over this, Richard. This is simply another assignment ...of precaution, at this point. We should take things one step at a time. Our organization has a long history of being thorough; seven sites, seven chambers. I grant you that the way we handled that last chamber in Iran was a political nightmare... it should have been handled more diplomatically. It was too messy, too public."

"The military never should have gotten involved." Richard interjected.

"We have full faith in you handling this local concern. Frankly, I think everyone is just nervous to keep a lid on things, as it were, especially when considering the proximity of a particular female colleague of yours."

"Moira Fennessey?" Richard grumbled at the thought of her. "She should be easy enough to deal with, from your position."

"My position," Paul corrected Richard's casualty swiftly, "is my concern. Now, it is your place to get this dismissed, destroyed or covered up. Use whatever resources you must, but keep it discrete. If it is anything like the others and it tells of the Academy's existence, it could be detrimental to us all."

"Well, is the site currently being contained, is access being restricted?"

"Yes, in the usual sense, but we have never had to deal with anything like this inside the U.S. The legal system is more protective here, there are many transparencies. Also… well, Dr. Fennessey has already heard of its existence."

Richard grumbled again.

"So we do have a situation, if the identification is correct?"

"Yes, and we need you on the ground floor of this."

With the normal formalities, Richard was dismissed and carried his folder up the stairwells and hallways back to the inner lounge for quiet thought and the space to review the details of what was provided to him. He had to concoct a plan, but until he identified the site he couldn't be sure what his approach should be.

He admitted to himself that both Moira's and the mayor's involvement might create some delicate conflicts …depending. The reference to his memories of Tehran was alone enough to raise his blood pressure, but the thought of there being another chamber excited him with the thrill of a mystery. He still had questions of his own. Now he had even more. How could the Academy be wrong after so many years?

* * * *

Soon after Dr. Martin began her lecture, she entered what she sometimes referred to as her "zone." Some call it the "flow." Almost every cell in her body was singularly focused on channeling the logical progression of material that her students needed to build a foundation for the more complicated topics at the end of the semester. It was almost a meditative space except that it was much more energetic than what most people experience when they meditate.

"Look," she said, "the struggle has always been over land."

She welcomed the normalcy of this lecture which she knew like the back of her hand, but by the time her lecture ended she was agitated again and the banging resumed an echo in her mind. Now she was just anxious to get to her office and check her messages.

"Good morning Dr. Martin," the secretary chirped as Alex walked into the office suite.

"Good morning Susan, how are you today?" Alex asked sincerely. She had been wondering if other people experienced the disruptions and nervousness she felt all morning, but hadn't yet seen anyone she could truly ask.

"Oh, I had a great morning, as it turns out. D'ove in early, didn't have a p'oblem; even found a pa'king spot." Susan spoke with a thick accent that indicated she grew up on Boston's south shore.

"You know, one of those with the b'oken meet-ahs?" She really didn't pronounce many "r's." And she explained, "Anyway, then I hea-hr as people start gettin' in, that there was this pow-a fail-ya in the 'T' subway. I'd have been late, if I took it. Didn't see you befo'e class, is that what happened to you?"

"Yes, I was later than usual…" she responded, "but I also had to be in court."

"Oh, by the way, Docto' Martin," Susan interrupted, ignoring Alex's response, "here ahe ya messages. Docto' Lyons called. Says he wants you to meet him fo' lunch. Like usual, at the Haah-v'd Club. Say's it's impo'tant."

Alexandra raised an eyebrow as she clutched the stack of pink slips Susan handed to her. She was suspicious. It wasn't that she didn't have the utmost respect for Richard Lyons. Certainly the fact that he was an old friend of her parents gave her a sense of obligation in working with him, but over the years he had proven to be a knowledgeable and significant resource. In any event, she was sure he wasn't calling only to have lunch. Richard never just had lunch.

"Call and tell him I can meet him at two-thirty." As Susan agreed, Alex walked into her office to call her friend, Diana, who was just getting up.

* * * *

"Bang! Bang! Another Roxbury Shooting!" the headline read. Diana Wolfe sat reading the Boston Times, sipping on her morning cappuccino. She was much too artistic for regular coffee, although she did enjoy the flavor of a strong cup of Goya or Café Bustello. If truth be told, she had many other addictions than caffeine, but she bartered with herself years ago to indulge in this one, and not to feel guilty about it.

Still unaware of this morning's underground accident, Diana lit another cigarette and reflected upon all the destruction that surrounded her. She lived in lower Roxbury, a part of Boston targeted for revitalization but essentially still a ghetto. She chose this house for its marble mantles, mansard roof, and affordable price tag. It was close enough to the downtown for Diana to still consider herself an "urban dweller," but she was practically the first white person to cross the city's racial divide, further aggravated by the fact that she was a woman. She exhaled loudly, wondering what her commute into town to meet Alex would be like after last night's racial incident. This morning she too felt uneasy. Looking forward to seeing Alex for lunch, she still had to meditate, stretch canvases, and finish drafting a grant proposal for her goddess imagery ritual book.

I better check my horoscope, she thought to herself as she turned the page to erase the headline from her view. She found the table of contents and quickly rifled through the newsprint, careful not to knock over her cappuccino. Diana Wolfe was one of the few people in the world who considered astrology an exact science. She had lived long enough and was in tune enough with her own ancestral beat to know that the interconnection of the planets, the stars, the earth, and the elemental forces of life unfold in a complex pattern of cause and effect. To her dismay, the horoscope ambiguously told her to prepare for intrigue and set-backs today.

As she grimaced, her black cat, Night-Night, jumped and landed next to her. She purred, reminding Diana that it was time for breakfast and that she ought not to take astrology so seriously. Nothing was an exact science other than breakfast.

"Okay Night-Night." Diana snuffed out her cigarette, got up from the kitchen table and headed for her friend's food bowl. She rinsed it out in the deep basined, old porcelain coated farmhouse sink. It was salvaged from a large mansion located just outside the city, in a revitalized area called Jamaica Plain.

Diana placed a full bowl of kibble on the counter and looked out the window in search of some morning sun.

"I wouldn't have to meditate so much if it were ever sunny in this city, Night-Night," Diana said out loud. Boston is the kind of city that requires a person to stay perpetually on the top of their game. Unlike New York where this kind of frenzy can be exciting and contagious, Boston has an air of unspoken stress; a dis-ease.

Diana Wolf knew that this morning there was more than just the average day-to-day stress filling the city's atmosphere. She had been restless all night and Night-Night, true to her name, had also been up for most of it keeping vigil: waiting, wondering and yes, worrying.

"What's going on Night-Night?" Diana asked, knowing that her feline friend would be hard pressed to reveal her nocturnal knowledge.

She walked through the parlor doors of the dining room, into her living room adorned with a marble mantle. Standing in front of her altar she selected a stick of incense.

"Lavender will be best to quiet the nerves," she said out loud even though she was alone.

Night-Night had, of course, been feeling the vibration for some time. Dogs and cats know more than we imagine. And in this instance, Night-Night was not just Diana's familiar but a fellow traveler who when necessary brought her own special powers into play. Night-Night knew that Diana would eventually figure out what was going on, but she also knew that her mistress was not anywhere near prepared for the pervasiveness of it all. She figured she would have to have a long session helping Diana. She yawned and stretched at the thought of it.

Typical, Night-Night said, *thinking you are so evolved with your frontal lobe! Can you not hear the sounds of the Earth's waves as they approach you? I am here for you Diana but sometimes*...and with that, Night-Night found a spot in the sun, and began to groom herself.

The phone rang.

"Oh, I hate it when this happens!"

Trying to decide whether to light the incense and begin her meditation or allow herself to get distracted by the phone she thought, *I am never quite sure what to do when this happens.* She picked up the closest receiver to look at the caller ID and saw that it was Alex, *Alex is no distraction.* She quickly answered.

"Hey, good morning!"

Alex sounded rushed. She wanted Diana to postpone lunch until tomorrow, "I need to meet with Richard today."

Diana smirked, remembering her last encounter with Alex's godfather at the French bistro, Francoise. Richard and she had gotten into a more or less uncivil conflict regarding the existence or non-existence of matriarchal cultures[i]. Diana was not one to back down from her intellectual position, especially when she knew she was right.

"Yes, and is Dick still paternalistic?"

A moment of silence passed between them and Diana continued more softly than before, "Well, you'll need to decompress later on. Why don't you at least come by for some wine when you're through?"

"Hm... that sounds nice, Diana. Thanks, I knew you'd understand. I'll be by later, but for now I've got to run. I've got students waiting to see me. See you tonight, I'll bring the wine!" Alexandra was a connoisseur of fine wines, not a sommelier, but she had a definite knack for pairings and always enjoyed being the one to make an evening's selection.

"Ok, bye!" Diana hung up the phone only to discover that Night-Night had fallen asleep on her meditation pillow, and was probably making better use of it than she could this morning. She went upstairs to her studio to start a new painting, relieved that she didn't have to leave her house today, or ride on the Silver Line "T".

* * * *

By the time Alex arrived to meet Richard at the Harvard Club, he had reviewed the items in the folder at least a dozen times, looking for proof that it was a hoax. The photos were quite distorted and blurry. They were obviously taken in a hurry, probably with a cell phone camera. But the shapes were identifiable and there certainly was proof enough that some hollow of significance was found in the rock bed. He'd have to worry about "how" it got there and "why" there was another chamber that they didn't know about later. The steps he had decided to take first were innocent enough and proper for all of his responsibilities, regardless of what he determined the site to be; and they could buy him some time down the road, in case problems arose. He was sure that Alex would be a help to him either way.

Richard sat by a window sipping his scotch, always Glenlivet on the rocks. Alex knew exactly where to find him. The familiarity of the silk oriental rugs comforted her as she passed by the long mahogany bar into the dining room. She noticed how his wavy gray hair matched the worn leather elbows of his tweed jacket and how five years earlier the same scene would have been complemented by a cigar. At sixty-three years of age, Richard Lyons had spent most of his adult life in libraries and ancient sites around the world. He carried his own knowledge with an assured air of dignity. This was one of the reasons why Alexandra found him charming.

Richard looked like he had been thinking. His brow was almost frozen into place, but he saw her enter the room and rose to greet her warmly.

"Aahh, Alex! Good to see you, you look lovely as ever!" She was dressed in a stunning Armani suit that complemented her sleek auburn hair. "Sit down; let me order you a glass of that wine you like so much here." One of the benefits of the Harvard Club was that they stocked excellent wine. Alex's favorite afternoon blend was a fragrant floral Viognier mixed with a leathery Shiraz rooted in notes of dark chocolate.

"Thank you Richard, I would love a glass and certainly could use one." He signaled to the attendant.

She breathed in the familiarity of her surroundings and was grateful for the apparent good mood of her companion. Richard Lyons had known her all her life and although he was cold and unemotional, since her parents' death he had provided her with a sense of calm reassurance. They weren't close enough to fulfill the role of a family member for each other, but they both tried, out of mutual respect for Alex's father. Richard was her father's oldest friend and colleague. He was present on the night of his death and Richard was the closest thing to him that Alex had left.

"So Richard, how have you been?"

"I don't know Alex. That's like asking me how my elbow is." He said it rather curtly, and then changed his tone.

"You know me, I've been the same. I don't change but something very interesting has come up, which is why I called you."

"Really? What is it that has you so excited?"

"Fascinating stuff. Really, fascinating. But let's order some lunch first, shall we? And you can tell me about what happened in court this morning." Alexandra's jaw clutched tightly at the thought of it, but not enough for him to notice.

"Well… it wasn't good. It turns out that our transportation infrastructure and cost concerns trump the value of tribal sovereignty and cultural heritage. Poverty forced these people to build a casino on their land, but with their financial success came public demands for better access, et cetera, et cetera. In the end, the intergovernmental politics became the justification for moving forward with a station that the tribe never wanted in the first place." Alex let out a long deep sigh, "I'm sorry it's just been an off day for me and I get frustrated even thinking about it."

"Can't they appeal?"

"They should, but they already told me they didn't want to file an appeal. You know, to be honest, I'd rather not talk about it. It's over and done with now." As it was she didn't enjoy talking about the substance of her work with Richard. They both had strong opinions and as an anthropologist, his views on human rights policy often differed from her own. She had found it best to avoid the meat and bones of her cases rather than try to mediate her respect for him with her ethical principles.

"Are you representing any other tribes?"

"At the moment, no." She touched over the details of her classes while looking over the menu and was grateful when the well groomed waiter interrupted to take their order.

They continued casual conversation for a few more minutes until the caprese salad, looking delicious and healthy, was placed in front of her. Richard sat back in his chair sipping another scotch and began.

"Alex, I got word today from the Mayor's office. You've probably heard in the news, the various uh, ...unfortunate events, and the rumors of corruption associated with the Big Dig. Well... that's not even the half of it. But that's not important right now, what I want to talk to you about is this most recent incident which is very hush-hush."

He sat back abruptly, crossing his legs and pinching his lips as the waiter returned and reached down to replace his decorative charger plate with a pink cut of meatloaf served on fine china. Once they were alone again he continued.

"No doubt, you'll be brought in on this at some point, but I wanted you to hear about it directly from me. A man was killed this morning in a nasty explosion right down near your law school, where they are still digging for the Silver Line extension."

"Oh yes, is that what it was? I was caught up in something on the T just earlier today." Alex crunched her salad mindfully, trying not to show the depth of her instant intrigue.

Richard continued, "Well, aside from killing this poor soul, the blast tore out what appears to be a side wall from a small chamber room. Judging from its shape and design it could be thousands of years old. This is of course unheard of! And what's even more ridiculous is that it contains curious artifacts and a variety of ancient symbols. So I have been asked to consult and to help decipher its age and meaning while Harvard interprets the purpose of the chamber itself."

"Is it Native American?" Alex asked. During law school she was an intern with the Bureau of Indian Affairs and in her first years as a lawyer assisted one local tribe with the recovery of some sacred and cultural artifacts held by the federal government. "What about the local tribes, do they think it is one of their ancient sites?"

"Aah, well that's where you come in." He swallowed his bite and continued, hoping she would take the bait. "No one has been told about this yet. The funny thing is, the workers' crew that unearthed it in that blast, they're not sure which one of their men it was that got blown to bits! A few from that graveyard shift skipped out early." He couldn't restrain his slow scotchy chuckle. Alex's stomach churned.

"The City wants to keep it quiet until the body is identified and the family notified properly. Then they'll release some information, but probably not all. The Mayor is concerned about the heavy media attention that will surely follow the accident, and has managed to keep news of it undercover until its origins and significance can be ascertained. Issues of historical preservation aside, there has already been too much controversy and scandal surrounding the Big Dig. I would like you to work with the City this time. You'd be taking a different perspective, but still work with the people you're already committed to …it would probably be more beneficial for them as well. I haven't seen this chamber yet and I certainly don't know for sure what is down there, but either way this is a mysterious discovery and I'd think you would jump at this kind of opportunity." Richard resumed dismantling the thick slice of meatloaf and waited for her reaction.

Raising one perfectly arched eyebrow and taking another sip of wine, Alex adjusted herself in the leather chair. She knew that Richard and the Mayor were old friends. It had worked to her convenience in the past but the ink hadn't even dried from the judge's order this morning.

"Richard, how exactly do you see my role in this? You know I'm not accustomed to representing the city on these matters, especially after the hearing I had this morning."

"All I'm saying," he coyly replied, "is that the city doesn't want another billion dollars in delays and hold-ups, or the embarrassment of a legal battle over this forsaken Big-Dig project! The Mayor wants to know what he will be up against as soon as possible." Silence hung between them for a moment as they both contemplated the possibilities.

Alex finished the last few mouthfuls of the fresh mozzarella, swirling it first in an oaky bath of thick balsamic vinegar. Richard knew she was idealistic but couldn't help the timing. It wasn't an ideal situation for him either. If he could have it his way, the chamber would have disappeared as quickly as it was uncovered. But it was sure to become public knowledge.

"Look, Alex, you're not on retainer with either side, you're neutral here. The City wants this wrapped up quickly and an experienced outside attorney familiar with the tribes could help keep the discussions peaceful and below the radar, until we know what we are dealing with. Alex, I'll be honest with you. Of course it would be more convenient for the city if it is not a native site, because they could move forward with the Big Dig plans without further delay, but I have not formed my own assessment as of yet, you must remember."

She placed the fork down on the right side of her now empty plate and pushed it aside. Cautiously she responded, "Well Richard, it does sound like an intriguing situation. And when the public learns of it, especially if the artifacts and the chamber still haven't been identified and dated, the local tribes will clamor for preservation and custody. I'm sure the Mayor would prefer that it isn't connected to any of the remaining tribes, but it's more likely that it is." She made this point very clear and continued, "I think it is in everyone's best interests to identify the site and the artifacts as soon as possible, not to mention who ever this poor person's family is…and especially before the press gets wind of it! Have the artifacts been dated?"

"Harvard's working on that." His tone changed. He seemed almost tired, or full, which they both were, but unapologetic.

"Alex, I need you on my side with this."

"I know, but I can't say for sure yet Richard. Feel free to keep me informed but I'm going to wait until I hear from either the city, or one of the tribes and I'll make my own assessment. Thanks for lunch, but it's getting late, I have to get going."

"Alright then, go ahead. After all, we're on the same team, right?"

As she stood to leave, he raised to meet her with a handshake.

* * * *

The doorman kept taxis waiting outside. Stepping into one, Alex remembered that she promised to bring wine with her to Diana's. "Take me to West Newton Wines and then I'll be going to Dudley Square."

The cabbie grimaced at the final destination. Having picked her up at the Harvard Club, getting to the other side of town was not only difficult with the daily detour changes caused by the Big Dig, but would negate the possibility of a decent return fare on his way back into the nicer sections of the downtown. He obliged with a curt nod of his head and dutifully waited at their first stop where she selected a Syrah from Washington State, an expensive Bordeaux, and an accompanying aged Gouda.

Heading south, toward Dudley Square, the cabbie streamed down Washington Street, recently named the "gateway" to Boston. Alex watched through the taxi's windows as the meticulously preserved townhomes with wrought iron ornamentation and cobbled stone streets gave way to the stark institutional drab of urban projects and garbage-littered concrete that still defined lower Roxbury. This land had once been very prominent, equally graced with the hallmarks of wealth and splendor that were now restricted to the northern length of the "gateway". Much of the architectural proof of that history was plowed over at a time when ignorance and bigotry instituted segregation of the less desirable, less affluent, less white communities of Boston. *The struggle is still over land and the telling of history*, she thought.

The vehicle swerved between orange cones and Big-Dig detour signs, driving together the thoughts in her mind. Something about her conversation with Richard irritated her. She was well aware of his friendship with the Mayor, but it was contrary to the normal protocols to begin processing such a find without a formal and public declaration of its discovery. State and Federal laws demanded it. *What is he into?* She buried the thought that she didn't trust him but realized that Richard was placing her in a potentially political position. Whether there could be a risk of that would depend on the history and use of the chamber, which Richard was interpreting. Alex's mouth was dry and her mind was racing, but it clasped at nothing.

The taxi stopped for the red light at the last major intersection between her and her destination. Trucks, buses and cars of all sizes blared through the streets, seemingly competing for both speed and noise. It was a busy intersection, sitting at the edges of the Dudley Square neighborhoods, the industrial outskirts of the Medical Center, the Columbus Street projects, and the Ruggles Street side of Northeastern University. The cross street was called Melnea Cass Boulevard, named for a local advocate of human and civil rights presumably to inspire some unidentified change in the spirits of the poor and oppressed. A biking path ran along both sides of the tree lined boulevard and empty lots sat at each of the four corners of the intersection, but there was nothing that felt natural or green about it.

The sun had almost set and with the aid of the gateway's decorative street lamps, Alex watched a young girl standing at a bus stop on the other side of the street. Bundled in cozy winter attire Alex could see very little of her features other than the pig tails dangling from the sides of the girl's hat, like fastening ties. She was eating what appeared to be a fast food sandwich, wrapped in wax or metal lined paper. She took one last bite and threw the wrapper to the ground, unconcerned by the waste-bin standing conspicuously to her side. *This area needs a more active kind of inspiration,* Alex thought, cringing. An oversized dump truck roared with the force of a locomotive as it crashed over the uneven pavement. Litter and dust swirled across the surface of the asphalt, coming to rest as the traffic lights changed color.

The cabbie eased through the intersection, slowing for pedestrians, shopping carts and heroin addicts. They then turned onto Diana's small, one-way street. It was one of the most well preserved in all of Dudley Square and still boasted the original Victorian architecture. Taking the corner they passed on the left, a loft condominium building with a carved Carrera marble façade, followed by a lone strip of Victorian, mansard-styled town houses built in the eighteen hundreds. On the right sat the brick four storey international market that fronted Washington Street. It was decorated with a colorful urban mural of smiling faces of multiple ethnicities. Passing the back side of the unkempt market acrid aromas of garbage sludge, disinfectant, and butchered cattle wafted into the car. Alex tried to force the rank air back out of her nostrils as they proceeded down the short side street. The smell dissipated but the taste lingered.

The other buildings on the right hand side of the street had been leveled years ago to make a parking lot for the market. This orientation provided unobstructed views of the city skyline for the town houses on the left side of the street. Diana's was the last one in the row. Alex found her wallet and counted out the fare as the vehicle pulled to the end building.

* * * *

Diana had been hurrying about her purpose, "cleansing" the living room with carefully selected essential oils, incense and candles. She was intent on creating an atmosphere of calm, knowing that Alex would likely be stressed; she often was after a meeting with Richard. She prepared the room with an acknowledgement of each element, as though she were beginning a ritual. She placed a white candle in the east, red in the south, blue in the west and a green candle in the north. *Alex has a tendency to internalize patriarchal energy*, Diana thought to herself. *She is sure to be a basket of false neuroses.*

Diana herself never internalized patriarchal law. At an early age she witnessed women who did, and they became crushed by the loss of their own voices. She naturally tended to identify herself with women's laws and modes of being, and she knew this often made her an outsider. Being a social deviant had always appealed to her. She consciously chose to develop a radical voice and took society's reaction to her as a good sign that she was succeeding. As a pagan and a lesbian, she could concretely identify some of the things that set her apart from common society; obvious political differences and so forth. But it was her spiritual gift, her knack for negotiating the energy world and its creative void that prevented her from more common minglings.

Aside from the fact that Alex was a consistently staunch heterosexual, Diana found her personal power and competence seductive. And they trusted each other implicitly. Alex did not have many friends, or have time for them, but she had known Diana since they were school girls at the Day School on the flat of Beacon Hill. They became fast friends and when Diana's family relocated to Seattle, they kept occasional correspondence, enough so that when Diana moved back to Boston as a fine arts student, they decided to share an apartment together. Not that they traveled in the same social circles, but they were good companions together throughout graduate school and helped each other through finals, critiques, broken hearts and frayed dreams.

As Diana stacked wood and prepared the fire, she felt an inward rush of anticipation. The kindling took nicely, the fire was lit. Diana sensed her friend's presence before Alex had a chance to ring the doorbell.

"Come in and get out of this cold air," she said, hugging Alex hello. Alex was clearly relieved to be inside the warmth of the house. The old wooden floors, marble fireplace and crown moldings reminded her of earlier times and she could see why Diana bought this property, despite its location.

Always the risk taker, Alex thought to herself, proud and envious of the courage that accompanied Diana's free spirit.

"I brought the wine!" Alex said, handing off her briefcase. "Wow, thanks for the fire, it feels great in here! How was your day?"

"Good, I got a painting started. Here, let me take your coat."

"Great," Alex said. "I got your favorite cheese," and she moved with the groceries into the kitchen. "Sorry I cancelled lunch but at least you didn't have to go out. It is miserably cold out there and traffic is always so stressful." Alex unwrapped the cheese and set it on a plate. She grabbed two wine goblets and selected a bottle to open.

"This is much better anyway! I've even prepared the atmosphere in here for you to unwind," Diana spoke from the living room coat closet.

"Yes, it feels perfect," Alex said as she emerged from the back with two full goblets. "Here, your glass."

They met in the plush living room and Diana said, "I know exactly what you are talking about outside, with the Big Dig, I mean. No one knows where they are going anymore. You can't get from one place to another the same way twice." Diana loathed public transportation but she also refused to own a vehicle so Alex usually disregarded her complaints in these matters. The mention of the Big Dig, however, caused her to wince and the coincidence of Diana's chosen words made her queasy.

Diana continued, "Last night I had another strange dream."

Whereas Alex almost never remembered her dreams, Diana almost always did and the detailed fantasy lands that she concocted in her subconscious and unconscious states were mind blowing to Alex, in both their particularity and Diana's description. Since they were young school girls, Diana had shared the stories of her reveries with her friend. She loved to talk about them. They were resources for both Diana's art work and her spiritual practices. Alex had always appreciated the entertainment value; Diana was remarkably funny and a visual story teller. It offered a sort of replacement for Alex's sleeping mind's lack of creativity. But Diana had been complaining about her dreams lately. She said they have been changing, becoming more dull and dark …threatening. Last week Diana kept talking about the Tower card, from the major arcana of the tarot deck, appearing in her dreams.

Alex prepared to listen and felt a slight touch of relief that she didn't recall her own dreams more frequently.

Diana sat down, cross legged on her carved mahogany couch in the formal receiving parlor of her town home. The rich upholstery shone pink from the texture of the Queen Anne brocade. The radiators clanked rat-a-tat-tat as the great boiler in the basement pumped steam throughout the house.

After a pause Diana continued, "there was this old woman." She talked with her head down, as if she was examining the tips of her fingers for clues, "a powerful crone archetype, standing in the middle of a circle deep within the earth. She had a lantern or a ball of fire and she kept waving it and screaming. And there was dancing or something, it was almost tribal, but I couldn't understand what she was saying. I don't know if it was a warning, but she was definitely agitated."

Alex said nothing. Her jaw clenched and she stared obsessively at the rug beneath her feet.

Diana kept talking, "I can't help but think that they shouldn't be cutting up the Earth under Boston. The city is going crazy from all the detours, dizziness and circumventing and I'm afraid it's all going to make the Puritans lose it any day now! There's so much hostility in the air, I think that's what my dream is about."

"Hmm…" Alex hardly knew what to say. She loved her friend but never knew what to do with these coincidences. *Why is she connecting a dream to the Big Dig, today of all days!*

Alex chose to merely respond to the more pedantic aspects of what her friend had just revealed, "You know, when they first started digging up this city, I thought it made sense. It was such an important project that I thought it would be beneficial. Now they're saying that our population increases have already outgrown the Big Dig's capacity goals, so what's the point of it all? Maybe I can't say for sure factually, but it seems like it has only created more problems..." She drifted off into her thoughts of the project's latest unnamed victim that Diana didn't even know about.

Alex could not deny that Diana's timing was relatively impressive in light of the surprise events in her life of late. Her friend had always displayed a keen sensitivity, not psychic abilities per se, but an ability to read out patterns, generally, and be in tune with Alex's life, more specifically. But Alex did not share in all of the same beliefs that Diana did. She didn't take any of it seriously and she liked to push Diana's boundaries on the topic. Sometimes they bantered philosophically and metaphysically, an intellectual exercise that they both enjoyed and they were well matched.

"What do you do," Alex facetiously challenged, "if you have a dream in which someone that you don't know tells you, no orders you, that you must grow wheat? ...I mean *really*..." The note of her voice rang with a trill sharpness that neither had expected. Rather than sounding like an invitation to debate, it vibrated nastiness, projecting the roughness she'd acquired through her tiresome day. Alex looked to her friend and saw the look of betrayal in Diana's eyes, caused by her own cynicism. Alex then back stepped and over compensated much too quickly.

She let it slip, "Ah... I'm sorry. It's just that... Speaking of the Big Dig, I have to tell you about the conversation I had with Richard." Alex took a slow sip of wine, digesting that she was about to share her secret with Diana. It certainly wasn't the first time. Richard would be perturbed, because it was Diana, but she wasn't really under any obligation. The city's invitation of her counsel, if Richard's conversation could even be considered one, certainly didn't follow the usual formalities that would trigger fiduciary duties or confidentiality. Still, she chose her words carefully from the many voices in her head.

"Something has been unearthed and …I might be getting more politically involved than I'd like." The room was dark, causing her words to hang very slowly in the air, silhouetted against the light of the fire.

"Unearthed?" Diana noted her friend's chosen phrasing and tone. Diana knew something was bothering Alex, she felt it in the cold that blew Alex through the threshold when she first arrived. Now Alex was finally talking about whatever it was that had her wound so tight. Alex was always a much happier person when she talked about the things that produced her anxiety, usually either work or family. This involved both. As close as they were, Diana would still have to be careful not to hit a nerve when ever Richard was involved in Alex's professional world.

For casual comfort Diana commented, "Odd that much could be unearthed. Most of Boston is land fill, well, except for where we are here, around Washington Street." Diana spoke gently but the light of curiosity in her eyes revealed her intense level of interest. "The fact that there's so little solid ground under the city is the first problem I've ever had with the Big Dig."

Part of the reason Washington Street was named the "gateway" was that it was originally the only road in and out of the area we now call Boston because it used to be surrounded by water. Boston as we know it today was born from three large hills sitting at the tip of a thinly necked peninsula surrounded by marsh swamps and the bay. The

Seventeenth Century European colonists leveled two of the three massive hills, selling off the dirt to fellow settlers who used it as fill to create more land mass over the wet marshes. Remnants of the third, named Beacon Hill, remain to this day crowned by the golden dome of the state house.

Alex nodded, the muscles in her face relaxing, "And everyone knows from the news that there have been allegations of corruption and scandals of all sorts associated with the Big Dig."

Diana agreed saying, "I saw in this morning's paper that Governor O'Reilly is suing another one of the contractors."

"Right, well in addition to all of that, there now seems to be an archaeological site in Boston's underground. Not in the fill area of course, but under Washington Street, by Downtown, where they're connecting the Silver line."

"The Silver line, you're kidding!" Diana said vivaciously, "what was it that they found, exactly?"

"I'm not entirely sure," Alex responded. "Richard was quite vague, even for him." She left out mention of the unfortunate human casualty saying, "I think they don't know what it is yet, but Richard said it is some kind of ancient chamber." Alex let out a smile as she spoke; she knew Diana would want to hear about this. She was always reading about the past and had that little collection of sculptures, small reproductions of artifacts from various ancient sacred sites around the world. She continued, "The city might be consulting with me; I probably shouldn't even be sharing news of it."

"I bet this is exactly what my dream was about!" Diana blurted out in excitement. Alex tensed again, her heart beat loudly inside her chest.

"I don't really know what's going on yet," Alex asserted, "but it got me thinking about your argument with Richard, about the existence of early matriarchal cultures. I could never understand, I had never seen him as angry as he was that night."

"Oh please, Alex," lighting a long, slender cigarette Diana inhaled deeply, "Do not even get me started." She exhaled gracefully despite the reminder of one of her not-so-graceful moments. "It just drives me crazy that so many of the male scholars in Richard's field try to claim that matriarchal cultures didn't ever exist."

"Well, frankly, I can't see why it matters?"

"Oh, Alex, come on now! This is more than just a scholars' debate for Richard, or the other scholars like him for that matter, and it's more than that for me too. Richard has a stake in all this Alex, whether you or he is aware of it. It's been born and bred right into him. For him it's about the control and preservation of our current social institutions... and I don't mean that lightly, either. I mean, really, think about it! If matriarchal cultures ever existed as cooperative societies, then patriarchy is wrong. Not just wrong about the existence of matriarchy, but wrong about everything... morally, wrong. That's why it's such a huge debate for them. Well, he must be rather puffed up over this, having control over the site, having control over the interpretation of our history. He'll love the publicity, I'm sure. How many strings did he have to pull to get this assignment?"

"Well, you know Diana, Richard and the Mayor are old friends from college."

"Mm, that's right, interesting." Diana responded, "Well, then he'll *have* to be his usual, neutral and objective self, won't he?" The wine had started to relax Diana, and she laughed carelessly at Richard's expense.

Alex noticed the row of clay statutes on a shelf near the window on the North wall of the room. The eight statues represented various goddesses found across Europe, many from matriarchal cult civilizations, like the Greek *Baubo* and the *Sheela-na-gig* of Ireland. Diana claimed to have a personal spiritual connection with the ancient magic that each of the mythical characters depict. And she had visited the archeological sites where the original artifacts were first uncovered. *Pilgrimages, she calls them.* They formed the ancestral pantheon of a modern feminist spirituality that was uniquely Diana's. The night that she and Richard last met erupted into chaos and animosity when Richard dismissed these and similar goddess artifacts as pornographic figurines that lacked any divine significance.

"But really, Alex, what are you going to do? Are you going to follow in Richard's footsteps and do the most politically rewarding thing? Sign on with the devil and try to play an angel of truth?"

Alex shot her a sharp eye of contempt, "Oh, please, Diana!"

"Alex, you know Richard will have an agenda. I've warned you about him before. At some point, it will force you to have to choose and you've never had to. Richard made his choice a long time ago. He is committed to maintaining that which is convenient for his comfort. And by comfort I don't mean physical luxuries alone… "

"Alright, that's enough Diana!" Alex tried to temper the distance between her best friend's spiritual beliefs and the last living member of her parents' family she had left, "…besides, he was making a philosophical argument that night."

"No, Alex, do not mistake Richard for a fool!" Diana tried calming her agitation with a deep drag of her cigarette. She quickly exhaled, "He is trained in a field that is supposed to appreciate symbolic meaning and context, but he is wed to an institution that re-writes history by writing *his*-story, and forgets large portions of inconvenient truths. Richard understands the consequences of what it would mean to admit that the cornerstone of western civilization was matriarchy. All of our myths are patriarchal and teach dominance and submission, not interconnection, creativity and cooperation. That would undermine everything. People like Richard," now she reached for her glass, drawing her eyes down as she added, "and I'm sorry to say you too Alex, think that the origin of society is patriarchy, with its laws and religions." Looking back at her friend she charged, "And you uphold those values."

Alex said nothing and Diana sipped her wine.

"The question about the existence of matriarchal cultures has to do with the evidence. Richard was right when he said, 'Paleolithic cave drawings are hardly conclusive.' I know what he means, but one has to look deeper at the subcultures and what lies beneath. By five hundred B.C.E., goddess worship had already gone underground. There is no evidence by today's standards because there is no record. Nothing has survived, if it was ever written down. He still doesn't get it, and he'll probably rip to shreds the truth about the cultures that built the chamber here in Boston, too. How can you even consider working on this if he is going to be involved?"

Alex scoffed. Her mind was racing from Diana's comment comparing her to Richard and supporting of patriarchy, dismissing her own struggles and successes against the oppression of modern day sexual politics. She tempered her desire to get defensive. Alex had always feared that her decision to fight for change from the inside of the legal institution might backfire and she could end up supporting the destructive aspects of the system itself. Diana hit a chord, but Alex remained silent.

"It's a whole other way of knowing. I know why Richard feels threatened, but I worry about you." Diana said slowly.

Alex kept listening and her defensiveness now cooled, she took a deliberate sip of wine.

"Well," she replied, "of course I understand what you are saying. Take oral tradition for example. I have had to deal with similar frustrations in the law, in the courts just this morning for instance. Tribal customs and ways of knowing don't always translate their breadth and significance of meaning within our legal parameters. Even I wonder sometimes whether justice doesn't get sterilized away by the 'objectification' of legal rules and court procedure."

Diana threw another log on the fire and refilled their glasses. Alex's profile was dramatic, framed against the flickering orange flames, reflecting brightly off her sleek auburn hair. Her cool brown eyes rarely revealed their feelings, but always tended to suggest a deep surging passion which, as far as Diana could tell, was reserved solely for Alex's work, human contact being just too messy.

These two friends had sat together fireside like this on many cold evenings over the years, forging a steadfast bond despite their radically different modes of expression. Stephen, the Nigerian geologist, broke Alex's heart the same time that Therese, Diana's college sweetheart, left Diana to travel through Spain. Diana felt her pain so intensely, as if helicopter blades were ripping through her solar plexus,that she couldn't eat. *Probably for the Running of the Bulls*, Alex quipped callously, trying to help Diana heal her pain through humor, while simply swallowing her own. Alex tended to guard her interiority and emotions. It came across to many as awkwardness and coldness, but Diana had always seen clearly in Alex that it was an homage she paid, with respect and sacredness, to her intense compassion and capacity for love.

Alex still felt the drumming of a familiar rhythm echo through her body. "You know Diana I am a little concerned over this thing with Richard, myself. There is something else going on here. I can't put my finger on it yet, but I'm left with a sense of unease. Like this is something I would not necessarily choose to do, but I have to do it. Only, I don't think that I feel obligated just because of Richard. I don't know Diana, maybe it's just the wine but I understand the old woman in your dream."

"What do you mean?" Diana asked.

"I think she was me, she is me. I know there's something terribly wrong, but I can't articulate it and all I want to do is yell and scream. And don't even get me started about court today!"

"Was it that bad, Alex," Diana asked.

"You know, sometimes I envy you Diana, your creativity is your own, mine gets usurped so often by the institution." At times, Alex really did envy Diana and this was one of them.

"You don't mean patriarchal institutions do you?" Diana smirked, "I don't believe they really exist."

Alex was slightly annoyed, but more so amused and stimulated by the discussion, so she responded, "Yes Diana, very cute, but matriarchal or patriarchal, the truth is that law needs to be objective and universally applied. So sure, my work supports the patriarchal process, if that's what you want to call it. And no, I don't like its history, but I don't know how else to work for justice."

"Breathing in, and then breathing out. That's a good place to start, Alex. But I do know exactly what you mean, and you are right that it does get more complicated than just that. I personally never know what to do on an ordinary Tuesday afternoon. I know thousands of women across the planet are dying every day for lack of justice!" Relishing in another sip of the fine wine, she added, "at least my cycle is always in tune with the full moon. I feel it. I drink wine, I love this cheese, and I wonder what to do, just like everyone else." Diana stretched over Alex's lap to reach the now empty goblet.

"Here, help me finish this." Diana looked at her friend and Alex looked softly back at her. "It's getting late," Alex said but not in protest.

They both smiled and Diana glanced down to steady her pour, dividing the remains of the bottle between both of their glasses.

"I've got to figure out what's going on," Alex said, the drumming in her ears slowly becoming chanting in her head.

"Sometimes you just need to *see* what's going on," Diana responded.

Alex's eyes came to rest again on the goddesses Diana so carefully selected for her spiritual expression and development. *How come Diana's vision is so clear when it comes to topics that seem so terribly murky to me?* She wondered whether the myth and folklore of these tiny objects held any real power.

[*] This re-telling of the Goddess myth is an adaptation of the re-telling told to us by Alexander Mulherin in 2008, emphasis ours.

[1] Many male scholars to this day still dispute that the Goddess artifacts painstakingly uncovered and documented by Gimbutas and many others, constitutes proof of the existence of matriarchal cultures. See, for instance users of Wikipedia quoting the *Encyclopaedia Britannica* that matriarchy is merely a hypothetical social system, http://en.wikipedia.org/wiki/Matriarchy .

Chapter Two

MODERN WEBS

Early the next morning, Richard Lyons got up to visit the site of the explosion. The winter sun wasn't strong enough to burn off the grey cloud cover, but Richard didn't notice, nor would he have particularly cared. He planned to spend most of the daylight hours underground, examining the chamber thoroughly.

He was also oblivious to the fact that all over the city that morning, when anyone tried to make a cell phone call, the line went dead. He was focused on one thing only, and it was taking too long to get through the traffic. He was on his way to meet a man named John Doherty who was told not to be late and stood waiting for him outside South Station.

Other than knowing Doherty's name, Richard didn't know the man he was supposed to be meeting but Richard was easy enough for Doherty to spot. He fit the description of an older academic, emerging from the taxicab in erudite attire and brown hiking boots. Born and raised in Boston, John could spot an academic a mile away.

"Richard Lyons?" Doherty stretched out his hand in traditional greeting.

Richard reciprocated but instinctively corrected him, "Yes, I am Dr. Lyons."

"John Doherty, sir. Please, follow me this way." Doherty introduced himself professionally but interpreted Richard's excited focus as distracted arrogance and led them away from the street thinking, *this one should be a real treat.* They walked behind the largest train station in the city. The busy rush hours had passed, so the area was fairly quiet.

Richard looked out over the Four Point Channel Waterfront District. The harbor looked silvery and grey, monochromatic. It seemed rather two dimensional in contrast to the complex dimensionality of stacked and multi textured sky scrapers to his right. But the sea gulls soaring overhead proved the expanse of the harbor.

The two men came to a gate. Doherty acknowledged the guard, a heavy set man with stout legs and languid eyes. He marked their names on his clipboard and waived them both through.

Excitement was building within Richard's mind. Only a handful of people knew that something so ancient and mysterious had been found here. He could tell that this guard had no idea, too much boredom in his face. Richard felt an advantage over the rest of the world. This was what he loved about his work and his life. He got a charge when he visited a site. He was in charge, entitled.

Doherty retrieved a large black duffle bag from a locker on the back side of the gatehouse, resumed walking through the open space of the entrance gate, and then turned down an aisle-like row of tall wooden fencing. Doherty kept a steady pace as he reached inside the black duffle and pulled out two hard hats. He placed one on his own head and then passed the other, extending his arm back behind him. Doherty was much younger than Richard, who was having trouble keeping up through the maze of the construction materials. But he quickened his step to clasp the protective hat, trading it for his own more stylish felt accessory.

Richard took note of their route so he could navigate when he was alone. But the next section of the path was enclosed by a ceiling and he lost sense of which direction they were heading. The light changed up ahead and the wooden walls turned into chain link fencing. Richard hoped there would be something to see.

What he learned from the view was that they had entered what looked like an opening to the belly of the Earth. The two men had been walking inside a metal framed catwalk structure along the outer edge of a crater-sized hole, intentionally constructed to facilitate the Big Dig. The sky was again visible above them and natural light filtered down through the clouds, exposing the scene.

The canyon-like chasm was at least fifteen stories deep, every twenty feet or so tied back with footers, piers and blocks, staged into stepped layers, like a hillside prepared for rice farming. The long necks of construction cranes towered high above them, some positioned at street level and others set onto lower tiers, providing make-shift elevator access to every story. A network of tunnels visibly ran into the sides of the cut back earth, some marked with planks or colored flags.

The ground below looked slushy and Richard registered the sound of water behind him. Walking further through this long cage, he gained perspective to see numerous unmanned sump pumps extracting water from the working tunnels. The gushing echoed like thunder as hundreds of gallons were deposited into an open holding tank, far to his left.

This section of the Big Dig had otherwise been silenced; all the pounding and explosives were halted yesterday morning with no explanation given. Rumors of an accident spread quickly amongst the workers though, and the current desolation lent the place the overall feel of a graveyard.

Large exposed steel girders seemed to hold back the skin of the city's surface in front of them, exposing a dark passageway straight ahead, illuminated by a single string of construction lights. The tunnel plunged into the shelter of the earth, enabling them to hear each other as they walked.

"Dr. Lyons, I'm sure I don't have to tell you how concerned the Mayor is. Your expertise and discretion is greatly appreciated here. We don't need any more setbacks and the implications of the finding of this site could greatly impact our outcome. The Mayor is anxious for work to be resumed and the last phase of the Big Dig completed without further delay."

"Tell the Mayor not to worry, Doherty. I'm not unaware of the political climate. My work here shouldn't cause any delays."

They were walking at a steep decline, now fully within the tunnel. The opening receded behind them and looked like a dim grey disc hanging in the darkness. The dangling bulbs strung from the tunnel wall beside them was not enough light for Richard to see clearly. It took some time for his eyes to adjust.

"How many people have seen the chamber so far?"

"Well first there was the worker who found it, after the accident of course. The city supervisor called the Mayor right away and we locked it up until we could get a grip on the situation. Only a few archaeologists and scientists, then now there's you, our interpreter!" Doherty was used to working with politicians and found that flattery usually worked best. "I understand that your specialty is ancient religious symbols and that you are here to examine the contents of the chamber."

"That is true." They walked in silence for several moments.

Returning to a dig site reminded Richard of his youth. Even as a college student, he had always been a member of the "old school", in his thinking, his dress, his scholarship. He originally mentored with one of the scholars modern critics referred to disparagingly as an "armchair anthropologist," or one who writes about past or foreign cultures without experiencing firsthand the actual culture being analyzed. With the subtle emergence of a more "politically correct" culture of the late twentieth century it lost public favor as agenda driven scholarship, as though that could be considered something new.

Richard, unlike his mentor, found that he legitimately enjoyed visiting digs. After graduation, Richard started taking volunteer positions on archaeological sites in Western Europe, the older the better. By this time, the Academy already had their eye on him. Richard enjoyed the stillness of a dig. Observing some captured moment in time from the remains of a people allowed Richard to preserve himself. It made him feel powerful. The sites became his own private space or, rather, the private frozen space of another that has no control over him. For this reason, he decided to specialize in the archaic past. There would be no living accounts.

Richard's approach worked well enough from his perspective. His graduate experience at Oxford and his family ties guaranteed him a starting position to teach at Harvard. As far as anyone else could tell, his genuine affection for books spurred an impressive showing of publications to ensure his permanent tenure. In the beginning, even he didn't realize that the Academy was helping him along quite as much as it was.

Richard wondered how much farther it would be down this tunnel. He felt the cool damp ground under his feet and the smell of ancient earth mixing with twenty-first century air. Doherty pointed his arm to the left, indicating their direction through the fork in the path that lay about thirty feet ahead.

After a while Richard asked, "Where are we exactly in relation to the city above?"

"We are right in the heart of it, Washington Street, the Gateway." Doherty explained. "Actually, we are one hundred twenty feet below the spot where the Liberty Tree once grew. This area wasn't all land fill, like most of the city. Of course, as you saw from the pit back there, the moisture content in much of the ground around the Big Dig sites still poses a problem. We've got it under control though, those pumps run day and night. They have their own power source and if they stop for any reason, we've calibrated the percolation rate sufficiently to allow for ample time to mediate any errors."

Richard thought it interesting that Doherty mentioned the Liberty Tree. Many Bostonians were unaware of its history or its old location. The story of the tree tells that it was a symbol of truth and freedom meant to greet all travelers at the gates of the city with good tidings. But in the days preceding the revolution, it became a harbinger of death, transformed into a tree for hanging those who didn't support the common cause of free speech and colonial liberation.

As they moved deeper through the dark maze of tunnels Richard thought they had come to a dead end, as the path seemed to fill with darkness.

"Here we are, Dr. Lyons," Doherty announced as Richard's eyes found a small rounded door-like opening in the jagged wall ahead. Doherty placed his hand on the rock, to the upper left edge of the opening, indicating the entrance. For a second or two Richard didn't understand why the entrance seemed to illuminate when Doherty touched it.

Then, Richard saw movement inside the chamber and his body clenched. His heart quickened. Someone else was in the chamber?

Doherty ducked his head at the opening. Richard could now just make out the space inside the small room and he saw a small woman in the darkened light. He was nervous at first, as it was difficult to see with the flashlight beams bouncing off the smooth surfaces. But he was sure he didn't know this woman. He was relieved.

"Hello," the female stranger said, her dark features now clearly visible.

Doherty started to respond, but abruptly a second voice interrupted from inside the chamber.

"Hello?" the second female voice quizzed as it bounced around the round interior. Richard couldn't quite make it out.

The second voice continued more smoothly this time, "oh, it is you Doherty! My, you did give us a fright."

Richard stopped breathing. For a fraction of a heartbeat he stood dead in his tracks. Unmistakably, that was the sound of Moira Fennessey's voice.

Incredulous that *she* was already in the chamber, Richard's nostrils flared and elbow hairs stood on end. He glared fiercely through the cut rock opening.

To everyone other than Richard, Moira looked like she belonged in the small round chamber and the sight of her gave him an eerie emasculated and threatened feeling.

"Hello, Moira. No surprise seeing you here. It is a bit early for you, though isn't it?" As it was Richard thought she was a foolish imp of a woman. Their history and mutual distaste for each other was obvious.

Moira's small and stout body masked the size of her presence well, until she wanted to be seen. She didn't like being interrupted when she was at a site and, although she was almost done here, at this moment she was giving critical instructions to her young assistant. She stopped mid sentence, turned only her head and looked across the chamber to Richard who was now squeezing through the rough stone opening.

"Yes Richard, Good Morning." She countered and then promptly resumed attention to her work and instructions so that they might ready to leave.

As a colleague, she was more than a mere annoyance to Richard Lyons. In faculty committee meetings she disrupted the flow of the agendas by taking issue with various procedures or institutional processes. But they were also students together, back in graduate school.

At one time, he even felt a strong attraction to her determination and insights. Despite Moira's meticulous research, dedication and talents, the gender politics of their schooling years dispelled any tolerance for her "absurd" interest in archaic goddess cults. When she refused to change the focus of her dissertation, one of her scholarships was yanked, and then given to Richard. He built his career on the backs of such institutional martyrs. Thus, Moira was to Richard a painful reminder of his own transgressions. And he feared that she knew too much about him. As a scholar, much to Richard's chagrin, Moira's work always had an underground following. It was now even internationally respected, even though it contradicted his own. Over the years, his fear had turned into loathing. And now he thought of her as a witch, an ugly, little, old crone, in mockery of the archetype that she found so empowering.

Seeing that they were preparing to leave, Richard Lyons bit his tongue and tried to ignore her. He did not come here to revisit their on-going debates. Instead, he studied the room. First he noticed how the dispersed lighting in the chamber created a strange low frequency hue. Then, he noted the overall shape. The room was semi-circular, approximately forty feet in diameter and Moira Fennessey stood at the far side, studying a small stone mound.

The room was dry, not damp, and somehow smelled sweet, sickeningly so. It was starting to give Richard a headache. He noticed that in the very center of the room an inverted bowl-like circular impression was cut from the stone floor. Within it sat the carving of a familiar symbol. Many of the surfaces were decorated with carvings of various shapes and sizes.

"Aah, fertility symbols," Richard provoked. "Very rudimentary, very ancient. This place must be thousands of years old. Nothing like this has ever been found around here."

"I know," Moira responded. She couldn't help herself, "of course it is clearly matriarchal."

"Come now, Moira, do not confuse fertility rituals with feminist politics. The existence of matriarchal cultures has never been proven to have existed."

"See Richard that is what I mean."

"Excuse me," Doherty interrupted, "Mr., I mean, Dr. Lyons, I must return to the surface." Doherty didn't step into the chamber, but he leaned into it, toward Richard, passing him a black duffel bag.

"This contains a radio to call me in case you find anything else of interest while you are down here, a flashlight, permitted hand tools and a letter from the Mayor. I see you already know Dr. Fennessey. Do your thing and call if you'd like a guide to the surface when you're done."

Doherty started to turn to go but the construction lights began to flicker on and off, then all the lights went dark. Everyone froze and felt for that moment the solitude and depth of the underground chamber's earthen darkness.

Doherty, already unnerved from not being used to such places, tried to stay calm by taking a long, slow, deep breath. Then, his cell phone started to ring, surprising him. He pulled it from his pocket and the blue light from the screen comforted him. But he was confused; the phone wasn't working five minutes ago. He lifted it to his eyes, casting the skin of his face in a rich glow of cerulean light and it stopped ringing. He realized that he was once again starring at an unresponsive phone, only this time in the dark and far under the dense surface of the earth.

"Why was this ringing down here?" he wondered out loud. He put the phone to his ear just as the construction lights came back on. In frustration and relief he thrust the phone back into his pocket.

Turning briefly to his company he said, "Well then, good day," and turned to leave. His footsteps echoed off the long, stone passageway.

"Raya," Moira looked to her assistant and packed up her belongings with seeming calm. "We have enough for now."

She was fully satisfied that they had sufficient data, more than she had ever hoped to find actually. Besides, she couldn't work peacefully alongside Richard in this small, powerful space. *I will be back*, she thought as she mustered her own "good day!" to her colleague. Moira and her assistant exited through the opening and Richard was glad to be left with his thoughts.

He had visited dozens of underground sites throughout his career, but he did not like this place very much. Trying to shrug it off to his agitation, he returned to studying the room.

The chamber was round all over with arched walls and a domed ceiling. The perimeter appeared to have been a perfect circle before the explosion, which ripped open one side. What remained revealed the skilled precision of its maker. It was entirely solid rock and resembled the inside of a geode, although the surfaces here were very smooth. The floor was decorated with carvings and an arrangement of stone mounds rising two to three feet in height. They appeared to be positioned in two concentric circles around the central basin shaped altar. The larger, outer circle of rock mounds was comprised of eight equally sized mounds, each at a height convenient for sitting, leaning or resting things. The rock looked polished and translucent; perhaps quartz or amethyst but he couldn't be sure in this light. Even though they were made of stone they appeared soft and malleable, inviting even. The inner and smaller circle was made up of rock mounds of a smaller size, but seemingly the same stone material. He counted these. They were also eight and circled the altar perfectly.

The convex altar was unlike anything Richard had ever seen before. It had been dug out from the earth, not constructed or placed upon it. Richard thought it seemed more like a fire-pit than an altar. He looked to the ceiling for an indication of a chimney. He noticed that the ceiling was also surprisingly smooth and plain. No signs of a vent or of any charring. *How did they make this*, he wondered, *and who?* The space was so quiet that except for the troubles with the lighting he would have forgotten that he was one hundred twenty feet underground. *How would they have gotten down here?* He knew that even though this room is far beneath the surface today it might not have always been. And even if it was, any passageway or continuous opening in the rocks would have been used advantageously in the blasting for the highway and subway tunnels and would already have been destroyed.

He noticed the shapes carved upon the walls; strange, biomorphic, fluid-like cellular creatures joining and intermingling like bubbles dancing in a spiral pattern. He wondered what else was destroyed by the explosion. *Had there been a door to this chamber, or was it sealed in solid rock? Hm, that makes no sense! There had to be a way in.* The function of the chamber would play a large part in his final assessment and the sheen of the rock surfaces indicated a lot of use.

Careful to step around the explosion debris, Richard entered the inner ring of mounds. He wanted to get a closer look at the inverted altar. The room's curious odor was strongest in the middle and it started to make his eyes water. Further complicated by the poor lighting, he decided to dig through the duffle for a flashlight. Finding it, he shone it on the ground. He was standing upon inscriptions. Shallow from wear, etched shapes were noticeable in the bright beam of light.

"Ah, there's a clue," he said aloud. He noticed there were a lot of these petroglyphs. He decided he had to take rubbings of these odd characters and realized that he was going to have to stay in this chamber for a while. He took advantage of the closest mound and sat down upon it. He rummaged through his leather valise until he found charcoal and paper tablets for rubbing. *This will take at least a few hours.*

Richard worked quickly, taking impressions of any marks in the floor that could have been deliberate. He hadn't even gotten to the center altar or the walls when his radio started beeping.

"Richard! Ah, Dr. Lyons, hello, are you there?" The voice on the hand held was Doherty. "I'm sorry sir, but I have to go. Something has happened."

Richard found the button and spoke into the speaker, "I hear you. Ah, thank you, but I can find my way back on my own. I don't need any more assistance. Good bye."

He looked at his watch. It was later than he thought, but he had a lot more work to do. There were many familiar fertility symbols; spirals, triple spirals connected at their center by a tiny rounded triangle, upside down triangles with a straight line drawn down the middle, and infinity symbols were etched everywhere. In the very most central spot of the room, where the rock had been cut back in the shape of a bowl, was the carving of a figure. Richard looked more closely.

It almost resembles a Venus, except... Hhhm? Ah! He glanced up to the dome above him, knowing full well what Moira would make of it.

* * * *

Moira wasted no time in returning to her office. It was true that she wasn't usually up this early and wanted to make the best of it, especially after what she had just seen.

She handed Raya a long list of assignments, notes she scribbled in the cab ride back to campus. She spoke quickly as she took off her coat and poured the coffee.

"No one knows it yet but this is an amazing archeological moment. Did you notice that the eight mounds formed an octogram?" Not waiting for an answer Moira quizzed, "tell me the significance of an octogram?"

"Octograms have magical implications. Despite having an even number of termini they can be formed by one continuous line. And, as a sacred symbol they are said to represent regeneration and parthenogenesis."

Raya Gupta had been Moira's assistant for only six months. She was a doctoral student from India, here at Harvard on scholarship. Moira selected her last summer as her teaching assistant largely because she was a woman with a strong sense of self. Moira could be difficult and demanding, at times even idiosyncratic, but Raya respected her expertise and was thrilled to be working for her.

"Yes, Raya, that is right. And why might we find an octogram's points imprinted upon the ground of a chamber?"

"Well," she answered, "early matriarchal societies used the interlacing path of a polygram drawn upon the ground in their religious rituals, to protect against various evils and negative energy. Depending on the number of points, different patterns were formed and each had their own qualities."

"Interlacement patterns are not only used for protection." Moira added, "Their energy forms a karmic imprint upon the time and space of the ritual. In this case the energy was even cast into the stone. And although they are used for magical circles, what we have here is a very high level magical rite. Why don't you get started on the research list I gave you? Remember Raya; speak to no one about this!"

"Of course, Dr. Fennessey!" And she left the room, clearly excited to complete her assignments.

Moira sat back, thinking about how best to present this material. *Academics tend to be conservative these days.*

This was no longer the hey-day of the feminist movement and discussions of early matriarchal cultures tended to make elbow pads shrivel. Still, she couldn't deny the connection between this chamber, and the symbols represented in it, with a myth she rediscovered years ago that linked ancient prophecies across various cultures.

At least the director of Harvard's Peabody Museum of Archaeology and Ethnology had recently been replaced and Moira would have a clean slate in working with the new one. His name was Nathan Grey and Moira had met him only once before at a faculty luncheon. Normally she wouldn't go to such things, but the event was a friend's retirement party. She didn't particularly enjoy the food, as little of it was vegetarian, but she paid her professional respect, as it were, and was preparing to leave when she was introduced to Nathan Grey. She was not in the mood for a conversation, but she liked his genuine enthusiasm and they seemed to have a ready rapport. Of course the new director was the least of her worries.

As Moira sat recoiling from the possibilities of meaning posed by the chamber, she recognized in this event the culmination not only of her life's work but of the last few thousand years of history. For Moira, viewing the chamber this morning was like a self-fulfilling prophecy.

The Earth is going to speak out! She thought. *Those eight mounds, they are not just breasts sitting down there!*

There were rare records of a similarly described site existing at Eleusis, back in ancient Greece, but as of yet no one had discovered any such chamber. And although the mountainous terrain at Eleusis revealed a few shallow caves, no evidence of tunneling or underground access had ever been found. The dominant view in her field was that the underground, magical chambers were only a myth. Still, she was compelled to search for clues and turned to the Eleusian Mysteries early in her career.

Written records about the people and spiritual customs of Eleusis are scant because the rites and beliefs of the Eleusian peoples were kept secret, earning their status as a "mystery cult." It is known, however, that the primary deity of their worship was Demeter, the provider of grain and mother to Persephone. It is also known that members were considered "seers" because at their initiation ceremonies Demeter was said to reveal her gifts to them, though what the gifts were still remains a mystery. Overall, the ceremony was described as one that creates a sense of "blessedness," in a non-Christian sense, as well as a mind-expanding, life altering, cosmic and blissfully ecstatic experience.

Moira had focused much of her career on unraveling their secrets and trying to get a clearer glimpse at their traditions and older matriarchal ancestors.

The Eleusian mysteries are among the most well known of the varied "mystery traditions" that reigned during the ten to five thousand years preceding the time of Christ. They are called mystery traditions on the one hand because the details of their ceremonies are not known to modern scholars, but also because their worship of the goddess was representative of their worshiping the mystery of life itself.

Moira followed each written account, mostly by non-initiated witnesses to their daily life and celebrations. Most of these, however, were relatively modern and were even written after the *telestarion*, or main temple, had been destroyed. Some documented the prophecies of the oracle. Most were terribly biased.

This must be one of the pulse points of the mother goddess! They'll really think I'm nuts this time. She took some time to decide how best to present the material before preparing for her next class.

* * * *

The deafening concussion from a thousand pounds of falling concrete reverberated through the air! It took only a second, and then it was over. Cars behind swerved, brakes screeched in horror. Traffic came to a full stop. The first completed tunnel of the Big-Dig had crumbled.

* * * *

Alex sat upon her favorite stool in the Twenty-First Amendment, commonly called the "Twenty-First," a local lunch and watering hole for lobbyists, tourists and the Suffolk University community.

"Cye, turn that back," she yelled to the man behind the bar. He was a native Bostonian and a friend. Alex had known Cye since the late nineteen eighties when she first started coming to this pub as a young assistant professor. She wasn't comfortable confiding in most people, but Cye was true to his function as the friendly neighborhood bartender and she found herself telling him things about her life. By now, not only did he know her name, he knew her favorite foods and drinks, how she preferred her coffee, how she preferred her men and why she usually avoided both. He was the closest thing to a long term relationship she had ever had.

Still flipping channels and reaching up to the TV, he eventually turned back to the last news station. "Breaking News Update" gleamed across the top of the screen in a bold blue hue. "Death by Big-Dig" scrolled underneath it.

A newscaster had already begun reporting and Alex's eyes were instantly glued to the screen: "The tunnel that collapsed had multiple exits and connected various parts of the city. As you can see behind me, the traffic has stopped and it appears that no one can come in or out of Boston by this highway. This is going to create a lot of difficulties for the city today. As you know, this tunnel which connects the city to the airport was a fashioned compromise between the Mayor and private resident interest groups, who have recently led the campaign of investigation for embezzlement and corruption. Attention now is sure to turn to their opponents, and of course the engineers who designed and monitored the construction at this location.

"It appears that at 1:18 this afternoon, an actual ceiling panel, which I am told is literally formed concrete and rebar, came crashing down upon the windshield of an unsuspecting vehicle. Full details have not yet been released but we do know that the rogue ceiling panel made impact with only one vehicle, that it was a Green Toyota Camry, and at least one passenger was dead before the arrival of the EMTs. The City is planning a full investigation. And we will keep you updated as soon as further details are released." Alex was stunned. Cye turned down the sound and activated the captions.

"Oh boy, that's awful," Cye said to her. "So many things have happened since the start of this Big Dig. Did you read last week how they had to re-do the same ceiling because it had leaks? Traffic was stopped then too. Can you imagine a multi-billion dollar project and it has leaks! It just goes to show: you do it nice 'cause you do it twice." Cye had been rated the best bartender in Boston five years in a row and it was largely because of his long pours and quick witticisms, this one not included.

Alex pushed her empty wine glass across the bar, towards Cye, for a refill. As he topped her glass she considered the implications of the accident, ignoring the possibility that it could be connected to the chamber. Still, she couldn't deny to herself that she had felt extremely anxious ever since Richard first told her about the chamber and news of this accident only made that anxiety grow stronger within her.

"The City is going to be forced to step in and do something," Alex responded. She arched her back against the stool and looked around the room. The atmosphere of today's lunch crowd was different; darker, cynical, quiet. It was not any less noisy than usual but the talk was serious and, except for the table of students joking amongst themselves, everyone was discussing the accident and their respective feelings about the Big Dig.

Two middle-aged women with shopping bags were talking at the table behind Alex. One was clearly more irate than the other, "What a joke! It has destroyed this city. Just the other day I was stuck in the underpass to the Mass Pike for forty-five minutes. Traffic was backed up from one end of the tunnel to the other. Given what happened, it's no wonder I felt like a sitting duck."

The waitress with the curly hair spoke up while delivering their lunch. She was a graduate student for urban planning and had followed the Big Dig closely. "This project was supposed to alleviate congestion and all it has done is make commuting more difficult. And what about all those green spaces and parks they promised the residents?"

The older dark man who was always at the bar spoke to Alex. "Did you hear, they are thinking of closing all the tunnels, even the smaller ones to the airport? First the leaking, now this! Who's to say we aren't all in danger."

Before Alex could reply, the female college professor on the other side responded, "I do not even know how to get to the airport anymore. I've been living in this city for twenty-five years and now I can't even get to work! Every day they change the signs and re-route the flow of traffic."

"Did you hear about the scaffolding falling down on the workers?" The well-dressed female professional with the heavy make-up and gold jewelry added from the other end of the bar. Alex took another sip of her wine and kept listening as the woman reported, "All this incompetence makes me nervous. It has been ten years since they started this project and the whole landscape of the city has changed. Boston used to be a great city, what's happening?"

The tall man with white hair in a blue suit stood up at the other end of the bar, drawing Alex's attention as he talked to Cye. She had seen him in here for years and occasionally they've had a drink together. He was a lobbyist at the State House. Alex watched them and watched Cye's expression as the voices from the room rang in her ears.

Nobody else knows. She was worried about what people's reactions would be when they found out. She also couldn't help but wonder if the city ever learned the name of the construction worker who died in yesterday's explosion. He was somebody's son, somebody's husband, maybe even somebody's father.

There was no doubt about it, the Twenty-First was a watering-hole for the discontent and it was getting busier by the minute. The stools at the bar were full and tables were quickly taken up. The well-worn floors and walls echoed with the spirit of true revolution from a more primitive time while its modern day occupants tried to figure out what was going wrong with their city.

Alex paid her bill and left, not feeling any better. She bundled up for the gusty wind and, heading to her office, walked toward Beacon Street. Turning the corner she heard the State House street prophet calling from his concrete, curb-shaped podium. He claimed to be a veteran and was always clad in patriotic gear. American flags were printed, embroidered and pinned to every garment draped over his frail little body. The travel sized shopping cart he towed donned two mini flag poles, complete with mini flags, strapped to either side and it held blankets and propaganda for the cause of the day. He yelled at no one and everyone, regardless of whether they listened.

"What are you people thinking?" he roared today. "Look around you!"

Alex usually enjoyed this guy. He was not a beggar and she couldn't tell whether he was homeless or not, but he was much older than the other street prophets in Boston. He didn't seem to want anything other than to be heard and his commentary was frequently more insightful than that of the evening news stations, so she didn't go out of her way to avoid him. The shortest path down Beacon Hill was to walk past him so without trepidation she crossed Beacon Street, towards his pulpit. He kept ranting.

"Something awful is about to happen! Stop giving up your rights! Stop taking what is not yours! Stop the government before it stops us all! I am a true American, I fought for our freedom. Where is it now? Look at what you have done, you, you and you!" He shouted pointing at pedestrians. He seemed to enjoy picking on those that wore the more expensive overcoats.

"You!" he screamed in a frenzy as he whirled around pointing a finger at Alex. He had never spoken to her before. She felt a muscle tighten in her solar plexus and now wished she had taken the other route down the hill. There was no time to turn back.

"You!" His voice dropped suddenly to a whisper as she approached. He captured her gaze. "You, you know, but you will not admit it. You have been shown the signs. Look below the surface. Look deeper!"

He started shouting again, "Look or it will be your end too!"

Her mind was racing over his words, "below the surface?" He held her gaze. "Underground, dear lady, underground."

Oh God, she thought and lowered her face against the onslaught of wind and verbiage, breaking his visual hold.

"It will be the end of us all, the end. The end, the end!" He kept screaming it like a refrain. Alex pulled her coat tighter and hurried down Park Street until his voice was barely audible over the noise of the traffic and the rhythm of the Big Dig's pounding.

* * * *

While Alex was leaving the Twenty-First, Diana sat at home, staring into her second cup of cappuccino as if she were crying. Night-Night would have enjoyed some, had she been given the chance. But Diana was intently focused on the cup. Not the cup really, because her mind was looking inward.

While she woke up early, she didn't get out of bed until ten and the past few hours of painting had been fruitless. Without reason, a sudden feeling of sorrow came over her and she was fighting the urge to go back to bed with another jolt of caffeine.

Diana was very *sensitive* and she knew it. She knew when something was wrong. She could feel it. All of her life she had a sense of things that others did not. Energy levels and astral planes were as real to her as the coffee she drank. She learned at a young age not to communicate everything she knew, lest she get an unfortunate label from unbelievers. But she never dismissed her gifts.

Fortunately, Diana's parents were well equipped to deal with their daughter's proclivities toward inner dimensions. Her mother, Phoebe, was also gifted - part psychic, part healer, and part Sunday school teacher. And Phoebe taught Diana how to cultivate her own gifts.

Her parents had owned and operated an alternative bookstore for spiritual seekers, lost hippies and theosophists since she was in the fifth grade, when they left Boston to move to Seattle. By the time she was fourteen Diana had been exposed to every major religious tradition, earth-based votive spiritualities, mysticism and various esoteric teachings, and was moving on to astrology, philosophy, yoga and meditation. Before graduating high school, she had familiarized herself with Alice A. Bailey and H. P. "Madame" Blavatsky. And her mother felt obliged to take her to psychic readings, past life regressions and aura cleanings. Diana thrived on all of it.

Diana never thought of herself as odd, rather she thought it odd that so many others live without ever seeing the truth of inner dimensions. She embraced the occult and developed her sight. She remembered a few times when she did not heed her own intuition, and each time was a learning experience!

Desiring to remain authentic to her creative and astral nature, Diana wanted to carve a life that would ensure her autonomy and self-expression. Being an artist was the solution. She had learned to trust her body and mind and her heart was genuinely over brimming with love - which is why one might describe her as a dolphin amongst the sharks. But with years she honed her fluidity into a toe shoe dance of balance and made a modest living practicing and learning from her arts.

She now sat smelling her coffee, contemplating what should be done. She looked to her familiar and determined, "Night-Night, I am going to have to do a meditation ritual, if I want to know what's going on. These feelings are far too heavy for me to grasp anything concrete. I am going to need to talk to my guides."

She reached over to scratch Night-Night's thin black ear.

Night-Night purred at her charge's action, and rolled over onto her back, exposing her belly.

"What do you think is happening?" Diana mocked, petting her.

Night-Night didn't answer Diana's prodding but she did know what was happening. She just couldn't tell Diana.

Having received enough attention, Night-Night jumped to her feet, yawned and stretched her long sleek legs. She looked to Diana, squinted her green feline eyes, and blinked.

I'm sorry there's nothing I can do to help you now. You have to figure it out for yourself. I'm only here for you when you are ready. In the meantime, I do not intend to work too hard. I'm going to find a little spot of sun.

After a moment or two, Night-Night moseyed over to the window seat, softly lit by the filtered glow of the winter sky, flicked her tail a few times, and then curled down into the perfect posture for a cat nap.

Of course Diana was not yet evolved enough to understand Night-Night's denial of assistance, but she was happy with her own chosen course of action. *It is better to act.* Diana put aside the cappuccino and began her stretching routine in preparation for a series of yoga asanas. After fully aligning her mind-body connection, Diana soaked in a rose petal bath to further cleanse and perfume her skin and aura in final preparation for her encounter.

She drew the curtains, closing out the world. She was ready to go into the land of magic and ritual, somewhere between consciousness and unconsciousness, between life and death, between spirit and matter. She set the altar. Green, red, blue and white candles were placed in a circle, respectively commemorating the east, south, west and north corners and corresponding to the four elementals: air, fire, water and earth. Diana felt that these things and all things are interconnected and she laid them in such a way as to remain mindful of what she was invoking. Air is life and holds the power of divine creativity, fire feeds our passions, water sustains us as we ebb and flow with the currents of our emotions, and the earth, she is our ground.

Diana lit the incense to purify the time and space and cast a protective circle of salt as she chanted three times,

Salt and sea, of ill stay free,
fire and air draw all that is fair,
around and around the circle is bound.

Diana sat, legs crossed in half lotus. The room was dark, except for the candles flickering about her.

She heard the noises from the street outside and the clunking breath of steam heat banging and rattling through old radiators.

Breathing in...

...and breathing out...

Diana acquired focus through her breath. Her mind calmed and the worldly senses faded. She began to forget the sounds and smells of the room, and her frazzled emotions. Diana knew that whatever answers she sought would be provided in "perfect love and perfect trust" with the universe.

Diana traveled inward, in search of her guide. She was ready to begin an alpha countdown.[1] It would transition her quickly.

In rhythm with her breathing, Diana visualized the number seven cast in a shroud of red. Red is the color of passion. She reflected and drew energy from all around her remembering the ways passions make us freely who we are. And where would we be without them?

Breathing in and breathing out, she next visualized an orange six. Orange is the color of vitality and she could feel its vibrations altering her consciousness going deeper and deeper.

A yellow five is for communication. Diana loved yellow and felt its inspiration open a new horizon of creative expression.

Concentrating deeper still, she visualized a green four. Green is healing energy, the color of grass.

Diana reflected on the blue three. Blue is for intuition and insights. She would need clarity too. She concentrated even more, now hypnotized by the ease of her breath.

An indigo two is the color of the rich earth and stands for stability.

Finally, the ultraviolet digit, one, brings forth potentiality, the all of magical possibilities.

Transcending the simple reality of the material plane, Diana was now embraced in clear white light and using her own sacred symbol as a kind of key, she unlocked a door and walked through the portal of the unconscious.

Diana always went to the same place. She created an astral portal for herself many years ago and only used it when all conventional ways of wisdom had failed.

On the other side of the portal was what Diana could only describe as Artemis' garden. *Artemis*, the Greek Goddess of Nature, is the equivalent to *Diana* from Roman Mythology, the Goddess of the Hunt. Since the first time Diana ever visited this astral garden, Artemis had always met her there. Diana appreciated Artemis as a powerful goddess and wild woman archetype.

Diana entered the garden. Everything was serene. And the colors... she always loved the colors here. Brilliant flowers and succulent ground cover of every kind and texture imbued the place with soft and fluid hues of green, pink and gold busting from themselves in the clear bright light. Trees and shrubs grew rich next to a small stream and Diana inhaled the lusciousness of the environment.

The air was alive.

Diana sat upon a bed of clover and waited, breathing in and breathing out. Butterflies danced past her and a few Monarchs stopped to land upon her shoulder. Some places on earth these Monarchs are almost extinct but here they fluttered eternally. The birds too were many and varied and were heard chirping, singing and courting. Next small animals started to peep out of the cover of the lush greens as if to welcome her.

Diana felt the presence of the goddess emerge. It is always an awkward moment when one encounters a goddess or any divinity for that matter, and Diana, although familiar with the experience, was perpetually taken aback at first.

Neither spoke, for the language of the goddess is beyond linear logic, subject and predicate. The goddess already knew what was needed. And so Diana just watched and felt. She listened with her inner ear and waited.

In the days of the ancient Greek Mystery traditions it was commonly believed that all power and knowledge came about only through a direct encounter with the Goddess herself. As Diana sat and waited for answers she started to feel something happen.

Projecting from the Goddess's heart Diana sensed her own heart expanding, becoming heavy and full. Joy and sorrow, rage and forgiveness, justice and passion all culminated and beat inside her like the pulse of the cosmos. She thought she was going to explode from ecstasy and pain. The love of the goddess was being poured into her but she also felt intense grief. A pale pink light emanated from the heart-center of the Goddess into Diana. It was brief and ecstatic, and then the Goddess was gone.

Oh my word, thought Diana. She reached down to touch the earth and reassure herself. It was warm and the soil smelled sweet. She noticed a coin pressed into the cover of clover, next to her foot.

Diana picked up the coin; no it was more like a rune. She turned it over, in hopes of a message. It bore the mark of an eight, an infinity symbol.

This puzzled Diana because this place was eternal. She already knew this.

She looked about for more clues. It was obvious that the goddess still surrounded her, in the lushness of the trees, in the birds and the bees. Love surrounded her.

A long legged hare lopped into the opening, where the Goddess gracefully stood a few minutes before. Diana looked in its direction and noticed a new horizon. It looked like Boston but cloaked in a dark fog, and at a far distance, perhaps from the harbor.

She rose to get a better view but it quickly disappeared, replaced with a waxy hedge, laden with ripe berries. Next, the rune dissolved in her hand, telling her that it was now time for her to go.

Diana followed the length of her golden astral tether and properly returned to her body. She opened her eyes to her candlelit room and thought, *we are all called to bear witness to what is... but what is it?*

To complete the ritual she gave her thanks to the guardians of the corners and closed the circle just as she'd begun, but in a counterclockwise direction. She blew out the candles and in conclusion blessed, "The peace of the Goddess."

So much pain, Diana thought as she returned her ritual objects to the altar. *The earth is in so much pain.* Diana did not know what to do first: think, write, take notes, drink. She was afraid that at any moment she would go yelling and screaming through the streets. *The earth is in pain, heal the earth, the earth is in pain!* Recalling her dream, she took a deep breath and tried to override her mind. Her intuition was telling her that there was a reason for all this, but she didn't know what it was.

* * * *

Raya Gupta sat in the front row of Dr. Fennessey's 'Archaeology of the Ancients' lecture class, taking meticulous notes. As Dr. Fennessey's Teaching Assistant she was responsible for ensuring that the students actually understood the lecture. She wanted to be prepared when they bombard her later with questions.

"Goddess mythologies were the earliest means of understanding the order of life and genesis of the universe." Moira Fennessey lectured, while sitting on her desk in the front of the classroom. Every so often she made a point that got her so excited she jumped down from the desk and ran to the blackboard to outline it for her students.

Moira spoke quickly and passionately: "The situation in the Aegean basin, the cradle of Greek thought, parallels in many ways that of early India which, in the late Neolithic Age saw a migration of semi-nomadic, herding, androcratic warriors into an area whose indigenous population was primarily agricultural and gynocentric. But, as the modern science of Ethnology is revealing, indigenous cultures are not so easily obliterated: the 'world-view' and ways of a subjugated people, as preserved in their art, religious rituals and especially their myths, is not so easily erased. Worship of the divine feminine principle is the oldest religion in the world. These earliest religions were centered on the worship of a single 'Triple-Goddess, so-called because of her three phases as maiden, mother and crone corresponding to the phases of life and the three seasons of spring, summer and winter. Since the reproductive cycles of plants and animals are governed by these seasons, she was also identified with Mother Earth. These Neolithic civilizations, centered on agriculture with a corresponding gynocentric and peaceful world-view, were subjected to a series of invasions by herding peoples whose culture was basically androcratic, patriarchal, patrilineal and militaristic. Beginning around 3,500 B.C.E., history can be viewed as the struggle of indigenous peoples to preserve their customs and religion, art and mythic lore, in the face of successive waves of invaders. Thus, the earliest myths testify to the oppression of patriarchal culture trying to subdue the matriarchal elements of indigenous traditions."

Raya always enjoyed Dr. Fennessey's lectures. She grew up in a small village just outside New Delhi. Unlike most of the American students, she was raised to respect the creative, rejuvenative powers of the feminine principle as celebrated through the goddess traditions, so Moira's lecture was not foreign to her. Like Moira, Raya could appreciate that certain value structures get coded into one's subconscious through acts of worship and the impact of myth.

Moira's lecture continued, "Despite the general reliance on oral myth and esoteric symbols to reveal the existence and attributes of these matriarchal ancestors, there are other references by well respected, historical figures such as Sophocles, Aristophanes, Clement of Alexandria, and even Plato. It is almost shocking therefore that there remains today a shadow of doubt over their existence within the academic community.

"Some of you might be familiar, for instance, with Plato's famous 'Myth of the Cave,' from his *Republic*. You should have learned about it in your Philosophy classes. In his myth Plato was talking about knowledge and used the metaphor of being kept in a cave, where everything you are allowed to see is merely a shadow cast from a puppet held against a fire light, at an unseen distance. Well, conventional wisdom of western scholars throughout the modern centuries teaches that Plato designed this myth to represent humanity's movement from the darkness of ignorance into the light of reason. But it is no accident that Plato selected the cave for this metaphor, if it is a metaphor at all. In reality, the cave is symbolic of the womb and was frequently used by some goddess cults for ceremonial events. Some scholars have argued that Plato himself was an initiate into one of the prevalent Goddess cults of his day. Bearing this in mind, Plato's metaphor was actually heralding the shift of power, the movement out of the womb of the Great Mother Worship into the light of patriarchal control. Remember it was Plato that went on to create the Academy that established patriarchal knowledge as the standard for education. That Plato was successful in overcoming what he perceived to be the irrational elements of Goddess worship is evident today by the fact that some of you cannot conceive of any other way to think."

Moira's reputation as the resident feminist on campus made her delivery of anything resembling feminist ideology less palpable to skeptical students. And every semester at least one student challenged that the only difference between matriarchy and patriarchy was gender – as in which sex holds the most power. It was Moira's goal to ensure that inevitably such a student would come to realize that this view simply arose from an inability to see beyond the patriarchal control paradigms.

Even still, Raya could see that the American students in particular did not have the cultural background to understand the full thrust of Moira's point about goddess mythology. It's about cooperation with the whole, not control. Moira recognized the look of uncertainty and doubt in the students' eyes, but she had faith in Raya's ability to answer their questions. Besides, Moira was much more concerned about her next audience with the new director.

In conclusion she said, "Utilizing the mythical conceptualizations the Goddess as the force of nature, as the wilds and as the Earth herself, draws dramatic attention to colonization practices that are harmful to humans, plants, animals and the earth. The earth is alive after all. It is whole and organic and does move in synch with the cosmos. Over the next week I'd like you all to consider whether you actually move in such synch with the cosmos."

As Moira ended her lecture, students packed up books and papers while Raya prepared for the onslaught of students that would be waiting for her after class.

Moira too gathered her pages of notes and turned to Raya, "after you collect the assignments, Raya, I would also like you to grade them this week. I have a lot of extra work now, as you know. How are you coming on that list of research?"

Raya replied, "Fine, Dr. Fennessey. I should be done with it by tomorrow morning."

"Great! Thank you. Leave it under my office door, or email it to me when you are done." Then, aware of the urgency of the situation, she added for encouragement, "This is a very exciting time, you know… for all of us."

"Yes, Dr. Fennessey, don't worry, I can handle this."

* * * *

Moira left the classroom quickly, she was anxious to get to the Peabody Museum and see Nathan Grey. When she heard yesterday that the Mayor specifically requested Richard's involvement she realized that she was going to have to act quickly. She knew too well that Richard's first response was habitually 'divide and conquer.'

Best case scenario, he will want to dismantle the chamber, move it into a lab for further study and then petrify it in a museum gallery. Worst case… he'll try to destroy it. From all the media heat the Mayor had recently gotten over the Big Dig there was no reason that Moira could see that the Mayor wouldn't share in Richard's own goals.

Having just lectured about matriarchal societies, Moira's body and mind were fully prepared to articulate to the new director why this chamber should not be touched or further disturbed. But she knew that Richard Lyons would likely also be meeting him this morning and she did not want to be drawn into another heated debate with Richard on what she knew otherwise to be true. The stakes were just too high.

Moira's work had taken her in directions that contradicted traditional academic scholarship and as far as she was concerned, so much the better. Archeology relies on science, yet so much of it is a matter of interpretation and in a male dominated field, those interpretations can tend to support the status quo. Scholars like Richard had long dismissed matriarchal artifacts as pornographic figurines and Moira believed this was simply self-serving scholarship.

This will be an interesting challenge for the new director, she thought to herself as she hurried through the cold.

The museum was located across campus on the other side of a small open field. As Moira approached the Museum she noticed how its flat façade accentuated the grey of the stone stairs and doorway, reflecting the color of the afternoon sky. Momentarily, she wondered whether the cool light surrounding her was an omen of some kind. She had an ancient oracle on her mind. But she also had a sense about this director, that he was intelligent and reasonable. He certainly was younger than the previous one, but in her brief introduction Moira found Nathan to be grounded, open minded and aware; like a wise old soul.

* * * *

Nathan Grey came to work very early this morning. Having been informed that Harvard could be making a large, possibly temporary acquisition he wanted to clear his desk and schedule for the coming weeks. He had been called to a meeting with the President. All he was told was that he must secure an exhibit hall within the next week, organize cataloguers, coordinate with the insurance carrier, schedule an opening day for the new exhibit and meet with the faculty who were working at the site. Since seven that morning he had already been inundated with paperwork, had the meeting with the President, another with the gallery coordinator, then Richard Lyons, and now knew that his next appointment, Moira Fennessey, would arrive at any moment. He wasn't used to working this way. And it was only his first week.

Nathan Grey was not a man who had difficulty dealing with powerful women. Having grown up in a household of seven sisters, without a father figure, Nathan knew how women typically either yield or wield their power. As a biracial American he understood oppression, but living with so much female energy taught him to cultivate his own knowledge of balancing power. He had been looking forward to conversing with Dr. Fennessey and hearing what she had to say about the chamber, especially since he had just met with Richard Lyons. Their reputation for rivalry preceded both of their appointments.

Moira arrived at Nathan's office looking a little disheveled. She was carrying her knapsack, books and papers all of which were now in a state of disarray. She was clearly windblown from her trek across campus.

"Hello again Mr. Grey."

"Please call me Nathan," he rose to greet her warmly as she put down her burden of books, unwrapped her simple brown plaid scarf, and removed her down parka before seating herself opposite his desk. She plopped into the chair with a jovial sigh.

Nathan's office was neat, nicely decorated and well organized. But Moira noticed there was a distinct lack of personal objects. There were no photos on his desk and no memorabilia on the book shelves. Nevertheless, the office had an aura of warmth and professionalism. Moira usually did not experience these two things together and she found herself wondering who Nathan Grey was as a person, rather than as an administrator.

"It is good to see you again, Moira," Nathan said sitting down into his leather chair. "Can I get you something, coffee or tea?"

"No thank you, Nathan. It's good to see you, too. I hope that you are settling in alright here in Cambridge," she responded. "How are you finding your situation?"

"To be honest it is a bit of an adjustment. But I seem to be managing."

"You are not from around here are you, Nathan?" Moira picked up on a slight accent for the first time.

"No, actually I'm not."

"Oh, that's right you worked at the Smithsonian for some time didn't you?'

"Yes, I was the assistant to the director of the Museum of Ancient History."

"Very impressive," Moira said genuinely. "Harvard and the Smithsonian have maintained a long and reciprocally fruitful relationship. I'm sure that your experience and success here will only continue to strengthen it. Actually, I do recall reading a little about your background when they announced you as a new hire."

"Well, good, and I know something of your work as well."

"Really," she responded, quite surprised. She studied his face and only discerned a genuine pleasantness in his expression, without prejudgment.

"Your books on ancient goddess traditions and early mystery cults were classics for some of us in graduate school. I remember reading your critique of the anthropologist who investigated the ancient site in Velea, Italy. I laughed when you described their methodology as anachronistic."

"Nathan, thank you. You have no idea how glad I am to hear that, especially in light of this chamber. I presume that you are making all the appropriate arrangements but... Well, Nathan, let me be blunt. I ought to warn you that I plan to protest any disruption of this site. It just can't be touched. At least, not until I have a chance to do some more research."

"Excuse me?" Nathan chuckled at Moira's feistiness. "There are no active plans to have it moved, yet."

"Yes, I realize that but you cannot move it at all. And Richard Lyon's *M.O.* has consistently been move first, ask questions later." She said emphatically.

"Just what exactly do you think it is, Moira?" asked Nathan.

"I do not want to say too much right now. Tell me, have you met with Richard Lyons?"

"Yes, earlier today in fact. He is waiting for some final reports and looking forward to examining the contents of the chamber in a more leisurely manner. He has a pretty firm idea about the nature of those symbols and showed me some of the rubbings he made. He believes it is a fertility chamber; a pagan temple where ancient rites were performed to ensure successful procreation and reproduction."

"I'm sure he does," Moira responded slowly.

"I take it you disagree?" Pushing a little further Nathan inquired, "In fact I suspect you often disagree?"

"Nathan, the problem is that a chamber of this kind, and the symbols within it, point to more than a mere celebration of intercourse and reproduction. The rites performed there are much more powerful. And most importantly, I suspect that it would not just lie dormant all these centuries and pop up like an empty tomb. This chamber is still . . . *charged*, if you know what I mean."

"You mean hexed?"

"In a manner of speaking."

"Huh, and I am sure that Richard would say it is only rock and clay."

Moira wasn't sure if he was being condescending or playful. He continued, "There are many legends about protective curses cast upon ancient sites and the quick demise of the archaeologist that doesn't heed its warning. But myths of these kinds were generally intended to keep robbers away from pyramids and tombs filled with treasure. Why would that be a concern here? Did you find a treasure?"

"Perhaps..." Nathan's eyes furrowed, so Moira explained.

"Look, this chamber may not be filled with gold, but what went on there pre-dates simple fertility rites and is much more powerful than what our post-modern brains can accept, especially when approached with the Frazierian attitude that our modern view of reality and science is superior and that ancient peoples were somehow lesser, underdeveloped, ignorant versions of ourselves. Richard believes the chamber celebrates intercourse and reproduction because the symbols celebrating life and feminine powers have been relegated to the singular role of birthing by outdated, closed minded scholars before him and he has no talent for independent thinking!"

Quickly realizing she didn't really know Nathan yet, Moira probably shouldn't have undermined Richard so blatantly, but she couldn't help herself. It slipped out. She downplayed the professional faux pas by making her point carefully.

"In my initial investigation I noted subtler images and symbols in this chamber that have been paid less attention through the years. And although there is no documentation that has ever been found together in one place before, there are oral histories and myths that talk of such places. Nathan, this discovery is potentially epic and indicates that some of those myths might be more than mere symbolism. If you have any understanding or appreciation for my work then you must be aware of the reputation for magic that is said to have been harnessed by some of the most ancient matriarchal civilizations?"

Nathan, now leaning forward on his elbows, just barely nodded while staring at her intently. She continued.

"I... I just need to be sure about how much time I have so that all of the connections I see can be drawn out and paid their due. In the meantime, I am just warning that I suspect it could be unstable and should not be disrupted until we have a better idea of what went on there. I know it is hard to believe that something this old is here in Boston but matriarchal temples are all over other continents, middle and central Europe, South America, the Middle East, the Far East, Africa, so why not here? It is only a question of geography."

"And time," Nathan smiled and smirked, or smirked and smiled, Moira couldn't quite tell. But he nodded his head again as if he understood and finished by saying, "I agree that everyone must have ample time to do their research. There is obviously a lot of controversy here and I want to protect the integrity of this project. Nothing is going to happen until I am sure we have everything we need for an accurate assessment."

"Thank you, Nathan. I am glad that you understand. I just want to make sure I have time to prove my findings."

Moira stood to leave and Nathan held the door open for her as she gathered up her belongings.

"We should meet for lunch sometime," Moira said. "I do not usually do lunch but I think we may have some things to talk about." Nathan admitted that she was the first faculty member to invite him for lunch and that he would be delighted.

* * * *

Marino stood by the long window in his home office that overlooked the Boston Common. A light snowfall had dusted the trees, softening the naked branches. He was thinking about the woman who lost her life only a few hours before. He always took himself quite seriously and felt rather responsible. As a Mayor he was a politician in the truest sense; he was very talented in the arts of sleight of hand. But as far as call to service went, he genuinely cared about the impact his term had upon the public and individuals. He heard his maid approach the room's grand double door entrance. Ever since his loving wife died tragically, he kept a maid on staff, just so there would be another person in the large and otherwise quiet building. He turned to face her. The old wooden door creaked slightly.

"Sir, Mr. Doherty has arrived."

"Ah, send him in."

John Doherty emerged from behind the young woman almost instantly. He stepped into the office which was furnished with antique wingback chairs and leather sofas. The room seemed to have been frozen in a different era. The gas light fixtures, now converted to electric, were original. Intricate plaster moldings and medallions were impeccably preserved and not one pane of the old leaded glass windows showed their age. They cast a light purple hue across the face of Marino. His modern tailored suit looked out of place in the historic home.

"Afternoon Sir." Doherty greeted the Mayor.

"That will be all for now Maria, thank you." She nodded, clasped the decorative brass door handle, and closed the massive paneled door.

"Here, Doherty, sit by the fire." The marble mantel was also dated, but classic in its beauty. In such a setting, the fire would be inviting in any season. Marino bore his own stresses from the growing chaos but Doherty spent the entire day running crisis intervention over the Big Dig. His morning involved leading the archeologists and academics in and out of the chamber. And his afternoon was absorbed by the police, news crews and engineers hammering out what to do over the fallen ceiling panel in the motorway tunnel. It all took longer than expected and it was a grave crisis. Marino could tell that John was tired and still very cold.

Marino sat down into a large leather chair and gestured for Doherty to sit beside him. "I have some good news," Doherty announced as he approached the chair and sat down into it.

"Thank you, I am certainly ready for some, fill me in."

"Well, the worker who was killed by the blast yesterday has been identified. The family is being contacted now."

"Excellent, now what is being done about today's accident with the ceiling panel? Is there a time line in place to check the soundness of the other panels and get that route open again?" Marino was very calm under the circumstances. When he heard that the panel fell, taking yet another life, he retreated into seclusion and hadn't left his house since.

"The entire ceiling is being checked as we speak. The chief is going to get me a report as soon as possible. And," Doherty continued, "There are the engineers. The liability for most of this should be shouldered by the contractors and the engineers. The contracts were very..."

Marino interrupted him, "Yes, I know about the contracts Doherty, but I'm the Mayor and this started as a city project!" Marino's voice was slightly raised. Doherty hit a nerve. His training was as a lawyer and in his career the government corruption which was historically so common place left him a bit sated. Sometimes he lacked the finesse to understand that legal liability is a very different beast than political liability. Plus, Marino's high ethics and honesty rebelled against Boston's politics, and he didn't appreciate the implication that another loss of life could be classified as a mere legal frustration. Catching himself, he continued more subdued.

"Never mind Doherty, that's not what we need to discuss right now, the press will have their field day and Graham is planning my strategy anyway." Meredith Graham was a parallel colleague to John Doherty.

"Right, sir. My staff is working with the Governor's team. The chamber has been examined by an outside engineer who's consulting with Public Works. Harvard's also cooperating, as you requested, to begin the identification and classification protocols. As it turns out

UMass and the State Museums don't have capacity anyway; they are still cataloguing the sites from Spectacle Island and the sea wall. Harvard does have availability for housing artifacts and the chamber itself when the excavation begins. All appropriate guarantees for confidentiality were properly secured."

"What excavation, Doherty?" Marino had previously directed his staff to ensure the chamber wouldn't be disturbed, that the Big-Dig should be re-routed around this find. Doherty on the other hand had already discussed the situation with the senior foreman. He had been underground and spent more time studying the maps and reports than the Mayor. He had waited until now to bring it up.

"The digging in that location cannot be redirected. The increase in expense that would result from rerouting will likely cost your administration the next election. Boston's underground is too crowded. Where the chamber is situated already perforates the recommended allowances between tunnels for that depth. The initial report was not ambiguous. While it is theoretically possible, there is a very high risk of further flooding and instability."

Turning his head back towards Doherty, Marino added, "and the Governor?"

Orange flames from the fireplace reflected off Doherty's glasses, shading any view of his eyes.

"Yes, the Governor is on board. We have been in regular communications with the state and the Governor's office will act as liaison with the federal agencies. It's not going to be as easy as it sounds. There are federal issues. Of course we have to comply with the Antiquities and Historic Preservation Acts and The Native American Grave Protection and Repatriation Act of 1990 might also apply to this site. We still don't know. When we know what it is and who built it, whether it's for burial or something else, we'll know for sure. But the local Indian Nations will surely want to have access to make their own decisions."

"You've seen the chamber, haven't you?" The Mayor was staring into the fire which cracked and popped in a hypnotic rhythm. He spoke as if they hadn't already been speaking, with a touch of enthusiasm. "Is it really very old?"

"It might be sir. I've never seen anything like it before. It doesn't clearly evidence a tribal connection from what I've seen. There didn't appear to be any human remains, or artifacts or even tools for that matter. Anyway, the staff has been preparing the required reports and we'll just have to hope for the best in negotiation. Our priority is just getting the site and any of its artifacts moved. It's just that it doesn't look like the kind of thing one could move. It's more of a space than a thing."

"Oh, Doherty, that reminds me, I want Dr. Alexandra Martin brought in on these negotiations. She's a law professor and comes very highly recommended by Richard Lyons. We need someone on our team that has experience working with the Tribes and Indian law."

"Sir, the state has a team."

"Listen, this is not just a shell heap." Before construction began on the Big Dig, teams of archaeologists first surveyed the areas to be impacted for artifacts and historic remains. One of the teams on Spectacle Island found a giant shell heap, or "midden", containing among other things, Native American fish harpoons.

"Harpoons are easier to negotiate over and move than a 'space,' as you put it, made of solid rock-wall. If this is a burial site, I want someone to consult with who really knows the people and the federal systems. From what I've heard she's worked with the Wampanoags before. She can work with the state's people too. Besides, it will free up your team to have an expert."

Marino knew from previous experience that Doherty didn't like working with outside consultants of any kind. There was a clear difference in working styles between government employees and those in private practice, especially with lawyers. And he was tired of dealing with academics who in his view were all overly opinionated, idealistic and naïve about the way government business actually gets done. But he knew better than to fight this decision. Richard Lyons and the Mayor were very good friends.

"Ok, I will have her contacted today. Dr. Alexandra Martin, you said?" Doherty wrote the name onto the same note pad, gathered his files, and prepared to leave.

"Yes, she works at the law school, here on the hill. She should be expecting you. I told Richard we would contact her."

"Ok, sir. Enjoy the fire, I'll keep you updated." Doherty rose from the chair and walked to the doors, leaving Marino alone with the fire and a few moments of peace.

* * * *

It was late in the afternoon. Alex had finished teaching her classes and welcomed the idea of going home. Rather than risk a delay on the Orange line, or a rogue ceiling panel on the turnpike, she decided it simplest just to walk. She recalled the earlier episode of the street prophet with a shudder, but she would be going in the opposite direction. Still, she resolved to walk quickly.

The air was crisp and cold as she hurried through the Commons. Half way home, the wind changed. It was wild. Chicago is sometimes referred to as the "windy city." Alex had visited Chicago a few times and observed that the wind blowing off the great lakes was exactly that, wind. But here in the heart of Boston the wind and the architecture created a vortex that could knock you down and blow you back up hill.

The tall buildings of the Financial District, Beacon Hill and the Back Bay were oriented to the harbor and flanked by the Charles River in such a way that they created a series of wind tunnels, amplifying the wind's force like a cyclone. Alex pushed on, determined not to be swept off course or blown into somebody. Everyone else on the sidewalk was also having difficulty. Gusts pushed in alternating currents. And looking up at the buildings, Alex wondered whether the architects ever considered such things. *No wonder there is always a mark of tension on people's faces in this city, just getting to and from work is a challenge.* Counterbalancing the forces and negotiating the crowds, she kept a healthy pace on her way down Boylston Street toward the safety of her condo.

* * * *

Diana had spent the rest of her afternoon rummaging through her home library trying to soothe her emotions and ignite her mind to the imagery of her encounter. She had been looking for something to help her unconscious process what she learned from the Goddess in her meditation. Trying to articulate what was down deep inside the recesses of her psyche, she poured through all of her books on magic and sacred symbols. She knew at least that the Goddess had commanded her to speak and to act. Diana determined that the Goddess was in pain, just like the earth, just like the city, just like its inhabitants, and everyone had to do their part to correct it – although she knew there was more to it. She also knew that there was no such thing as a coincidence.

Taking a long, slow, deep breath – this time for courage and strength – Diana reached for the phone to call Alex.

* * * *

The telephone rang just as Alex entered the front door of her condo.

"Hello."

"Hey, Alex, it's me. Are you busy?"

Alex could tell that Diana didn't sound like herself. Not waiting for an answer, Diana went on, "I need to speak with you. Can I come over?"

"What's the matter? I just walked in the door," Alex said while setting down her briefcase which she knew was full of papers that she still needed to grade.

"Well," responded Diana, "nothing I can talk about over the phone. The Patriot Act aside, I need to see you in person. This is important."

Alex wasn't sure at first, but Diana typically didn't invite herself over on a school night, so decided, "Sure, my grading isn't due till next week. Could you pick up some Thai food on your way over though? My fridge is empty."

* * * *

As the old adage goes, the journey to a friend's house is never long. For Diana, however, the journey between their two homes felt like an odyssey. She was infused with a purpose and the whole way there, she kept trying to figure out how she was going to convey all of what she had been experiencing to her friend. Alex was extremely rational and not prone to flights of the imagination or the spirit and Diana knew that she must be very controlled. She was going to need Alex's help.

She meditated as she walked. Dogs and commuters, out for their early evening constitutionals hardly noticed her as she passed by, reading quietly the aura of the city as she went. It throbbed with the coming storm like an open wound, still hot and sharp with pain. She barely felt the cold, dusk air as she proceeded to their favorite Thai restaurant where she picked up the order. On her way up the street to the wine cellar she noticed the lights on the top of the Prudential Center flashing red, indicating that bad weather was coming yet again.

The Pru, as it is affectionately called, is a landmark for many Bostonians. No longer the tallest building in

Boston, it still stands as a beacon in the heart of the Back Bay. Diana usually found it reassuring, but tonight it felt ominous lurking above the city, as though it was forecasting something other than the weather.

* * * *

Alex was fairly well relaxed by the time Diana arrived at her friend's ultra-contemporary condo. Unlike Diana's row house, which was an 1890's antique, Alex's penthouse did not shake, rattle or roll with the gusting wind outside. The windows were brand new and air tight, silencing the screaming sirens and bustle of the streets below. Diana carried in the packages of food and was happy to see that Alex had already set out plates and wine glasses on the coffee table in her living room, alongside the blazing gas fireplace.

She kicked off her shoes and made her way through Alex's living room which was meticulously furnished with some of her parents' antiques and her own collection of Scandinavian hardwoods. Diana glanced out at the sky as she passed in front of the small wrought-iron balcony, then sat down next to the coffee table on a very plush rug and leaned back against the base of an over-stuffed lounge chair. Alex poured the wine and arranged the plates and napkins.

"I am so hungry," she said to Diana, who loved the flavors of Thai food but never found it to be very filling. Both women ate absent mindedly as they chattered about the weather and their respective days. Maintaining good manners they skirted around the obvious until they finished their meal.

"So what is going on?" Alex asked, seeming quite relaxed as she sat back with her glass of wine.

Diana herself was anything but, and was grateful for Alex's demeanor. She knew she should tread lightly where Richard or Alex's work is involved but there was no way to be subtle so she watched her closely as she began.

"I was hoping you would tell me more about that chamber Richard was talking about. And... can you get me down there to see it?"

Alex's eyes narrowed quizzically but her reaction was not defensive.

"Sure... I mean... I can tell you what I know. But... I haven't decided what I am going to do. Why?"

Diana cautiously continued, "Alex do you remember when I had that dream about your father and tried to warn you that he was dying and you did not want to believe me? Well, this is a little like that only much worse." Alex wondered what could possibly be worse than the death of a parent as her friend explained.

"You remember the dream I had the other night. I think I told you about the screaming woman in it. Well, she was sending me a wakeup call so that I would listen to what is going on. Alex, I need you to believe me about something here." Taking another reflective sip of wine she continued, "It is about the Big Dig. I cannot explain to you how I know, but it's serious."

"Diana, you are not going to tell me that you think the Big Dig is cursed are you?"

Both women laughed knowing that Alex was only half joking. Alex knew her dear old friend had a new-age-ancient-wisdom-psychic-bent and tried to do more than just tolerate it. But, if truth be told, she could not understand it and often struggled with what to do when Diana's predictions and interpretations proved to be correct. Alex had come to believe that Diana's "sixth sense" (for Alex did not know what else to call it) was usually accurate and at least always insightful.

Gently Alex asked, "So, what are you trying to say then?"

"You know about global warming, we all know about global warming. You know about the environmental abuses all over the planet, the melting ice caps, the destruction of the land and its resources, the polluted waters and dirty air. We buy bottled water! We are told that the air and even the sun is unsafe and people seem to just sit back and accept it."

"Yes, Diana, I know but what does this have to do with the Big Dig?"

"It is exactly the same thing." Diana continued, "It is one thing to know that the earth is being destroyed. It is quite another to *feel* the earth's pain and that is what has happened to me. *I* feel it! The earth *IS* in pain. She is in pain. Mother-Nature is suffering."

Alex was about to respond with a dismissive air and a hopeful platitude but when she saw the intensity of emotion on Diana's face she stopped herself. Alex refilled both their glasses and let her friend continue uninterrupted.

Diana tried to back up a bit to explain, "I know you're going to want to make fun, but I'm being serious. I have been sensing a progression lately, a shifting in the energy fields around the city and the auras around people here, and the dreams I've had lately. Everything that I know has been saying 'wake up, pay attention,' so I went into meditation to talk to my guides. I was shown an image of a goddess pouring forth cosmic love and then a view of our city cloaked in darkness and filled with pain." She took a moment to study Alex's tired face, in case she was rolling her eyes, but she seemed to be listening.

Alex replied, "…Ok? That's what you mean about the earth being in pain?"

"Yes, and I think that we are on the brink of something monumental. The Big Dig is part of this," Diana continued. "You know Boston is more than just a hub, more than just a city, more than just the history that we know. This area is an energy vortex. It is crossed with multiple ley lines and it's no coincidence that the witch trials happened here. Something has been happening in this city for a long time now. We've talked about how much the city has changed ever since the Big Dig. But it's not just about the parking problems, the re-routing of traffic or smug politicians. Boston has lost its vitality. The weather patterns are changing, the demographics are changing, and attitudes are changing. It is more than just climate change. It's like the 'Stepford Wives.' People who live here don't seem the same anymore; there is less friendliness and stress runs rampant. No one looks happy. You remember how it used to be when we were in graduate school: Boston was an energetic city full of vitality. There was an air of freedom and creativity then. I have been in a state of melancholy over what has happened to this city, I just did not know what to call it until now. The energy and the joy are being sucked out of our city.

"This is what I think, feel, know, Alex, and I fear you are going to scoff. It is because of the Big Dig. The Big Dig cuts right into the heart of the city, its central artery; it is not just a metaphor. The Big Dig has cut open the very soul of the earth beneath this city. And the pain of all of the history that has been buried for so long within it is rising like a virus back up to the surface. This is more than geography. Boston has been violated. The Big Dig has ruptured the energy of this city and something has been exposed, released. I am not saying that it's cursed but a rupture has occurred. Come on, Alex, you are an intelligent woman, you have traveled extensively. You know cities and places have identities and those identities are defined by karmic energy patterns. Well, something, and I think it is the Big Dig, has destroyed the integrity of this city's core energy. You don't need to be a psychic to know that something is terribly wrong here."

Holding her glass close, Alex said flatly, "Things are always changing, places too. Maybe you are resisting the city's new energy patterns?"

Diana went on, "do you know that if you put a frog in boiling water it will jump out, but if you put the frog in cool water and heat it up slowly it will not feel the boiling water and it will die! What has happened here is like that. People do not feel the changes because they have been so gradual and we make excuses for them. Only the thing is we *do* feel it. We just think that the problem is with ourselves or it is this or that, some trivial distraction. We do not want to look at the whole picture because then we would realize the pervasiveness of what has happened and that leads to despair. So we all go on, status quo, and pretend that everything is all right. I think that most of this country is living in a state of denial. But the city feels it too."

"Well, I do agree about people's attitudes lately, but cities are always changing and the Big Dig is almost complete. Why is this an issue now?"

"It is because of that chamber, Alex, but there is more there than what meets the eye. Look, you and I are very close, but we are also two different types of people. You believe in what you can see and I believe in what I cannot see, but feel, and that is as real to me as what you perceive with your first five senses. I believe there was a reason you decided to tell me about the chamber in the first place"

Alex recognized that this was not one of their typical philosophical conversations. Reality for her was fixed and stable while Diana's world was fluid and mutable.

"What do you think you are going to find in the chamber?" asked Alex, trying to get the conversation back to solid ground. "You are not going to embarrass me by doing one of your rituals down there or anything are you?"

Diana scowled.

"And if you believe so much in all this psychic stuff why not just astral project yourself into the chamber."

Diana was hurt by her best friend's dismissal. She wanted to laugh and cry at the same time.

She replied surly, "because, Alex, I need to bring my physical body with me…and what if I did think a ritual could help?"

Alex had the nagging feeling that she would end up complying with her friend's request and was even a bit tickled at the thought of the two of them trekking down into a mysterious chamber like some new age descendants of Nancy Drew. Maybe she felt compelled simply because they were friends, and if Diana was truly losing it, it might be therapeutic for her to see there was nothing to her crazy notions, or maybe Alex herself was a little curious at this point and would feel more comfortable bringing Diana with her when she visited the archaic site. In any case, Alex was thinking through the pragmatics. She would first have to accept the role of consultant, and then secure their access. *What will I tell Richard? Should I tell Richard? Probably not, but he might find out anyway.*

"I thought you didn't want me to get involved in this?"

"I know. I thought it was just another one of those distractions from your life's path that the universe was throwing at you, but I was wrong. It is very important. I didn't see it before, but everything that is going on right now is connected. This city is heading in the wrong direction and I am not about to just sit back and do nothing. You asked me last night, facetiously I might add, what you should do if in a dream the goddess tells you to grow wheat. Well, you grow the darn wheat, Alex! You grow it! It doesn't hurt anyone to sow a seed and if it's not going to hurt you, even if you don't think you'll need the wheat, you should grow it! Boston has some heavy karma; it clouds the atmosphere in darkness and everyone in it with negativity."

"Every city has a history, Diana."

"Yes but this city has a portal too, a recently discovered ancient site connected to another time, another civilization. It's older than the histories we can know in this age. It would be a great opportunity to cleanse the city, attune the rupture and awaken it's heart center. It could make everything a-right! From the beginning! I know you've seen it too, everyone is cold and tense, hurting from their own imbalance. We are fragmented here, from our selves, from nature, from each other. And it's not as though performing a heart chakra opening ceremony could hurt! I mean all we would be doing is radiating images of love in pink and white hues from our mind's eye out to everyone in the city, for Christ sake! I mean what is the big deal, why are so many people uptight about *rituals*! If we are all able to pick up on each other's negative energy, why wouldn't love and joy be contagious too! What's wrong with that?"

"Look, Diana I don't want you to be upset. Calm down. The thing is, it's all just hitting too close to home for me right now. I haven't been myself this week. There's been a lot of weirdness, real fast. I mean today some homeless man started shouting at me, screaming about looking underground! How strange is that? I don't buy into outlandish delirium, but even I am starting to wonder if I need to look at things differently for a while. Like you said, how could it hurt? I mean, I'm single, even bitter at times. Maybe I'm freezing up? I don't know, I've just been thinking that I'm the one who's crazy."

"Alex, I know you don't believe in magic, but a lot of other people do. Historically, more people over the ages have believed in some form of magic than have not believed in it. Only since the very recent modern age did we sever and separate science and magic; discrediting the one because it can't be proved by the other. Magic falls outside the parameters of the scientific method; verification just isn't possible. Science can't either prove or disprove that magic exists. Accept, therefore, that it IS possible, that's all that I am asking from you. Because in that possibility, I think you might find hope. And don't turn down this assignment with the city out of fear. If you are being shown signs, it is because there is something coming that you will not be able to avoid. In the meantime, you are my dearest friend and as my friend, I need to tell you that I am being shown some signs. I, for one, know that I am not crazy…Just don't close your mind, or your heart, alright?"

* * * *

By the time Diana left Alex's condo it was snowing and sleeting and the freshly dusted streets glittered like diamonds in the light of the street lamps. Diana was worried that she had said too much about what she was sensing, but she needed Alex's help and just as importantly she wanted Alex to understand. Never before had she challenged her to play such an active role in her premonitions or "come to the other side," so to say, in terms of her meta-political understanding of reality. But this felt different. Diana suspected that this time there could be grave consequences for anyone refusing to acknowledge that there was a deeper and underlying order to things which worked according to its own laws and forces.

Trying to stay warm she waited for the Silver Line bus at the newly constructed "T" stop. The outdoor shelter was simply a clear plastic enclosure that barely kept out the wind. She huddled against the plastic barricade and thought of the fall of magic and the retreat of nature based religions to the underground.

The earth is calling us back, she thought and the sides of the shelter shook violently in the rattling wind, like a round of applause. The sound of splintering plastic silenced Diana in her last thought.

The gust split the East side of the shelter in half. The two parts, still stiffly tied by their fasteners flapped back and forth like saloon doors, and snow started to accumulate upon the bench's shiny silver surface. Nobody else seemed to care.

* * * *

While his wife, Lydia, slept Richard Lyons worked late into the dark hours of the night. He had waited for her to fall asleep before he left their bed and climbed down the stairs of their Cambridge home. He stepped lightly, trying not to make a sound, but he was anxious and stressed, which he wasn't accustomed to. Halfway down the carpeted stairwell he bumped into a potted plant, almost tipping it over. His silhouette cut through long shadows, cast from the double sets of floor length windows.

He closed the study door, found the switch for the overhead light, and the moonbeams scattered from sight.

Turning on the computer monitor, he sat down to pull his thoughts together. He had to devise a plan. He knew what the chamber was. Paul's presumptions were correct. He would continue to conduct all the tests and analyses that protocol dictated, but he already knew. If even half of the myths were true, Richard realized this chamber posed a real threat. The monitor lit and he searched for the file of photos and scanned rubbings.

When word about the find hits the news, Richard wanted to be ready with answers for the press and get his findings published quickly. It was the surest way of keeping opinions under control and fulfilling his duty to the Academy.

He studied the symbols he photographed in the cave. Shapes and spirals indicated to Richard these were primitive peoples. Many of the triangular images still showed remnants of an irony residue - possibly paint or blood. All of the edges were smooth, as though they had been cut out with a sophisticated tool. Richard made a notation about the nature of the ornamentation and began charting the number of times each symbol appeared in the room and where.

What do you do with a white elephant? Richard wondered. *And how could there be an eighth?*

How could he tell the Academy that Plato was wrong? He himself had seen the original writing of the myth of the seven maidens contained in Plato's allegedly lost Dialogue on the Good. He knew the ancient texts: seven sites, seven temples. The Academy had systematically surveyed and destroyed all of the main ancient Goddess temple sites. The existence of the seven had been successfully kept secret all of this time, now there was an eighth!

The possibility that the Academy was wrong about such a fundamental truth jeopardized Richard's sense of security. Knowledge is power. The only world Richard had ever known – competitive, hierarchal, and contentious – was all he could conceive of. While he knew that these temple sites did in fact exist and maintained great power, he refused to believe that a truly cooperative, non-competitive, non-hierarchical matriarchal society of people could exist, ever. A matriarchal culture in this sense was simply utopian idealism in Richard's eyes. And he looked condescendingly at Moira for thinking otherwise.

He went on to think about Moira – more from habit than from anything else. Since realizing that the site was what he didn't believe it could be, he had been worrying about her obsessively. He was comforted by knowing that he had already been guaranteed the publications required to be considered the leading authority. However, the myth that had guided them successfully through the last few centuries said that there were only seven sites. He was concerned that she would try to connect the site to the pre-Indo European goddess cults and risk exposing society to the knowledge of what these matriarchal temples housed.

He knew he was going to have to out maneuver her to dismiss the importance of the site. Getting her to cooperate was sure to be an issue; he only had one piece of leverage to use against her directly.

Richard's computer flashed and an instant message appeared on the screen, from an unknown sender named "urgent". He read it twice:

Brother, never forget:

> *"The mysteries... are really profanities, and solemn rites that are without sanctity.*
> *What manifest shamelessness! Quench the fire, thou priest....The fire is not acting a part; to convict and to punish is its duty".*

~V

To Richard the message was unambiguous. He recognized these words as those written by Clement, many centuries ago, warning mankind of the dangers of women and goddess worship, and leading the way for the membership of the Academy. Now he had his plan. *How do you hide a white elephant? ...in plain sight*, Richard mused to himself.

---

[1] This meditative technique is named "The Crystal Countdown" in LAURIE CABOT WITH TOM COWAN, POWER OF THE WITCH: THE EARTH, THE MOON, AND THE MAGICAL PATH TO ENLIGHTENMENT 183-187 (Delacorte Press 1989).

Chapter Three

FATE

The next morning was one of the coldest mornings in February on record. Of course most February mornings in Boston are the coldest on record. Meteorologists had predicted that a giant Nor'easter storm front would emerge from Canada later in the afternoon and the wind was blowing from various directions at the same time; from the ocean to the west and from the Charles River to the east. Meeting and careening down the cross streets, up and over and around tall buildings, picking up speed, it pierced through the best and finest winter clothing. Wool and down, cashmere and fleece, with or without earmuffs, are no match for Mother Nature when she has something to say. And today she was howling.

Richard never did go back to bed and it was still very early when Alex's phone rang.

"Good morning Alex, it's Richard. I hope I didn't wake you?"

"Richard? No… of course not, you know I'm an early riser. Is something the matter?" She was actually a bit surprised; he didn't usually call this early.

"No… I just wanted to continue our conversation from the other day. Can we meet at some point today?"

"Uh, sure, I have to be at the university today, but I'm free for a couple of hours after two. Are you going into town today?"

"I should also be finished around three." Richard said, "Why don't I take you for tea at the Bay Tower Room?"

"That sounds great Richard, I haven't been there in a while... See you then."

* * * *

Alex wasn't sure yet what she was going to say to Richard, or what she was going to tell the city authorities. She was trying to start her day with a good attitude, but so far she just felt alone.

Alex glanced across her spacious bedroom suite to check the state of things outside. Despite the forecast, the morning sun seemed to be rising successfully over the harbor and, even if temporarily, holding back the clouds. Remnants of yesterday's flurries still iced some of the sidewalks and grassy areas. She closed her eyes for a moment and tried to feel the sun's heat upon her skin. The wind looked fierce, but the cars, trucks, and buses below were moving along the streets in mass synchronicity.

Alex couldn't quite articulate to herself, or justify, the fear that she harbored about this chamber situation. As she lotioned her body and selected warm undergarments, she felt a knot of dread materialize in her belly. She tried to push it out of her mind.

Stopping in front of the mirror for a moment she asked out loud, "Why am I letting all of this get to me?" Startled by her own behavior, she resumed her search for the proper outfit. She selected a pair of woolen slacks and a cashmere sweater, thinking it would help her feel warm and fuzzy. Although nothing in her life was warm and fuzzy at the moment, she thought it would offer a good contrast and much needed balance.

Seeking reprieve from her nagging thoughts, she decided to check her email. She walked casually down her condo's sleek hallway and noticed how the bamboo floors reflected the light brightly, more brilliantly than usual. She suddenly realized that her feet were wet. Not wet still from the shower, but standing in an inch of water, wet. Instinctively she moved toward her office and gasped in horror as she entered the room. Cords, plugs, cables connecting her printer, fax and computer all sat on the ground under the water.

She heard gushing from the utility closet in the left corner of the room. She rushed to the closet and opened the door. Water was flooding from the water heater!

She remembered the homebuyer's inspection she purchased before closing on her condo - the one she thought was a waste of time because it was a brand new building that shouldn't have appliance failures.

Finding the shut-off valve she thought to herself, *Rightie-tightie-leftie-loosie.* She backed away as the water slowed. The sight of the mess in her office was too much to bear. As she started to gather towels to begin soaking the wetness up, she realized Diana would have something to say about the timing of the incident. Alex imagined her friend say, *I wonder if Mercury is in retrograde?* Diana always told Alex these electrical malfunctions coincide with astrological events.

"I hope the building manager and his plumber aren't into astrology." She muttered in frustration as she walked back toward the phone in the kitchen, arms full of drippy towels, "I just want a new hot water heater!"

* * * *

Meanwhile in Diana's house, Night-Night was just settling down to sleep again. She didn't need a weather broadcast to tell her that a storm was approaching. She had her own barometer: Night-Night had a headache. For as long as she could remember, she had always gotten headaches at intense, axiomatic moments. And even though Diana was not yet aware of it, her familiar remembered that the real storm was predicted centuries ago.

Diana had been Night-Night's "person" for the last five years. Diana thought that she had rescued her cat from the alleyway behind her house. At the time, however, Night-Night was actually wondering whether Diana would ever open the door to let her in. Night-Night had been sitting outside waiting there for almost a week and had come to realize that this new charge of hers was slow to "come around."

As she basked in the morning's sun she thought to herself, *this is one of those times*, but Night-Night liked Diana in spite of her airy irreverent attitude. From what she had observed so far, Diana was constant, she didn't crack under pressure, and she already had the historical training and correct metaphysical perspective that so many of Night-Night's other charges lacked before their initiations. She had concluded that Diana was well prepared for what she would have to do, but was also a bit too interested in other planes of reality, making her seem a bit absent-minded or distracted even.

Just as Night-Night started to enter a deep sleep, the shrill ring of Diana's telephone disturbed her. Diana answered in her studio.

"Hey, how are you doing?" Diana tucked the receiver under her chin and dragged her easel across the floor, shuffling paints and brushes between her fingertips.

"Hi," Alex said, "How did you know it was me?"

"I just did… what's up?"

"I'm having tea with Richard this afternoon. I'll get a better idea of what's going on. I wanted to know if you could meet me tonight, maybe at the Twenty-First?"

"Mmm… Richard, tea, really?"

"Yes, Richard, tea, really. Do you want to see the chamber or not?"

"Of course, and sure I'll meet you at the Twenty-First. What time?"

"Five-ish?"

"Sure. How's everything else going this morning?" Diana asked, wondering how her friend was coping with the added stress that she had likely caused. Quite to character, Alex avoided the more obvious meaning of Diana's question and replied to the mundane.

"Ugh, I've flooded my office! My water heater broke and has soaked everything." With levity, Alex added, "I thought of you, is Mercury in retrograde?"

"No," Diana hesitated as she adjusted between the two levels of dialogue, "but I do know what you mean. This morning all my light bulbs blew out and my cable hasn't been working. Even Night-Night is more insomniacle than usual. It's like Mercury *is* in retrograde," she said sincerely, "but it's not." Diana chose a gentler route and refrained from mentioning the cosmic significance.

"I can look outside and it seems so peaceful right now." Alex said, labeling her own anxiety through the contrast.

"Here too, and I'm practically in the ghetto! You know they are predicting a storm."

Alex sighed and inclined her head to the phone, "It does feel like the calm before the storm."

"I think it might be," Diana practically whispered it into the mouthpiece. "Sorry to hear about your office, Alex. Be careful today, alright?"

"Ok," Alex uttered. "Thanks. See you tonight!"

"Alright, see you tonight, bye." Diana placed the phone into the receiver cradle and looked out the window at her wintery backyard. She noticed a large flock of birds flying in formation above the open lot bordering the back of her property.

She reiterated, "the calm before the storm," because from where she stood it still looked orderly and serene. Children marched down the main road alongside the open lot, heading to school. Businessmen passed in the other direction, toward the downtown. The clusters of young men that lingered at various alleyways, arranged by color and ethnicity, were surprisingly quiet, although they still hooted at the ladies.

As the birds finished their bend to the west, they made one last swoop to the north and were then outside Diana's view. She decided to return to the work in her studio. The birds lifted into the sky and they saw what Diana could not yet see. In the heart of the downtown, at the top of Beacon Hill and outside the state house, the traffic signals were malfunctioning, blinking and glaring red. They were demanding an intensity and authenticity that hadn't been expressed within the city for years.

The governor was not at the state house today. Had he been, he would have seen that the backup of traffic at the crest of Beacon Hill was no longer moving.

It started slowly and would have seemed insignificant. The single light at the top of Beacon Street controlled the traffic encircling the state house and connected the financial district to the Back Bay. It was not a major intersection. It was only one traffic light, and yet, the timing of one little traffic light changed the tempo of the day for an entire city.

For years, vehicles of every kind had crowded and inched, ever so slowly, across this spot at the top of the city's central Beacon Hill; shifting gears and idling heavily, waiting for the next push towards the light. Moving only five or ten feet at a time, drivers got frustrated every time. The accumulation of all that negativity caused strange side effects: erratic blinking, for one.

Like a beacon of chaos, the city's efficient flow of traffic was falling apart. Traffic started and stopped, and started and stopped again, trying to keep up with the signal's tempo. Were the light to go out completely, the drivers might have figured it out for themselves, but it taunted instead with the allure of restored order. It was as though a karmic switch had been thrown, triggering this specific malfunction. At eight thirty on a week day morning, this congestion created a domino effect that whiplashed into the surrounding connector streets. Gridlock spread quickly, flooding exit ways and major arteries.

* * * *

By the time Alex left her condo and stepped out onto the chic sidewalks of downtown Dartmouth Street, the wind had slowed, but bumper-to-bumper traffic had already reached the Back Bay.

This is ridiculous, she thought. *What is going on?* She had never seen the morning flow of vehicles inch so slowly along the road and one could barely cross her street. It was obviously no morning to take a cab into work. Looking above her, she saw that the sky was still clear and pale blue, so she decided to walk to the university.

At least I can count on my two feet. She felt like she was finally taking total control of her day and was grateful for the comfort of her favorite Italian leather boots.

Turning towards Copley Plaza, she negotiated gracefully through the throngs of pedestrians and vendors. There seemed to be people everywhere; even the dog walkers were having difficulty traversing the confusion. Normal patterns of movement were thwarted by the unusual and impermeable line of traffic. Pedestrians everywhere strained their muscle memories to adapt to an obstacle course of new directions.

Alex glanced at her watch as she maneuvered between bumpers and tried to cross over the Arlington Street intersection to reach the entrance of the Public Gardens. It had taken her twice as long to walk three blocks and she still had to trek through the Commons before reaching the Law School.

The wind was starting to pick up again. It tugged and pulled at her coattails. She stepped up onto the curb and took a moment to adjust her bag strap. The urban landscape of bone grey branches and dark blue evergreens looked wild, bending and swaying against the backdrop of high rises and construction cranes. She proceeded into the Public Garden.

Designed as a sanctuary dedicated to the beauty and grace of civilized nature, this garden was dressed seasonally with various species of flowers, trees and shrubs. Always meticulously well-manicured, its swan shaped paddle boats are famous. During the summer months tourists and lovers rent them to float upon the pond and enjoy the peace and serenity. Today the gardens weren't peaceful at all, it was too overrun with people and the half frozen geese looked intimidating.

Alex stayed to her path and passed the bronze sculpture, *Make Way for Ducklings,* noting that she felt a bit like the little duckling that had been stolen time and time again. She made her way through to Charles Street, wind gusts increasingly yanking at her pants legs and textiles. To her relief, a state trooper was posted at the intersection and he tried bringing order to the vehicular mayhem. He held the tide behind the cross walk as she approached and hurried across to the lawns of the Boston Commons.

In colonial days the "Commons" received its name from being the common grazing field for cattle. Today, it is a quintessential city park hosting everything from picnics and Shakespeare productions to ice skating and holiday tree lighting ceremonies.

Alex began her ascent up its southern slope and heard a flock of geese coasting above her. They landed in the open field further ahead and to the right. She laughed as she saw a small Jack Russell Terrier running and nipping after one. Apparently, geese are more formidable than one might imagine. The goose, not to be undone by the ratter, straightened its knees, protruded its chest and bearing its wing span squawked loudly in the little dog's face. Fortunately, the terrier ran fast enough and made it safely back to its owner's side. But the threat created its own chain reaction. The agitated geese rallied into a simultaneous dance of knee jerking, wing flapping and squawking, looking as though they had been purposely choreographed.

Then Alex noticed a mounted trooper approach from the other side of the clearing. The geese, still focused on the dog, all had their backs to the horse and rider. The wind pushed Alex's back a little harder, now blowing from the South, and she realized that the horse was upwind of the flock.

The state trooper apparently didn't consider this because he encouraged his horse forward, right up to the rear of the ensemble. Suddenly and uniformly the geese all turned to face the mounted beast. They resumed the frantic squawking parade with greater gusto and in goose step, strutted across the horse's path. The trooper could barely calm the animal beneath him and pulled at the left reign in an attempt to redirect the horse. The bridle was equipped with blinders, however, and the horse threw its head at the suggestion that it should lose sight of the feathered aggressors. The trooper urged the mare with vocals and she began to walk sideways. The geese followed their lead and also stepped sideways. Next, the mounted pair tried to the right. Again, the geese blocked their path, honking and howling all the way. It looked like a battle over territory and Alex wanted to stay and see its resolution, but the wind swirled again with such ferocity that she opted for the shelter of her school. The gusts were increasing as she approached the heart of the downtown.

Nearing the university, the clock tower at Park Street Church told her how late it was. She was looking up, calculating her remaining minutes before class and didn't see the man crossing the street. He stepped up onto the curb right beside her.

"Got some change?" The raspy voice rang familiar to Alex's ears. It startled her with a jolt, but she tried not to look at him.

He walked alongside her in long, languid paces. The steady gait matched his awkward cantor while he spoke.

"Got some change?" He berated, "I got change?" Then he bent down and pushed his face towards Alex's. He got in her way and shouted, "Change is a comin'!"

"Change is a comin'," he screamed again, throwing his long arms up in the air, blocking off the sidewalk with his vast span. Alex recoiled, putting her hand in front of her face and bending away from him.

"The rapture is here!" he cried, "Wash your sins, young soldiers, wash your sins. Change is a comin', pray for mercy! 'Cause I can hear the hooves a 'comin!"

His arms fell and his stature shrank. His volume also dropped and he practically stuttered as he resumed.

"Judgment day. Ha – Hhaah! I got some change. Change is a comin'! The knights are a comin', wash your hands!" As his volume declined, his gaze fell from Alex to the ground, and the crowd seemed to somehow just push him aside into the mob. Alex managed to squeeze into the flow of other people crossing in the direction of her building.

The encounter was very disturbing. He seemed to be targeting her and yet, no one else around her really paid any attention. Was he mad at her for bumping into him the other day? Was he after money?

Another roadside attraction on the highway to funky town? she joked with herself and noticed a sweaty trickle that had formed on the inside of her cashmere sweater, at the small of her back. *Nothing seems normal anymore. I don't think I can take any more of this,* but she remembered Diana's words last night, "…just don't close your mind, or your heart…"

Walking into the law school building, she opted for the stairs, hoping they might flex her mind back around her responsibilities. When Alex got to her office suite, she could tell that Susan Coffey still wasn't in. *Uh, oh*, she thought as she unlocked her own door, *I hope she isn't stuck in that traffic.*

Alex turned on the lights and shut the door to her office, then aimed for her phone. *Time enough to act*, she determined and dialed his direct line. She exhaled slowly into the receiver and heard ringing on the other end. After the second ring he answered.

"Yes, John Doherty, please," she said.

A timbre voice replied, "This is, who's calling?"

"Good morning. This is Dr. Alexandra Martin returning your call."

"Oh yes, hello Dr. Martin. Thank you for getting back to me. I believe you know Dr. Lyons."

"Yes, yes I do."

"Great, and he did give you an idea of what is going on down here and the assistance that the Mayor would like from you ...or shall I update you?" He sounded a bit distracted and Alex was hoping that he would do most of the talking.

Choosing her words carefully she said, "Well I do have some further questions... I know that there was a find and there are some concerns as to whether it might belong to an Indian Nation or even be a burial ground."

"Actually, Dr. Martin that is looking like less of a possibility than it did yesterday." Alex was relieved. She wanted to wash away the anxiety that a conflict might erupt between her ethics and familial duty, but that thought was followed by wondering whether they would need her involvement any longer.

Wanting an explanation she asked, "Really, what? You mean that it's not Indian?"

"Listen, we would still appreciate your assistance in this, you are highly regarded by Dr. Lyons. The Mayor is holding a press conference this morning to tell the public what has been found, but all indications point to an origin predating the regional tribes and it is not a burial site, that we do know. There are no human remains."

"What type of assistance does the Mayor want from me?"

"Look Dr. Martin, I'm sure you know the Mayor wants this wrapped up as quickly as possible. As I said, you are very highly regarded by Dr. Lyons and the Mayor would be grateful to receive any consultation you might be willing to give. We do have our own legal staff for the technical matters, as you are aware. On the other hand, it could be fortuitous for us to have the benefit of your being outside counsel …without the formal ensnaring that constricts us government employees. I understand you have worked with the city before. An extra mind can come in handy, given all the red tape these days. There might be a Tribal Nation or two, or their attorneys, who will want to view the site, or our reports, to protect their interests and make their own determination. In any event, you know the main players in these circles and the Mayor wants your experience for insight into how to deal with them; strategy and probability assessment, that sort of thing. So he knows what to expect, no more surprises! Do you understand? We aren't looking for another attorney, *per se*, but an informal consult."

"I… would be happy to offer my opinions, Mr. Doherty …but any information that I may have about a nation that I represented in the past could be confidential."

"Of course, Dr. Martin. The Mayor would never expect or suggest that you jeopardize your professional obligations, goodness no. As I said before you were highly recommended and this has been kept quiet for a few days now, much longer than it should have been probably. But here it is and if you are on our team to buffer a sticky situation, if one arises, it could help. Obviously, if there is a risk of a client conflict, we won't have the full liberty of your assistance. As for other conditions …let me see. Ah, we will be scheduling a status meeting for tomorrow, depending on this storm, which you will have to attend and there will be regularly scheduled weekly meetings and others as needed."

"I see, well then we shouldn't have any problems of that sort." Alex says cheerfully. "Will I be able to visit the chamber personally, to draw my own opinion about its possible connection to earlier tribes?"

"Of course," Doherty responded, "And, I should mention that your services would be provided to the City as an honorarium."

Hmm! Alex scoffed to herself. She wasn't really expecting to get paid. Once he said it though, she felt dismissed, patronized even. Doherty had already made it evident that she was only being allowed to "consult," as he put it, to flatter Richard's friendship with Mayor Marino.

No matter, she determined. She was getting what she wanted, what Diana wanted. She would have access to the site, independent of Richard. And she was sure she would be able to get Diana in too …if she decided to do so.

"Mr. Doherty, please tell the Mayor I would be happy to assist the city in any way that I can. When will this first meeting be held?"

"Alright, great. Congratulations. Ah, the meeting isn't scheduled yet. Someone from my office will call and let you or your secretary know. Well I've got to go. I'll look forward to meeting you soon then, good bye."

"Ok, Mr. Doherty, good bye." Alex hung up the receiver feeling as though she had finally dried her feet of the water that leaked out of her hot water heater that morning. She set out to begin her day again renewed, and free to focus on her next lecture.

* * * *

Moira decided late the previous night, or rather very early that morning, that she couldn't wait. She had to see Nathan now, so she spent most of her moonlight hours researching Nathan's background. *Could he really be trusted?* She found no reason not to. But she still wanted to catch him before he had too much time to get twisted by inter-collegial politics. She wanted to probe his own intentions and inclinations.

The connections and clues she had gathered about the chamber were energizing her and she barely felt the lagging yawn of last night's late workings. She dressed quickly, selecting practical clothes that would keep her warm and dry from the approaching storm.

She wondered what revelations would come from the research she assigned to Raya, *it would certainly be helpful to be armed with additional material before meeting with Nathan.* Raya had indicated she would finish everything yesterday, so it should already be waiting for her at the office. She could hardly wait to get there and see it. There was a particular myth she had been tracking her entire life that is associated with the secret "mystery traditions" of ancient Eleusis. She had been trying to decode its meaning for many years. She suspected that if she could, it would hold the key for understanding the chamber's esoteric purpose.

Readying to leave, she went to her study and reached into an ornately carved cabinet. She pulled out a well-worn and crumpled manila folder. It was Moira's prized possession: the sum culmination of her work on ancient ways of knowing, magic and prophecy. Some people might be disappointed if their most important accomplishment could fit between two flimsy flaps of cardstock, but Moira was proud. She had been patient and always knew its time would come. She wasn't so overconfident as to think that the material itself held all the answers, it was merely the chart of the beginning of the mysteries. Most of the data and findings would even be indecipherable to others because its substance was so obscure, especially at this point, while she was still collecting the clues. But as she clasped the folder in her hand she could feel the charge and weight of its significance, and power.

The folder consisted of an astral chart of the ancient energy centers of civilization's earliest goddess worshippers. Twenty-five thousand years of ceremonial utterances had marked energy patterns within the earth's biosphere. Moira was beginning to understand the meaning of these patterns. Years ago, her interest was perked by discussions of ley lines. Her own archaeological scholarship coupled with her initiation into the ways of magic led her to realize that early matriarchal rituals, parthenogenic rites, and secret ceremonies had literally forged nexuses of energy, creating astral temples in much the same way that Stonehenge is more than a mere pile of rocks.

This folder pulsed with the charge of Moira's own life force and with the truths that were mapped by its contents. She had never removed this packet from her study before, let alone taken it out of her house. Even though she knew it all by heart, she slipped the folder into a larger envelope, closed it carefully and wedged it deep within her sack to protect it while she walked to campus.

When Moira arrived at her office, she immediately knew that the heat was out. The hallway was lukewarm but her office was freezing and she both heard and felt the cold racing in through the gaps in the old windows. Her office was on a third floor corner of Harvard's oldest brick building. The ceilings were low and the wooden beams, immense. It looked over a small quad. Through the window she saw the old oak trees waving bony fingers as students in scarves and earmuffs hurried along with their heads down, using their books for protection from the wind.

She found a new stack of papers on her desk along with a computer disk. Shuffling through it all, she was pleased to see that Raya had been successful in getting copies of the ancient maps and imagery she requested. These documented various oral traditions, myths and folklore. Still cloaked in her heavy coat, Moira sat down at her desk. She organized her notes and called a few international archives.

She stopped her work just before noon and noticed that her timing today had been perfect. With such a great flow of productivity building, she didn't want to get distracted or involved in departmental small talk so she exited her office and left by the back stairwell. From there it was just a short walk to the Peabody Museum.

* * * *

She had practically memorized the former director's Wednesday morning routine and expected that Nathan would be completing the same weekly gallery review right about now and would probably be hungry for lunch. Nathan was, in fact, just completing that very task in the foyer gallery and, being rather beleaguered from his own morning communication difficulties, was genuinely pleased to see Moira enter.

"Dr. Fennessey, good morning! Or is it good afternoon by now?" Nathan said as he glided toward her with an open hand.

"Yes, I have trouble keeping up with that myself! Good afternoon I suppose, and do call me Moira."

"To what do I owe this surprise, Moira?" he asked with a bright smile.

"Well Nathan, I was wondering if you are free for lunch today. I know it's rather abrupt, but thought you might be hungry."

"Actually, I am." He turned back toward the staff waiting in the gallery and said, "We're all done for now aren't we? Are there any other questions?" The staff was satisfied, so he turned back to Moira and charmingly responded, "Moira would you wait right here a few moments while I grab my coat?"

"Of course, take your time." Moira utilized the opportunity to study the lines of a mystical statue by the entrance to the East Gallery.

* * * *

Settling into a corner booth at a local bistro, Moira realized that she might have to engage in small talk. She would have liked to get right to the point but prudence dictated that she broach the subject of the chamber carefully.

* * * *

Nathan took off his overcoat and suit jacket and hung them on the hooks bracketed to the edge of their booth. Moira noticed how nicely pressed his suit shirt was even after a long morning of meetings. The creases were so crisp that they looked sharp and made of something hard, though the shirt was actually made of fine cotton. The attention paid to his appearance indicated to Moira that he understood subtle realities and she trusted that the creases were more than mere fashion. After all, he had acquired a significant position and would have had to finesse political challenges to make it this far. Moira considered him an interesting study.

As Nathan slid into the booth across from her Moira asked without pretense, "So Nathan, what is your story?"

"Not nearly as interesting as one may imagine, I fear." His smile was captivating and he chuckled lightly at her straight forward tone. Moira also responded with a smile,

"Oh, I'm sorry. I don't mean to be so direct."

"Really?"

"Well, no, I am direct. I'm a very direct person. That's why so many people take issue with my approach." She retorted, "So what is your story, anyway? I'm curious."

"Would you like some coffee, Moira? Let's have some coffee," Nathan's smile was unrelenting. He looked up over the tables and with the aid of his height effortlessly made eye contact with the waitress. She walked toward their table.

"The truth is, Moira, that I always wanted to be an archaeologist. I just can't stand getting dirty." And his light chuckle deepened into the heartiest belly laugh she had ever witnessed from a colleague. The waitress stepped up to meet them and Nathan ordered the house brew, "And for you Moira?"

Moira, equally taken aback by Nathan's candor, decided to follow his lead with a coffee, "Ok, I guess I will also try the house brew. And a bowl of vegetable soup."

"Oh great, you know what you want," Nathan added, "I'll have the cheeseburger in paradise with onion rings," he told the waitress, "cooked medium well." She jotted down their order and disappeared toward the kitchen.

"I always know what I want, Nathan," Moira returned his playful innuendo with a smirk of her own.

"What do you want Moira?"

"The truth, I want to know how a man like you came to be interested in matriarchal cultures."

"That's a fair question. I understand your concerns and battles more than you may realize. Knowledge is oppressed in many ways, and truth is buried by more than just dirt. The way I see it, if you archaeologists in the field can unearth it, I want to make sure it gets displayed to the public for what it is. One interpretation never tells the whole story.

"But I believe I mentioned to you that I was exposed to one of your books in graduate school. I was an intern preparing for an exhibit of artifacts from a burial site believed to house the body of an Amazon warrior woman. I was aware that for centuries she was thought to be only a myth. The female archeologist who compiled the artifacts for the show was the one who discovered the burial site. Her research and interpretations proved clearly that the primary person buried there was an actual Amazon warrior verifying that she was real. The exhibit was a raving success, by the way." Moira was keenly aware of the Amazon Warrior Woman but she was surprised to hear that he had worked on that exhibit.

He continued, "I didn't realize there was such opposition amongst the different schools of thought about matriarchal pasts until later, when I read the lead archaeologist's autobiography. When I worked with her, I heard her comment about some of her male colleagues, but I merely assumed that they had personal or private conflicts between themselves. I mean, her findings were so impeccably verified it sounded absurd that they would still argue that these women never existed. Anyway, I started looking around for other work involving pre-historic matriarchal civilizations and that's when I came across your work on the Eleusian mysteries."

"And what do you think?"

"Your sources were also properly documented, in context. Modern methodologies don't lend themselves equally to every segment of time or culture. But contrary interpretations don't have any greater or lesser form of documentation than yours. Both views should be treated with equal validity and respected - and debated openly. It must have been difficult over the years, working so closely with Richard."

Moira expected Nathan would be as familiar with Richard's scholarship as he was with her own. She and Richard were Harvard's top producers, so to say. They were also arch enemies in the world of academia and their areas of interest often overlapped. Four months after

Moira's book on images of archaic female divinities was released, Richard challenged her thesis with a book of his own that argued the images were an early version of pornography and intended for a strictly male audience, rather than inspiring of the divine. The gesture alone infuriated her, but worse, he didn't engage in any of his own research, he merely piggybacked on her sources. Over the years it had become obvious that their competitiveness was personal.

"Well Nathan, I hope you understand that Amazon Warrior Women still exist!" She was still unsure whether he was merely paying lip service or whether he agreed with the ideas he could so cleverly recite.

"Oh, yes Moira, and believe me, I was raised by one."

"I'm sure you were," she sung and to the point added, "good, I'm glad that we can speak the same language together. And I'm relieved that you're not uninitiated. I have some things to discuss with you regarding the chamber, so it's helpful that you already know about these matters."

"I presumed lunch had something to do with your findings," he replied. The waitress served the specialty coffees and they both fell silent for a moment, inhaling the strong, warm aroma.

Once the waitress left the table Moira leaned forward and said, "The data is revealing that the chamber is older than anyone had imagined. I'm sure that you are familiar with the secret rites of the Mystery cults in Egypt, Babylon and Greece."

"Yes and no. I am familiar with the thinking that the rituals were very secretive and because of that, it is almost impossible to determine what actually went on."

"Yes, that's the common thinking." Moira blew upon the steaming mug as she raised it to her lips. "But I have been tracking and researching those rites for decades."

She took a short, hot sip. "Tell me Nathan, do you believe in esoteric forms of magic?"

"Ah Moira, you are direct aren't you? I should think your experience with such matters might warn against certain levels of honesty."

"Oh quite to the contrary! Some levels of magic might be referred to as the intersection of causality and will. Do those words make you more comfortable? How about laws of attraction?" Somebody dropped a heavy dinner plate in the back of the room, distracting their conversation momentarily.

"Perhaps, but not to beat around the bush, I spent a lot of time as a teenager with an Aunt in New Orleans. Let's just say that I have had my own experiences with elemental knowledge."

"Good," Moira responded, the light in his eyes revealed all that she needed to know. "The rituals involved a sacred reenactment of an earth goddess's parthenogenesis; her eternal story of life-death-and-rebirth. What most scholars won't admit, actually it would never occur to most of them, is that this reenactment, as they call it, is an actual magical happening that created an astral charge upon the earth at that very geographic location. Many of these, I have determined actually correlate with the locations of ley lines. If parthenogenesis is about creation and rejuvenation, then the magic triggered by these rituals manifests energy eruptions of spontaneous rejuvenation, and may have the potential for ushering forward the collective consciousness of humanity to higher levels of awareness." Noticing a hint of skepticism in his temples she explained, "Through myth or direct worship, every religion and culture from Islam and Christianity to Indigenous Cults recognizes in some form the existence of such powerful ancient loci, often more generally referred to as a 'holy land' and usually associated with either the birth or death of either a religion or existence itself."

"Ok, well tell me this, how does this cavern differ from the small Celtic temple that was found recently in Vermont, the one that dated back 3000 years and seems to merely catalog the winter solstice?"

"That's just it Nathan, it's the design. Temple sites indicate different functions. The site in Vermont rests on the top of a mountain and looks to the sky. It merely charts the cycle of time, although it is also said to sit on a ley line. Our site retreats to the underground, it is womb-like and naturally transformative. It was likely designed for upper level magical rites and its charge may be as intense and real as the inner protective chambers of the great Egyptian pyramids. And, actually, it's not just the design. It's also the numerosity of similar sites that we have to compare it with. Unfortunately, most of these have already been destroyed. Add to the equation of analysis knowledge of Newgrange and Stonehenge. If we only had knowledge of any one of these, we wouldn't know for sure whether the annual viewing or marking of an astrological event was the main purpose of any of these sites until we had the others, a number of other similar sites to indicate a consistent focus on that orientation and function. Only then did the sociological, archaeological and archaeogeodeseological communities all agree that the astrological function was an intentional part of the design.

"Now let's take a look at our chamber. Well, this is the first, the only chamber of this sort ever found still intact. Its symbolism, design and intersection with these particular ley lines is key to a possibly near-cataclysmic event as referenced in various archaic cult myths including one from Mesopotamia, at least one I'm aware of in a remote Persian text, one of the hymns to Demeter, as well as numerous others. I'm still mapping it all together, but, my point is that we should be very hesitant in any plans to disturb the physical and psychic integrity of the chamber!"

Nathan teased, "So not only do you think its pre-Indo-European, but you're intimidated by its Mojo?" Even though Moira was being very serious, she couldn't help but laugh along with him.

Nathan added, "besides I already told you that there are no plans as of yet and I will make sure you have the time you need. I hope you didn't ask me to lunch just to hear me reassure you of that?" Another waitress stopped briefly with a full steaming pot to top off their mugs.

"No, Nathan, of course not," Moira gratefully wrapped her fingers around the warm drink and stirred in a healthy dose of sugar and cream. "To be honest, I am truly just excited again. And from your background, I thought you might be a good resource for working out some of my thoughts. Honestly, I'm rather shocked. I didn't expect this to happen in my lifetime. But I believe I might know what it is that the city has found, and it could change everything."

"Well, Moira, I must say I'm flattered, but if what you are saying could be possible, if there is that legitimate risk, wouldn't it already be too late? I mean, how does one stop an apocalypse?" Nathan turned his attention to the proportions of his own rich coffee.

Moira paused for a moment. She appeared to be mulling something over in her mind. "I don't know Nathan, but that's the point. We are talking about the unleashing of ancient magic. Maybe not quite apocalyptic ...although that is a marvelous connection! There is certainly something worth looking into, the sources are old enough... anyway," she leaned in close over the table. "I was saying that the mythical references differ slightly. Some indicate this kind of chamber is like a tool that must be wielded by humans to bring about its charge, to ignite it, so to speak. Others imply that it is already charged, more like a ticking time bomb."

"Moira, aren't you supposed to be a scientist? Are you saying that you're willing to abandon everything scientific in favor of magical thinking?"

"Science and magic are closely related. The existence of energy fields is a proven scientific fact. That's one of the things science *can* prove. We can't even prove that matter exists, other than energy. Consider for example Sheldrake's biomorphic resonance field. The connection between matter and energy has long since been established. Magical thinking is just one step beyond science in a direction of holistic awareness of causality's being not only temporal, linear and horizontal, but also vertical, quantum leaping through time and space, if you know what I mean!" Before Nathan could answer, the waitress sliced the air with plates of food being placed on the table in front of them.

* * * *

Boston was built on its pride and sense of community. First, there were the Red Sox. Then it was blessed with the Patriots and the Celtics. Today, that harmonizing camaraderie of team spirit, the kind that makes men want to sweat together in an open field of mud for sport, while others watch hooting and hollering, had a new source: Boston's Big Dig. Digging paraphernalia had crept up across the open markets, town squares, and even online. The Big Dig manifested in the strangest of ways. Brigham's Ice Cream Shops, equally classic to the New England landscape as maple syrup and Dunkin' Donuts, offered a salute to the boys digging underground: a Big Dig Sundae. If man enough, one could consume four scoops of Oreo cookie ice cream, crumbled Oreo cookies, walnuts, hot fudge, peanut butter sauce, real whipped cream, and a cherry, all for just $4.99!

Alex was getting sick of it. As she entered the grand foyer of her destination, her snobbery and classist tendencies got the best of her when she saw that the ritzy

Bay Tower Room was now promoting its own $7 Big Dig dessert. Her spine straightened and she bit her lower lip as she read the description chalked across a gilded slate menu board — cheesecake mousse garnished with marshmallow sauce, caramel, and dusted cocoa, served with a shovel shaped cookie.

Attempting to ignore the lurking persistence of the project that seemed to be haunting her, she proceeded to select a comfortable leather couch, with coffee table, beside a floor length window.

I am surprised Richard isn't here already, she thought as she sat down and noticed that the glass bud vase was adorned with a delicate peach colored rose. *He is usually early.*

The waiter introduced himself and she ordered a glass of wine to sip on while she waited for Richard and admired the view of the city. Cars and pedestrians were on the move again but the days' worth of forceful winds had ushered in a thick blanket of storm clouds that now fully consumed the sky.

The Pru's weather tower was still blinking red, but Alex felt like she could relax and enjoy a few moments of solitude. Her earlier conversation with John Doherty offered great relief to her nerves. She had now concluded that Richard was merely trying to do her a favor in mentioning her name to the Mayor and she trusted that it was not the case that Richard had his own agenda for her, the thought of which had really weighed on her conscience. *Where did that fear and judgment come from? He's family after all.*

Still, she had to decide whether she should tell Richard that she planned to take Diana into the chamber. *If he finds out on his own, he will take it the wrong way.* Tension resumed within her body, this time targeting her shoulders and neck. *Why is everyone so obsessed with the Big Dig,* she wondered. *...And that chamber? Richard* *might really be pissed when he finds out about Diana. He is so threatened by her. She is right though, there is something quite provocative about this chamber. I can feel it too. I don't know why it unnerves me so, but just thinking about it gives me chills. What was it Diana said? Or no, maybe it wasn't something Diana said. Maybe it was just the tone of her voice that night...? Oh I wish I could shake this feeling of trepidation!*

Richard arrived and saw her staring pensively out the window. She sensed him approach and looked up from her thoughts to find he had stopped to speak with one of the waiters, no doubt to order a scotch. She stood to greet him and observed that he looked tight and flummoxed.

"Alex, sorry to make you wait. I got tied up at the office," he said sitting into the leather arm chair next to her.

"Actually," she said "you're not late, I was a bit early."

"Did you see on the news? The Mayor made the announcement."

"No, did he?" Alex was immediately enthralled. "Oh, I wanted to see that press conference!" She couldn't believe she actually forgot after class to go straight to the lounge and watch it. "I already feel so involved in this. I'd almost forgotten the public doesn't know about it already." She noticed a waiter heading towards them and she was worried she might have said too much.

"So you did speak with the Mayor's office then," Richard inquired in response to her comment as the waiter placed the warming liquid in front of him. He took a sip.

"Yes, as a matter of fact I have."

"And you're on board?" His face lit up but he didn't say it like there ever was a question.

"I am consulting..." She didn't want to say too much about her decision, or how she came to make it. "But tell me about the press conference, what was the response?"

"Oh! It was the damnedest thing." He excitedly put down his glass and asked, "I take it you really didn't hear anything at all about it?"

"No, I came straight here after class. Doherty told me it was this afternoon, but I had other things on my mind." Like trying to make sense of why he wanted her involved and why he got so irate that night when Diana mentioned matriarchal cultures.

"Hmph, that's not like you. Well, before the Mayor could get into the details or start taking questions, the cable feed was lost. Apparently it's a major issue because cable is out across the city. That's one of the reasons why I didn't get here early. I was at the office and I thought it was just my set, so I went down the hall to the faculty room and they didn't have a picture either. I called the technicians and they said that all the service was down. I think it still is."

"What did the Mayor have time to say?"

"There were normal introductions and condolences were made to the family of the worker who died. Al even had a special plaque made to commemorate his sacrifice to the 'historic event.' That's the nickname for it, an 'historic event.' Not very creative is it. Anyway he was very vague and non-committal about the nature and age of the chamber, for obvious reasons. He just had enough time to say that they found it, when there was a pop and the screen went to snow."

"Hmm, that's odd." Alex grappled with another oddity surrounding this chamber.

"It's not odd, Alex," Richard bombastically struck, "It's unfortunate! It is only going to fuel all the superstitions of hysterics! I know at least one woman who is going to try to spin a tale of magic over this disaster. Oh, and the media of course. It will create more publicity, that's guaranteed."

"Maybe that was why that guy was shouting about the apocalypse," Alex mumbled trying to ignore the comment about magic, which could have been meant to be directed towards Diana, "no…, no, that was too early, that was in the morning…"

"Huh?" Richard asked, "What man?"

"Oh, nothing," Alex saw this as a good opportunity to get from Richard more information about what he thought the chamber was. "Just a noisy beggar in the park. Tell me, what *have* you learned so far about the chamber, Richard?"

"Well, there are still some tests pending, but we won't get the results for a while. Carbon dating takes a few weeks, but it is much older than we originally supposed. It's quite possibly Neolithic."

"Really, that old!" Alex found relief in knowing that the older any site or artifact was, the more difficult it would be to prove with legal sufficiency a direct genetic or cultural connection to a Tribe, making it less likely for an Indian Nation to file any claims. But then she wondered why she kept worrying any way; why did she feel like she couldn't trust Richard, she always had? Besides, Doherty told her it was not a burial site.

Alex kept identifying the surges that had been building within her as angst or fear of being put in an unethical conflict. She didn't know that she actually had a much more important and personal affiliation with the site and that the positive, energetic connection was what she was experiencing as stress. She felt drawn to the site and was rationalizing that she needed to check for herself the representations made by Doherty and Richard. She had also been telling herself that she was getting involved for very clear reasons: her career, Richard, and now Diana. But there were other motivations working from within her body and she did not yet understand them. At least her intuition had told her that she must walk through this door and, because she didn't often hear her intuition speak to her, she was compelled to respond.

"You know," Richard said with pride in his voice, "this is an amazing archaeological find, especially in this region. It is almost unprecedented. Tools have been found in New York's Catskills dating from 70,000 B.C.E. but this chamber is unique, it will make a great display."

"Unique, huh? Then that will make it easier to identify, if it is ancestral to any of the Indian tribes."

Richard lowered his voice and urged her, "Listen to me, Alex, this site has nothing to do with any of the Indian Tribes."

"I thought you didn't know what it was yet, Richard?"

"There are certain things that I do know about it Alex."

"Oh I see, like it isn't Indian but it will make a nice display? What are you going to do, anyway? What's really going on here Richard?"

"Nothing's going on Alex. Look, you know there was Meadowbrook, the rock shelter in Pennsylvania," Richard tried to deflect, "but this chamber is like a perfectly preserved room that had a single specific purpose. It is a fertility chamber, plain and simple. It's only real novelty being that it was found on this continent. But that even isn't such a big deal. There is rogue evidence of nomadic Viking fishermen traveling westward from the Nordic seas. It fits the timelines. In any event, Meadowbrook was inhabited throughout time. This place that was found here in Boston was almost frozen in time. So it's undisturbed, that's all. The symbols indicate a religious cannon and it is self-contained. We can move it and Harvard can house it."

"Mmm, it sounds fascinating. I wonder what kind of function it could have served, being so far removed from everything else."

"Well, it is obviously ritualistic, the circular orientation and the stones make that clear."

"I can't wait to see it Richard." Alex said authentically, "It will be interesting." She noted what Richard just told her about the chamber affirmed Diana's interest and persistence. She prodded a little further, deciding it was pointless to try to avoid telling him.

"You know I asked Doherty for access to view the site?" He acknowledged with a casual shrug of his shoulders while he continued to swirl the dirty, amber stained ice around in the fancy glass tumbler.

With a quick inhale she prepared herself and then confessed, "I am thinking about bringing Diana with me." But as she heard it spoken out loud, she quickly realized that she should have told him in a different way.

He first ignored the mention of Diana and then calmly replied, "Alex, I can understand your curiosity but do you think it is necessary for you to go down there? Surely, you can rely on the reports and protocols. It may not be safe." Failing to get her complicity he said more strongly, "What do you need to go down there for? And what does that woman Diana have to do with this?" His rage grew quickly and Alex could see that he was terribly annoyed. She expected as much, but for which reason exactly, she wasn't quite sure.

"Richard, I know that you do not think it is necessary, but I want to perform my due diligence here."

"I have already determined that this site predates any registered tribes," he said through his teeth, "and that is just fine Alex, if you want to second guess my work, but what does this have to do with your friend Diana? Do you expect that the mayor's office will really allow for any Tom, Dick, Harry, or Witch for that matter to go see the chamber? I didn't get you involved so that you could bring her into it!" Now he was really very surly. "Especially now that the public knows, it will be in the spotlight and under constant scrutiny!"

"Richard, Diana considers herself Neo Pagan," replied Alex.

Grumbling, he said, "Yes, I know. As I said, witch."

"Ok, but I do not think you mean it in the same way. She does actually consider herself a witch also, but she worships life, nature and the changing seasons; evolution, Richard, not the devil."

"Pagan, witch, whatever! Diana has no business going into that chamber and I am surprised that you would compromise your professional responsibilities this way."

"Richard I do not see any compromise in bringing an assistant. I admit it is not usual but in order to do a thorough job for the city I have a right to consult my own sources."

"Alex, since when has Diana been your consultant? You simply cannot take her down there!"

"Richard, there is no harm really, and she asked me specifically to do this for her. She is my friend after all."

"I understand, Alex, but you must admit your friend has a way of getting carried away and taking things too far. I suppose she told you she had a vision or something when she was visiting some other dimension."

What could she say, that was pretty much what happened. "Oh, Richard, please do not be snide. What is it with you and her? Why were you so angry the other night… what about her beliefs gets to you so? You are my family, but she is also my friend."

"Alex, maybe you do not realize what is at stake here."

She defended on point, "Diana's presence is not going to influence my role in this, if that is what you are afraid of." Stress is stress and Alex began to feel a headache coming on. She didn't really understand why she was in the middle of this conflict, what she was fighting for, or why she felt so emotionally invested. Her head began to pound. Looking for visual reprieve she looked out the window again to the city's skyline. The dark, thick clouds had now blanketed the entire horizon, like the thoughts in her mind. Looking out toward the harbor, the islands were barely brown streaks behind the strokes of the clouds. Thinking still of Diana, she heard the voice in her head from when Diana once told her, "Storms are nothing other than an explosion of force." This one was now tightening around Alex's temples and she pulled her coat around her shoulders for protection. Turning back to Richard she spoke slowly and gently, not to compound the pressure in her forehead.

"Look, Richard, there are more people involved here than just you and me. I am going to attend the city's meetings and I'm not going to do anything rash, ok?" She felt the cold emanating from the full length wall of glass beside her and clutched the coat's fur collar closer. The softness caressed her neck.

"I've got a terrible headache," she added, "and I must get going soon. I'm meeting someone for dinner." She didn't have the strength to add that it was Diana whom she would be meeting. Richard was anything but comfortable with dropping the topic of conversation. He felt betrayed in the worst way, but also discerned the genuineness of her physical discomfort and didn't ask for details. He let it and her go.

* * * *

As Diana looked out the window of her third floor art studio, there were at least two entities in lower Roxbury who understood that climactic forces are about more than just the weather. She knew that storms purify. And purification is necessary for any rite or transformation, which goes to explain why she wasn't surprised that neither her cable nor telephone was working today. Getting ready to meet Alex at the Twenty-First, she thought, *this is why people used to use smoke signals, they're more reliable than most of our modern technology.* Diana grabbed her coat and bundled up. Night-Night was also aware that communication systems were starting to fail and the looming storm indicated that time was running short. She wondered how late Diana would really be.

"Good night, Night-Night," Diana sang from the foyer, chuckling at her choice of words as she pulled the door closed behind her.

* * * *

Night-Night had been a cat for the past thirty, or so, centuries. Not the same cat, of course, but she always chose the same form for efficiency purposes. She had been around since the time of Isis, helping to unveil the Great Mysteries. Over the years she had initiated hundreds of women, each with their own purpose and complete with their own gifts and fears. Some assignments had been better than others. She found it sad when the Goddess religions went underground, at the start of patriarchy and monotheism. She found the Middle Ages even sadder still. And though she didn't fully understand where her "assignments" came from or "who" or "what" controlled it, she knew more or less how it would be played out. Having been here since the beginning she had seen clearly the turning of the wheel. *Here it comes around again.* She thought to herself, settling down to wait and watch.

* * * *

Opening the heavy wooden door of the Twenty-First, Alex was looking forward to its warm woods, familiarity and casual comfort. Upon entering the front room however she was taken aback to see a stranger, a small blonde woman with massively curly hair and dark eyes, manning Cye's post behind the bar. Alex surveyed the room of chatty customers in search of Cye and realized the air didn't seem as friendly as usual. She was used to hearing Cye say, "Hey there, Alex!" but no one said it this time when she walked up to the bar. She took a seat and noticed that all the television sets were turned off. *The cable must still be out*, she thought to herself.

She heard the stress in her own voice as she asked the woman, "Where's Cye today?"

The stranger was washing glasses. She looked up from the sink to respond, "Cye quit!" She said it as though the words had no meaning, as though it was a simple fact that wouldn't impact anyone's existence.

"What do you mean, Cye quit? Where did he go?" Alex was frantic.

The bartender replied, "I heard that he just came in one day, said he was quitting. He left for the Bahamas, near Paradise Island, to open a pizza shop."

Alex was so shocked she could barely mumble, "A pizza shop! I didn't know he was going, he never said anything to me!"

One waitress walked through the room at the same time and in answer shouted, "He didn't tell anyone he was planning to leave. All he said was, 'Confucius says a wise person knows when it's time to go.'"

Alex was stunned and grief stricken. Aside from being a pillar in her own life, Cye was a great bartender and always claimed to love it. "Why would he do anything else," she said out loud and then to herself, "why would he leave without saying goodbye?"

Alex felt like she was about to cry, even though she didn't cry very easily or very often. But an anchor had just been ripped from her soul.

The intersections of human relations are funny things. Alex hadn't fully appreciated the intimate junctions of habit, time and frequency. She thought of Cye as a friend but also as an institution. She felt something in the recesses of her psyche starting to crack. While Alex was an independent woman and learned years ago not to get too attached, everyone needs connections in order to feel human and Alex was very human and very sensitive. Her quintessential Boston bartender, better than a therapist, gave solace to people all around the city. Cye's bar was a watering hole for all walks of life and he really did know the regulars by name.

The woman behind the bar moved toward her and interrupted her pining, "Don't worry, the music hasn't died yet! What can I get for you?"

"A glass of merlot, please, but Cye usually kept a special bottle under the bar for me." The pressure in her head was now overshadowed by the pressure in her heart.

"Aaah! Yeah, I heard about you, you're the professor right!" She shook her head in a backwards motion and laughed out loud. She bent under the bar and pulled out a dark bottle and started to work on its cork. After it was opened, she set it down and jammed her hand across the bar, into Alex's space.

"My name's Yana," she said in an exotic European accent. "Nice to meet you."

Feeling obliged, Alex took her hand to shake it. This woman had a very strong grip and Alex was unprepared for its authenticity. She returned the introduction.

"Hello. Please, call me Alex. I teach at the law school and... sorry, it's not that I'm not thrilled to meet you, it's just that I am used to seeing Cye when I come here, no offense."

"Ah, none taken," Yana said lightly as she buffed a wide rimmed glass and then filled it. Alex watched her pour and checked the color. Dark red indicated the bottle hasn't turned or corked. *Cye always stored the wine properly*, she recalled in her mind. She noticed Yana's slight accent and unique angular features so she asked, "Where are you from, Yana?"

Pushing the full glass towards Alex she answered, "You're asking about my terroir, no? Hm... well, I moved here from Bulgaria. Originally I came to study international economics, at the urging of my parents. But I've decided I'm really a gypsy. I am too much like my grandmother – who was a gypsy through and through - to work in finance. So for now, I tend bar."

Alex laughed a little at her response, and pondered the archetype of the gypsy. She enjoyed the leathery aroma of the fragrant wine and swirled it gently in the glass.

"Sounds symbolic," posing a question, rather than a comment.

"Everything is symbolic. In my country, gypsies have knowledge. They see and they know."

"Hm, I see..." Alex paused, and took a slow taste. "So what are you doing here in Boston?"

"I see that I must stay for now. I'm waiting for something, you know? My grandmother taught me to listen to such feelings. There is something that I must do before I can go. So, I stay. Boston is a cold city though, and I'm not just talking about the weather. It is not a good place for some Europeans, I think. Not that it doesn't get cold in Bulgaria, it gets especially cold in the mountains. Back home, though, we work! We hang out! We eat with friends, and it is relaxed! Here, it is severe. I try to do the same things, but it is frenzied. There's too much repression of energy. I thought I would find here the opposite. Boston being the birthplace of freedom in this country and all the universities, I thought it would be illuminating and enlightening. Didn't the puritans come here to escape persecution and oppression? It's just like Marx said." She paused for a moment and as if she skipped her thought, she resounded, "There is some heavy karma in this city." Yana turned around to another customer who was waiving a small black leather bill jacket at her.

"Marx talked about karma?" Alex asked quizzically, recoiling from the fact that Diana gave her a similar lecture last night and seeing that she wasn't sure of this new bartender yet, Alex wasn't about to allow her to skip a logical progression.

"Well no," Yana responded and then to the departing customer chimed, "Thank you, have a nice day."

She walked back to her computer to close the check and return to their conversation.

"When I was a little girl, my country, its culture, its way of life, had already been tainted and transformed by the blight of communism. I was lucky; my grandmother lived through most of my adolescent years and shared with me the way it was before and the hope of things to come... My parents were the biggest victims, born in the forties just after the Soviets took control, living the bulk of their lives under it, losing their spirit, losing respect for their heritage, losing the true mystery that comes with life." Yana paused for a moment in thought, and then continued.

"Like I said, my generation was lucky. Still, they taught us all kinds of things about Marx in school. Much of it was true, much wasn't. I don't mock Marx. Marx is Marx, but communism is communism. He acknowledged that power has its own oppressive cycle. Those that fight to resist oppression often turn around and inflict it once they have the power. You know my girlfriends and I used to have to skip class to sneak into churches and temples. The doors to all spiritual and religious places were guarded by police with machine guns. We weren't allowed to learn about religion or spirituality, except what was permitted by the government. And the Communists said they would bring our country prosperity, freedom! No, there was less! The allure of power is seductive. And in the end, the Puritans did burn the witches."

Yana kept pressing the computer screen as she searched for the right check and Alex replied, "You sound like my friend, Diana, she thinks the Big-Dig is cursed."

"Oh, right. Well, you know, with that ancient chamber it might be, but I think it is more than just the Big-

Dig. It's the *terroir*." Yana's pronunciation of the French swirled through her Slavic accent like an exotic wine.

Considering the metaphor as she examined the aromas of the wine in her goblet Alex replied, "Yes, a wine's flavor is determined by the history and content of the vineyard's soil."

Just as she said it, Yana's computer screen started to fade and then blackened. "Damn!" she shrieked and looked up to Alex. "It has been one thing after another today in this crazy bar! Now what?" Yana's blonde hair made her look frantic, yet Alex sensed she was actually calm, although Alex was still harried by her erratic migraine and didn't make the best judge.

Sympathetically she shared, "I've had the same kind of day and a throbbing head to go along with it."

"Really?" Yana leaned over the bar and quietly said, "The owner is going to think I'm incompetent with computers. I had to call him three times already. And I don't know why it keeps shutting down. I know how to use this system; I've used it before in other bars." Her volume increased, "It is just being temperamental and he has to key in his security numbers each time we re-boot." Yana threw her arms out from her sides, gesturing a kind of resignation. She emptied the money from the black receipt book, and then placed the book on top of a stack behind her.

"Plus, the TV has been down ever since the Mayor's crazy announcement about a Paleolithic cave! Maybe Mercury is in retrograde?" Yana said slamming shut the register's drawer. She noticed Alex's glass was already half empty and wrapped her fingers around the bottle.

"Better to get it topped off when the computer is out, don't you think?" Yana smiled.

"Thank you, that's very generous." Hoping to avoid another conversation about the chamber she added, "Oh, and no, by the way, Mercury is not in retrograde." She smiled as she realized that now she too was talking about these astrological connections.

"I already asked my friend about it, and she always keeps track."

Yana said, "See then there it is. Maybe your friend is right, or maybe it's the city itself that's cursed. Remember the witches…"

* * * *

Diana stepped off the Silver Line bus at downtown crossing, thankful to have made it in one piece. She was easily disgruntled by public transportation. She was a single white woman riding on overcrowded buses that crossed a plethora of cultural and economic barriers. The bus picked up riders of various colors, shapes and sizes and passed by everything from elaborate brownstones and multimillion dollar condos to low-grade rehabs and subsidized housing. It could all either be seen as a celebration of diversity or a recipe for disaster! But this week she felt particularly unsafe. There was a mounting tension amongst the public that Diana picked up on. She had felt it since the start of the Big Dig and this week it had accelerated. Others were beginning to feel something too. A volatile kind of hysteria rooted in fear and ignorance was brewing. This was the worst kind.

When the bus pulled out from the cathedral at its midway point on the route, it narrowly escaped becoming the center of a bloody incidence of gang violence. The passengers watched as the brutality erupted from behind the safety of the shatterproof windows while the driver crossed himself with emphatic gestures of his right hand and pumped at the bus accelerator with his right foot. If that wasn't enough, the satellite communications between the driver and his dispatch faltered the rest of the way into town, causing him to miss the alternate route that might have spared them from driving right into the heart of the gridlock traffic. Most of the traffic signals were still going haywire. The parody reminded everyone on board of the strange interruption in the Mayor's announcement only hours before. Hushed, frantic voices spread rumors like wildfire across the interior of the bus.

When the driver pulled the vehicle into the last downtown station, where Diana already planned to get off, he announced that everyone would have to disembark. The bus service would be discontinued temporarily, he emphasized. Diana wasn't surprised, or convinced that it'd be working again before the storm.

Getting off the bus, Diana overheard two teenage schoolgirls, dressed in the black watch plaid kilt that was signature to the private Sacred Heart school, say something about the radio and the closing of the bus as a weird coincidence. *Far from it*, Diana thought as she walked on, through the crowd of stranded passengers.

Glancing at the Park Street clock tower she confirmed that her three mile bus ride down Washington Street had taken over an hour. It was no surprise she was already hungry. Climbing Beacon Hill toward the state house she looked forward to the Twenty First's Baked Potato Soup that she had been craving all afternoon. She could almost taste its rich, thick warmth in a hearty stick-to-your-bones kind of way. And, most importantly, she was looking forward to talking with Alex.

* * * *

Alex was still sitting on the same barstool when Diana arrived.

"Hi Alex," Diana stretched her words as she spoke to intonate the many delays she faced on the Silver Line bus that almost didn't get her here.

"Sorry I am so late! It is a mess out there. The traffic lights on Washington Street are all crazy. Some work, some don't and those that do are sporadic. I almost got out to walk, but it is too cold and the people, I think, are getting ready to snap any minute now!"

Alex slid down her stool and stepped toward her friend to give her a hug. As they embraced, Diana's cold skin was soothed by Alex's warmth.

"Oh don't worry about it Diana, I really couldn't do another thing this evening anyway. I was more than happy just sitting still for a while. Plus I got a chance to get to know the new bartender here," Alex gestured to the other end of the bar where Yana was mixing a martini.

"What do you mean? Did your buddy Cye leave?" Diana also enjoyed his sense of humor and knew he was a stabilizing influence for Alex. So much so that Alex's friend always suspected that Alex and he had a romantic relationship but Alex never admitted to it.

"Yes, he did. Apparently he is opening a pizza parlor in the Bahamas, of all things. And I don't know why I'm so upset about it, but that's for later… Let's get you something to drink and settled …and warmed up a bit. You are so cold didn't they have heaters working on that 'T'?" Diana looked up and caught a glimpse of the bartender strutting towards them. Alex removed her hand from her friend's arm and saw that Diana was captivated by something. Seeing that it was Yana she introduced them.

"Oh, Diana, this is Yana, the new barkeep here." Alex then turned to Yana and continued, "And Yana, I'd like to introduce you to my friend, Diana, the one I was telling you about."

Yana extended her arm from behind the mahogany bar and Diana's lifted in response. The two women shook hands without either of their eyes breaking connection.

"It's a pleasure to meet you, Diana! Alex has told me a lot about you. Don't worry; she spoke only of wonderful things." The angular lines of Yana's face curved with a smile. She smiled as if she had nothing to hide, as if she was free. Alex recognized an immediate connection bouncing between them.

Yana casually continued, "I hear you think the Big-Dig is cursed? I happen to agree with you, in a way, but I was telling your friend that it is more likely that a curse would come from the earth and the city itself; karma and all."

Diana's lips didn't move because she wasn't sure how to respond. The personal connection she felt to Yana could have vast implications, not to mention her comment about the Big Dig. But Diana had to speak privately about the chamber with Alex right now. Otherwise, Yana would have become an enticing distraction.

Before she had a chance to respond Yana continued, "What can I pour for you?"

"Thank you, umm..." Diana considered her options, "I'll have whatever Alex is drinking. Thank you, very much! It's nice to meet you as well."

"Alright," Yana said as she filled a wide rimmed goblet and passed it to her. "Aah! ...excuse me, ladies! It looks like the boss has finally arrived to straighten things out." Yana smiled again, specifically to Diana, then headed away to talk with the owner.

Diana saw that the dining room was filling up quickly. "I do think we should get a table, it's more comfortable for dining."

Both women gathered their things and walked to the back booth in the corner, under a diamond paned window. The low ceilings, heavy wooden beams and gas fireplace gave the little dining room the realistic revolutionary feel of an eighteenth-century New England pub. The building might in fact have been historic and one could almost still hear the British coming. As the women sat down, a waitress delivered menus.

Diana took hers, and pushed it aside firmly, "You look tired, Alex. Are you alright?"

"No not really, but let us order first and then we can talk." Alex sounded more severe and solemn than usual.

Both women ordered the house specialty, the baked potato soup, which by the way is really very delicious.

"Already cultivating that new bartender, Alex?" Diana asked, teasing and hoping to learn something more about the Bulgarian beauty.

"Sorry ladies," the waitress spun around and returned to the table saying, "but I almost forgot. The kitchen has already eighty-sixed the baked potato soup today."

Remembering her days as a waitress, Diana translated the meaning: they are out of the soup they had both been craving all day long!

"Uh!" Diana squeaked and moaned sympathetically, "I am so disappointed!"

Alex reluctantly took back the menu and they both tried to adjust their taste buds. Diana could adapt, but Alex looked positively devastated. Diana ordered a filet of sole and Alex, the pasta special. With the culinary decisions out the way, both women were content to return concentration to the conversation they both came to have.

"Are you ok?" Diana asked becoming concerned as her friend's face grew more and more forlorn.

"I just wanted some of that soup!" Alex said quietly and tensely, emanating more anger than soup should normally inspire in a person.

"Ok Alex, I know you are upset about something and I am sorry that my asking to see the chamber is probably a hassle, especially if Richard is involved but . . ."

"No," Alex interrupted, "it is not about you, or Richard... I just do not know that *I* want to see the chamber... I have a *foreboding*."

"What do you mean?" Diana repressed her urge to comment on the fine line between a foreboding and a psychic intuition.

Alex resumed by saying in a matter of fact way: "Look Diana, I've thought a lot about what you said. And I don't agree with all of it. On the one hand when you talk about it, it makes sense that places have… what is it you call it, a karmic history? And Boston has violated it? …Ok, so even if I accept that, it does not necessarily mean the chamber has anything to do with what you are talking about, karma or otherwise. Still… I did speak with the Mayor's office and you can come with me to view the site but what do you hope to discover? I guess I just do not really get what this is all about!"

"You do get it, Alex!" Diana said it not in self-defense, but as an assertion of Alex's higher understanding.

"What I am saying is that the environment has an effect on people's psyches but it works both ways: peoples' psyches also have an effect on the environment. That chamber means something about our environment and might explain part of what is going on with it lately. Try looking at our city as a living entity. Did you know that ancient alchemists and healers of India and China taught that there are both energy centers and energy pathways in the body? In the holistic tradition of Ayurvedic medicine, they are viewed as deep seated patterns of energy connecting life force to life force, matter to spirit, and history to nature. They identified seven chakras or energy points in the body and when those energy centers are violated or blocked an imbalance occurs in the system and becomes manifest. The same too must be true with places and also might be true of the earth itself. Do you know what I mean? Am I making any sense to you?"

Alex was nearing the end of her patience and reason.

"Listen," she said taking a short sip of wine to swallow her irritation, "I just do not understand this, and I know that you want me to. And yes, I work with arguably arbitrary laws but they are firmly established and, more or less, objectively agreed upon. What you are saying goes beyond reasonable parameters of the real world."

Diana continued her appeal adding, "This is absolutely about what you study and work and know! It is about the connections between land and people. The chamber is important not just because of its history or what it represents, but it is sacred space. We do not live on the land we live with it and the land has a right not to be violated. I do not know why that chamber is important but I do know that it is there for a reason. Twentieth century technology has come up against an ancient cave! Don't you see Alex, it is there. It has just been sitting there, and that is all it is doing, but potentially it could change everything. I was thinking last night, what if they cannot continue with the Big Dig project because of it? I mean what are they going to do? Re-route the tunnel, change course? The problem is Boston has never paid its respect to nature, to its environment. And now the multi-billion dollar project is at a standstill because of some unforeseen cave. It makes sense that the city comes face to face with its own unconsciousness. My fear, and perhaps yours as well, for the last few years has been that the city will turn back on itself and implode from its own negativity and destruction. We are not different from our environment. The cause and effect is reciprocal. This area is suffering the effects of spiritual anorexia, and our land here, the earth our roots burrow into for nutrition and protection, is densely packed full of holes dug in the name of progress. Now amongst all that empty space we find this chamber, and it is not just a hole or a cave, it is a source, of sorts, a vortex.

"The weather, the accidents, the birds, the traffic, Night-Night, the chamber, all of these disruptions and changes in our environmental behavior are signs, manifestations of the imbalance cultivated by the glamour and illusion of society's mono-focused, linear notion of progress. In your legal work, you have helped people to hold on to their sacred spaces, why? It's not just about property rights or money to you …or is it?"

"Listen," Alex put her elbows on the table and pulled herself a little closer to Diana saying, "I feel what you are talking about and I hear the passion in your voice. I know this means a lot to you, but honestly I can't digest it. I don't know how to understand what you are saying, but that's okay. You can't convince me this is all some divine plan or karmic puzzle that needs your interpretation. It is a historic site and that might come with a lot of mystery, but as far as I've been told it isn't affiliated with any tribe or culture still alive today. That human element just isn't there. So, for me, it simply is just a site. Regardless, I am going to take you with me to see it. Tomorrow, I think we can go. I have an afternoon meeting but we can go afterwards. What's your day like tomorrow?"

"I'll be free, just let me know when." Diana said as she saw Yana returning with the bottle. Yana stepped up to the table and set it down between their two glasses. Alex felt her head throbbing and realized she had a distinct ringing in her ears. Yana reached for their empty glasses and was about to pour them more wine when she noticed that the bottle was shaking ever so slightly. Diana noticed it too and felt that the table was also vibrating subtly.

"Do you see that?" Yana asked, "This is not San Francisco. We do not have earthquakes here."

Diana placed both of her hands, palms and fingertips spread flat, on the table so that she could feel the full force of the vibration's pulse. Yana felt it through the balls of her feet upon the old wooden floor boards.

"That's not just the Big-Dig, is it?" Diana rhetorically replied, "...it pounds, this is more like a buzz or humming."

Nevertheless the rumbling continued as if it was a comment in response from the earth herself.

"It feels like a galloping herd," Alex murmured. She was still adjusting to the ringing in her ears but glanced around the room to see if others were aware of the current.

Most of the customers were absorbed in their own conversations and seemed to be unmoved. Those that might have been able to sense the shaking dismissed it immediately as peripheral.

The patrons continued eating and drinking as these three women, intuitively awakened, stared back at each other in wonder and concern, texturized by their earlier discussions of the chamber and a curse.

"There is nothing to fear, you know," Yana spoke, and both Diana and Alex's hearts beat faster from the simplicity of her statement and the conviction in her heavily accented tone. "In my country curses are not the same as they are understood here. A curse is simply a challenge between forces. If the earth is going to open up, then you can either let it swallow you whole, or you can plant a seed. Any cause put into motion can be offset by another force. We have the power to travel another course. Do you see what I mean?"

Neither answered and the rumbling slowly subsided, but only to a vibration faint enough to lead those people on the surface of the city who did perceive its tremors to believe it was over. Yana returned to her work, desiring not to intrude further into the private, shielded conversation that Diana and Alex were having. And the two old friends avoided discussion of Yana's implied knowledge and strangely familiar calm.

* * * *

Ring, ring. . . Doherty decided to answer his phone even though he was about to sit down to a late dinner with his family.

"Hello?" It had been an unbearably long week, but his job required availability whenever the shit hit the fan, symbolically or otherwise.

"Sir, this is Ron Osterman, I'm the night supervisor for the tunnel site. My crew is down here assessing the stability of the chamber."

"Yes," Doherty said, "Ron, what is the problem?"

"It's about the chamber."

"What about it?"

"Well," Osterman continued slowly not sure which words to choose, "there is something strange going on."

Doherty ducked down the hallway of his classic, center chimney, cape styled home into another room, "what do you mean strange? What is going on?"

Ron Osterman took a deep breath. He would have liked a cigarette but his wife of thirty years was making him quit. Unfortunately, nicorette gum does not cut it in situations like this and Ron spoke as directly as he could.

"The chamber is making sounds," he said, "earlier there was a rumbling that felt like a small earthquake but nothing registered on the machines. They might be broken. The crew is already concerned because of the last incident, but now it is making sounds, groaning noises. We cannot account for it sir. I think you need to see this."

Doherty had worked with Ron Osterman many times before and knew him to be dependable and smart, certainly not prone to overreaction.

"Well it must just be wind, Osterman. There is a Nor'easter that's due to hit any second now." Doherty was a bit perturbed as he was hungry and would rather talk to his third grader than struggle with the traffic back into town.

"No, sir. I'm sorry John, but you have to see this for yourself. I really do think you should get down here, before the storm hits us."

"Ok, Ron," he reluctantly obliged, "I'll be there shortly. Secure the site until I arrive."

"Thank you," Ron said as he hung up the phone, relieved that Doherty did not ask him any more questions. He really did not want to explain tonight's happenings over the phone. Heading back down the tunnel he could hear his crew talking loudly and then another groaning noise from the chamber sounding and feeling like a freight train. As he approached he saw the small crew of men gathering at a short distance from the chamber door. He was about to order them back to the surface just as a bright light flashed and erupted inside the chamber. The men quickly moved back, whispering about angry spirits and the worker that died a few days before.

"What the hell was that?" someone shouted. Lights and colors flickered and flashed in the chamber. Sounds rumbled up from underneath the earth and the men backed further away. Osterman didn't think he could explain this and in truth he had never seen anything like it before. He glanced up and down the rock hallways to assess the electrical cables and lights. Some of the lights were flickering, but not uniformly.

"It must be a surge," he said to himself. "It must be a surge!" he shouted loudly to the men in an attempt to regain morale and calm nerves. With his arms in the air he made himself heard, "Everybody back away!" He tried to settle the group but everyone was talking in unison. He looked back to the chamber's opening feeling unconvinced himself, watching and thinking that Doherty had better get there soon.

* * * *

By the time Doherty arrived, Osterman and his crew were standing outside the tunnel's entrance. Ron, his resolve broken down, was smoking a cigarette he bummed from one of his men. Usually cigarettes don't taste so good in the cold, but Ron was smoking this one with gusto. As Doherty stepped out of his SUV he could hear the chamber's sounds echoing to the surface. The orange construction lights were still blinking on and off and the tunnel entrance refracted with colors of light and sound.

"It's like a damn concert with strobe lights," one of the workers said as Doherty walked toward Ron. The two men met in greeting and stepped away from the others for privacy. Standing in the frigid night air, the wind howled around them and the snow started to fall as the light show continued in the background of the tunnel walls.

"This is surreal," Doherty said, "what's going on?"

"I do not know what to tell you," Ron said rather stupefied.

"How long has this been happening?" Doherty asked, not really sure of what else to ask.

"A couple of hours. The men were assessing the possibility of moving the chamber, as you requested, when the rumbling started. Then this eerie pinkish light started to appear from inside the chamber. We couldn't find the source, it just hovered."

"Well there has to be an explanation," Doherty said in his best authoritative voice.

"Yes, of course, but you need to understand who you are dealing with here. These men are scared, what after the mayor's announcement this afternoon. I can't hardly convince them to get too close to it. I've got to stand by them. What do you want to do?" Ron asked skeptically.

After a moment Doherty went to his vehicle and grabbed his hard hat and flash light and headed toward the entrance. Ron Osterman told his crew to stay put as he went with Doherty into the tunnel to investigate, trying not to show his angst. By the time they got half way to the chamber, Doherty realized that the interior overhead construction lights were out and that the chamber itself was illuminating the passageway. He felt the ground beneath his feet start to vibrate as they got closer and heard a lower grade mumbling of the earth as the moaning increased.

They stopped when they got about ten feet from the chamber's entrance. The tunnels and chamber seemed secure enough even though the shaking was more intense around it. Both men grabbed the rock walls for balance. They looked to each other for encouragement and made their way toward the light.

Brightness glared forth making Doherty's pupils contract as he stepped inside the chamber. Once inside, he realized that the light and noise was all around him. It surrounded him but seemingly came from nowhere. Standing in the chamber's center both men took a moment of speechlessness to absorb what was happening around and to them. It was like being in the center of a cyclone. The intensity of both the light and sound was overwhelming and made it difficult to communicate or even to think. Ron gestured that they leave the space.

Walking back toward the surface he said, "We do not know what it is. What do you think?" Doherty was lost for an explanation and nodded in affirmation of the confusion. "Have your crew secure the entrance to the tunnel. I need to speak with the Mayor." Doherty said realizing that whatever this extraordinary event was it would cost the city more time and money to resolve.

* * * *

The falling sky in Boston this late night was a dark plum grey, made fuzzy from the motion of oversized snowflakes splashing tall sides of skyscrapers and pelting the asphalt. This type of precipitation accumulates almost instantly; wet and heavy, firm and sticky. Thunder cracked and rolled high above the dense cloud cover and late night drivers moved quickly but carefully home, while the roads were still barely passable. Dispatchers called long lists of plow-driver crews. Salt and sand supplies were rationed and New England residents prepared for nature's next intrusion into their routine and re-organization of realities. Snow dropped quickly and swirled with gusts of wind that whirled them around street lights and alleyways.

Al Marino decided to return to City Hall earlier this evening. He enjoyed watching blizzard scenes from his office window and it didn't feel right to him to go home, to an empty house, with the day's disruptions still unresolved.

Silence echoed inside Al's ears and the weight of the information just conveyed to him smothered the writhing anxiety of a long day full of frustrations and chaos. John Doherty had finally reached him on his office line after many failed attempts and explained the chamber's strange episode as best as he could to the already dazed politician.

There's nothing else I can do but resign and let go, Marino thought. He was practicing a relaxation mantra, not thinking about a career change. He had been introduced to yoga and meditation through his wife, who developed a variety of techniques for him as a stress management aid. He recognized that this late hour was deserving of the practice.

The view from his desk of a wide open horizon reminded him of humility and the relative insignificance of each individual on this planet. Government Plaza stretched out behind the full length wall of glass and was framed by Beacon Hill behind it. He liked the idea of looking to the West, in the direction of the rest of the country. It represented the future to him, in contrast to the present and recent past, which had already been very taxing. On this dark night, he had had enough of both. The sides of his desk chair propped him up and he sat in the dark, breathing for peace to the pace of the rapid snowfall.

The quiet emptiness surrounding him after the phone call seemed to create a heaviness on his brain that felt like a shrinking sieve and he was in need of some relief or distraction. The room and the snow were noiseless but he could not quiet his mind. Recollections of the day plagued his consciousness.

Absurdity! He screamed mentally, forgetting for a moment his resolve toward enlightenment and letting go. He was right, though. The chain of events for him earlier this day was absurd. First, he had to coordinate storm preparations and service adjustments, and then confess the death of the worker and the find of a prehistoric chamber.

He thought he was the object of an assassination attempt in the middle of the press conference when a TV camera exploded. After everyone in the room picked themselves up off the ground and realized all broadcasts had failed, the Mayor was forced to walk away without completing his announcement. He wanted to convey a sense of order and calm along with a demonstration of unity and pride in relation to the city and the historic find. The site was sure to bring good things in the future: international attention, media intrigue, public events - all resulting in increased profits to the businesses and tourism industries. This was his message. He wanted to detract from the unfortunate losses, not merely because it was good politics, but because cabin fever produced by long, cold, desolate winters makes people scared, on edge. Superstitions grow in the dark.

Idealistically, perhaps, Al wanted the mysterious find to bring the city hope, not a focus on death or the delays that have actually occurred. And now, there was no way to gauge public reaction and no way to send messages out into the city's living rooms. Radios weren't working neither were the cable and satellites, and there was no explanation for it either.

One low note bellowed from the oak faced clock mounted on the office's south wall. The brass pendulum swung, telling the early morning hour. Now there was little that Marino could do but watch the snow and breathe.

He had already unbuttoned his shirt collar and top few buttons hours ago. The starched oxford stretched across his chest. *Inhale – two – three – four, Exhale – two – three – four.* His soft cotton undershirt pulled with the lift of his chest against the crisp but slightly wilted outer garment. His shoes sat neatly off to the side in the space under his desk and his toes gently combed, in unison, the woolen carpeting through his thinning cashmere socks.

Occasionally he'd come to, realizing that he was still awake, and held his feet still. Then as he'd get lost again in the horizon, his toes returned to their stroking, back and forth.

* * * *

Night-Night sat at home staring out the window and swayed her tail to the beat of her own thoughts. *The Earth seeks justice and the evolution of consciousness is spinning another wheel. This will be an eruption of life, but there is still work to be done. The force of an illuminated collective consciousness cannot be bought off with consumerism, religious fanaticism, nationalism, political distractions, wasted time, money, all other social-isms and distracters. Fellow earth-walkers and free spirits will know when the time has come. And they know who they are. They are beginning to feel it. Good, good, good, good vibrations!* She purred slowly.

[1] Many male scholars to this day still dispute that the Goddess artifacts painstakingly uncovered and documented by Gimbutas and many others, constitutes proof of the existence of matriarchal cultures. See, for instance users of Wikipedia quoting the *Encyclopaedia Britannica* that matriarchy is merely a hypothetical social system, http://en.wikipedia.org/wiki/Matriarchy .

Chapter Four

ELEMENTAL HAPPENINGS

The following morning's back lit sky was muddy and yellow. A strange silence fell upon the city along with the snow which must now be measured in meters. It seemed relentless, piling up on sidewalks, roadways, sagging trees and rooftops. Store fronts were closed and the morning's newspapers laid stacked in frosty piles that scattered occasionally in the wind. Aside from the main highways, most city streets had not yet been plowed. Too much snow and too little resources has paralyzed public transportation across the state. Logan Airport had been closed most of the night. Schools and business had shut down late the previous day. The storm's force created a curfew premised on survival that strong armed the habits of boredom, turning attention away from the chamber and towards the storm.

The sun couldn't break through the dense grey cloud cover and the persistent wind gusts facilitated the accumulation of house-sized snow drifts and obscenely poor visibility. The Pru's weather tower still flashed red, although it too was hard to see, through the thick sheets of pounding snow. In the light of this storm its hue was a hazy yellow, and pinkish, blinking meekly against the backdrop of a foreboding sky.

* * * *

Paul Schroder and other masters of the Academy were grateful for the bewildering storm. They had studied human nature and mob mentality enough to know that with sufficient distractions and dissuasions, curiosity could be replaced with complacency and knowledge could be turned into fear. If the Academy could control the weather, they would have done the same thing Mother Nature did, but for different reasons: follow the Mayor's announcement with a deep freeze, and then spread rumors that the chamber was associated with an evil curse.

Their resources had been substantial enough to support the workings of their organization throughout the centuries, despite hundreds of wars and natural disasters. They were unimpeded by this storm or the temporary failure of public telecommunications devices. Paul got word to Richard to meet him at the Vault in the early afternoon.

* * * *

Clunk-ity, Clunk-ity, Clunk! James McKennan's big rig plowed through the slushy snow, with little concern for the extreme conditions, and the chugging of the mighty engine drowned out the music from his radio. He was driving south on Interstate 93, making his way through the city from New Hampshire. Heading for the Storrow Drive exit, he had just crossed over the new Zappata Bridge. The suspension bridge's design was considered a real marvel. In truth it looked like it was held up by Q-tips and the ramps connecting to it arched out high above the snowy city, and would typically funnel traffic down into the tunnels of the Big Dig, promising to spit you out on the other end of Boston. But on this particular day, there was no other traffic.

It seemed ridiculous to him that the city planners hadn't designed the new highway to re-route long distance drivers around the city altogether. In college, he used to party with them. He too dreamt of building bridges, but dropped out of the program when his girlfriend got pregnant. He had driven trucks ever since. Driving in the early morning on the south-bound side of I-93 made him feel like he was a part of the same old crew.

Most of his drinking buddies completed the program and his old roommate had since become the Senior Plan Reviewer for one of the biggest firms in New England. If he had known this, he might have thought to take a different route. His old classmate never learned the art of moderation or, for that matter, meditation. If he had he might have noticed a mistake in the calculations. As it was, the plans for the bridge ramp were approved as designed and it was built to the exact specifications.

James himself never mastered moderation either, so he allowed his rig to barrel over the highway without much concern for the extreme snowy conditions. Coming around the final bend, the driving wheel's strong resistance told him something was wrong. He downshifted as fast as he could but the right side of his eighteen wheeler crashed into the guard rail.

"What the hell kind of grade is this!" he shouted as he struggled with the wheel on the outside lane of the turn. He could feel the tires grinding against the side-rails as the inertia pulled the truck to one side. Braking, shifting and leaning into the turn he gripped the steering wheel hard and tried to correct his trajectory. The force of a fractional error, a slight difference in grade and pitch from what would have otherwise ensured his safe return home, was irreversible. The only thing left for him to do was brake. But there was no time.

"Ho-ly shiiiiiiiiittttttttttttttt!"

In the blink of an eye he felt the front end be pulled by the force of gravity. He realized he wasn't going to make the turn. The weight and momentum of several tons of metal and cargo propelled the cab as it pierced the steel guard rail, slicing through it like a hot knife through butter. A snow cloaked gravel pit, eighty-five feet below, was the last thing he saw before leaving his body.

"Holy shit!" was the mantra of the day.

* * * *

Not even the dog walkers were out. Contrary to some human beliefs many dogs prefer to come in out of the rain . . .or in this case, snow. Dogs also seem to come equipped with hefty bladders allowing them to ride out the most persistent of weather fronts. Boston, like most cities, typically uses a chemically enhanced salt and sand mix to melt ice from the roads and sidewalks. This helps with the shoveling and plowing process that restores the use of roads and travel ways. Custodians and building maintenance personnel liberally, as if with a vengeance, sprinkle the concoction over the white snow and ice forming a milky paste as it liquefies and leaves a toxic residue. It is quite effective in melting snow, ice, and even unprotected skin. Dogs know this better than anyone. The chemical in the salt burns the pads of the poochie paws, causing pain and irritation. Pathetically, the four legged friends limp and whine, as they are unable to stand or walk through the salt rocks for very long. Some owners resort to purchasing doggie booties and place them on all four paws. Others are found repeatedly kneeling at the side of their furry companions, brushing the salt substance off and soothing the burns. Local dog owners have for years petitioned the city and business owners to become more dog friendly, green friendly, open space friendly, environmentally friendly and *just plain friendly* by using a different product. But the painfully popular product sells well, and the political bark is not backed with a sufficiently sized bite.

In any case, and in spite of the salt, no dogs were out *this* morning. The snow drifts in most neighborhoods were simply too insurmountable for five and six foot uprights, let alone eighteen inch quadrupeds. Bichon Frises and small white dogs in particular were staying in.

Cats, on the other hand, have different issues all together and Night-Night could not help but feel her feline wiles. A self-professed indoor cat, Night-Night's only concern with snow had ever been the glaring and unusual quantity of light it reflected into her eyes when napping in her favorite window seat. But that wasn't a concern this morning for she was basking in a different kind of light, more like a cosmic radiation. Rotations, revolutions and evolutions were happening in the circles and to the people that surrounded her. Orbits were coming together and Diana was gliding into place.

Night-Night consciously flicked her tail in the air as if to give her charge a pat on the back. She was excited and a bit impatient. She had been sitting in the front bay window, waiting and watching the morning clouds above the sky. It was still cluttered with snowflakes.

Night-Night appreciated the urban location of Diana's townhouse because there was always something to see outside her windows. The short block was framed on one end by an African Muslim Mosque and on the other end by a Caribbean Spirit and Tea Room, as well as a Botanika. At every hour something was going on, even if it was merely a discrete drug transaction on the corner. This morning she had been entertained by the neighbors attempting to dig out of their houses. The street and all the cars parked upon it were completely covered in snow. But neighbors had been busy shoveling their front steps as though they might get a visitor or go somewhere.

She heard footsteps and water running in the kitchen. *Finally*, thought Night-Night, knowing Diana was up and starting to make her cappuccino, *there is work to be done and we must be awake and alert.* She heard Diana transfer the water to the machine, turn it on, then disappear to the bathroom. Night-Night heard the sounds of the machine. It gurgled and bubbled and a dark, aromatic espresso was squeezed from the finely ground beans. Next, the sound of steam overtook the other sounds, followed by Diana shouting as she burst out of the bathroom, hoping that she hadn't destroyed her much needed cappuccino.

"Wait, wait, wait!"

Apparently, she made it on time because the sound of milk frothing was distinctive and this machine didn't froth on its own. Night-Night may have been proud of Diana's evolutionary receptivity, but she was unimpressed with her charge's morning routine. She heard the satisfactory placement of a dense mug upon the kitchen island's marble slab and the click of a cigarette lighter. She wondered whether she would have to remind Diana about her breakfast again this morning and realized that she'd better start to take a more proactive approach in helping Diana make sense of the signs that surrounded them.

A loud knock sounded from the front doors and the inner foyer doors rattled. Night-night looked back out the window while Diana set her cigarette in the ashtray and walked toward the hallway, exhaling.

* * * *

Diana pulled open the inner foyer door. "Oh, great," she murmured, seeing that snow had even accumulated inside the house, blown in from under the doors and through the mail slot. She tip-toed around the icy pile and peered through the glass to see if she could find the source of the loud noise. *A chunk of ice maybe?* Although it was still snowing rapidly, some of the sidewalk had been cleared back of snow by her neighbors. Diana saw a tall drift where her car once stood and a few trenches through the otherwise unshoveled sidewalk that passed in front of her property. She looked down at the white mounds that used to be her front steps and saw a plastic baggie peeking up from the dent at the top.

"Excellent," she exclaimed, "the newspaper! Hmm," she apologetically moaned, feeling pangs of guilt that the paper boy always managed to bring the paper and she never salted or even attempted to clear off her sidewalk. "Maybe I should shovel," she said to no one.

Feeling the wind through the cracks in the doors, she pulled her flannel tighter around her in preparation. She reached for the broom that she kept in the foyer corner and then unlatched the front deadbolts. Diana stepped aside, swung open the door, and in two quick gestures she swept the snow from the foyer floorboards back to the outside. The blast of sub-zero temperatures quickly realigned her senses and the notion that she might, on her own, battle the unconquerable task of clearing a sidewalk during a storm of these proportions, when it was still snowing brutally, became a fleeting fancy. Her fingers pinched the broom handle as if slipping might result in a hypothermic deep freeze. She dug with the broom through layers of snow that had formed over the top step until she found the newspaper. She grabbed its protective baggie and slammed the door shut in disgust; being so tuned in to other worlds often made Diana annoyed and impatient with the material limitations of this one, especially when it came to the cold. The muscles in her hands trembled, creating heat, as she carefully bolted the outer doors then shuffled through the inner ones, returning to the warm Victorian hallway. She double checked that the inner doors were shut tightly, to help keep any chill out and, still thinking about the cigarette burning in the kitchen, returned to her coffee.

She stopped first over the farm-house sink in her kitchen and clutching the wet bag at one end, shook the paper out of its plastic sleeve. She left the bag in the sink to dry and took the paper to the island counter. As though she were being reunited with a lost lover, she wrapped both hands around the glazed curves of the large mug. Her long fingers were soothed by the warmth and she took a frothy sip.

The Boston Globe's bold headline read, "Mystery Chamber Brings Cursed Storm?" It boasted photos from the media command post that had been established at the opening of the now legendary chamber tunnel and an early morning photo of an urban park whose trees had branches that looked like they were about ready to fall off from the weight of the precipitation. Smaller news titles indicated just about every public school was closed, that cable TV, satellite and many radio stations weren't working throughout the city and most land-line telephone grids had failed. A state of emergency had been declared.

Reaching for her cell phone, Diana was a bit startled when it started to ring.

"Diana? Hello, are you there?" Alex sounded like she was straining against the phone on the other end of the line.

"Yes, Alex. Hello! I thought nothing was working? Seems like a snow-in doesn't it!" Diana was glad that Alex had called. She had been worrying about her after the strange earthquake last night. It was a curious evening for both of them, and Alex had that terrible headache.

"I've been trying to get through for the past fifteen minutes! The cell phone circuits are clogging with overuse. It's the only way to reach anyone, you know."

"Oh, well how are you feeling today, Alex?"

"A bit bewildered. Listen, classes are cancelled for me, obviously. I was thinking I might make my way over to your house for food, wine and a warm fire. Kind of a slumber party I guess."

"Ahh, the essentials in a storm!"

"Well, almost. But I do need to talk to you, shall I bring some supplies?"

"Sure, let's ride out this storm together! It will be fun. Bring some extra candles and wine, if you have any. Most stores are likely closed." Diana said and then added, "Alex, do you still have that headache?"

"Yeah, I do. It could be sinuses or the barometric pressure from this storm. I'll see you later on."

Diana hung up the phone and went to feed Night-Night her breakfast, but Night-Night was nowhere to be found. She looked in the living room and saw her black cat sitting at the altar, on the meditation pillow. Her green eyes peered back at Diana in a beckoning manner and Diana decided to take a cue from Night-Night by starting her day with a meditation. She still needed more insight about the tension rising in the city and the electronic chaos. A meditation would at least clear her own mind and if she was being called to something her guides should be ready to speak.

Diana passed through the dining room and as she approached the alcove designated as her home's primary sacred space, her cat waived her closer with gentle movements of her tail. The architectural nook defining the meditation area was painted with peaceful shades of dusty rose and the purest of whites. Pastel silks of gold and pink adorned the wall behind the antique rosewood shoe-shine box that Diana used for her spiritual altar and magic box. It held the mementoes that were closest to her heart; photos of long past ancestors, clippings of fur from every pet she had ever had and elementals such as shells, sea salt and crystals. As if knowing Diana's purpose, Night-Night rose from the pillow and stepped down so Diana might sit and begin. Night-Night circled her charge and purred slowly. She rubbed her whiskered face and furry shoulders against Diana's side while Diana adjusted her legs into a comfortable lotus posture.

Ritualistically, Diana drew a circle with salt on the ground around her and then struck a match. She selected a pine incense for cleansing, clarifying and for personal growth. After the aroma had filtered the space, Diana ignited the wick of the prominent central white candle. She closed her eyes and let her hands come to a rest upon the tops of her knees. Her meditation took her through the customary channels of inward descent. Deep rolling inhales navigated her path into the subconscious, through the unconscious entering the astral underground. Eventually she traveled down a long stairwell, to a wooden door. In tempo with the exhale that she was no longer even aware of, the door opened very smoothly and she coasted straight into a circular and domed rose-quartz room. The interior was luminous and the quartz surfaces radiated with an energy charge of the most ultimate sensation.

She came to be in the center of the room and participated in a reciprocal exchange of positivity and expansion. Once she was fully atoned, awareness of the astral temple melted away and a large picture screen was presented to her third eye. With clarity she saw in the light a symbol. This was familiar to her. She recognized the experience from her childhood. Her first guided meditation brought her to an inner chamber where she was able to conjure her animal spirit guide and reveal to her conscious mind her personal symbol, a kind of spiritual or astral signature. What was being revealed to her this time was distinctly a crescent moon. The product of an eclipse, Diana was keenly aware that the crescent is only revealed when the majority of the moon's surface is concealed by the Earth's shadow. It represents both illusion and reality, the paradox of truth. Curious for more, Diana's arms lifted up to reach for the image. As she did so, she was abruptly pulled out of the temple and consciousness returned to her living room at the sound of a very loud and distracting, heavy thud!

Diana relaxed her forehead and, pacing her frustration at being interrupted, took another breath. Her head felt light and she was slightly disoriented from being pulled back so quickly. She rubbed her face with the palms of her hands and took another full breath. Then she opened her eyes.

When she glanced around the room she saw that Night-Night was precariously perched on the narrow ledge of one of her bookshelves. On the floor below the guilty feline was a book that seemed to have been the source of the loud disruption. It was lying spine side up with its pages spread out and open upon the floor.

"Night-Night," Diana scolded, after making sense of what had happened. "Can't you be more careful?" She rolled onto her knees and scooted a couple of feet to get to the fallen book. Before lifting it, she slid one finger under the spine to mark the page where it had landed - these things sometimes have meaning. The book that Night-Night toppled was Walker's *The Woman's Dictionary of Symbols and Sacred Objects.*[1]

Diana rotated her wrist to turn the book over and what she saw gave her instant goose bumps. Shards of knowledge and intuitions of meaning coursed through her body in multiple directions. The top image on page 347 was a crescent moon and the word printed alongside it read, "Night." The connection between her cat, her meditation and the book would be bizarre at best under normal circumstances, but the timing of this combined with her intuition and the week's events all foretold that there was more significance involved than a mere coincidence.

Diana ignored the awkward distribution of weight on her palm and wrist as she clutched the tome and looked up in wonder to her guide. Night-Night was still perched on the shelf where Walker's *Dictionary* used to sit. She stared casually back to Diana, with a slightly sarcastic air about her.

"What are you up to Night-Night?" Diana meant it. She already knew that the universe had been trying to tell her something. Could Night-Night be a direct player in conveying that message?

"It's got part of your name on the page, you know? What does this mean, Night-Night?" Instead of responding, Night-Night leapt, in one giant sweep, from her perch to the seat of a side chair at the edge of the dining room. She then, casually, exited and retired to the kitchen to eat the breakfast that Diana had left out for her.

Diana on the other hand, was disappointed by Night-Night's lack of apparent insight into the symbol from her meditation. She looked back to the page detailing the image and read about its history:

According to Hesiod, Mother Night gave birth to all the gods. She stood for the darkness of the womb in which all things are generated, for the blackness of the abyss, and for infinite space, source of stars and other heavenly bodies. She preceded creation. The Orphic creation myth said that even the heavenly father stood in awe of primal black-winged Night, who first laid the silver egg of the cosmos in the womb of Darkness. From this egg (sometimes equated with the moon) hatched the double-sexed deity Eros who gave motion to the universe. Night was a Triple Goddess, her other two personae being Order and Justice. In Egypt, she was Nut or Nuit.

In terms of psychological archetypes, Mother-Night represents the unconscious, from which all images arise.[1]

After reading about the crescent she noticed another symbol on the page to the left. It was simply the capital letter "M," labeled "mountain." She read,

The letter M seems to have been based on symbols of the twin peaks of the holy mountain, which were often seen as the breast of the Great Mother. The Epic of Gilgamesh describes such a holy mountain, Mashu, whose 'paps' reach down to the underworld; she gives birth to the sun and she is as high as the wall to heaven. . . . The oldest deity in Greece was the Divine Mountain Mother, Gaea Olympia, the first owner of Mount Olympus before its takeover by upstart grandson Zeus. She was called Universal Mother, Oldest of Deities, and Deep-Breasted One. She controlled several mountain shrines including the Delphic oracle, which was later usurped by Apollo. One of the oldest deities in India was Chomo-Lung-Ma, 'Goddess Mother of the Universe' whose mountain shrine is now known by Westerners by a man's name, Everest...

Magic mountains throughout Europe remain sacred to the Goddess and so acquired the reputation of witch shrines...

"Oh, my word!" Diana said out loud, causing Night-Night to look up from her breakfast. Diana sat on the floor, reading intently and absentmindedly twirling her hair around one finger.

"I wonder if any of those witch shrines were built underground?" Diana asked the universe and continued twirling her hair as she recalled that the terrain now known as Boston used to be crowned by three small mountains reduced by the European colonists to a single mound they named Beacon Hill. *Triple mountains,* Diana thought ...could *it be connected to the triple goddess?*

* * * *

Sometimes, Night-Night reflected with the crunch of a kibble, *enlightenment comes in a flash and sometimes it takes a while.*

* * * *

Al Marino was on the verge of abandoning his own search for enlightenment after the week he had had. At this point would trade every mantra he'd ever tried for a little Cartesian order. He barely slept last night and only went home to shower and change for another early morning. He had coordinated with the Governor to declare the state of emergency. This ensured supplemental state and possibly federal resources for salt, supplies, snow removal and emergency management. Then he held another press conference to announce the city's progress, keep the peace and clarify that he was in fact still alive and unharmed.

Across the country, many eyes were now watching Boston. This storm was measuring up to become the storm of many centuries, and news of the archaic underground chamber and the bizarre happening with the Mayor on TV the night before was ripe material for every good morning show around the nation. His message stretched far and wide to those who still had cable or satellite service, which ironically included everyone except Marino's constituency. He delivered his address to the newspaper journalists, knowing they were his closest, most direct link. But the morning paper laid on the desk in front of him and it did little for conveying his tone or furthering his agenda. Rumors had already been bred, from certain particularly disposed neighborhoods, that the ancient find was a cursed pagan temple and that the deceased worker, crushed motorist and, in Al's mind let's add the Mayor to the list, were its first intended victims. In many ways this might have been true, because Al Marino felt like his hands were tied. With nothing going his way, he clung to the hope that Doherty would have some answers.

* * * *

Doherty didn't make it back home last night either. The snowfall and the light and sound phenomenon both necessitated that he stay in a nearby hotel, walking distance to city hall and the tunnel. Doherty entered Marino's outer office concerned that he lacked viable data to share with the Mayor. What he did have to say might cause Marino to question his competence. Nonetheless, he determinedly knocked.

"Come in," Marino called from his desk and Doherty entered.

"Good morning Mayor." He said as he approached the desk and sat down into one of the stuffed leather chairs. It was hard to tell which man looked more exhausted.

"Quite a mess still?" Marino gestured with his head to the winter landscape outside the window.

"Yes, it is. And the media isn't helping. The supernatural makes for popular news these days."

"Is your cell phone still working?"

"Yes, I think so. The circuits jam periodically and it's a bit temperamental near the Big Dig sites. But I've been able to get through to each of my staff members and they are equipped to keep working, even if from home. The nation knows about the conditions here so we will have the benefit of some grace time, so to say, and federal aid."

"Update me about the chamber."

"Well, the first comprehensive status meeting that was scheduled for this afternoon has been cancelled. Until telecommunications devices are restored, there's no point in trying to hold it, not to mention the roads being impassable."

"And last night's phenomenon; has it stopped?"

"I visited the site about an hour ago. It was completely dark and quiet. It felt still, sir." Doherty paused then was about to tell him about his conversation with Nathan Grey but was interrupted by the Mayor.

"Can you tell me how they come up with this crap, Doherty?" Al had grabbed the newspaper and shook it in the air as he spoke. "It's not bad enough there are actual noises erupting from this chamber, but now they are saying that we're all cursed? What are they talking about?"

"Well, it's a complicated situation. I've spoken with the engineers and the people at Harvard. One working hypothesis for these manifestations is that the chamber is sitting on a ley line."

"What exactly is a ley line?" he asked indignantly.

"Ley lines were first discovered, or coined rather, by an amateur archaeologist of the name Watkins, in the early 1920's. Their existence is quite controversial and many consider it pseudo-science. They are described as path ways or energy line patterns connecting sacred sites and holy places around the world. Simply put, they can be seen as energy pathways, or routes, traveled by our ancient ancestors between various holy sites over thousands of years. Boston, for instance was designed with all major roads leading to the state house, Washington with all leading to the White House, and similarly it is said that ancient peoples traveled the shortest path, or line, between sacred sites."

"Telling me the chamber is aligned with an old road doesn't give any explanation for why or what is happening down there!" Al said in frustration.

"Hypothetically, sir, it is said that the sacred sites are positioned in relation to each other upon certain lines because there is a unique magical affiliation to their placement."

"Doherty, this is very interesting but you are talking curses, magic and witchcraft here, tell me something I can use!"

"I understand sir, and there's not much to work with, but let me continue." With an exhausted nod from Marino, Doherty went on.

"Electromagnetic anomalies are often associated with particular points along ley lines, like at Stone Hedge or the Egyptian Pyramids. Actually, the causal connection is not clear, making it all the more controversial. Either the heavy pattern of repeated use has somehow imprinted or infused a pathway with an electromagnetic resonance, or individual lines and points are inherently magical and volatile, thus explaining why it originally came to be recognized as 'holy' or 'sacred' in the first place. But the climax of the theory is that when multiple ley lines intersect, especially if one of them is heavily 'charged,' strange occurrences happen there such as earth lights, vibrations and poltergeist activity, even UFO sightings are said to coincide with ley lines. Proponents believe that their intersections connect with and affect the electromagnetic energy of the surrounding area. Apparently, one of the archaeologists at Harvard has studied the ley line phenomena before and considers this chamber a likely candidate for this classification of study, claiming that the chamber lies directly at the point of intersection for at least three, possibly more separate ley lines.

"So I wanted to get a look into this myself and found out, you're never going to believe this, but apparently, the Seattle Arts Commission once paid $5,000 to a group of dowsers, the New Age Geo Group, to map out the city's ley lines. There was a great deal of skepticism and debate regarding the city's funding what some believed to be a religious, pagan mission. The Geo Group, however, maintains that Seattle is the first city to heal the earth's energies within its limits. Their report claims that," he lowered his eyes to the notebook in his left hand, "and I quote, the 'project made Seattle the first city on Earth to balance and tune its line system.'[1] It goes on to say that by identifying ley-line power centers they have neutralized negative energy and amplified the positive potential and health of the city's inhabitants. As you might imagine, the group's claim that reduced anxiety and disease will result is not only unsubstantiated, but has made them a laughing stock."

Marino took a deep breath in the ringing silence. "I'm not ready to end my career," he said. It would be easy enough for his opposition to roast him over the coals as a New-Age Guru Mayor if much of *this* got out. "Keep Harvard quiet for a while. I'll talk to Richard Lyons myself. Let me know if anything new comes about."

* * * *

Whales are very intelligent mammals; all of their waste is organic. And they are very sensitive. Whales are completely tuned in to their environment. Maybe that is because their physical bodies live in water and their world view is thus framed from the perspective of dense interconnectivity. In any event, they know that they are a part of an organic system and have felt a keen lack of balance in the waters over the last few generations. But with the energy released from every earth-conscious or green act performed by humans in an attempt to consciously re-institute balance, whales are inspired with hope and will, and that feeds their spiritual natures. This is of course also due to their astral sensitivity and notion of interconnection, but they really thrive on it. It's like a high.

Whales were originally quite grateful when the city of Boston's waste management agency decided to modernize its sewage treatment plant and implement a recycling program: most solids and semi-solids got processed into a marketable fertilizer nugget and is thus re-used in an immediately productive, organic way. This benefited the whales in two ways: it minimizes the risk of supersaturating any of their extended and local environments with waste, and it feeds their hearts and spirits with the energy charge released by the compassionate, mindful act. But the modernizations came to also include the pumping of semi-semi-solids and semi-processed waste liquids off shore and into the whales' waters, fifty miles out into the ocean.

It was lived with and adjustments were made to manage the impact. But Boston had grown a lot over the years. The quantities changed. And in order to accommodate the increasing human populations, more seafood had to be harvested. So of course boating and shipping increased. Then another few tons of over-board garbage was added to the mix and, of course, let's not forget tourism and the Big Dig's planned attack on marine life. OK, so it was done with the best interest of fish in mind but, regardless of the motives, some neighboring creatures were very upset that a policy of fear, through the use of false explosions, was used to usher fish and baby seals from their homes in order to make way for another round of tunnel blasting.

"Just plain rude," one crab reported.

"Fish terrorism," a flounder said.

Needless to say, these whales were tapped in and ravenous for some random act of kindness or senseful act of beauty. And whales have a very wet sense of humor, which is why, after all they have endured and witnessed, it was decided that a protest was in order. So, they devised a plan to send a few scouts into the Harbor to deliver a message.

* * * *

Meanwhile, Richard had already made his way through the lumpy streets of Cambridge and sat in Paul's office discussing with Paul the episode in the chamber last night. It frightened him more than any of the others who knew of its occurrence. It further proved that the Academy's identification was correct. But over the past couple days Richard had practically proven that there were absolutely no references made to an eighth chamber, not by Plato, not by any of the Goddess Cults, and not by any scholar or historian since. This left him in a precarious and unfamiliar state of not knowing. He didn't like feeling powerless and it was becoming clear that he had made a few too many mistakes in the past.

Richard repeated Paul's words back to him, "Lights and sounds?" He asked astonished, "and not just lights and sounds, but movement …activity?" He huffed as he struggled through the densely packed information that was garbled in his head.

The Academy is not as clandestine as what normally comes to mind when one mentions a "secret society," although it is the oldest and the most discrete. Their mission had always been to preserve a way of life and a structure of power, based on control of public knowledge – not just information, but thinking; and not just thinking, but thought forms, and thus reality, if Plato is to be believed. It was Plato after all who first organized the

Academy. His purpose was the proliferation of patriarchal reason, designed to stop the growing power of the mother goddess in her proverbial cycles.

A memory of Moira flashed through Richard's mind. "The gendering of knowledge", she once screamed it to his face, "It's all about the control of knowledge, Richard, isn't it? You think you can hoard it, like knowledge is a finite thing and you have it all? Knowledge is not a commodity to be shared only amongst men!" She screamed it to him on their last night together in Tehran, when she found him destroying the last of the scrolls that she pulled from that chamber. Richard also realized, now more than ever, that he never should have let her keep the one that he did.

"Perhaps such a phenomenon did previously occur at one of the other sites, but I truly don't think so." Richard said, he didn't have a good feeling about this and neither did Paul.

"And Moira has already drawn a connection between the chamber and the ley line hypothesis." Paul replied.

"Is it true, though? Do we have any sources that make that connection?"

"Our organization hasn't had to deal with even the question in centuries. Aside from the Persian chamber we don't have record of any other chamber being a concern for over twelve hundred years. It's a bazaar anomaly that we'd see two in our life time. Look, Richard, it has become painfully obvious to all of us that this plan of yours about hiding the chamber in the plain sight of our museum isn't going to work. The publicity is only going to increase, especially with Moira nosing around."

"She'll probably say this is the resurrection of the Goddess, or something hysterical like that," Richard replied, not so facetiously. In fact, he was trying to cover his own ass knowing full well that it was prophesized in the scroll that he let her keep – the one he never told the Academy about.

"You had better plan to spend the rest of your day in the Vault. I've ordered a few assistants in to help you with your research. We want this thoroughly explored. If something more is to be found, we've got to be prepared, and the first to know about it. I'm putting you in charge of answering all our questions about this site. But I will also be directing the decisions about this particular chamber from here on out."

The message was bittersweet. On the one hand, Richard was being demoted, punished for the publicity surrounding the chamber caused by circumstances outside of his control. On the other side of the token, however, he was put in charge of providing the answers to the Academy itself. It was an opportunity to interject the information only he knew about from the scroll Moira and he had secreted all these years. Still, in Richard's latest years, he had become unaccustomed to taking orders.

"What would you like me to do first?" he proffered.

"One of the state's men that is working with you and the Mayor has allowed for some... prior indiscretions, let's say, regarding his career. I have ensured that you will have his full complicity in executing the proper corrective action, given whatever means necessary."

Richard understood his meaning.

"Together, your bases should be covered. The two of you should be able to control the perceptions and implement the plan. You already know him, his name is Doherty."

* * * *

The snow kept blowing into Alex's face, stinging her cheeks and making her eyes water as she trudged through the snow to Diana's house. Even though it was still the middle of the afternoon, it was dark like the night had already set in. She was bundled up like a child going sledding. Her nose kept running and she had to practically leap and climb over snow banks to cross both the plowed and the unplowed streets. Luckily, both Massachusetts Avenue and Washington Street got plowed at some point during the storm, providing a route of least resistance. She couldn't see the asphalt on either of these main streets, in fact she couldn't really see much in front of her through the cluttering of falling snow flakes. The snow had been falling too quickly, but at least the plowing created a more even terrain for negotiating her footing.

Aside from the physical exertion of walking in this weather, Alex was exhausted from the new sensations that had been running rampant through her own body and she welcomed Diana's comfort and familiarity with these matters. By the time she got to Diana's street she could smell the intense aroma of her wood burning fireplace pierce the cold air like a trusted friend. The sun was setting behind the building as she approached the entrance to the old mansard structure.

Diana was waiting in the foyer and both women smiled in greeting when they saw each other through the glass. Diana opened the door but neither could speak rightly in the frigid cold. She urged Alex in with the flutter of her hand and quickly slammed the door behind her.

"Jesus! It is cold. I cannot believe you walked over here." Diana said as she pushed Alex into the hallway warmth and opened the parlor doors to their right. She gestured towards the blazing fire.

"Go defrost by the fire. You'll feel better in a minute." Diana checked that the front sets of doors were properly latched and joined her friend in the parlor. Alex's teeth chattered as she warmed her hands in front of the orange flames. Nodding to her friend's remark and with her body still shaking Alex said, "I had the day off, I thought it would be fun. I needed to think, but after that hike I'm glad that I am not going out again. It's a good thing I brought an overnight bag! Here, I also brought the supplies: candles and wine."

"Great," Diana handed Alex a full red glass. "This has been breathing. I made a pot of vegetable soup figuring we would need some sustenance."

Alex's nose picked up a variety of flavors in the air. "Mmm, I guess so," she said, "It smells delicious, but why all the incense? It's a little overwhelming."

"I needed the smoke," Diana replied matter of factly, as if this would make sense to anyone. Alex understood how her friend's mind bridged meaning, however, and presumed that she meant she engaged in some heavy meditation or ritual work today.

"Did it work?" Alex asked in response.

"In some strange ways!" Diana said with a curious note of righteousness as she disappeared into the kitchen to stir the soup.

Alex didn't pick up on what Diana had insinuated and proceeded to tell her friend how bewildering last night's experience was for her. "Nothing feels the way it should, Diana," she said with a raised voice so it might be heard in the kitchen, "ever since last night at the Twenty-First. I am beginning to think that you may be right. There is something profound going on, but I need to see it in a way that makes sense to me." Alex sat down on the leather sofa and removed the quilt from the back of the couch. Placing her wine beside her on the end table she wrapped the flowery cover around her and felt ready to settle in. Before leaning back, she adjusted the throw pillows just as Night-Night jumped up on the sofa next to her.

"Well, hello, Night-Night," Alex exclaimed. "You aren't usually so friendly! Good to see you, what's up?"

"Don't ask her that!" Diana yelled from the kitchen with a wooden spoon in her hand, "She will tell you!"

Diana's comment was too late. Night-Night worked quickly when she had to and Alex was ill prepared for any kind of feline intervention. All Night-Night had to do was to blink her green eyes. Cats' eyes are powerful. One should never look into them directly unless one is willing to trust the cat.

Night-Night held Alex's eyes in her own only long enough for Alex to feel the truth of what she herself already knew.

In a fraction of an instant, Alex saw in her mind a crystal clear image of her past. It felt like a memory but she didn't know where it came from or why she thought of it just then.

Meow! Night-Night cried as her tail danced graceful gestures from the rolled arm at the other end of the couch.

By the time Diana returned to the living room, Alex's face showed confusion. "She spoke to you, didn't she?" Diana charged.

Alex opened her mouth slowly, uncertain, like someone coming out of a deep sleep. The picture was in her mind so briefly, but it was so vivid that she could still see it, as if by a replay. Shaking it from the foreground of her mind, she looked to Diana then to Night-Night now lying innocently on the couch next to her.

"Spoke to me? I don't know, but something happened." Alex mumbled.

"She has been very active all day." Diana said by way of an explanation which really offered none to Alex. "We need to get into that chamber." Diana said.

"What are you talking about?" Alex asked sitting up straight and willing herself back into the conscious reality most familiar to her.

"Night-Night knows about the chamber," Diana quickly said before her friend could fully regain reason.

"What does your cat have to do with the chamber," Alex asked, reaching for her wine. One of the things she loved about Diana was her gift of levity. The direction she was going here would surely deserve a sip.

"I am serious, Alex. I don't know exactly what's going on but the chamber is definitely involved in all the electromagnetic disruptions to the city. Nature is finally lashing back, with the help of something that's down there, in the chamber. We have to see it for ourselves and I am sure we will find some answers once we get there. All day long today Night-Night has been giving me clues, guiding me."

"What kind of clues, what are you talking about?" Obviously Diana was not being humorous.

"She's been knocking books off their places on my bookshelves."

"And that's a clue! Seriously, Diana, I'm trying to stay with you in all this craziness, but are you losing it? What is the fact that your cat is bored or is looking for attention, a clue of?" Alex was already having enough of a problem adapting to Diana's journeys into other dimensions with regard to the chamber.

"She's not bored, she's aware. Look, Alex it's more than coincidence. It may even be more than synchronicity. Ok, you have to see this." Diana pulled her knees in underneath her to stand up. She walked to a conspicuous stack of books with yellow tabs sticking out of their pages, towering alongside her altar and meditation pillow.

"These are all the books that Night-Night has knocked off the shelf today. This one," she grabbed the book on top, "this book was the fifth book to be pushed over the edge. And she did it after I looked her square in the eye and asked, 'Night-Night I don't get it, what are you trying to tell me?' And you know which book this is? This is Mary Daly's *Quintessence*. It landed open to a page on inter-species communication!" Alex's head began to shake as she wondered whether Night-Night could have telepathically conveyed the strange image she saw moments ago insider her head.

"This book," Diana continued, "is about the lost and found continent of enlightened women and animals. It is set in the year 2058 and tells the story of women after the Earth's ecological disaster." Diana was practically ranting now, "See the apocalypse is about to happen; only it's going to be ecological! The destruction is environmental! This chamber marks the beginning of it!" Diana could see that her friend wasn't following all of her connections. Quickly, her hand lashed out and selected another book from the middle of the stack.

"See, this one! This is the Bible! It fell open to Revelations and the four horses of the apocalypse." Getting more excited she went on, "Here, look at this one. This is about Einstein's theory of relativity. Oh, and here, this one. This was the first time it happened. Do you know I was in a meditation!" Now she was clearly agitated, "And in my meditation, I saw a symbol, a crescent moon! And then I was interrupted by the sound of a book falling off this book shelf." Diana pointed to the shelf. "The page it opened to had a picture of the same symbol and described the meaning of it. Don't you see? Night-Night has been giving me clues to piece everything together!"

"Diana, I think you have seriously gone over the edge. I am worried about you. I think you need to take a rest. Maybe I should make you some tea?"

"Of course I've gone over the edge! Don't you see? It's an ancient prophecy. I don't need tea, I need to get inside that chamber and listen for the past. I think I might hear something. It all makes sense that I've been building up to this my whole life. I have trained and tuned my intuition and senses for something, I've known that, and I think this is what I've been expecting."

"What have you been expecting?"

"I don't know fully. I can only see these glimpses. That's the point, I think I can get another perspective from the chamber, tap into some primal memory or karmic imprint on the space. I'm not sure exactly how. Hey I wouldn't have expected Night-Night's method."

A loud response was heard from the other room, "Meow!"

Both women paused for a moment, looking into each other's eyes in recognition.

"I don't know about any of this Diana," Alex kept staring intently at her friend. The wind howled again, shaking the eastern facing panes in their sashes like a rattle.

"It's one thing to pick up on patterns and coincidences, hell you can call them psychic vibrations if you want to. Even I can admit that you tend to be 'tuned in,' so to say. But it's another thing altogether to think that you have been called upon to reenact an ancient prophecy. Have you been self-medicating with homeopathic herbs again?"

"Look," Diana took a long swallow of the Washingtonian Syrah. She sat back on the couch with her friend, who looked concerned. She poured them both a refill and said, "I know I sound hysterical, but tell me what did Night-Night say to you, anyway?"

Alex turned her eyes away. She didn't want to admit to Diana the contents of the image that flashed into her head when Night-Night was staring at her. She didn't say a word.

Diana broke the silence, adding, "Not with words, Alex. Didn't she show you something?" Alex's jaw clenched and her eyes darted back to Diana in response to the words she chose.

Alex started to speak with hesitation, "I've got all this chamber stuff in my head. Anything I might have seen has nothing to do with Night-Night.

"Well, then share it."

"It was… a very brief image, more like a memory or a fantasy. I don't know, maybe it was just a dream. We were both there… actually in a cave, which I find very disturbing under the circumstances and there were lots of other women around. It was rather cryptic, really." She paused before telling her friend the rest of it.

"Okay, see!" Diana interrupted, "that might be a memory of the past, or an omen even, of something still to come! We must visit the chamber! Go on, please, what else happened?"

Alex's expression changed to an apology as she considered keeping the further details of the vision to herself. "You're putting all of this in my head Diana, and words in my mouth. Nothing really *happened*. It was just like I said, it felt like a memory."

"But there was more to it than that?" Seeing the hope and sincerity in Diana's face reminded Alex of the trust between them and she was consoled to continue.

"It was positive... hopeful. I also felt a force of *intention* from everyone present, as if something wonderful and big was happening or was coming to fruition. Oh, listen to me! I mean after all, it was very brief and happened in a flash, but I heard my name being called out and then I moved into the center of the cave, inside a circle. I was holding a piece of parchment paper. I know I was responsible for reading it out loud. I don't remember what it said, but I think it contained some kind of law or declaration."

Diana looked mesmerized. "Alex, you have to get your thinking aright with this," she said slowly so that her tone didn't run away with her emotions. "You're involved in this too. Don't you see? We cannot deny what we know any longer, the truth has been unearthed and we are staring it in the face. Look outside; does this look like a normal storm to you?"

"Diana, nothing about this week has been normal." The resignation in Alex's voice was unexpected to them both.

"That is exactly right, Alex, nothing has been normal, and I do not know if it ever will be again," Diana couldn't help sounding melodramatic at this point.

"Oh for god's sake Diana," Alex pleaded, "be reasonable. You are not seriously telling me that the chamber is the start of an environmental meltdown. I can't accept that. I can only accept that I don't know."

"It's not the start," Diana countered, "it's the effect. The environmental meltdown, as you call it, has already started years ago, in fact, but we have been in denial. The chamber means something. One way or another, it's a magical vortex. If your vision doesn't convince you that you are already involved then consider it from another angle. You know that the law isn't completely arbitrary. Nothing is. And your vision is telling you something. You hold a key to all of this. There are no coincidences, it's meant to happen this way."

"What are you talking about?" Alex challenged Diana, "I believe in free will, not prophecy or myth. That is why I teach law; it tries to balance standard consequences with the choices we all make freely." Her discomfort with the abstractions in Diana's language had risen, but before Diana had a chance to respond, Night-Night jumped back onto the couch and nestled in between them. Her little black body was soft and warm, comforting them both. Diana reached down and stroked her velvety head and ears. Alex looked skeptically at the strange feline.

"Could we bring her?" Diana broke the momentary silence.

"Bring her? Who? Where?" Alex asked and Diana kept stroking Night-Night's slender tail.

"Night-Night?" Alex asked with horror in her voice. Diana sheepishly nodded her head.

"You want to take your cat to the chamber?" Anger swam through Alex's question, which she only meant rhetorically. Diana's eyes widened with concern as she realized she might have pushed her dearest friend too far.

"No, you've got to be kidding me Diana, seriously?" After staring silently at each other for a moment Alex dropped to a more compassionate tone, "are you serious?"

* * * *

By the time Alex and Diana put down the many books scattered across the living room floor and drifted into sleep, Moira was just rising from her evening nap to begin another session of work. Her biological rhythms were somewhat eschewed from the normal daily patterns of most workers. She wrote with the moon.

But at this late hour, she was not writing. She was still sifting through her life's worth of theories, research and charts collected about everything esoteric, mystical, mythical and relevant to the known cultures that had displayed the various symbols housed in the chamber. But now that she was sure, she didn't know what to do. The ley line hypothesis would keep minds and wits churning for some time – she needed more time to decide what to do - she had counted on it, but knew that it would quickly be discredited as pseudo-science even without any better explanation.

Like the snow crusted city, Moira was frozen this evening in the sense that she was stagnant and unable to move within the confines of the current reality that her past choices had created and long ago solidified. Finding this chamber was something that she had both hoped for and dreaded her entire life. But she couldn't tell anyone *how* she knew. Her proof couldn't be authenticated… that is, not any longer. Her past was catching up with her.

She looked down to the ancient Persian papyrus that lied on her desk. She ran her finger softly across the dry, delicate edges and traced the outline of the symbols drawn across its back side. The snake and the almond shaped eye have been represented since the dawn of human kind.

She smuggled this scroll out of a dig during the hostage crisis in Tehran, back in the Reagan years of the eighties, to protect it from sure destruction. It told the tale of our ancient foremothers and foresisters who crafted magic upon the earth herself. It first explained how their teachings of inner alchemy had been stolen and bastardized by Plato and the Academy in their quest for power and later, during the Middle Ages, their quest for gold. It went on to explain the herstory of the Goddess and how her magic was powerful enough to be cursed by the churches of Christianity and sensitive enough to awaken at the time when we, her descendants, would need her most, causing her to rise again. In one woman's words a message was sent to the daughters of them all, to share the knowledge that was rightfully theirs. Up until now, that knowledge had been successfully contained by the Academy.

Moira had spent hours this week rifling through accepted sources for additional direct references to the message on this scroll that she could now use. Of course she had already been looking for such further proof for years to no avail! Though she didn't ever know it, there were several other scrolls that told the same story, but the Academy had successfully destroyed every text except this one. Now time was running out. She would have to keep referencing her own works and their previously authenticated theses.

Feeling like she didn't have a choice, she decided it best to precede status quo: remain silent about the papyrus, for now, and build the best argument she could from her other sources. Some of the dating tests she ordered would take at least another week. It had yet to be established whether the iron coloration in some of the petroglyphs was blood, paint or natural mineral deposits. *Surely,* she told herself, *I have more time.*

185

She sat down to work at her computer and decided that all she really needed right now was a draft. She constructed an outline as though she were free to use the hidden artifact that told the prophecy enshrined in what was otherwise known as the Myth of the Caves. She typed until her eyes started to twitch and she knew she was being forced to stop and sleep once more.

The sun would soon rise. Before returning to her queen sized brass bed and alternative down comforter, she pulled her curtains and closed them tightly. Knowing that there was much more at stake here than just her reputation, she was prepared to do whatever was necessary – when the time came. Before going back to sleep, she let down her long silvery hair and asked the great Mother Goddess for strength and courage.

* * * *

In the Back Bay the locals were waking from their lavishly plush slumbers to the rank smell of oozing sewage flooding over toilets onto the marble floors of garden duplexes. Some unknown force was causing the harbor pumping system to back up and actually take on water, instead of flushing the city's waste fifty miles into the ocean. The Back Bay, being the lowest region of the city became a holding tank and leeching field almost instantly.

* * * *

Meanwhile, the Oceanic Institute in Nahant was watching two oddly behaving pairs of humpback whales along the harbor's inner coastline.

---

[1] BARBARA G. WALKER, THE WOMAN'S DICTIONARY OF SYMBOLS AND SACRED OBJECTS (Harper San Francisco 1988).
[1] *Id.*, 347.
[1] *See* http://geo.org/qa.htm

Chapter Five

INITIATION

Alex's solar plexus woke her early, before the morning sun that flooded Diana's guest bedroom on the occasional clear day. She and Diana had spent the evening perusing the various books spread across the dining room table and living room floor. Diana awoke soon after her, when the oily fragrance of a strong pot of Café Bustello rose to meet her well shaded bedroom.

Alex and Diana were both a little surprised that the snowfall had subsided and the main roads looked almost passable. The storm's calm was predicted to be short lived, something of more significance was sure to follow. Still, few workers would be around so they decided that today should be the day to visit the chamber. Alex wanted to get them in when no one else would be there. She wasn't concerned professionally, she was sure that no one would ask her any questions once she got an okay from Doherty, but she certainly didn't want to take Diana when Richard or one of his colleagues might be there.

In the clear light of morning Alex also resolved that there was no way she could entertain the idea of taking Night-Night down into the chamber. The feline would only complicate a sufficiently delicate situation.

What was Diana thinking? Alex wondered. *Is she really claiming that the cat is her guide now? Nothing against Night-Night but...what was I thinking?* Alex might be willing to follow an intuitive hunch, but she wasn't about to throw out all rational and sane judgment.

The sky was perfectly clear and a dark, tropical shade of blue as if no storm had ever occurred, although the blinding white proof was all about her as she walked home.

Blue skies this rich typically only showed in Boston during really cold temperatures, as if even the air pollution had frozen and fallen to the ground. But the snow didn't look polluted. It was brilliant, pure and bleached. The reflected sunlight that shined in every direction was so unusually strong that Alex's sunglasses were hardly enough of a filter to see comfortably, nor were her boots tall enough to keep her legs dry as she waded down Diana's unplowed street. What she really needed was an adult sized, waterproof onesie.

The block was short and she made it through the drifts to Washington Street. A thick layer of ice had formed over the asphalt, now visible in places from the melting power of the chemically enhanced rock salts. Plows and salt trucks worked incessantly to clear this thoroughfare but none of the smaller roads had been touched.

In keeping with Boston's hearty spirit, men, women, children and merchants were up and out, contributing their sweaty back-aches to clear the sidewalks and start to uncover their automobiles. Like the rest of them this morning, Alex had to get up and get out. Without telephone lines, television, or radio, the only way to participate with the world was to get out into it. She squinted her way to her condo building's main entrance. The slow two miles gave her plenty of time to think quietly.

She entered the building's warm foyer and pushed Night-Night out of her mind. *At least I can get this over with.* She was determined to focus on the task at hand and not let herself get spooked. Although Alex would never admit it, spooked was definitely the right word for what she was currently feeling.

In addition, Alex missed Cye. *He would be able to put this in its right perspective*, she mused. He would say something real and then offer a wise-crack about how "out there" Diana could be. They would both laugh and Alex would feel better. *But the thing is*, countered Alex again to herself, *Diana makes a lot a sense when you listen to her. She can be quite convincing . . .although many of the things she believes in are not part of me. And until now have had nothing to do with me. How did I do this to myself? Here I am involved. First through Richard and now through Diana! I thought the city would be difficult to deal with. All of this pressure and force and I haven't even seen the damn chamber yet myself.* And with that thought Alex got off the elevator at her floor and entered her condo.

She walked directly to her bedroom suite and drew a hot bath. Peeling off each woolen layer, one at a time, she stood before her closet mirror for a moment to study the tactility of her own body, *something real and familiar.* She studied the shape of her shoulders and reviewed the round curves of her breasts and hips... her lean muscular thighs. She closed her eyes and felt the air on her skin, defining what she liked to think of as clear boundaries between herself and the outside world. Her stomach was heavy, not to mention empty, and the beating of her heart sounded in her ears. She tried to focus on her breath but the rhythm reminded her of drumming, the Big Dig, and the varied creation myths told to her by tribal elders. She desperately wanted to know what she should do and what all this meant about her world, and reality.

In a flash, the street prophet invaded her thinking with the memory of him screaming, "look underground!" Then, before she could control it, memory upon memory flooded over her. The noxious pounding of the Big Dig synchronized with what now seemed to be regular migraines, the earthquake, the beggar, the honking of the geese, Diana's insistence, Richard's detachment, and now, standing by her closet in her underwear, she recalled again, with vivid accuracy, the vision she had last night that Diana believed was a telepathic message from Night-Night.

"Damn," she said out loud. "I don't want to think about this nonsense anymore!"

But just in the next instant her mind grabbed itself from behind and stopped her from screaming ferociously. She sat down on her bed, brushed her hair back from her eyes and took a moment to compose herself. She then walked to the bath, stepped into the tub and tried to put reality back into its proper perspective.

* * * *

By the time Moira got to campus, Harvard had already shoveled out their walkways and students were plowing through snowdrifts. Her office was cold, but the radiators promised some heat as they were working audibly. At least Raya had already come in to organize her files and messages. She read a note from Nathan saying that he needed to meet with both her and Richard this afternoon. *Now what?* She wondered and, shaking off the thought, cleared her mind for class.

She wasn't sure if her students in Cultural Anthropology were ready for what she had to say. *Sometimes ideas are more threatening than a gun.* Parthenogenesis wasn't a new idea but she was about to give it a radical twist.

"I want to talk to you today about how the universe is not like your living room," she started out. "It is not comprised of things that you can clean up and throw away. In fact it is not comprised of things at all, rather energy and force fields – through a fluid network of interconnection where nothing is wasted and everything is shared in a delicate dance of perpetual redistribution. How many of you are familiar with the idea of parthenogenesis?"

Not waiting for a response she continued, "The word 'parthenogenesis' comes from the Greek: *parthenos genesis.*" As Moira began her lecture, Raya took attendance and noted that the majority of students were present and seemingly prepared, in spite of the debilitating weather. Moira paused to make sure she had her audience's attention and continued on thoughtfully.

"Traditionally this term describes a natural reproductive process in just a handful of animals and some vertebrates where reproduction is self-generated, without the need for fertilization from an external source. But the pre-ancient mythical notion of Parthenogenesis is not about reproduction *per se*. It is about an ongoing genesis of the universe and the creative powers of the Great-Mother Goddess as divine *Creatrix*. Please note, as many feminist writers have, that the word 'creatrix,' the feminine version of creator, is not in your average American Dictionary. Perhaps we should be thankful that we can even speak of Her at all! It should come as no surprise that the universe was originally represented in female imagery. The pre-ancient and ancient goddess cults celebrated the female form because when you look to nature, females are eternally the life givers, from generation to generation."

Moira continued on point, "The essence of her true creativity lies not only in her ability to give and sustain life, but also in that she can rejuvenate and transform life, even herself and the earth. Her creative powers are still hidden in the rituals, ideologies, myths and doctrines of the present. Her presence and influence in modern-day world religions still allows us to experience the primal connection between the human and divine, because re-creation is, and it is continual. We stand here today as the proof." Moira looked out at the blank faces.

"You do not get it?" she asked. "You do not understand why this is so important? Look, I am sure that you are all familiar with and believe in Einstein's theory of relativity. Einstein was interested in a unified field theory, a theory to explain everything. He identified two of the forces in the universe as gravity and electro-magnetic energy. You cannot see either of these forces and yet scientists study them and you believe that they really exist. Look at post-Newtonian physics and quantum mechanics which teach us that atoms are not things, but energy. They are comprised primarily of empty space. And their protons, neutrons and electrons are also primarily composed of empty space. Atoms are merely a series of relationships and energy exchanges. On a sub-atomic level also, matter truly does not exist, only forces which we might anticipate through probability. Electrons cannot be determined, fixed or held fast, they quantum leap; spontaneously appearing and then reappearing in different locations. We live in a magical universe where quantum leaping is happening all around us. Electrons do in fact leap out of their orbits. Reality is dynamic and alive. This is what the ancient goddess myths have to teach us: life is creative energy, pure potentiality.

"Parthenogenesis is possible, because the universe is alive. The Earth is alive. She is a living being capable of self-motion and self-transformation. In terms of matriarchal thought, if I may be so bold, symbolically speaking, the Earth is the body of the Great-Mother. She is the living breathing Womb of Life. The creation of the universe was not a onetime event as popular thought or traditional creation myths would have us believe. The creation of the universe is an ongoing process. It is happening all the time. We do not see it, but we see its effects. Quantum leaping is happening and if electrons can quantum leap so can we. We all need to leap into a different orbit!" Moira's voice resonated throughout the classroom. Students thought they should be writing this down but most of them had no idea what she meant.

"The concept of parthenogenesis has been personified through goddess mythologies in numerous ways through hundreds of cultures because without an internal source for growth and rebirth, we have no inner source for personal responsibility, betterment and hope. The idea of the triple goddess is more ancient than our current codified and documented histories. The triple goddess, depicted as maiden-maid-crone represents the re-creation of the self-insinuating evolution across generations as well as inspiring radical, though responsible, freedom in each individual participating in the now - what Nietzsche was grasping at when he named the 'will to power' and dubbed man both the creator and the murderer of the gods. But god as he has been understood in the modern era is external and dictatorial, resulting in a dualistic world view where an end or apocalypse is perpetually imminent. Goddesses on the other hand have a womb - an actual cavernous womb where eternity is touched through the spark of creation. The internalization of the source for life, death and rebirth inspires the power to choose to grow and change for the better in the present. In fact I call upon each of you today to reach into your own divine wombs and pull forth a positive force to contribute to the betterment of the world that we and our ancestors have co-created.

"In any event, I am sure that you can see how this represents a completely different paradigm through which reality and nature might be perceived and participated with. It also creates a different role and purpose for religion and ritual than that which we are familiar with today. This difference is paramount when you as anthropologists or archaeologists are peering back at the lives of the ancients and attempt to decode the messages they have left for us to find.

"I leave you with a challenge. Considering that such a paradigm was woven into the foundational fabric of many ancient cult societies, interpret for me what the real mystery of the Eleusian mysteries is. Clement of Alexandria, a particularly biased Christian missionary from the third century, quoted in his text from someone who allegedly participated in an Eleusian mystery rite and then betrayed the secrecy of that rite by publicly proclaiming the following description of the mystery: 'I fasted; I drank the draught; I took from the chest; having done my task, I placed in the basket, and from the basket into the chest.'

Mysteries, mind you, are often housed in the obvious, even the simple. Reference my footnotes on ritual baskets in your textbook, the *kiste* (or covered basket), as well as the *kalathos* (or open basket), and, considering the significant role that wheat plays in the Eleusian society's mythology and lifestyle, describe how the process of photosynthesis and growth is similar to the concept of parthenogenesis described today in class. If you have trouble, review the Burkert book referenced in your syllabus, good day. "

Moira glanced at the clock and abruptly closed her notes, preparing to leave. If her realization about the chamber was right, she did not have much time and unfortunately, her students would have to wait. The students were perplexed and looked once more to their Teaching Assistant for help. Raya moved to the front of the room and waited for their onslaught alongside Dr. Fennessey's podium. Students gathered around her not sure that they understood the meaning of today's lecture, asking silly questions like "will it be on the exam?"

* * * *

Raya knew that Moira's lecture was more than just a deviation from the syllabus and that Moira was working something out in her own mind, but what was she going to say to the students? Something like, "No, Dr. Fennessey was not propagating Goddess religions, just offering a different perspective?" just wouldn't cut it and wasn't wholly true. As Moira left the classroom she smiled at Raya, looked in her eyes knowingly and said, "do what you can." Raya nodded in agreement and looked to the student's confused faces as they all spoke at once.

"What does she mean by interconnection being like gravity?"

"What's quantum leaping and do we all have to do it?"

"My boyfriend said that all feminists are really lesbians. If you're a feminist can you still get married?"

"What is this stuff about ecology and Goddess religions, what difference does it make?"

"Is there really any archaeological proof that Goddess religions ever existed?"

"Can I be a feminist if I am going to be an archeologist, or is it bad for my career?"

* * * *

Later that afternoon, Moira sat with Richard in Nathan's office listening to him announce the strange occurrences in the chamber Wednesday night, just as the storm began.

"Lights and sound you said?" asked Richard, interrupting Nathan's re-telling of the strange events.

"Yes, that's correct," Nathan replied, "and the Mayor's office, along with their structural engineers, is looking for an explanation." Turning to Moira, Nathan added, "Moira, I hope you don't mind, but I relayed your information about ley lines. He isn't convinced but is willing to look into it. Even so, the light and audio phenomenon is a pretty remarkable happening and the Mayor's office would like our input."

"You think the chamber is on a ley line?" Richard cleverly gasped, turning to Moira without really looking at her.

"Well," she responded, reluctant to say too much, "I think it is possible, it would explain the lights and sounds. Ley lines are known to create electromagnetic disturbances and you can't tell me that the citywide breakdown of TV, radio waves, and telephone lines isn't somehow connected. Nathan, have you ever heard of anything like this happening before?"

"There was an ancient cavern discovered in Peru in the early 1940's that emitted noises and lights."

Richard looked skeptically at Nathan and then to Moira, "At least no one in this room is suggesting it is cursed," referencing the now popular headlines, and continued, "I am sure that the engineers will determine the *scientific* cause of the phenomenon." His emphasis on the word scientific made Moira's stomach churn. "In the meantime, I would like to get back down there to re-examine some of my findings on the symbols."

Nathan replied, "Yes, the symbols! What have your findings indicated so far?"

Moira lowered her gaze to more comfortably roll her eyes at what she knew Richard was about to say. *Here he goes again,* she thought. *No matter what Richard is looking at he always sees the same thing.* Hearing Richard say fertility cult for the umpteenth time was more than she could bear. She somehow managed to remain quiet, knowing that what she had discovered about the chamber was much more important to both of them than either her pride or their rivalry.

Richard answered just as she had expected.

"What is interesting about these fertility symbols is that they are from distinctly different cultures and geographical locations but they collectively indicate that this cavern might have held female initiation ceremonies. Caves are symbols of the womb. Before the construction of temples caves were used for religious rites and fertility shrines by primitive peoples. The reproductive cycles of women. . . ."

"Oh, please," interrupted Moira, surprising herself because she thought she was only thinking the words. "Richard this is not simply a fertility chamber in the sense that you mean it. I thought we already had this discussion."

"Of course, it is a fertility chamber," Richard said, clearly becoming increasingly annoyed at his colleague's remarks. "Those symbols are distinct and each has been used at fertility sites throughout the ancient world: India, Sumer, Greece, Egypt, and Rome. For centuries, they have represented female fertility and its reproductive aspects. The 'S' shape is the oldest symbol of the serpent, representing the power of life and procreation. In India, she is the kundalini herself. And, and, the 'M' shape goes back to the Greek *Gaia Olympica* and as representative of the deep breasted Earth Mother speaks directly to reproduction. You cannot argue with history, Moira."

"History and symbology are all premised upon fallible interpretation, Richard, and that is precisely what I am arguing against, your interpretation. It is not the symbols that make the chamber unique it is the octagram."

"Excuse me, Moira," Nathan interrupted their feud to ask, "what octagram? There is no mention of an octagram in the reports."

Moira replied, "That's because I have not yet submitted my report. It is not a displayed symbol, rather it is a pattern. You have to see it. The mounds in the chamber form an octagram around the circle; that is why it cannot be a fertility cult."

"I don't understand, Moira," Nathan said gently, "Why can't it be a fertility shrine?"

"An octagram," Moira explained matter of factly, "is formed with a continuous line. This provides it with its integrity of use for high magical rites like regeneration and parthenogenesis, not simply procreation or sexual reproduction. Formed by one continuous line, it is gateless. There is no way into the symbol and no way out. It is completely whole in itself, inviolate." Furthering the old feud building fiercely between them, she added, "To put it in terms you might understand, Richard, it cannot be penetrated. That is why this is not about mere fertility or reproduction."

With the conviction of truth in her voice she concluded, "Nathan, It was not a cult celebrating fertilization. It wasn't a fertility cult at all, but a mystery cult. I believe this cave is connected to the prophecies relayed in the Myth of the Caves…"

"Oh, here we go again!" Richard shouted in anger. He too had connected this chamber to the scroll and the myth from Tehran. Her swift conclusion-made him hate her all the more.

Without losing a single beat he continued, "Moira, I've said it before, and I'll say it again. If the Myth of the Caves contains any prophecy or notes from the Delphic oracle we, so far, don't know it. It was never proven to exist and I can't operate as though it does exist." Richard was, of course, lying. He had seen the texts, inside the Vault, that proved the contents and made the same connections that Moira had been making. But Richard never actually believed the magical powers were real. He only ever read the references to them metaphorically.

"I mean seriously, are we supposed to divine its contents?" He added with calculated drama. "One or two cryptic references can't dictate our actions here today. It's poor scholarship, not to mention simply unprofessional.

"Besides, your analysis is incorrect. The mounds are not primary." Richard continued, "It is the pit that is crucial. That is where the high priest would deposit their semen."

Moira glanced quickly to Nathan to see whether he was as horrified about the possible layers of meaning suggested by Richard's pit hypothesis. Nathan's face was unreadable and placid as he inclined his head towards Richard, waiting for one of them to continue. Moira smiled and shook her head openly as she slowly looked back to Richard, trying to brush aside the image in her mind of an ornately clad cult priest jerking off into an altar.

"You know, Richard, it is sad. You think the primary purpose of the Womb is a receptacle. Not everything is about intercourse or semen. What went on in that chamber is a different kind of ecstasy."

Moira stormed out of Nathan's office and a few minutes later, Richard raced after her. He was fast and determined.

"Moira!" he shouted as he rounded the corner, catching sight of her at the end of the long corridor. He rushed toward her and she pretended not to hear him.

"Moira," his voice lowered with a quick grumble as he took hold of the back of her shoulder, swinging her around to face him, towering over her. "We need to discuss the chamber, privately."

Moira felt trapped. *Fight or flight* was all she could think, but she wasn't sure. She did not retreat into her office for fear that he would follow her and disrupt the sanctity of her own space. Recalling the wisdom of "The Tao of War," she sighed and determined to turn and face him, smiling.

"Yes, let's do discuss the chamber, or shall I say energy center? I am sure we are not going to agree, publicly, but it could be like old times, back in the day, perhaps over a nice cup of tea?" She crossed her arms and tried to sound nonchalant. The reference to an energy center wasn't lost on him. It was the precise information he hoped to gain in speaking with her. He was giving her one last chance.

"Moira, I think we have long passed the stage of nice intellectual discussions, don't you? Listen, this is about politics and survival. You need to be on board with this. I'm offering that we work together here."

"Richard, you and I cannot work together. We fundamentally do not agree and I have no intention of putting aside the truth of my findings, do you? Nor will I sacrifice the opportunity to finally reveal what you have tried so hard for all these years to cover up."

"Moira, I am not trying to cover up anything! There is nothing to cover up, science has already shown that. You have no more proof of the existence of the goddess cultures than you did two days ago, or twenty years ago for that matter." Richard paused and thought, *at least none that you can use.*

"Don't forget, I was there with you in Tehran. You put yourself in a precarious situation... I'd be more careful if I were you, you could lose your tenure! Frankly, I do not understand why you don't just cooperate!"

"You listen to me, Richard! I will not be threatened about what happened in Tehran nor will I allow you to use *our* past against me. I have far from forgotten what happened. In fact, as I recall, your behavior was anything but above reproach, and your motives have always been questionable. My only regret is that I didn't take more scrolls out from underneath you!"

"Moira, don't mistake my position. You've been tolerated, so far, but that could change at any moment."

"Oh Richard, let's not forget that I have seen you afraid, afraid that you might lose everything. It was not a pretty sight. If that temple in Tehran had not been destroyed, you might not even be teaching here. I didn't allow you to silence me then and I won't allow you to silence me now!" She strutted to the stairwell doorway, exited and closed the door in his face.

The tao of war, done! she thought, though trembling, and understood that this was her one, and likely only, warning.

Knowledge controls everything.

* * * *

Mayor Marino put down the phone and shouted at Doherty, who just walked in.

"Do you realize I have a gaping hole in the middle of my city?" His voice was loud enough to be heard resonating throughout the entire office suite. "Even the pedestrians are out right dizzy from all the orange cones!"

Doherty quickly closed the door behind him as Al continued in a more regular voice, "I just spoke to Richard who is very favorable about moving the room into a museum. Without a doubt, Doherty this is the best plan, and from what he said the engineers are worried about its structural integrity anyway. If we could resume the work, this section is only months from completion."

"Certainly," he replied, relieved that Richard had apparently already worked on Al. "The sooner we get started the better. We are expediting the waivers from the remaining tribes and then we can get this catastrophe behind us."

"Catastrophe," Marino noted his extreme expression, "it has wreaked havoc upon the entire city, but it's amazing we ever found it without destroying it in the first place!"

"Yes," Doherty replied heavily, thinking of the new direction he was being forced into, "well at least we still have control of the entrance."

"So I've been told," Marino mumbled under his breath unaware of Doherty's meaning. "Right now though, we are in a state of emergency. The whole country is watching us."

Doherty replied to the pedantic, "Under the circumstances, everything is moving along very swiftly."

"Yes, but we only have eight months or so until the elections."

"If I may speak frankly sir," Doherty taunted at Marino's moral fiber, "we need to get the chamber out of the way quickly and quietly, otherwise you can forget about the next election."

* * * *

Marino was experienced enough to read where Doherty was trying to take this conversation. His voice was unflinching and unambiguous as he paced toward him from in front of the oversized windows, "For Christ's sake, think, John! I will not be single-handedly responsible for intentional delays or sabotage! Come on, there's already one hole in this city!"

Doherty's blackberry beeped a welcomed interruption. He pulled it from his waist, excited that it was working.

"Excellent!" he exclaimed after reading the email. Doherty replaced the device to its holster and shared, "I just got confirmation for a meeting this afternoon with the Tribal Historic Preservation Officer of the Wampanoag Tribe. He said that he is also going to represent the Nipmucs, which will help speed things along. He wants to see the chamber and I've already coordinated with Dr. Martin to join us." He waited for a reply of enthusiasm or a nod of appreciation from Marino but the Mayor's face remained frozen as he paced around the room in his socks.

Doherty explained, "Once we get the tribal issue resolved formally, the removal process might come sooner than you think. The regulations articulate a different type of protection for naturally occurring sites than for artificially constructed ones. If the site is classified as artificial, excavation should begin right away."

Marino looked like he was still thinking. He scratched his head and asked, "Do you know anything more about those strange occurrences the other night?"

"The best explanation is that it was a prank. There's still talk of hauntings and ley lines. Some of the crew from the night shift have quit …just walked off the job."

"People, people… come on!" Marino wailed as he sat down in front of his desk. He crossed his leg; revealing the worn, threadbare bottom of his socks.

"When are you meeting him at the chamber?" Marino added.

John's eyes darted from Marino's sock to the silver faced watch on his own wrist, "About an hour and a half."

"Excellent," he replied and dropped his foot back down to the floor, "I want you to take me to see the chamber." Marino put his hands on his knees and pushed himself up to get his boots and outer layers.

"Now?" Doherty asked.

"Yes, now."

* * * *

Stepping out of the taxi, Alex wasn't sure what was making her shiver. She was anxious to see the chamber but wished Doherty had given her more notice. He called her cell phone only an hour or so ago about a meeting with a tribal rep. She hadn't been able to reach Diana and she would have preferred meeting in a more neutral setting, after she had already seen the chamber for herself. She worked with this tribe once before and the rep could have been someone she knew. Nevertheless, she found herself walking across the construction site to the outermost entrance of the chamber, not knowing who exactly was going to meet her.

Two or three journalists huddled with covered hands and faces around a white van just at the edge of the construction gates, clutching steaming Styrofoam cups and cameras. They watched her approach with stealthy eyes and assessed her newsworthiness. Eventually they returned their attention to the warmth of their beverages and she was relieved that she didn't make their cut.

Ron Osterman was supervising the entrance. She introduced herself and showed her driver's license. He found her on the list and checked her identification.

"Alright Dr. Martin, John Doherty and the chief are already in the tunnel. They're expecting you. They just started down a minute before. If you hurry, you should be able to catch up with them." He handed her a flashlight and a hardhat, pointing to the back of the tunnel and indicating that she should follow the right hand path and then straight to the chamber's opening. As she started to leave he added, "Cell phones don't work down there lately." The words sent another chill up Alex's spine. She tried to shake the feeling.

Before she left she turned to him to ask, "Am I listed with clearance to return to the site?"

"It says you have clearance, doctor."

Keeping her grace, Alex placed the dome atop her head, nodded to him in thanks and strode toward the tunnel's shaft. Chicly clad in her long brown wool coat, matching leather boots and orange hardhat, Osterman couldn't help but notice that while few women look good in a hard hat, Alex was certainly one of them.

She was grateful that it was daylight. She heard the sound of flapping wings and looked up into the sky. A large hawk flew above, hunting for its lunch. *It must be difficult to find in the snow*, she considered as she surveyed the ground around her. The metal and concrete environment made her feel vulnerable and small. She realized that there was much less snow on the ground in here, behind the construction gates, than on the street. With all of the activity, machinery and high wattage light fixtures, the ground here was probably warmer. *Like an open wound,* she thought. Another chill ran through her body and she turned on the flashlight in preparation. Before entering the tunnel she paused. Looking left and then right she took one last visibly vaporous breath upon the surface and began her descent.

The first thing to come to mind was anger and annoyance at the taxi driver. If he had taken the waterfront route, as she had wanted him to, she might have gotten here a few minutes sooner and she wouldn't have had to walk through these tunnels all alone. They branched off the main corridor and could be difficult to tell which way was straight. The sounds of her heels against the cold hard stone echoed loudly, ringing down around the curved ceiling. The earthy tunnel was damp and dark. From time to time the string of lights flickered and she clutched her flashlight tighter, fearing they would go out completely. But they stayed lit. She stopped for a moment to listen for sounds of other people. She heard nothing, then a slow drip. She turned to look behind her. The strong musty smells made her eyes water. What she could see was that the tunnel stretched beyond her view in both directions and it seemed endless. She felt like she was inside the large intestine of a massive living organism. *How long have I been walking?* She looked to her watch but it could tell her nothing for she didn't know when she had started.

"Hello!" she called out. Her voice bounced around the stone and vibrated in her ears, but she heard no reply. She walked on.

Up ahead she could see that the next section of lights was out. The shaft seemed to end in total darkness, like a bottomless well, spread out before her. She tried to keep her negativity at bay but the darkness ahead was suffocating. She held her breath as she proceeded into it. The beam from her flashlight was strong enough to watch for holes and power cords lying on the ground. She kept her mind on what she could see and the speed of her breath, trying to maintain calm. The whole experience reminded her of a guided meditation: focused breathing, visualizing a descent into the unconscious, etc. *This is enough*, she thought as all feelings of excitement and curiosity morphed into disorientation and frustration. Then she heard something, or someone.

"Hello?" She spoke out one more time into the darkness. She directed the flashlight's beam along the wall to her right. As her eyes came into focus, she saw a doorway. She thought she had finally found the chamber when something large and dark came at her from the shadows. She heard a loud screech and something knocked into her, pushing her over. She hit the ground hard, losing consciousness. The damp earth engulfed her.

* * * *

Buzz! Buzz! Buzz! Diana almost didn't answer the doorbell that afternoon. She was upstairs in her studio working. If not for the persistent rudeness of the buzzing she would have ignored the distraction. Running down the stairs to answer the door her annoyance quickly gave way from finding Alex at her threshold.

"Oh God!" Alex cried as she rushed in, "We have got to go back to the chamber! You won't believe what happened!"

Diana rarely saw Alex this excited. She was breathing rapidly, talking fast and gesturing like a court appointed attorney.

"What's going on?" she asked, trying to get a handle on things.

"I went to the chamber but something happened in the tunnel on my way down. I met this shaman ...I took flight with an eagle. You were right!" Alex tried to get everything she had just experienced captured into simple sentences but there was no way for it all to fit between her quick shallow breaths.

"Wait, you saw the chamber?"

"Kind of, that's what I am trying to tell you." Alex responded, though still hyperventilating. "I tried to get a hold of you. I called and called. I had a meeting with the Mayor and Doherty and one of the tribal reps. I can get you into the chamber today, but... oh, just come on, we need to go!"

"Ok, ok slow down! Of course we'll go, but calm down first. Do we really have to rush, or do we have a few moments?" Assessing her reaction, Diana continued to soothe, "Tell me what has happened, you need to catch your breath. Take your coat off, sit down and tell me what happened, and then we can go. I think you could use a cup of chamomile-mint tea; it will soothe you. Is that ok, do we have the time or not?" Diana said getting over the shock of Alex's obvious and unusual lack of composure.

"Alright, alright, maybe that's a good idea." Diana had set out to prepare the cups and boil the water. Alex's body still shook, but her breath started to slow. She sat down on the couch and closed her eyes.

After a few minutes the tea kettle blew a proud whistle and Diana brought in their tea. She set the tray on the marble coffee table and then picked up Alex's hand by the fingertips. She felt her friend's nerves pulsing.

"Are you ok?" Diana asked releasing her touch.

"Yes, no... I don't know. You have to see the chamber and so do I. I had a kind of mystical experience before I got there." Alex said blowing on the hot liquid and sipping it carefully.

Diana looked closely at Alex. She looked the same, objectively speaking. She had the same auburn hair and high cheekbones, the same beautiful eyes and she was still impeccably dressed. But something else was different, Diana could tell. Alex's aura had changed its color. Alex hadn't just had an experience. Quite to the contrary, an experience just had her and it was transformative!

"Take a deep breath and tell me everything that happened. Start at the beginning and then we will go to the chamber together."

"Ok." Alex complied with a deep inhale. "Doherty called me late this morning for a last minute meeting with a rep for the Nipmuc and Wampanoag tribes. I can tell you more about him later, but I was to meet them in the chamber. I got there and while I was walking down the tunnel into the chamber I had the strangest sensations. I started to get dizzy and I thought I was going to faint or pass out. I couldn't breathe. They sent me down into the tunnel all by myself. I was standing in the tunnel about to approach a doorway, I think it was the opening to the chamber when I saw an eagle fly out and come straight at me! It flew right into me and knocked me over. The eagle circled around and flew over my head and then, the next thing I knew, I was flying with the eagle through the tunnel and into the chamber. You know Diana I don't know what to think about any of this, but there I was flying. I didn't think this could be happening, but it seemed so real. Of course now I don't even know if it was real or not. I don't know what it was that I saw even, they were strange unfamiliar lands, and other sights that I couldn't quite make out, but I know what I felt. I felt so peaceful, even blissful. And the flash that I saw in the chamber was like the experience I had yesterday with Night-Night. Well, the next thing I knew, I heard someone calling my name. 'Dr. Martin, Dr. Martin are you alright?' When I came to, I was on the wet floor leaning against the side of the tunnel and these men were standing over me, looking terribly concerned. I was so embarrassed and disoriented!"

"Alex, you met your spirit guide! That is wonderful!"

"I guess so," Alex whispered, "That is what Chief Thundercloud said."

"Chief?" queried Diana.

"Chief Thundercloud, he is the Wampanoag lawyer but he is also a medicine man, very interesting! He told me that the eagle was the totem of freedom and necessity. He also said I need to see with the eyes of the eagle. And I really don't know what that means either. But the thing is, you were right about that chamber. I saw the symbols, well in my vision I mean, they were etched in the center of the chamber."

"What symbols, Alex? You mean the ones that…"

"Yes, yes the ones that Night-Night showed you. I cannot believe I am saying this! In my vision, the chamber had those very same symbols. It was so real. I want to go back and check the chamber, just to be sure. But I kid you not… I'd swear they're there and I'm not going back alone to find out. Where is Night-Night anyway?" Alex looked around.

As if on cue, Night-Night appeared looking perfectly like the kitty-cat who saved the world or ate the canary…depending. In any case Night-Night was certainly full of herself. She jumped onto the table in a single boundless and graceful leap, landing softly in front of Alex. *I told you so.* Of course, anyone who has ever lived with or loved an animal of a different species knows that communication is not confined to words and Night-Night's message came across loud and clear: *I told you!* Both women felt inclined to laugh at themselves but Night-Night's demeanor prevented too much frivolity.

"Ok, Night-Night," Diana scooped up her feline friend and placing her on the floor in front of them asked, "what should we do now?"

Alex answered immediately, which pleased Night-Night immensely, "We need to go to the chamber and we need to go, now!"

* * * *

"When we get there, we first go through a security check," Alex was habitually attempting to regain rational composure, even though her intense feelings were obvious. "There might be reporters or news crews."

"News crews!" Diana shouted in shock and horror, competing with the noise of the taxi catapulting slush and slosh out of a pothole the size of a bathtub. Slushy, salty, snow-sludge sloshed against the metal, paint and glass along Diana's side of the car.

"Better hold on!" She continued, grabbing the handle on the roof above her. The tires returned to the pavement and they continued toward the city.

"Don't worry. They hardly even paid attention to me when I went in earlier. I don't think it will be a problem. I just wanted you to know, so you'd be prepared for everything." Being prepared for everything was not very likely. They were dealing with forces far beyond their full comprehension and control.

Alex continued, "This is definitely a strange and intense place. Getting there is unworldly to begin with. The long dark tunnels make you feel lost even though they seem to travel straight *and* down!" Alex was obviously talking through the preparations because she was a bit nervous. Her totemic experience earlier in the day was mind blowing and life altering for her. But she hadn't yet digested the full meaning, let alone the greater implications to her own life and the world around her. She needed to stay focused on following her instincts. She didn't have the time to digest it all right now, nor did she feel ready to get walloped with another such episode when she headed into the tunnel this time. *Fear again!* She stopped herself from continuing down that trail of thought.

"Got it?" She asked and smiled nervously. Alex felt the dizzy anxiety of distractions like whether Richard might show up and insult Diana, or whether she was going to grow the reputation of a nut case for bringing a friendly psychic to the site. Letting go of all that messy stuff, she remembered Diana's description of a dream from a few days before. She said she was shouting that they would all see the white light.

"I don't think I am ready," Alex said to Diana as though Diana had also been inside Alex's head.

"This is all going to work out the way it is meant to." Diana eased just as the taxi rounded the last corner to their destination. She took the folded bills from her left hand and passed them to the driver.

They both thanked the driver and got out of the cab. They climbed over a snow bank to get to the sidewalk on the right side of the street. Despite the sunny sky all day, no snow had melted. The temperatures had been too low and ice grew over every inch of concrete that hadn't been salted.

They stepped carefully up to the security gate and Alex was overjoyed to see that Ron Osterman was still on post.

"Greetings again, sir!"

"Hello Dr. Martin!" Ron's eyes twinkled with an Irish light, probably from his mother's side, at seeing Alex again.

"What can I do for you, Doc? Shouldn't you be home relaxing; what are you doing out in the cold again?" He was obviously quite taken by her and spoke with legitimate concern.

"Oh, thank you for the concern but I'm fine, really! Never better!" Alex smiled and shook his hand firmly. Turning to Diana she added, "This is my friend and colleague, Diana Wolf. She will be accompanying me down this afternoon. Do we need to sign in?"

Ron shook his head with the biggest grin, "That's a good idea, I don't suppose you should be trying to go down there alone again anytime soon, right? I'll just make a note in my log, I know who you are. And," He reached into his booth and located two hard hats, two flashlights and one walkie-talkie. "You know the drill," he said as he handed them each a hard orange hat and a heavy flashlight. "Now, these started working again about an hour ago. But they went out again oh, maybe twenty minutes later. Do you want to take it or just rely on each other and the shouting method?" He held the radio device up in front of them and the two women looked back and forth to each other.

Ron replied to Diana's quizzical expression, "I have to stay up here. Cellphones don't work around here and these walkie-talkies aren't reliable. Ever since that big light show we had down here." He dropped his voice like he wasn't supposed to mention Wednesday night's happenings even though no one else was around. "Anyway, after this afternoon you might feel more comfortable?"

"Thank you, but no thanks. We'll stay together and I believe I do remember which way to go. We will be fine, thanks." Alex smiled back to Ron and Diana nodded in agreement. Both ladies placed the bulky hats upon the tops of their heads and Alex lead the way toward the tunnel. Diana waved a "Thank you" to Ron and followed behind her.

* * * *

The hike down into the chamber was, in comparison to Alex's previous descent, uneventful. The musty smells in the tunnels didn't bother Alex this time around and as they journeyed deeper, they both realized that the air was getting warmer. They had left the chilling cold at the surface. Other than Diana's making a comment that the chamber was the earth's metaphoric womb, they didn't say much to each other. Alex just led them straight to the chamber's opening.

* * * *

Alex was grateful to have Diana's company but remained silent. She was paying close attention to where they were in relation to her hike that morning. Navigating through the semi-darkness, she struggled to let down her guard. She wanted to understand why she had the vision that she did. Each step of descent seemed a little bit easier, a little bit lighter for her. But she lacked the confidence that her questions could be answered.

* * * *

Diana's silence was merely external. She communicated with her surroundings every step of the way. She ran her open palms along the balmy stone walls of the tunnel, feeling the inside of the earth. She wanted to feel it all. Diana conjured ancient magis and priestesses for guidance, asking only for positive illumination. She felt safe and listened to their stories.

They walked together in silence for a good forty five minutes, or so, to the bottom of the tunnel. They knew when they were getting close and together they approached.

* * * *

Very little ever surprises Diana. Spirits, apparitions, astral planes and cosmic paradoxes were practically second nature to her. But when she stepped over the stone threshold shockwaves reverberated through her body from every possible direction in reaction to what she saw. Diana had been getting psychic "hits" from all over. It was her psychic abilities and her own spirit guides that led her here in the first place, so it was not surprising to her that the ceiling would, rather literally, speak to her, or that the walls would bring back ancient memories of past magic, in the same sense that it dramatically happened to Alex that morning. What she didn't expect, however, was who she saw standing there in full corporal stature, or what she was standing upon.

"Well, hello," Moira said. Diana recognized her instantly as the woman with grey hair who was screaming in her nightmare and she was standing right on top of a large familiar carving. The symbol of the 'M', rendered in exactly the same way as the one from Night-Night and her meditation.

Diana was stunned not because her intuition had been right, but because she got confirmation so quickly upon arrival. She could barely peel her eyes off the woman that scared her so in her dream, but she could see each and every symbol from the past week of meditation laid out across the floor and walls of the room. Voices telling tales of omens and magic and ritual clamored in her inner ears and the symbols marched through her inner mind right into the recesses of her psyche. Her entire awareness was permeated with the understanding that this woman was not meant in her dream as a warning of danger, but that she, like Diana, was a link. *Who is she? Does she know it too, or will she be skeptical, like Alex?* Unsure of how to proceed, she just stared and listened, inhaling the odor of ancient wisdom.

Stepping forward, Alex was the first to respond. "Hello," she said, "I didn't expect anyone to be here. I'm Alexandra Martin from the Law School. I'm here for the city." Extending her hand as she introduced herself, Alex also acknowledged Diana. "And this is Diana Wolfe." Alex gestured toward Diana and her anxiety crept up again. The chamber had a strong power over Alex. Being back within it, she could not deny that it held a unique and dizzying energy. In the dark light she turned her head around to regain her bearings.

"I'm Moira Fennessey, from Harvard," the funny looking woman said, standing in a rumpled flannel shirt, baggy jeans, and dirty work boots.

"You are the archaeologist, then?" Alex asked. "You must know Richard Lyons."

"Yes, and yes, I've known Richard for years." Moira responded.

"I have as well. Funny, I don't recall him ever speaking of you." Alex didn't mean to be rude, but it sounded that way.

"Hm, I like your honesty. I'm not surprised, though. I'm unspeakable, didn't you know," Moira chuckled with just the right touch of sarcasm for Alex to perceive her meaning. Then, even though Moira was shorter than Alex, the archaeologist bent toward her as though she were looking down upon her. Studying and glaring, Moira asked, "You're not here to meet with Richard are you?"

"No!" Alex retorted, "Why, is he on his way?"

Moira's pinched face relaxed as she interpreted that Alex was telling the truth, "As far as I know, Richard is meeting with the Mayor this afternoon. I came down here thinking I could get a little quiet time without worrying that he'll get me agitated."

"I know what you mean. Don't worry we'll try not to disturb you." Alex said and realized that Diana hadn't said a word. Alex turned to her and asked, "Diana, are you okay?" But clearly Diana needed another moment, or perhaps a whole lot longer to listen to all the ancient voices whispering in her head. Her body was perfectly still and she just stood there, gazing at Moira. She didn't even seem to hear Alex's question.

Eventually, she said, "I know you."

"Really," Moira replied, "have we met, were you a student?"

"No," Diana replied, "you were in my dream. But… I mean, …I know you from before. In my dream, though, you knew something big and powerful. It scared me at first."

Alex couldn't believe what she was hearing, "Diana!!!" she interrupted from under her breath.

Moira laughed and offered back, "I've scared a lot of people over the years, but I doubt that I could scare you." Changing the subject, Moira asked, "So, why are you girls here?"

"I asked my friend to bring me here." Diana sounded almost mesmerized, "I am here because I was called here. This chamber holds some powerful magic. I had to see it and, apparently, you. I think this is an energy vortex, created by our ancient ancestors in the past for a purpose here in the present. I think that you and Alex and me, we are all a part of that purpose. I think that it is our destiny."

Alex was going out of her mind thinking, *couldn't she be a little less direct? I would have thought she could have come up with something better than that! We just clarified that this woman does work with Richard!* She was trying desperately to be open and receptive to everything, no matter how "out there" it got. After all, she had had her own share of convincing experiences this week. But hearing it said out loud to another person, especially a colleague of Richard's, made it sound insane.

Quizzically, Moira replied, "Interesting theory..." and turning to Alex continued, "She doesn't strike me as one of Richard Lyon's cronies." Alex said nothing but the stress was visible in the way she clenched her jaw. She waited to see what would happen next.

Moira replied, "She isn't totally crazy, you know." Moira was referring to Diana. "Well, she might be crazy, but what she said about this place isn't all wrong. It is powerful and it *is* saturated with ancient magic."

Alex saw that Moira was being totally serious. Then she noticed that as they had each come into the space, the three of them had come to stand upon the outside perimeter of the chamber's inner circle. They now stood in a circle, facing each other. It felt familiar to each of them and reminded Alex of her vision.

Then Moira responded, "In fact, you're absolutely right. It is an energy vortex but it is much more than that also. I take it you have studied the ancient ways?"

Worried about where the conversation was going, Alex interrupted. "Richard tells me that he believes this was a fertility chamber, what do you think?"

Moira gruffly replied, "Well of course Richard thinks that. But this wasn't used for lust or sex or fertilization. On this site there was performed a much more esoteric rite, and the most powerful magic was performed inside these walls." Moira's hand lifted to caress the stone wall of the chamber. The air grew thicker as she talked. Her face whirled toward Diana and she said, "I don't mean sex magic or anything childish like that! The ceremonies held here inspired parthenogenesis amongst the priestesses. Parthenogenesis is not an individual matter but it is a cosmological process because of the interconnection of everything, especially women's direct creative connection to the natural forces of the universe."

Alex wasn't sure whether to be more shocked over the fact that this woman seemed to be advocating a feminist metaphysics or over the fact that she and Richard actually worked in the same department.

Moira continued, "The difference is that fertility chambers have to do with an external fertilization. Nature's creative energies are often symbolized in the feminine because of our sexual and procreative powers. And that is where male and female scholars get confused, distracted by the lore of their own sexual attractions. Magic this powerful is not about sex or child birth, as this birthing image might seem to depict," Moira pointed to a graphic etching in the outer circle. "It is about an internal transformation born from awareness through the use of elemental energies and interconnectivity!"

"Do you mean like inner alchemy?" Diana asked.

"Inner and outer," Moira retorted, "the earth has been demanding what this magic remembers: an embodied state of personal responsibility."

Diana proclaimed, "we three are here because we have been here before! Look, it does make sense actually." Diana said in a more forceful and unfamiliar voice, "maybe this chamber should never have been unearthed. It should never have been violated, but it was inevitable from the inertia of the many generations of destructive choices we have made throughout time. The earth's self-generating energy vortex has been disrupted and is now turning back on itself. That's why the surrounding EMs are going haywire! It needs to be realigned and we are the ones that need to do it. Don't you see? We did it the first time and we have to do it again."

* * * *

A presence swept through the chamber. Diana had invoked ancient memories from the room's energy body. While Diana's body-mind had been electrified by the charge of the space since her and Alex's descent, she had suddenly consciously awoken to the energy. And in contagious unison, Moira and Alex each silently started to notice a similar recollection within the muscle memory of their astral bodies. A surge rose through the three of them all simultaneously.

Alex hugged her arms across her chest to ease the goose bumps prickling her shoulders. The soft blonde hairs on the lower base of her neck lifted as the surge increased and then dropped to the fronts of her thighs. Moira stood still with her eyes wide open and Diana stretched her arms upward over her head with closed eyes and a deep inhale.

A warm wind, blowing in from nowhere, encapsulated the room. It moved in a circle around them and the lights in the hallway started blinking erratically and quickly in a lively rhythm. They blinked faster and faster. Startled by the lights, the three women stepped forward instinctively and in unison clasped hands around the smaller inner circle on the chamber's floor. The stone mounds on the ground closest to each of them started emitting a strange orange hue with a radiance that caused each of them to notice.

"What's that on the floor?" Alex yelled over the growing sound of the wind, careful not to let go of Moira's hand as she gestured to the floor behind her. Diana had also noticed it, "It's glowing," she shouted.

"The two behind both of you are glowing too!" Moira spoke without a shred of fear or nervousness in her voice, "But notice that there is a fourth!" The inner circle of the chamber was defined by eight mounds enshrining the convex altar, four of which were glowing. The three mounds directly behind each of the women glowed a strong amber light but the fourth glowed dim. They were obviously at least missing someone. The wind continued gaining speed, circling like a twister and howling.

"We're not all here!" Diana screamed, "We need a fourth!" From her own ritual work she knew what it meant, that balance would have to be attained, so she decided to break the circle. She let go of her clasped hands and stepped out of their incomplete circle. The wind suddenly stopped. The orbs of light quickly grew dim and faded.

"See," she said to her stunned companions, "we are meant to be here." Diana hadn't expected any of what had happened but she was completely in synch with it. Alex and Moira on the other hand were not yet able to speak.

Diana continued, "We have to find the fourth corner. It makes perfect sense, we must perform the ritual but we need the fourth corner to represent the four material elementals. We are missing a participant and we have to find out who it is!"

Alex was still journeying between the worlds. She had followed Diana's memory and was now having a full body memory experience of her own.

"It's easy," Alex murmured.

"What Alex?" Diana asked, "What's easy?" Getting no response she tried again, "What's easy, Alex? Are you okay?"

"What?" Alex blinked as she came to, "Oh, I don't know. I almost had it… I was remembering about…" her voice slowed, "I wanted to remember…" Shaking her head she added, "Something about it is easy, but I can't remember what. It's okay, I'm okay I mean. It will come to me later, I know it is important."

"Well that's encouraging," Moira interjected, coming back from her own internal combustions and the realization that her life was more than just the 'study of'. She was beginning to see how all of her collected knowledge served this intended purpose. Diana was right, they had been called.

"Ladies, we should go. We can't do much more here for now. I think we should all come back to my house, where we can talk and even have a glass of wine!" Diana added to Moira, "My place isn't far, will you join us?"

Moira was processing. She had never met these women before but she recognized an auspicious occasion when she saw one. All of her research and knowledge had led her to this moment. Connections were forging with the new knowledge of her own experience. She replied, "Well you can't very well do it without me. Let's go," Moira turned to gather her supplies, now scattered around the chamber.

"Alex?" Diana asked, "Are you coming …are you with us?"

* * * *

Diana turned the key into the front set of double doors, letting them in from the growing darkness. Realizing, amongst other things, that it was getting late and that she was now the hostess, she stepped inside and ushered Alex and Moira in behind her.

"Okay, here we are!" she welcomed, "And just before the sun set too!" She opened the next set of doors and making her way down the hall, threw open the side parlor doors as she went.

"Alex," Diana gestured to the parlor, "why don't you show Moira around and where to hang her coat, maybe open some wine? I'm going to throw some pasta on the stove. Everyone must be hungry. We should replenish ourselves before we get too deep into this stuff!"

"Good idea," Alex replied and stomped her feet to shake off the snow.

"Oh thank you, it's nice and warm in here," Moira said. She walked into the hallway and looked around. Night-Night awakened instantly when she heard the sound of Moira's voice and came bounding down the hall to greet her. If not for the bell on her collar no one would have heard her light feet. Night-Night didn't greet them with her usual catwalk swagger of indifference, oh no, Night-Night was bounding, pouncing and bouncing. Her paws barely touched the floor and she stared directly at Moira the whole way. Her attention was fixed and her excitement was obvious.

"Does she think that I'm lunch?" Moira asked rhetorically watching the feline leaping her way. Although Moira had a principled respect and appreciation for animals generally, she wasn't what you'd call a "cat person" or even a "dog person" for that matter.

Everyone thought that Night-Night was going to land right on top of Moira's face. But once the fur settled, Night-Night was perched on the arm of a chair up close to Moira, looking at her with her tail swishing. *Good that you finally showed up!* Night-Night said, *I've had to handle this myself and frankly, I'm exhausted. I hope you brought your bag of tricks with you, we are going to need it.*

"You better say something to her," Diana shouted, watching the funny exchange from the kitchen "she seems to like you.

"I think she's already spoken," Moira facetiously replied, then asked Alex, "does she always act like this?"

Alex answered, "Lately. Her name's Night-Night."

Moira addressed the cat directly, "Hello, Night-Night, It's nice to meet you, my name's Moira." She patted her new friend on the head, oblivious to the fact that Night-Night already knew who she was. Then Moira noticed that Diana had left several books spread out across the dining room table open as though someone had been working on a project. In true professorial fashion, Moira wanted to see which books they were and went directly to them. Night-Night followed her, weaving in between her feet and staying close by. Alex attended to her tasks: coats and wine.

The blue book right on top looked familiar. *Hmm,* she thought to herself. *That looks… Yes! It is Walker.* She spun the book on its spine and tilted it to her eye. Walker's *Women's Dictionary of Women's Symbols* was open and two of the symbols on the pages matched those found in the chamber. She heard the clamor of stainless steel from the kitchen and running water.

"How, ah…" Moira hesitated mentioning him, "How do you know Richard, Alex?"

"My parents," Alex replied working the corkscrew into the bottle. "I've known him all my life."

"I see."

"And you?" Alex retorted as she poured the wine into the tall glasses.

"Most of mine; since graduate school. Richard and I don't… we're not what you'd call friendly. We've had too much history, literally, if you know what I mean."

Returning her attention to the books, Moira glanced across the table to the other titles and pages.

"These are all Diana's books?"

"Yes." Alex answered, "I'm only vaguely familiar with a few of these, but Diana… well, she grew up in a book store."

Jung, Nostradamus, Starhawk, Daly, Gimbutas, Jane Harrison; there were at least eighty books in all. Some more academic, others rather new-age, but the variety created an eclectic research array of mythology, archaeology, symbology, astrology, herbology, color-ology, dream interpretation, meditation studies and techniques, witchcraft, the occult, etc. Moira returned the blue book to its pile, with the pages undisturbed. She reverently breathed in a deep breath and took a moment to reflect on the reality that was being presented to her.

Moira asked loudly so she could be heard in the other room, "Have you been in the chamber before, Diana?"

Alex presented Moira with a glass of wine and answered for her friend. "No, this was her first time seeing it. Bizarre, don't you think?" Moira took the wine and tasted a small sip while Alex explained, "I went to the chamber earlier this morning. But, Diana showed me these pages yesterday." Alex ran her fingers across the book. "She saw them in a meditation she said, then Night-Night knocked this book off its shelf and it opened right to this page."

Moira sat down at the table to examine the books more closely and Night-Night immediately jumped into her lap.

Alex pulled out a chair to join them and explained, "I went to the chamber earlier today, only I passed out before having a chance to actually walk into it. While I was unconscious though, I had a kind of out of body experience... which is really bizarre for me to be saying, but while I was unconscious, I remember visiting the chamber and I saw these symbols in it. I absolutely had to confirm if they were really there, or if it was just... a dream. I asked Diana to go with me which was when we bumped into you."

Moira listened intently to the story of how Alex came to bring Diana to the chamber. Night-Night jumped off Moira's lap, onto the dining room table. She encircled one of the open books and then laid down upon it, giving Moira a big yawn before resting her chin on her paws in a hypnotic cat pose.

"I don't know who's spookier Diana, you or the cat," Moira said it loud enough for Diana to hear her in the kitchen.

* * * *

I wish she'd stop calling me "the cat," Night-Night said. *I am a benevolent spirit guide! Highly trained and quite advanced, as far as evolved beings go. I am surprised at you, Moira, for not remembering.*

* * * *

Actually, Moira was starting to remember. She went into archaeology because she loved mysteries that came from the earth. But this experience had awakened something more about her inherent knowledge that she had finally become ready to confront. When she was a young girl growing up in Connecticut a field of sunflowers spoke to her. Like most people who have mystical moments however, as the years passed and Moira grew into adulthood she came to regard the experience as a childhood fancy, doubting its reality and relegating it to mere sentiment. Until now, Moira had never let her adult mind consider that her conviction and knowledge wasn't a direct result of her training.

Chuckling proudly at Moira's observation about Night-Night, Diana placed bowls of pasta on the table as if this were a casual meal and not an evolution revolution .

"It has a purpose." Diana said, "the chamber I mean, not Night-Night, it has been waiting for something hasn't it, and the Big-Dig has triggered it?"

"You know," said Moira in her professorial voice, "that's not far off the mark. This, what is happening that we and this chamber are all a part of, is the subject of my life's work. In the ancient times, civilizations all over the world worshipped and celebrated the goddess. They were all believed to be manifestations of the same goddess and she came to be known as the Goddess of A Thousand Names. According to ancient myth and folklore, at the dawn of creation the goddess arose out of chaos and gave birth to herself. This is the myth of parthenogenesis.

"Prior to the advent of Christianity, in anticipation of the so-called 'holy wars,' goddess worshipping purposefully went underground. In order to preserve their secret knowledge of cosmogenesis and magic, high priestesses were chosen from the seven great civilizations of the ancient world to be light keepers and knowledge bearers during the great slumber of humanity that was sure to follow. Legend has it that these priestesses were entrusted to bury their teachings along with the magic of the Earth's sacred regenerative powers in underground caves and caverns. Although the fact of these caves has never been made public, many medieval churches were built upon the sites where they were said to exist. And proof of their existence, destroyed. Other goddess temples or sites of worship that have been located through the years have also been leveled by war or papal decree."

"What?" Alex asked skeptically, "you mean these sites have been destroyed on purpose? Why would there be such a conspiracy?"

"For the same reason all wars are fought: ultimate wealth and power. These chambers were each constructed at the same time and for the same purpose; to realign the dis-ease and disharmony of the planet before the imbalance of patriarchal practices reaches disastrous proportions for humanity and the planet. They are the storehouses of our ancient fore-sisters' planetary wisdom and energy. Look, here, I have maps although I never would have suspected there would be one in Boston! The seven I have looked for are in different locations." Moira's arms flapped like wings as she searched through her knapsack for the right folder. Getting more excited as she pulled it out she said, "I've got maps showing holy sites, ley lines, and..." she paused and turned to Diana. With reverent silence and attention, Moira produced a dry, fibrous piece of papyrus housed in a plastic sleeve from her worn manila folder. Its text was faded and displayed a foreign collection of drawings and script.

"Look here, this explains what happened. This papyrus scroll documents what is known as the Myth of the Caves. It is thousands of years old and what it speaks of has only been referenced, and rather remotely I might add, by Plato around 500BCE. It provides essentially a reinterpretation of the apocalypse myth. Our ancient ancestors, the high priestesses, in preparation of the coming onslaught used their magic to forge into the earth sacred temples, in the most sacred energy centers around the globe; ritual chambers which would help future seers awaken the goddess. At a future pinnacle moment in time, the ancient oracles foresaw that ecological and political crises would jeopardize the life of the planet, and everyone on it forever, just before the dawning of the Age of Aquarius. Think of it as a kind of acceleration of karma: an astral cleansing to usher forth a higher state of being, or goddess consciousness. At that time, now apparently *this* time, humanity is said to have a choice. It is the fall of patriarchy, brought about by the habits of destruction accumulated over dozens of centuries. It says that it is up to the few who can tap into that ancient parthenogenic magic to divert the destruction of an apocalypse with an awakening of the goddess and evolved states of individual and collective consciousness; contagious love, light and ecstatic being."

"We are the few, Moira, aren't we?" Diana exclaimed, "it will be up to us to tap into that ancient magic. Yes, that's it isn't it? If what you say is true we just need to perform a magical rite to realign our loving creative energy with the planet and the cosmos?"

"What?" Alex exclaimed.

"I'm talking about the rebirth of the Goddess, Alex." Diana replied.

"Look," Alex protested to both of them, "Diana, when I asked if you were planning a ritual in the chamber, I didn't mean I would go along with it. I mean this is kind of crazy! We have glowing rocks and, and, what's next?" She was so frantic she was almost stuttering. *Will I have to admit this? To others… to Richard?*

Moira and Diana could sense the fear in Alex. Moira carefully continued, "Listen, Alex we," she drew a circle in the air with her finger tip, "have an affinity to this chamber. Either it was us, or some parts of us, that engaged with this chamber's power many decades ago, but some part of that magic has survived within us. Maybe we are just tapping into what once was. I am not sure, but either way we have been called."

"Listen to what Moira is saying, Alex, she's right, but even more precisely, magic is women's power. We don't express our energy as power over," Diana interjected, "we are interconnected. The struggle between matriarchy and patriarchy has always been between magic and power. That's why it's always been so loathed by the churches. Look Alex, if we're wrong, the worst that can happen is that we'll have made fools of ourselves in private – it's not like I'm suggesting we make the ritual public or invite the press. And if we're right, no one will believe us anyway, so we don't need to tell anybody."

"Alex," Moira continued sternly, "I've learned from my many years of research and investigation, and yes from my many years of living too, that the purpose of life is not to be comfortable, but the purpose of life is to evolve. Our ancient ancestors and foremothers were visionaries. They were not just concerned with themselves and their own survival. They were concerned with the future, the evolution of life on this planet for future generations. We are a link in time between the past and the future, don't you see they had a vision, they had a plan. And no, I cannot trace back the causal orbits and give you demonstrated proof. But I can tell you that this was indeed recorded and foretold centuries ago. The myth is real. And we are a part of this myth. Whatever knowledge or energy is in that chamber is meant to help heal the planet. That is what all of this is about. So I don't care if you do or if you don't believe in magic. But you do believe in life don't you?"

Silence underscored Moira's last comment.

"How?" Alex asked the simplest, sanest question. They each longed to know the answer.

Alex took a mouthful of pasta. Diana watched her intently and with sincerity responded, "I know you are worried about perceptions, Alex, and your professionalism. You always feel better when you label what's bothering you and I'm sure Richard is weighing heavily on you as well?" While Alex swallowed, Moira interjected.

"Yes, Richard. There's something I must tell you about him." Moira clasped the worn research file, wanting to show them her life's collection of first-source texts and maps which help explain the history, and the legends. She spread a dozen more documents across the table, rearranging Diana's book piles and pushing aside her dishes.

"Simply put," she moved another stack in detached, nonchalant gestures, "Richard isn't to be trusted."

"He's my godfather; he's the only family I have left."

"I'm sorry, Alex, I won't beat around the bush, but you do have to hear me. I suspect that Richard is going to destroy the chamber."

"What? That's absurd!" Alex practically choked on the pasta.

"Look, I've known him longer than you've even been alive. I've witnessed him destroy artifacts, sacred matriarchal scrolls, ones that I recovered from a chamber site almost identical to this one."

Diana, who had just gotten up from the table to move Moira's plate into the kitchen, was equally shocked, but not surprised about Richard and quickly returned to her seat with eyes wide open to hear what was to come next.

"Wait, you've seen another chamber like this one? Where is it, why haven't we heard of it before?"

"Yes, it's true. There was another chamber unearthed during my lifetime. As I said a moment ago, there were supposed to be seven of them around the globe. Now I think there are eight. Each one that has been found so far has been destroyed. The site I worked on last with Richard was obliterated by a US military air strike. He helped plan it, to keep knowledge of its existence covered up. It was meticulously successful. He will never again admit to it and I am quite aware that he couldn't be doing it alone, but ...I don't know." Then she continued to Alex,

"I'm sorry. I don't know what to say. I'm sure this must be very painful to hear, but it is true."

Anxious for details about the other chamber, Diana asked, "how many have been found so far?"

"I can't say for sure."

Alex threw her napkin aside and charged, "Diana are you buying this?"

Diana couldn't lie to her friend, "Alex, I'm sorry but I've never trusted him. You saw for yourself how he reacted with me when I mentioned matriarchy and goddess mythology. I told you the other night what my intuition has told me right along: he's invested. His concern is the preservation of patriarchy. This is what I warned; you are going to have to choose."

"You are going too far," Alex exclaimed, "both of you!"

Diana didn't know how to respond.

Moira calmly replied, "I'm just sharing with you a few of the facts that I know to be true and pertinent to our situation at hand, facts that others have tried so hard to cover up. I do believe that we have been called. The few references to ley lines, audio visual phenomenon and goddess mystery cults that have managed to survive throughout history have one thing in common: each other. They only appear together. I know it and Richard knows it, and I saw him destroy the document that tied them all together with these chambers.

"Here, I do still have topographical maps, ley line patterning grids pinpointing three intersections of ley lines right where the chamber is, tidal charts, astrological charts. Look! Look at this one, it is a chart showing cult artifacts uncovered within the direct vicinity of medieval cathedrals throughout central and Eastern Europe, as well as the Mediterranean."

Moira pointed quickly to one of multiple columns on a very large page before Alex could protest again, "I have catalogued the corresponding creation myths, oral traditions, and rituals customary to each region." She gestured over the pages laid across the table, "this, Alex, is just the tip of the iceberg on the type of data and knowledge that Richard's cronies have been actively trying to deny and destroy for centuries."

"Enough!" Alex screamed and stood to leave. "Lots of strange things, maybe even seemingly magical things, have been happening around that chamber and to me personally. Now you're telling me that probably Richard and some unknown group of lunatics have been out there destroying these chambers right along! Well this sounds more like a self fulfilling prophecy. Forget magic, they're probably just playing tricks on us. Especially if Richard is involved, he's the one that got me involved in the first place!"

Coat in hand, Alex stopped for a moment. Looking down at her boots, she was shaking her head. "Of course, those lights were probably all just a hoax. I've been such a fool!" Still shaking her head Alex looked them both in the eye. "I'm sorry ladies... I've got to go. I need some time to think."

Diana complained, "Alex, you can't just walk out on this!"

"It was nice meeting you Moira. Diana, I'll talk to you tomorrow."

Moira also protested, addressing Alex's rational concerns. "There have been other episodes than just yours. Specialists have scoured that site. The light phenomenon isn't a hoax. I can assure you of that. So probably would Richard if you asked him. This isn't the kind of thing you *can* walk away from. You can only choose what you do from here."

Diana repeated herself, "Alex don't just walk out on this."

Alex shouted back, "I'm not..." then reduced her volume, "walking out on this, or walking away from it. I'm just calling it quits for the night, okay? We'll talk tomorrow."

Chapter Six

COURAGE

Alex looked out over the city's morning skyline from the window of her bedroom. The hazy pink sky warned of the next looming storm. *Just as the city had begun to recover from the last one*, she thought. The Bostonians did a remarkable job cleaning up the snow this time. The biggest problem had been finding a place to put the vast quantities once it had been plowed out of the main streets. Tall glaciers littered the asphalt landscape below, but even most of the suburban roads were now passable. Logan had finally opened its runways and was catching up on its missed flights. The appearance of choreography in the streets soothed Alex's yearning for familiarity.

She was in her own stupor, struggling to regain rational control. Old habits die hard. Her mind was tired from all the intellectual juggling she did last night after getting home, when she should have been sleeping. She probed the possibility that if this conspiracy theory was true, it would be so pervasive that there wouldn't be anything three women could practically do about it. And it would also mean that everything she had been taught to believe was wrong. And in the dark confusion that accompanied this jolt to her rational compass, she fell into circular concerns and double negatives, pondering the meaning of everything being "wrong." *Would that mean, then, that Diana and Moira would be wrong too?* She fretted most of the night, hoping to find a way out of her predicament.

She came to think about the intensity with which both Diana and Moira believed themselves to be right.

One's force of conviction is hardly proof of one's legitimacy. It is a gimmick that works well for sages and con artists alike. She tried to imagine considering the world as they would like to see it, dismantled of its existing institutional structures. And she wondered what was so different about her that she didn't feel the same drive to change things. The fact that this had all been so very coincidental just made Alex suspicious, and now even a little protective of Richard. She realized quite easily that perhaps Diana and Moira were the conspirators. But while she knew that was likely true in some sense, neither of them were after any direct or tangible personal gain, so their scheme seemed more innocent, not to mention naïve. In truth, all they were planning to do was burn some candles and say a prayer or something, privately, in a place where Dr. Fennessey had full, legal license to access. It was hooky, but peaceful and certainly not illegal.

She also thought about the suggestion that knowledge had been selectively secreted by an organized, fraternal power brokerage. For Alex, the idea wasn't very foreign to begin with. Deconstructing the notion, she even came to realize that it probably was true, though far from covert. The government often contains information for the protection of individuals and whole societies. The restriction of information isn't always a bad thing, knowledge does have social utility. In the United States, privacy is a protected right, information is often considered intellectual property, and artifacts can be owned privately, legally destroyed and never shared with the public. The entire legal system actually encourages the secreting of information. It is done frequently and legitimately throughout all society: the courts, the churches, the media, the schools, the universities.

But the suggestion that Richard could be a member of a clandestine fraternity also implicated Alex's father. The two were so close; he also would have had to be involved. Did her father have a secret life that she wasn't aware of? As it was, she wasn't sure which side she would choose to be on, if she had a choice. The chamber had essentially been haunting her and she might prefer to have someone just blow the damn thing up, and destroy this confusion. If her own father thought it best to protect the world from this chamber, maybe he was right.

In any event, she was sure that the meeting she was about to attend might bring answers to some of her questions. She grabbed her warmest trench coat from the closet and rang the doorman on her intercom.

"Mark? Hello this is Alex Martin!"

"Good Morning! What can I do for you?" The speaker provided such a clear sound Alex could hear pedestrians and traffic in the background.

"I would like to have a taxi ready to take me to Beacon Hill, I'll be right down."

"Certainly, whenever you're ready!"

She checked her briefcase and headed out the door to the status conference that was called earlier this morning. She knew that Richard would also be there.

* * * *

A security guard ushered Alex down the central hallway of the state house, which sat in tribute to order and democracy at the top of Beacon Hill. The building's sounds echoed loudly in Alex's head. Voices, footsteps and file drawer sounds reverberated violently off the dark mahogany moldings, lofty colonial ceilings, and then back and forth horizontally through the extended tile passage way. Alex had a growing tightness in her stomach, which she would later learn was her body's way of sending her a warning.

She nodded at a few familiar faces. A handful of properly suited men and women were crowded around a fruit and pastry display to the left of a large conference table. She noticed that there were less than a dozen upholstered executive chairs around the table and wondered how many people were actually involved with the chamber at this level. *It must be a closed meeting.* She selected a chair and claimed it with her briefcase. She could feel someone watching her as she moved around the standing crowd and chose a white porcelain cup and an exotic jasmine green tea. She took a sip and turned to see whose eyes were following her.

Nathan tried not to be too obvious about it, but he couldn't help wanting to stare at her. She distinctly felt it.

"Hello," a warm voice greeted as she turned to a handsome smile and an extended arm.

"My name is Nathan Gray." He had the longest lashes of any man Alex had ever seen. His beautifully colored skin, sensitive eyes and muscular features were offset by the starkness of his crisp white shirt. She took his hand and felt an immediate rush of heat.

"Yes, I'm Alexandra Martin. It's nice to meet you." She shook his hand and then released it, although a bit reluctantly. She would have liked to explore the sensation further. It was hot and comforting.

"Do you work for the government?" he asked.

"Actually I teach," she said, "over at Suffolk law school. I'm consulting for the city."

When he reached for a pastry the pull of his sport coat revealed bold plaid suspenders as opposed to the customary leather belt. He had a very playful style. Over Nathan's shoulder Alex saw that Richard had just walked in with the mayor. *Get a grip, Alex,* she prepared herself.

"I am the Director of Harvard's Peabody Museum of Archaeology and Ethnology," he told her.

"Harvard?" she hoped she didn't sound too startled.

The room erupted in applause and Nathan turned his attention to the mayor. The clamor caught Alex off guard and it took her an extra minute to calm the churning in her stomach. Bodies swirled around her as cups were filled and seats were selected.

"May I sit next to you?" Nathan asked as he turned toward the table and reached for the chair next to her briefcase. Richard walked towards them.

She quickly replied, "Certainly," set down her cup and turned to Richard.

"Good to see you Alex," he said as he leaned in and placed his hands on her shoulders. They exchanged a quick, rather awkward embrace.

"You two know each other?" Nathan asked.

Patting Alex on the back, Richard replied proudly, "Why, Alex is like a daughter to me, known her since she was a child." Alex smiled in confirmation and the room started to settle as everyone sat down in their seats.

"She's a great girl!" Richard added as he took the chair on the other side of Nathan. Alex's cheeks burned with a confusing mix of humiliation, anger and guilt. She didn't want to have to own any of those emotions.

The mayor sat down in between Doherty and Richard. Alex only knew two others. Kristina Yau was sitting at the other end. They worked together as legislative interns, back in law school, along with Marshall Banks, the mayor's chief counsel.

A skinny young man moved quickly around the table, handing out pamphlets and binders. Alex overheard someone mention a suicidal truck driver and then the meeting began. Much of the discussion was informative. Alex had been looking forward to a rudimentary briefing on the chamber's real, physical characteristics.

Tangible descriptions packaged into perfectly calibrated and easily digestible facts and statistics reminded her that it was the first time she had ever actually heard the scientific data. *Hmmmm, I have been kept in the dark about a lot of things*, she thought to herself as records and reports were presented.

Alex started to notice a theme surfacing amongst the speakers. Weight-load analysts and structural engineers had concluded that the chamber was structurally unsound. Polls revealed that public support for Marino had declined since the finding of the chamber. Economists concluded the Big Dig project couldn't afford even a six month delay and written waiver and consent forms were received, signed from all appropriate sources, indicating no tribal claim would be made. When the mayor stood to say that he was handing the floor over to Richard to present Harvard's report on the history of the chamber, the knot in Alex's stomach clenched her core as never before and she noticed that Nathan also had assumed a more aggressive posture in his chair.

What Alex was observing in Nathan's reaction to Richard was that Nathan had been informed by Harvard that the University was specifically not prepared to make any formal statement at this meeting. Although she didn't know it Nathan had also been misinformed. Nathan was told it was supposed to be a workshop and status conference, only. Harvard doesn't make premature pronouncements.

* * * *

But Richard began by acknowledging the honor of presenting the report on behalf of Harvard University. Then he shuffled across the table his stack of yellow-bound packets. It appeared to be a formal report, bearing the Harvard seal and emblem. The title indicated that "Historical and Cultural Conclusions on the Underground Chamber" had already been made.

Richard's delivery and choice of language reminded everyone in the room that he was more accustomed to speaking in front of students. He spent a bit too long explaining the philosophical angle of his presumptions and methodology and unsuccessfully tried to make people laugh. He made a reference back to the conclusions made by earlier speakers and how willing Harvard was to house the chamber and the artifacts.

Alex wasn't sure which side Nathan was on but she could feel his tension growing. He kept his composure, but he was reeling inside. His reputation was on the line and he didn't know what was happening. The President specifically confirmed with him yesterday that no acquisition would be acted upon without his full involvement. And Nathan had given Moira his word.

Alex's attention returned to Richard as he continued, "The cultural connection to modern societies is very slight and isolated. Although the symbols found within the site surface in a variety of later communities around the globe, their further reference forward into modern eras are equally remote. The primary asset of the chamber, which is a mere fertility chamber, a pagan 'red tent' used to house menstruating maidens awaiting fertilization, is the awe inspired by the fertilization process. And this can be recreated inside a museum, where it would be more accessible and a safer environment for education, without any adverse effects to the integrity of its cultural and historic value."

Richard was proposing that there was no worth or value to the site although to Alex it seemed to have a mind of its own and it was obviously impacting the city more than Richard had acknowledged. Alex recognized what Richard was saying as sleight of hand and she started drawing connections in her mind, thinking about what Moira and Diana said about the comparisons between history and storytelling, science and magic. And she wondered about the attractive man sitting next to her, what was his role in this?

"Now I'm by no means an extraction specialist," Richard continued, flashing his well-worn elbow pads. "But I'm sure those boys in the back room will come up with a fail-proof plan for protecting the carvings and we'll have it reassembled in no time, safely in the climate controlled wing of the Peabody!" Richard's pink cheeks grinned with glee, like a young and inexperienced salesman.

Alex noticed Nathan's eyes dart around the room at Richard's mention of the museum. A man in Nathan's position would be in charge of the Peabody. His eyes were the only part of him moving. Next, when Richard announced that Harvard officially recommended the entire site to be extracted within the very next week, Nathan's cheekbones contracted from the muscles tightening in his jaw.

Alex kept thinking about Moira, her conspiracy theory and how Richard's insistence about dismantling the chamber squared with her claim that he'd rather destroy it.

Richard went on, "Of course I have worked with Meyer and Associates on four other projects. I highly recommend them to ensure maximum preservation. We hired them in Egypt and in Johannesburg. I have also worked with them here, in New England, under similar conditions with massive layers of granite and quartz." Seeing Alex's disconcerted posture and trying again for humor, he awkwardly delivered, "although perhaps you'd have another suggestion, Alex? Hmph, perhaps your friends might prefer trying to levitate the chamber to the surface, eh?"

Alex near about thought she died. The shock of the sudden attention and attempted humiliation sent the room spinning. The meeting had gone from the absurd to the surreal. She did her best to hold her locked stare upon Richard, daring him to go on. He just looked back at her with a clever smile and raised eyebrow.

Without warning, and motivated by his own disgust, Nathan created a distraction. He threw both hands in the air and then slammed them down upon the surface of the conference table. He laughed facetiously in response to his colleague's lame joke, diverting some of Alex's embarrassment.

Of course, Alex had no idea that Nathan's actions were out of pride and anger that he had been railroaded by Richard and Harvard, nor did she know that he was instantly taken by her and his chivalrous tendencies also wanted to protect her from Richard's inappropriate comment.

What was painfully obvious to Alex was that this wasn't a participatory conference meeting. It was more of a closed room announcement. Tribal permissions had arrived suddenly and without any effort on her part - which was supposed to be why Richard ever needed her involvement in the first place. She had experiences that week which made her question everything, especially the monologue Richard just delivered. He gratuitously tried to undermine her professionalism and yet there she sat, lined up next to the two men from Harvard, as though she endorsed them. Having done nothing to support the excavation, she remained quiet, doing nothing to prevent it.

* * * *

Al Marino ended the meeting the same way he started it, by walking through the door with Richard following close behind. They left the room which was now buzzing in debate over institutional waivers, excavation contracts and federal regulations.

As the two friends entered the decorative hallway Richard said, "Nicely done," and patted the mayor on the back as though he were congratulating himself.

"Well, good!" The mayor pronounced. The sound of finely tailored wool careened the two gentlemen as they walked.

As far as either of them could tell, the meeting was a success. Richard was very pleased with his presentation and the written report was impeccable. Richard had done his job well and Al was pleased that there wasn't much dissention voiced over his decision to dismantle the chamber. Why should there be, it was an economically and scientifically justified decision that no one had legal standing to dispute. Al believed in political expediency and in regards to the chamber, Richard was more than happy to cooperate.

"Maybe now we can get this city back to normal."

Richard wasn't quite as sure. Getting the chamber approved for excavation and dismantling was only half of his problem.

They passed through the hallway toward the coatroom. A well pressed bodyguard met them and escorted them through the public rotunda. Light streamed through the glass doors as they marched through the large round gallery. It was bright for February and the shiny floors reflected the glare strongly, making it seem sunny. Richard noticed a few tourists stop to take second looks at them, recognizing his companion as the Mayor. Marino kept walking.

They said goodbye at the double French doors and Marino exited, going home through the Commons.

* * * *

Richard returned to the conference room to meet up with Doherty. He walked back through the rotunda, hoping to find him alone. Turning a corner, he saw Alex up ahead. She had Doherty cornered.

What did she want, he fumed, not wanting the distraction. He'd talk to her later. Doherty understood. Luckily, her back was to Richard so he could easily gesture to Doherty that he'd wait around the corner. He settled down onto a bench and studied the timeline that he and Paul had agreed to.

He waited only a minute or so until Doherty joined him.

"What was that about?" Richard demanded.

"Nothing, everything's fine. She just wanted to follow up from yesterday when she passed out in the tunnel."

"Hhmmph?" Richard hadn't heard about her accident.

Doherty added, "I think she was embarrassed."

Richard dismissed further discussion of Alex by saying, "Yeah, well, she'll get over it."

Doherty insisted that he was hungry and suggested a little pub he knew.

"It's just across the street from the State House, called the Twenty-First. On an early Saturday afternoon it should be pretty quiet."

The pub had obviously just opened when the two men walked in through the heavy door. Richard selected a wooden table under the window close to the bar. Except for the pretty young bartender and the cook, the place was nearly empty. A stock boy was loading cans of beer near the bar preparing for the Saturday night crowd.

"What can I get you?" asked the curly-headed bartender handing them menus and a smile.

"Glenlivit, on the rocks," Richard ordered without looking at her.

"And a Guinness for me, thanks." Doherty returned the bartenders pretty feminine smile with a cheeky grin. She walked off with a nod.

Richard didn't like Doherty but had been assured that Doherty always performed his assignments with diligence and discretion.

"Paul informed me that he has spoken to Governor O'Rielly and that we have resolved our mutual concerns in ensuring the safety of the city." Richard spoke softly, maintaining eye contact while at the same time being acutely aware of those around him. When the bartender returned to deliver their orders, for instance, he sat back in his chair silently thinking, *this is why I prefer the Harvard club.*

"Anything else for you gentleman?" she asked with a slight accent.

Richard let Doherty interact with her, not wanting to draw attention to himself. Forgetting that he hadn't ordered any food Doherty said, "No thanks, that is all for now."

Once she left Doherty said, "Well, the meeting went over much better than I would have expected. Not one person protested."

"This has always been the simplest solution, John. It just takes a little ingenuity, and a few men that you can trust. After all, there has already been one explosion." Richard swept it away as if it were an idle thing. "But we cannot fail to act too swiftly at this point. The structural instability has been very carefully emphasized by our leading experts…but still…the political pressures from the media will bring independent scientific and historic communities …there're already too many people snooping around."

"This was precisely why we are not briefing the mayor. I'm well aware of my assignment!" Doherty interjected, objecting to the tone of the conversation, Richard's plan, and his newly asserted authority.

Richard explained, "Too much has already gotten out of hand and too many people have gotten involved. The faster this chamber is destroyed, the better, and Paul agrees. This is like water surging behind a dam."

Doherty listened as intently as he could while trying to get the bartender's attention again. She was so close to their table but seemed to be preoccupied washing glasses.

"John," Richard continued aggressively, "we can't wait."

"Tomorrow night," Doherty swatted, "I told you, I know my job!" His tone was a bit too terse for Richard's liking. Doherty's stomach growled when he saw the bartender approach, suddenly giving him her full attention.

"No," Richard corrected, trying not to be too loud, "that's too much time, there's too much at stake. Paul's already worked out the timeline. The chamber has to be destroyed tonight." His voice fell to a grumble when she reached their table.

"I am sorry," she said, "Did you want something?" Doherty asked, "what's your house soup?"

"Baked potato."

"Sounds good for an early lunch, bring me a bowl." Doherty said. "Thanks, ah… Ms.…?"

"Yana," she replied as she retreated into the kitchen.

The two men worked out the remaining details with another round of drinks while Doherty gulped down the comforting soup. After he begrudgingly agreed to meet Richard outside the chamber at the midnight shift change, they paid their tab and went their separate ways.

* * * *

Nathan Grey wasted no time leaving the State House after the meeting. He was a man on a mission; he had to tell Moira what happened. He called Moira immediately after the meeting and invited himself over to her house.

Not only did Richard blindside him, Moira and Richard were supposed to compose Harvard's official findings together and Moira had no part in Richard's latest display. He was sure of that. The whole way to her apartment, Nathan kept thinking about how Richard's suggestion to remove the chamber "as soon as possible" was blatantly motivated by a desire to deprive Moira from further access to the site and the artifacts.

Heading down the small, icy, tree-lined street, so quintessential to Cambridge, he walked briskly to Moira's apartment building. *This is ridiculous*, he thought to himself. *The city is so fixated on completing the Big Dig they are not taking the time to really assess the discovery. And Moira knows more about the nature of that chamber than what she is saying and why was she so convinced that this was going to be an issue?* He jogged up the steps and rang the outside buzzer of her building.

* * * *

Moira had seen the look before. She had it once or twice herself... the look of having just been run over by a committee. Nathan Grey was wearing that look when she opened the door to welcome him inside.

"What happened?" she asked trying not to sound too concerned.

"You were right. They've decided to move the chamber."

Moira's apartment was not as cluttered as Nathan thought it might be. She gestured for him to sit on the delicate settee placed in front of the picture window.

"Coffee, tea . . . something stronger?" she said to him, studying his demeanor. Moira went to the small hand built walnut cabinet and uncorked a dark bottle of port. Handing Nathan a glass she said, "Here, it's the best thing for you."

"Thank you." he replied. He raised his glass in appreciation and took a hearty sip as Moira sat down across from him.

Moira continued, "I figured they would. They had no choice, Richard was there."

"He behaved like an ass. Furthermore his report indicated that the site is something that is able to be moved and should be. He supported the state's position and gave the mayor's office a justification for moving the site claiming that it is too volatile to be allowed to remain 'as is' if it is an historic site. I tried to argue that Harvard needs more time to evaluate the significance but Richard said the archeological findings could be preserved through the extraction. I think he has been speaking with both the mayor and the president of Harvard behind my back. I was told I had final approval on when and if that site was going to be moved. I do not like being rushed and I certainly do not like being told what to think."

Moira said pensively, "We are always being told what to think. There is more going on here than meets the eye... Do you remember how you mentioned the Amazon warrior woman? You said you were shocked that there were disagreements when the evidence was indisputable. There was a subversion of information. There was no other record of its existence other than the thing itself yet still it was disputed. We have been told a lot of things don't exist. And there's no record of half the sophisticated knowledge that our ancient ancestors knew. Where would all that knowledge have gone? Don't you think that's odd?"

"Well, Moira, scholars and historians have often hypothesized about what might have been contained in the library of Alexandria before it was destroyed."

"A likely story indeed," Moira quipped, "so likely in fact it is precisely my point. Certain knowledge and access to knowledge has been sculpted and controlled since the days of the ancient Greeks - since Plato first built his Academy. His works and those of his students have survived, but nothing else has. Where are all the writings by women? We only have scant traces of Sappho! Throughout history writings by women have rarely been accessible. How is this possible? Women's knowledge has been hidden, buried, covered up and stolen!"

Moira lowered her voice to a whisper, "The same is true of cultures that don't fit white, western notions of sophistication. Nathan, have you ever heard it said that the Academy still exists?"

"The Academy?" he echoed raising an eyebrow. "I have heard... but I have never given it much credence. I certainly haven't known anyone claiming to be affiliated. The organization, if it does exist, would have good reason to remain inconspicuous. But Moira, realistically, who needs another conspiracy theory when you already have the good ole boys." Nathan chuckled, "why, are you trying to recruit me as a member?"

Moira looked unamused.

"Oh Moira," Nathan protested, "you can't honestly tell me that you believe in a secret conspiracy pact amongst men. You know as well as I do, talk like that gives feminism a bad name."

"Nathan, you know that it wasn't originally simply a matter of gender, it was about power. Plato wanted the status that had previously only been afforded to women due to their particular... magical characteristics and abilities. Female symbolism was very powerful politically in his day. He was quite clever really, to unite a group that we know thousands of years later as the status quo. And I certainly didn't say that every man is a member of the Academy, that's poppycock! Do not think that you don't know anyone directly connected with the Academy, Nathan. Richard's arguments are all smoke and mirrors. He has no intention of preserving the chamber and letting you have it for display. Richard intends to destroy it."

"Destroy it!" Nathan gasped. "Come on now. That is a bit extreme. What is so important in that chamber that you think Richard would destroy it? And what are you implying about the Academy anyway?"

"The chamber contains evidence of the Academy's existence and the original Myth of the Caves. Oh but, not what you might think of as evidence. I found no scrolls in this chamber like the ones I found in Persia. That's right, I was together with Richard in a similar Persian temple. I was able to locate a bundle of scrolls that documented the patriarchal invasion that had originated in Greece. Like so many others of women's writings, they were destroyed. They bore the proof. That was the evidence, I had thought, and I had hoped to find similar ones here, only there was nothing. As it turns out, the real evidence is housed in this chamber. Only, it is more sophisticated than text, it is the thing itself. The other chambers were meant to lead the Academy away from this one. This is *the* chamber, the one that contains the source of the goddess' magic and ancient women's knowledge. It's like the mother of all chambers. Only, to prove it, I need the Ring of Baubo and we need it quickly."

Nathan's eye's flashed. "Are you sure you are not just a little paranoid?"

"I do not know. You were at this morning's meeting."

"Moira …I know the history of that old ring from working at the Smithsonian, but... What in the world are you planning to do with anyway?

* * * *

Lynn, Lynn!
The city of sin!
You never come out!
The way you go in!

Or something like that. Diana couldn't help thinking and chanting the local rhyme. Sitting on the northbound commuter rail, Diana was on her way to Salem to speak with her astrologer and to shop for supplies. Lynn was farther north than Salem but nevertheless the rhyme seemed appropriate. Diana was going over the list of what she needed for the ritual. *Mugwort for binding, lavender for healing, iron for strength.* She systematically went through her lists in her mind knowing that each substance was sacred.

Everything had its purpose.

What else will we need? She tugged at her memory. *Does saving the planet really depend upon the right herb?*

She worried. She knew that Alex had not fully processed what was happening, but at least Moira understood and of course so did Night-Night. Night-Night, though, could hardly be called upon to give testimony to Diana's sanity.

Salem held a strange fixation for Diana, but not because of the witch trials. For Diana, the witch hunt was still alive and well. Women and nature were both still seen as commodities.

There remains still a dark cloud of oppression over Salem, and in the face of global warming the expression 'the burning times' takes on a whole new meaning. Her stop was announced over the crackling intercom and she got ready to disembark. *Off to market we go!*

She stepped out of the station into the salty air that unmistakably confessed the close proximity of a harbor. She walked briskly westward, with the hem of her woolen cape brushing the sides of her ankles.

As she walked down the old, decorative street she noticed that some people were hurrying past her, heading in the other direction. First it was a young man, college aged. Then a small group of school kids scrambled over the cobblestone, one of them shouting something about Shamu. She sensed that everyone was going to the same place and it was a perfect opportunity to find out why.

A well-dressed middle aged couple also came around the corner, arms hooked, and hanging on to each other's elbows. They slipped across a section of ice right in front of Diana and fell almost at her feet. The young woman's long emerald colored over coat spread out across the white ice revealing her rich velvet skirt of a similar shade.

"Here let me help you," Diana extended a paint-splattered gloved hand to each of them.

"Thank you," the gentleman responded, and with legitimate concern asked his companion, "are you alright dear?"

"Yes, yes Adam, I'm fine." She certainly wasn't hurt, physically that is. She tried to adjust herself and prepared to stand, gathering her expansive green layers about her.

"Excuse me," Diana jumped in, "but do you know what's going on? Why is everyone rushing towards the harbor?"

As Diana helped the woman to her feet she enthusiastically shared that whales had been seen all morning along the coast line of Massachusetts, from Salem all the way down to Nahant. They seemed to be heading for Boston. Diana wanted to know more. She was sure it was not insignificant, so she asked, "Are whales that uncommon in the harbor? I mean, is it really that abnormal?"

The woman's woolen overcoat was wet and salt encrusted from where she landed. Unperturbed, she answered, "Well, I don't honestly know, but what is so spectacular is that one of the local panhandlers calls himself an oracle, and he was seen along the docks yesterday shouting that the whales would rise up and seek revenge upon humanity for the pollution we caused to the oceans." She paused a moment to adjust her handbag.

Her male counterpart thoroughly checked his coat for staining while she continued, "Yes, I think he will show again today. We had better get going!" She patted Adam's chest to indicate that they were through with conversing and they continued downhill, more gingerly than before.

* * * *

Between lunch and dinner there is, for the lucky few, cocktail hour.

The Twenty-First caters to the lunch crowd, the dinner crowd and especially the in-between crowd. Yana was clearing the bar as Alex strode in. Her hair was windblown and tossed out of place. Her agitation walked in front of her to the bar. Alex sat, but before she could speak, Yana poured her favorite wine from the stash under the bar.

Alex quickly concluded that Yana must have restocked the supply.

"It's that obvious?" she asked rhetorically, trying to rub the rage out of her furrowed brow with her fingertips.

"Yes," Yana replied, "...and no." Smiling through the European lines of her mouth she ended with, "It is my job to know," and headed to the other end of the bar. Alex recognized that restocking the wine was a gesture. The prominent leather and wood flavors were why she loved this vintage. She also got some satisfaction out of the label: Pan gaily trotting a dance, flashing a ripe bundle of grapes in hedonistic fashion. It was made in limited quantities and was very difficult to come by. Yana's kindness was refreshing.

Alex took a slow taste of the oaky syrah. *Yeah it's my job to know, too. How could I not have expected Richard would be so miserable and condescending?* She remembered feeling such an intense rush of dread in the hallway before she stepped into the meeting. *I guess I did expect it, but I ignored it. He deliberately sabotaged that meeting. And now that they are going to move the chamber, they'll more likely destroy it.*

"So what's up?" Yana asked returning a few minutes later and drying her hands with a towel. "It looks like you weren't spared from it either."

"Spared? Spared from what?"

"Chaos Alex, don't you know? Chaos has taken over. Everyone is talking about what a mess the city is in from the sewage flood and that truck driving over the side of the expressway. Not to mention everyone's heightened foul mood, although that might be from the weather and this maddening news of yet another storm! It's either chaos, or karma. Nothing has been right since they found it. And look at you! You do not look happy!" Yana seemed almost eagerly concerned. "Where is your friend, Diana, anyway?"

Alex checked the clock above the bar. "She should be here soon, but what sewage, what truck?" She was perplexed that she could be so unaware of the past few days' events.

Yana slid over a copy of the newspaper. "Here, read this." She said and strutted away to fill another empty glass. Alex scanned the articles.

"Oh the poor man," she said reading about James McKennan and wondering who was liable this time. "Was it an accident? How did this happen?" She went on to read the next article which described how the sewage plant in south Boston failed. It was supposed to pump the waste out into the ocean for nature to recycle but instead the pump brought water in, flushing the sewage into people's living rooms.

A week ago, she reflected sentimentally, it would have been Cye who'd talk over the news with her. And as she tried to imagine him hopping a plane and starting the adventure of a new life in the tropics, her eyes caught the small line at the bottom of the page, "Humpback whales coming to Town?"

Alex looked up and tried to orient her mind. "See I told you the city really is in chaos." Yana said slicing lemons and philosophizing. "Chaos is the necessary outcome of all bureaucracies. It is a contradiction to think that tyranny, lies and incompetence can serve the greater good. That is why I serve drinks. No shame in that."

"Do you have the potato soup today? I need something with substance," Alex pleaded almost forlornly, as if it were too much to hope for. And not wishing to seem rude by not engaging in discussion added, "if these were just random isolated events. . ."

"That's the point," Yana interrupted. "Nothing is random or isolated. You should hear the people from the Statehouse talk when they come in here." Yana glanced around to make sure they were not. "They can't fix *this* problem because of *that* problem and they do not know what is going on *there* because they do not know what is going on *here*, and so on. All they want to do is destroy things. You can imagine. Did you say you wanted the soup? I'm sorry but . . ."

"Don't tell me! I know, I know," Alex said with resignation "…it got eighty-sixed at lunch? Uh, he needs to start making more."

A chilling air swept across her back as the big wooden door blew open and with a gust of cold, Moira hurried in looking normally disheveled and a tad frantic. As her eyes adjusted to the darker light inside, she spotted Alex at the bar and trotted over. "I got your message. I came right over. I take it you know about the decision to move the chamber?" Moira was speaking quickly and quite out of breath. Yana prepared a tray of drinks, close enough to overhear conversational similarities with that of her earlier customers.

"Yes, I was there. I saw the whole thing." Alex replied, giving Moira a moment to unwrap her scarf and fling her coat over two barstools. "Richard had an obvious agenda. I hate to admit it but he was obnoxious, as I probably should have expected. He was just so adamant about it. I don't understand. And the city really wants to just be rid of the problem and move on with the Big Dig. Nobody seemed to care about it. I've spent the last few hours reading every footnote of his report. I'm just sick of it."

"Oh Alex, it's worse than your personal disgust. But I saw Nathan Grey after the meeting… he's going to help."

"Nathan did you say?" Her tone slightly altered, "I met him today as well, at the meeting."

"What did you think? Interesting isn't he?"

"Yes." Alex replied wondering how Moira had meant *interesting*. "And something more than that." She stopped herself from saying anything further.

"Right behind you," Yana spoke over Alex's shoulder, warning her not to lean back into the tray of drinks she was balancing. Acknowledging Moira as a new customer she added, "Be right back!"

"Holy Shit!" all three women heard a familiar voice and they turned to see Diana, getting ushered in by yet another gust of cold. The inside warmth sent painful shocks to her half frozen goose bumps, but her eyes quickly spotted her friends at the bar.

She said it again for effect, "Holy shit," and excitedly approached them.

"You are not going to believe this!" Moira and Alex welcomed Diana who was wearing a hooded black cape and looking as powerful and exuberant as Alex had ever seen her. Hugging Alex first and Moira second, Diana continued.

"Sorry I'm late. I've been in Salem all morning. I had a great day and made some finds at the apothecary. I have so much to tell you both! I now know what is happening!" She faced Moira, "We've had it all backwards! Those damn reversals again."

Yana returned with her tray now empty. "Hi," she said to Diana, "Good to see you again!" Diana returned the compliment but didn't take a seat. Alex briefly introduced Moira, who didn't feel the need to get to know the bar help, and Yana took their order. She also took the opportunity to give Diana a little tease, "did I hear you say you went to Salem? Are you conjuring something?" Diana blushed.

"You know you might just need a gypsy," Yana said.

Alex pulled back a bar stool for Diana and touching the cushion ushered, "Here, sit down." Moira scooted her stool over to give Diana room between them. Diana understood. As she moved toward the seat the televisions at the end of the bar blasted on, startling everyone in the room with a loud interruption.

"Holy shit," Yana playfully echoed Diana's earlier sentiment as she rushed to the volume controls. "I guess the cable is back!"

"Oh good, maybe we can get some more information," Alex said optimistically, thinking of all the news she'd missed.

"I doubt it," interjected Moira. "Nothing they say on television is going to help us."

"Looks like you three *are* conjuring something." Yana stared at Diana. "What are you up to?"

Diana still hadn't settled down. She was barely on the stool. A new discovery was vibrating its truth up her spine and energy was running wild through her body.

Yana resumed her post at the bar and poured their glasses. Yana knowingly commented to Diana, "no one else can tell, you know?" Diana raised her gaze to meet Yana's in recognition of what she thought Yana might have meant.

"Tell what?" she asked directly.

"Your aura, I can see it. You cannot run that kind of energy by yourself. You will fry your synapses! *What* is going on in that head of yours?" Yana slid the wine glasses over to Diana first and then to Moira.

Diana took a taste and said facetiously, "Actually, it's my body, or it's the climate change depending on how you look at it… if you know what I mean."

Realizing that Diana was talking about something other than the dismal forecast, Yana quirked, "You mean like thunder and lightning?"

"Exactly," said Diana and placing her hands on Moira and Alex added, "we have earth, fire and water, we are just missing air!"

"Lucky for you I'm an Aquarius," Yana said flashing Diana a knowing smile.

Diana sat back in her stool and nodded to Yana, then turned to her fellow evolutionaries pronouncing, "It's the coming of the Age of Aquarius, that's what I learned today! It's a transition into a higher state of consciousness. Moira, you were right, it's not the apocalypse, it's the rebirth of goddess consciousness!"

"It's Her Underground!" Moira added. Yana inclined her head, intrigued further by Moira's use of words.

"Well that may be true," Alex responded, trying not to be dismissive. "But there are current pressing problems." She dropped her tone and Yana quietly backed away to attend to another customer and give them a few minutes of seeming privacy.

Alex continued, "Diana, I was called to an emergency meeting with the city today. Richard made a presentation and announced that they are going to remove the chamber very soon. He's started the clock, they're getting ready to move forward. But, it just doesn't seem right to me, I don't…"

Moira leaned in to interrupt, "I still think Richard is going to destroy it." Moira explained, "Alex and I were just starting to talk about it when you arrived."

Alex said sternly, "this is all very upsetting for me!"

"Don't worry Alex," Diana responded. "It doesn't matter if they want to move it or destroy it; we just have to get there first. We should go tonight."

"Tonight?" Moira and Alex replied in unison with slight trepidation causing both of their voices to sound an octave higher.

"Look," said Diana in a tone of sanity, "we are all a little agitated. Let's sit down at a table and talk." She gestured to Yana, indicating that they were moving to a nearby table. Just for fun she added a little wink. Alex followed, wondering again how she became so invested in magic and myth in the first place.

"I'm sorry Diana," Alex said as she slid into the mahogany chair. "I understand the urgency about all of this and as crazy as it seems, I'm going to go through with this because, like you said, there's nothing to lose. But honestly, I cannot seriously accept that this chamber is somehow going to cause disastrous global effects if we don't light a few candles, sprinkle salt and hold hands!" Alex continued without taking a breath, "And Moira, I know that you have an affiliation and sympathy with this. It is your field and you understand it from your research. But I am right where I started. I do not understand my role in this… or Richard's for that matter. In spite of the strange events from last night, I can't seem to find any hope in this." She swallowed the remains of her wine and the others gave her time to finish. "Besides, I just do not think you are being realistic. I do not think that one woman, or three women and one cat, to be precise, can change the world." She returned her empty glass to the table and with an edge of self-defense finished, "There! I've said it."

"Well actually, Alex, *four* women and Night-Night *can* change the world." Diana spoke calmly and matter of factly as if they were discussing the dry cleaners. "Magic works because once released, it is contagious. It is about hope. But not naïve hope, 'Hopping Hope'[1] as Mary Daly calls it!"

"Precisely," Moira chimed in, "that is what the myth is all about. Matriarchal myth is about hope, not about an apocalypse! The church and state have created a self-fulfilling prophecy out of humanity's fears. The 'End of the world-ers' have us paralyzed but the myth itself speaks to the abundance of life, not the lack of it. We need only reorient our paradigms: reverse the reversals. Personally, I am sick to death of the 'four horsemen.'" Moira was almost hopping in animation herself, "for the first time in my life I feel I can do something instead of just talking or writing about it. You see, Alex, this chamber is like an amplifier for the kind of positive creative fluidity produced within the ancient rituals. You are right about the timing, however. The clock is ticking."

"You see, Alex," Diana said, "it is necessary and just that we make this cause for growth now, today! Or else it will never come about. We only have the present. We are here together because it must be done now, because it is needed now. The fact that you have told me the city is going to remove this ancient site doesn't surprise me. Nor does it matter for our purposes yet. I mean, I think corruption sucks and it's completely asinine that a government would risk and disrupt such an ancient part of our global heritage for a new roadway, but that's actually typical. After all we're even blowing up Mesopotamia. The wisdom and sight of our archaic and wild past has been obliterated again and again. But we cannot survive pretending to be sterile and independent of our internal and external environment and everything else natural. The cosmic timing of the naysayer's and doomsayers all talk about the end of the world. Even the Mayan calendar has been misunderstood! And for all I know, that one might have been right in pinpointing the date, but it's not about the end of the world! It's about its transformation and the creation of a new one; the evolution of life and consciousness! We must move from primitive through 'cultured' to balanced, from civilization and institutions to a new understanding of community."

Excited by the energy in the room, Moira's jovial, feminist self came out and sung, "it's the end of patriarchy."

"But we're not ready!" Alex practically screamed it from her reddening face, "...I mean, I am not ready."

"Yes you are Alex," Diana spoke softly and laid her hand upon her friend's arm for consolation. "Let me tell you what else I learned today about the timing. Maybe this will help. I was walking up the plaza and everyone else was rushing in the other direction. Did you hear about the whales?" Both women nodded and she continued, "Well everyone was going to see them. Of course I was going the other way so people kept rushing by me and all of a sudden I saw Christina coming toward me, she's an astrologer I know from Seattle. Apparently we have been experiencing a major progression she said. She moved to Salem because this astronomical event is expected to occur that she thought might bring about the worst earthquake ever seen on the west coast. The primary girth of her interpretations are always on point. The positioning of the sun and moon, earth and Venus are supposed to culminate in a pattern unlike that seen for thousands of years. It's supposed to occur on the winter solstice of 2012, which is also the end of the Mayan calendar symbolizing the start of a new cycle and the Age of Aquarius. Well, we have just entered the preparation period which has eight threshold astrological stages to it. The first is considered a major gateway and represents harmony. It occurs tonight. It is the ideal time to perform such a ritual; it is the opening that will unite our intention.

"But you are also right, though Alex. I am not ready either. None of us is ready. Only in the moment of us actually taking a leap and doing are we ever ready. It doesn't matter whether we think or feel we are ready. It is necessary, so we must be ready. You know, now or never. There is only ever the now, after all. By the way, I did see the whales."

Alex's face perked up, "you did?"

"Christina walked with me to the store, and then she took me to the harbor. Their survival is our survival. None of us exist separately; they came to remind us this. Night-Night has reminded us of this and we must remember this today, tonight."

There was a moment of silence and recognition that everyone's glasses were empty and probably shouldn't be refilled before Diana continued, "The chamber is here and waiting for us. The planets are in alignment, the stars are in their courses. Now is the time to balance ourselves and the elements. Meet me at midnight."

"Midnight, Diana?" Alex asked, not yet ready to commit, "couldn't we do this at a less dramatic time, like sometime tomorrow when the sun's out? Must it be midnight?"

"Oh, come on! It must, midnight. And, besides, it'll be fun!!!"

[1] Mary Daly calls for "Hopping Hope;" hope which is not latent and passive, but active verb-bound hope that inspires difference through its inherent quantum conjuring of action into the Now. *See* MARY DALY, PURE LUST; ELEMENTAL FEMINIST PHILOSOPHY 308, 311-312 (HarperSanFrancisco 1984).

Chapter Seven

MAGIC

Nathan's plane didn't land all at once, it landed three times. Tha-thud, tha-thud! And again the wheels hit the ground, tha-thud! Taxiing up to the gate, he was already twenty minutes late. The 4 o'clock shuttle from Logan to Reagan in DC had run true to form and was, in fact, forty percent on time. Luckily, Nathan was bumped up to first class so he could disembark quickly.

He sprinted for the airport's nearest exit and hailed a cab for the Smithsonian knowing that his old mentor and friend, Sebastian Sanders, was waiting for him. Had this been a more casual visit they would have met at the Capitol Grille, but Nathan was doing this favor for Moira and documentation was important. It was best to go through proper channels. The choice sirloin would have to wait, but he planned to be back soon enough.

The cherry trees that in the spring time decorate the capital's Mall and parks with abundant petals and floral bundles were now bleak and naked. They looked like they would never bloom again. Nathan adjusted his tie and shirt collar. He called Sebastian just a couple hours before, after speaking with Moira, and secured his assistance with little effort.

"An institutional loan to Harvard can't actually pose a problem for the Smithsonian, can it?" Nathan repeated Moira's words when he talked to Sebastian over the phone.

"Lending an artifact to you, Nathan, isn't the problem," Sebastian sincerely replied, "but this particular artifact?"

"Look, I can accommodate any restrictions you need. We can discuss it once I get there," was all Nathan answered. Then he called the airlines to book a ticket.

Here he was in front of the Smithsonian, walking into the plum colored, castle shaped building. He was happy to be back and a little sad to acknowledge that it was no longer his home, but it would be difficult for him to forget the prestige and challenge of his new position at Harvard, irrespective of the oddities that had been presented by the chamber personally, politically and professionally. He shook away any thought of regret. Besides, he was getting a kick out of this spontaneous jet-setting to stealthily acquire possession of a cryptic archaic artifact.

He headed up the stairs to Sebastian's office and noted as he turned the corner on the second floor that he was only forty three minutes late. He straightened the breast of his jacket and put on a brilliant smile while entering the outer office properly adorned with a secretary and a marble bust of Plato.

The secretary was still working. She looked too young to know the ropes very well and her long bright red finger nails made Nathan wonder whether she could physically type. *Another temp secretary,* he deduced and was relieved he didn't have to put up with the Smithsonian's support staff policies any longer. He greeted her cordially and glanced around the office suites he lived in for eight years. He recognized the distinct blend of coffee mixing with antiquity. It created a pungent aroma.

Sebastian had been growing impatient waiting for Nathan and was glad when his younger friend finally arrived.

"Sorry I am late," Nathan said as he entered Sebastian's office and greeted him at his desk. "Thank you for seeing me."

"No problem, Nathan! Glad to be able to help you out. There are only a few forms for you to sign and then you can tell me about Boston over dinner, I especially want to hear about that chamber they found under your new city," Sebastian said while handing Nathan the paperwork.

"Oh, yes," Nathan said taking the pages, "amazing isn't it? They found quite a lot of artifacts with the Big Dig, but I imagine no one expected something like this."

"I've heard that Harvard is involved, UMass got the boot, eh?"

Looking up, Nathan reluctantly said, "Uuuh, something like that."

"Well," Sebastian exclaimed, "good for you! I do believe congratulations are in order. You always have exceptional timing, Nathan, I will say that." He clasped his hands in a gesture expressing pride at the success of his apprentice. Without trying to be abrupt he asked, "So, why did you say you wanted to borrow the ring?"

Nathan finished scanning the pages and casually responded, "Well actually... I didn't say... I'm involved in a... personal research project."

His evasiveness only intensified Sebastian's curiosity. Part of Nathan's knack for organizing a successful exhibit came from his penchant for the controversial and effective timing for its display, an approach modeled after Sebastian's. "You know," Sebastian continued, "how the Ring of Baubo got its name, don't you?" Of course they were both very familiar with its provenance, but this was Sebastian's way of probing.

Foiling his attempts, Nathan jaunted, "Please, enlighten me." He penned his name on the page as though the ring's background was insignificant for his purposes and handed the signed copy to the secretary to duplicate. She left the room and Sebastian continued.

"The ring was discovered by a German archeologist in the 1930's. It was found at the heart of the Temple of

Demeter in Eleusis, Greece. It is said that after Persephone was stolen by Hades, the God of the underworld, her mother, the Goddess Demeter sought out consolation from Baubo. She found Baubo at a well and Demeter filled that well with her tears, mourning the loss of her daughter." He pulled out a package from one of his desk drawers and carefully unwrapped it as he spoke, "It was found at the bottom of that well and some hold that it has transformative powers because Baubo changed Demeter's tears to laughter. Scholar's disagree on its purpose but I have always found it interesting."

Sebastian lifted the ring and both men examined it. It looked rather like a stone donut. He explained, "It looks circular but when you examine it closely you will note that its circumference is askew."

Nathan remained silent as he ran his fingers across the markings. The circumference was more like an ellipse than a perfect circle and he recognized some of the etchings as infinity signs but others seemed incomplete, perhaps they were mere portions of a larger shape.

Sebastian added inquisitively, "The Mystery rites at Eleusis were said to be so powerful that the government of Athens could not contain them. That is why, after over thousands of years of prevalence, they had to go underground." He paused to assess any response in Nathan's facial muscles but he was too composed, his expressions gave nothing away.

* * * *

Night-Night was growing weary and bored from waiting. Perched on the back of the arm chair by the window she could see the whole block lit up by a single street light and although she had spent many lifetimes waiting, these last few hours had been the hardest. Washing her face with her paws and rubbing her chin she thought, *Ok, I know it's hard, you have to find a new way to live with Nature, to dance the dance we all have to catch a new vibration.* She hummed a few refrains to herself just for the pleasure of the beat ...*good, good, good, good vibrations...* And even though Night-Night couldn't remember all the words exactly, she rose up slowly with tail in the air and began to sway and butt-swagger as each little paw stepped back and forth on the edge of the chair in perfect rhythm and balance... *Ah . . . my, my what elations, . . . got to keep those lovin' good vibrations a happenin' a with her, . . . got to keep those lovin' good vibrations a happenin' with her . . . ahhhhhhh . . . good, good, good, good vibrations.*

She danced, knowing that the real secret lies in reaching a higher rhythm. The beat took her and she started to get excited.

Oh, for Goddess' sake Diana, hurry up! Her tail and feet kept lifting and descending, pumping energy until in exasperation she flopped down, laid her head on her paws and let her eyes glaze over into a trance-like state. She hummed to herself *good vibrations,* over and over again letting this positive pulse seep through the universe, travel through the city, find Diana and remind her not to forget Night-Night tonight.

* * * *

Coming out of the Commons, Marino wished he had gone straight home instead of trying to take a "peaceful stroll". It was easy walking down the hill, however getting back up it was a different matter. The path he chose was short and direct, straight down the mud streaked hillside to the frozen fountain that looked so artistic at a distance. He didn't think ahead.

Walking down the hill made him feel light and carefree. Knowing that a resolution was reached with the chamber alleviated a great deal of pressure off of his mind and stress off of his body. And for a find with such mystique and intrigue, the critical first "Assessment and Containment Stage" had been completed in record time.

When he got to the fountain the first thing he noticed was the color of the icy slush that accumulated from the earlier snow fall: it was brown. It looked as if a flat cola slushy had been dumped over the entire fountain and smeared across the faces of the carven angels, gods and goddesses.

He stood for a few minutes and starred at it. It reminded him of something but he couldn't put his finger on what that was. Then the setting sun broke through the temperamental clouds again. The sun had already moved to the western sky, but the dimming orange orb could be seen clearly through the trees and reflected off of the surrounding buildings like a prism. In the light he could see Peggy's face again, looking alive and so real. But of course, he knew it wasn't. He shivered a bit as there was no heat in the light, not in February.

He decided to sit for a little longer in the sun. One of the benches was brightly lit and buffered from busy Tremont Street by a row of hedges and trees. He sat down, tipped his face to the light and closed his eyes. He was trying to remember her voice. All he could recall lately were her conversations about yoga. She would nag him about creating a practice that would sustain his soul and his career.

Ping, ping...

As he was rewinding the sounds of her words in his head he felt something land on his shoulder.

...ping...

That was enough. He opened his eyes and found a foreign white and brown substance dribbled across the breast of his over coat. Realizing it was dropped from above he quickly stood and looked into the branches above the bench. They were full of pigeons and covered in droppings! He also noticed that the bench was filthy and his coat probably ruined!

Angry, he yelled obscenities at the tree. With stains on both sides of his coat he looked like a drunken bum. Meanwhile, a few Canadian geese detoured from their flight path to land in the park near the fountain for some bread hand-outs. As Marino swiftly determined he couldn't get any satisfaction from the pigeons for ruining his coat, he regained his composure and turned to leave. The street lights were already on and it was time to get home.

He had just passed around the fountain when for no apparent reason all seven of the geese lunged at him, squawking and honking and squealing. They chased him until he ran.

Now he was practically pulling himself out of the Commons as he climbed the slippery steep stairs that would take him to his street. The geese didn't chase him all the way back up the hill, but a good portion of it and now he was winded.

At least this week's saga was short lived, he thought trying to turn his attention to something successful about the day.

Beacon Street was again backed up with traffic and he took in a deep chalky mouthful of exhaust, making his nose itch and stomach sick. He was still catching his breath. He imagined that he felt accomplished and successful, but all he felt was alone.

He shrugged it off and, careful not to get run over by the vehicles swerving slowly in between the snow banks, crossed the road and left the Commons behind him. He was trying to remain positive. He needed to be able to turn his attention back to his campaign and now he was free to do so. *Maybe Richard is right*, he thought. *I should celebrate.* He wondered whether being with another woman would make him feel virile.

Destiny waits while everyone else is busy.

* * * *

Alex, Diana and Moira agreed that it would be best to separate early and get ready, gather any tools or supplies they may need and then regroup at the chamber just before midnight. The three of them were preparing to leave the Twenty-first when Yana stopped them at the table assuredly. She sat down next to Diana and explained herself.

"I didn't mean to eavesdrop, but I overheard Moira refer to 'her underground', I know you guys have been talking about the chamber. Alex, I told you, it's all about the *terroir*. I think you should know that I have overheard a similar conversation earlier this morning between a couple of men from the State House."

Then she leaned in real close, looked over both shoulders and scooted her chair a bit closer saying, "But theirs was a bit more sinister. I'm afraid you might be getting your selves into a little bit of danger, ...perhaps a whole lot, certainly more than you know."

* * * *

The bar was bustling with customers now streaming in for the beginning of happy hour, but Yana was unmoved by the responsibility. The bar back worked frantically behind the counter in her stead. There was a surreal moment of tension. Alex didn't breathe, Moira pinched her brow and showed obvious signs of offense. Diana noticed it and defended Yana's intrusion. "There are no coincidences," Diana said to her friends, "I may believe in a lot, but I don't believe in coincidences. Yana, please go on, continue!"

"I know the legend of her underground. This is part of my tradition. I am a direct descendant of the gypsies that still inhabit Bulgaria's Black Mountain Ranges, my grandmother's people. In the mountains there are many caves. Alex, I explained to you how my mother chose a different life for herself, opting for a more bourgeois lifestyle. So my grandmother's wisdom passed directly to me. This is my destiny as told by the oral histories of my grandmother and hers before her. I am being called to that chamber for the same reasons you all are: to awaken the goddess and none of us can do it alone. You don't even know."

Moira spoke up, "her underground, ...what? Yana, are you actually telling me that your ancestral myths actually reference a myth called her underground? Did you say Bulgaria?"

Yana affirmed, "Yes, on both counts. I was called here as I imagine each of you were. In fact, up until today I didn't know what I was still doing in Boston. But I would guess that... you don't know the half of it. In my tradition, there were signs that foretold the coming of the chamber. Now, today, we each must choose to acknowledge the signs that are being presented before us."

Alex was still stuck on Yana's reference to her earlier customers and asked, "Wait, Yana, which other customers? I am sure lots of people are talking about the chamber, the whole city thinks it's cursed. Are you sure you know what you heard?"

"Who? Oh, I don't know who... No! I do. Wait here a moment, the older one paid with his credit card."

Yana jumped up and went behind the bar, avoiding eye contact with the thirsty patrons. The ladies talked, more quietly this time.

"I never checked Bulgaria," Moira was stunned. "There is a direct connection to the Far Eastern traditions, but... why didn't I check it thoroughly?"

When Yana came back she said, "Lyons."

"Richard!!!" The three women gasped in unison.

"Yes, that was the name. You know him?" Yana queried, "you aren't working with him are you?"

"Not quite," Moira answered. "He's my colleague, but he's spent most of his life working against me. He also happens to be Alex's godfather."

They all looked to Alex as Yana explained, "I'm sorry, Alex, but he wants to destroy it, the chamber. He's planning on blowing it up."

"I knew it!" Moira exclaimed with both her voice and her body, now glad that this gypsy seemed to be more than a bartender.

"Yes, and from what they said, time is running out!"

* * * *

Alex decided to go home and seek the comfort of her finally dried and restored home office. Standing in the center of the room she could feel the order of the books on the shelves, the sheer weight of time sanctioned tomes that alone gave testament to the law. The room was a reflection of everything she had tried to become: clear, rational, precise, and principled. Everything was systemized and catalogued.

Nice. Neat. There is no magic or mysticism in this room, she thought gratefully, *it all seems as it should be. But it could be so much more than this,* she heard herself say. *...Hope, huh? Well, what exactly is it I am supposed to be preparing for anyway? According to Diana one minute, the world is coming to an end, and the next, we are supposedly bringing about world peace, or some wacky feminist utopia... Oh, Jesus, now I am starting to sound like Richard.*

Her thoughts turned dark with fear of sabotage, destruction and murder. She wondered whether he would risk her bodily harm.

Thinking and staring at the bookcases, Alex found no answers to her questions, but did notice the dust. Walking over to one of the taller shelves, she ran her hand along the smoothly finished grain. She rubbed her thumb and index finger together and examined the soft, minuscule residue. *We ought to be able to generate something more than dust.*

* * * *

Night-Night's ear twitched, her paws flickered at the knuckle joints. Involuntarily her body stretched as she came into consciousness. Diana was coming home. She got up and sat by the door. Diana pulled the key quickly from the lock and pushed open the inside doors. Immediately looking down, "oh good! Are you ready Night-Night? We need to prepare." Tossing her coat and hat over the wooden baluster she headed toward the kitchen with Night-Night at her feet. Jumping up on the table, the feline conveyed the thought that some nourishment might first be in order.

"Ok, Night-Night you are probably right."

After filling Night-Night's bowl and making herself a strong cup of cappuccino Diana rolled up the sleeves of her sweater and gathered up the items she brought from Salem. Unrolling her altar cloth and placing its contents on the table with Night–Night watching over her, she smiled gently at her fellow traveler and asked, "Ready to get to work?"

Woman and cat mixed ingredients, gathered spells and notes, herbs, protection and healing potions. When they were done, Diana finished her tasks by cleaning up the kitchen and headed toward her mediation cushion with Night-Night again at her heels. After a centering and blessing meditation, Diana packed up her knapsack with the herbs and supplies, altar cloth and magic book full of spells.

When it was time, the three pairs of feet and paws moved in unison down the hallway to the double sets of front doors. Diana started bundling herself up. She put on dry boots and a down winter jacket. Night-Night sat next to her, waiting. Diana put on her back-pack and prepared to leave when she noticed that she was humming to herself . . . *good, good, good, good vibrations.* She started to zip her jacket but stopped mid-way, bent down and scooped up Night-Night, tucking her inside the puffy lining.

* * * *

Moira went straight to her office after leaving the Twenty-First. In addition to worrying whether Nathan could get back in time, she had been gathering a small collection of artifacts for the rite that they were going to perform. Each item held a unique mythical significance that she intuited would be a positive influence upon the energy in the chamber when *it* happened. *I wonder what is really going to happen.*

She unlocked her office door but could barely tell the difference in temperature between the outside and the inside. *No welcoming warmth*, she shivered and grabbed the telephone receiver. *Where is his cell phone number? I know I wrote it down somewhere.* Moira searched frenetically with one hand until she found a small piece of paper tucked under the phone's base. The number she wanted was scribbled across it. She dialed... but the voicemail answered so she could only leave a message.

"Nathan, it's Moira. I hope your mission was successful. You have to come back tonight! Call me back or just meet me at the chamber, just before midnight. Until then, I'm at the office."

She reached into her knapsack and carefully removed the worn out manila folder that she had been carrying. She searched through the pages for the hand written notes she made to herself decades ago, when she was working as a graduate honors student on a dig in Macedonia. One of the Persian texts uncovered there was full of illustrations, documenting the oral myths of a traveling, goddess-worshiping society. She came across the note pad page where she drew a crude rendition of an illustration that seemed to depict the Ring of Baubo, although it was referred to in that text as the "Ring of Iambe."

Much of her own scholarship, and that of a handful of others, has proven a correlation across cultures between

Baubo and Iambe, as well as goddesses from other cultures, but no one else has made the connection between these two rings. They are the same. The Persian reference is considered mere folklore because it was written in a manner consistent with their mythical song-like lyrical poetry, whereas the Ring of Baubo is an artifact representative of a ritual tool from the Greek Eleusian Mystery rites. But as far as anyone knows there is only one. The Ring of Baubo and the Ring of Iambe are likely the same, and it will soon be in Boston, and in the chamber.

She thought instantly of the ring when the chamber was first found. The Persian text made a crude reference to the "myth of the caves," that was believed lost to the bombing, but which Moira actually rescued and secreted away. Scholars referred to it as the "myth of the caves," but its title translated literally read "her underground."

She studied the drawing and wondered what the ring would feel like in her hand. *What weight and temperature will it have?* She had seen the Ring of Baubo up close and in person many times, but if Nathan was successful she would be able to do so much more.

Poor Baubo, for centuries scholars have scorned her, dismissing her divine powers and relegating her to the role of a handmaiden known for her lewd jokes and obscene gestures.

As Moira sat back in her chair reviewing her notes she chuckled to herself, "The joke is on the scholars."

According to the myth, when Demeter, the great Mother-Goddess of the ancient Greek world, lost her daughter Persephone to Hades, God of the underworld, Demeter climbed to the top of Mount Eleusis and wept over her loss. She was inconsolable with rage and grief. As she wept her tears fell into the well from which Baubo appeared to give her comfort. It is said that Baubo cajoled Demeter with her fecundity by telling her jokes and finally performing the one crude act that has made scholars cringe and keep references about her to a minimum.

Moira read on the side of the margin "ana-suromai."

They even gave it a name, she thought to herself. *But, of course they would have to... The act for which there is no forgiveness, that is misinterpreted as obscene, because for them it is sexual. The gesture is as blatant and magnanimous as life itself!*

In the midst of Demeter's pain and grief, Baubo laughed her great belly-laugh and raised her skirt high to reveal her magical womb to Demeter. The magical vulva was more than a mere reference to sex, fertility and procreation. In revelation, Baubo was performing an act of empowerment, reminding Demeter of her great powers as the Mother-Goddess, as Creatrix, and as giver of birth and life. How can one with such powers of rejuvenation grieve?

It is because of Baubo's colorful reminder that Demeter found the power within herself to secure the return of her daughter from the underworld and resume the growth of wheat, which was her gift to the mortals, and through which the seasons were created. Summer, Fall, Winter, Spring: Birth, Life, Death, Return.

Female power!!! Moira thought when she first heard the myth. As her research continued she found Baubo throughout the world, in ancient Greece, Egypt, Africa, Old Europe and the Middle East. In ancient Sumer she was the Goddess Bau. Yet she was universal, beyond history and culture reminding women everywhere of their energy and creative powers. Apparently she was in the mountains of Bulgaria as well.

On the next page, Moira found a translation from yet another ancient text that delivered Baubo's message in a powerfully relevant way:

We are the life-givers, never forget that! We cannot become the destroyers, for our role is that of the recyclers . . . Lighten up!!! We must somehow manage it so that, as creators, we can continue to keep everything spinning, everything in balance. You must not turn your back on the whole mess, for it is our vulvas, our wombs, that are the center. We are the transformers!!! This is not mere exhibitionism.[1]

* * * *

With the paperwork complete, Nathan and Sebastian moved their meeting to a charming but noisy little boutique cocktail bistro in the historic D.C. neighborhood called Georgetown. At Nathan's side sat his brown leather knapsack, now a few pounds heavier.

"So Nathan, any love interest in Boston or are you still a confirmed bachelor?" Sebastian was being coy. He knew that Nathan didn't like to offer information about his romantic life. Sebastian relished in the moment and then serendipitously took the pressure off of Nathan by talking about himself, something he was never shy of doing.

"You know, Joanna and I have been so happy all of these years. I always buy her flowers and diamonds! A man like you ought to find an independent, intelligent woman," Sebastian added trying to sound vital and not like a man who was aging in his years.

Nathan smiled and winced at Sebastian's technique. "I keep my eyes open," he said careful not to sound dismissive of his friend's claim to happiness. "But at the moment I am not looking for a relationship. I am in a new city, in a new position. I haven't finished unpacking yet. Harvard and the Museum take up most of my time." Nathan's phone started vibrating in his pocket. He glanced down to it.

"Excuse me," he pushed a button on his phone, trying to retrieve information about the last caller. While Nathan checked his message, Sebastian straightened his titanium cuff links and sipped his martini.

"Aw, dear friend," Nathan said genuinely as he closed his phone, "I am sorry but I don't think I can stay, it seems I have to be going." He glanced at his watch. He could easily make the nine o'clock, ...even the ten would land in Boston by eleven or so.

"Have to go?" Sebastian still hadn't learned any details about why Nathan needed to borrow the ring, "don't you have time to finish your drink first?"

Relaxing back into his seat, Nathan agreed, "Yeah, I suppose that's a good idea isn't it."

"So, Nathan, why don't you tell me the details of your research project, ...and the ring? You know it is a very isolated piece. It's even kept in the permanent collection's back storage. You couldn't be doing too much research with it. There really aren't many threads to follow, unless you have a new thesis. What is this about?"

"Nothing too exciting I'm afraid... I'm just trying to do my job, and remain diplomatic in the midst of a tryst between some of my colleagues. Let's say I'm leveling the playing field. You know me, I'm always very thorough."

"That's what I'm afraid of Nathan. Look, I am sorry, but I must insist that whatever your project, the ring cannot be used in an exhibit or display."

Despite the touch of intrigue produced by the nature of Sebastian's prohibition, Nathan affirmed his compliance unmistakably, "it is understood. Don't worry Sebastian, I won't cause any problems."

"When the ring was first discovered, there was a group of anthropologists who were very interested in its significance. Still, few findings have ever been published. It is a carefully monitored piece; I must impress that upon you. I would not let it outside of the Smithsonian custody to just anybody, Nathan."

The warning didn't go unnoticed. "Well, I appreciate your confidence in me Sebastian. Certainly, by now I should think I had earned it."

"You are part of the Smithsonian family. Do you understand what I am saying?" Nathan understood and the emphasis made him reconsider Moira's conspiracy theory about institutional control of information.

"Yes and thank you, Sebastian. I will be sure to get it back to you as soon as possible."

* * * *

By the time Nathan finished his drink, got to the airport, flew all the way back to Boston and landed, Yana still hadn't finished her second double shift of the week. It was a good thing she trained quickly. After all, she had only just started at the Twenty-first.

"Damn!" she blurted when she glanced to the clock. She needed to cash-out early but now it was already late. She turned to her Bar Back and told him to use only the one register as she was leaving early. She instructed him on how to close up after the last customer left then headed out into the night.

The cold hit her in the face when she stepped out of the building. It stung her cheeks, made her eyes water, sucked the air out of her lungs, and freeze-dried the hairs lining her nasal passages. Her knees were resistant and didn't want to bend in this kind of cold. Even her gypsy sense wasn't working right in the frigid air. Luckily, it had been working all day.

Tonight, she was beginning to understand a greater part of her life's purpose, as well as her own life goals, which was why on this frigid February night she headed around the corner to Beacon Street where she knew she could catch a fast cab.

* * * *

Speaking of understanding one's purpose, Sebastian assessed that Nathan properly misunderstood his own. Of course Nathan had no reason to know that Sebastian kept Richard on his speed dial. Just after Nathan left, he called him.

"Everything is in motion as planned." Richard reported.

"That may be, but his plans have changed; something about a tryst between colleagues. He's coming back tonight." Sebastian replied. "I recommend that you bury both the ring and the chamber. The last thing we want is some parliament of women taking over. You make sure none of this gets out."

"Well, Moira," Richard said to himself. He glanced at his watch knowing he was supposed to meet Doherty at the chamber in a couple of hours, "it looks like we'll find out if that magic of yours really works, won't we."

* * * *

The entrance to the chamber was waiting. It was bathed in the harsh hue of overhead construction lights and was overwrought with do not enter signs, billboards and police tape. It looked like a crime scene, but with political and religious messages plastered to the street side of the barricades. At this late and chilly hour, the news crews and fanatics had all deserted their posts. Alex was quite relieved to have a bit of privacy and to see that they shouldn't be interrupted. She waited in the light, in front of the gates wondering about Richard and whether this was a good idea.

She spoke with the security guard to warn him that there would be a small group with her. But his attitude gave her further cause for concern. The tunnels provided access to the vulnerable heart of the city and he was generally distracted and didn't seem to care whether her name was even on the access list.

Alex brought with her the list of things she agreed to collect: flashlights, lanterns, blankets, candles, matches, a thermos of coffee and a bottle of brandy. Alex wondered why Diana didn't ask her to bring glasses. She did anyway, of course, adding that touch of class which was quintessentially Alex. It also made her bag heavy. She adjusted the weight on her shoulders. She saw headlights approach. As the car slowed Alex's heart began to race.

Diana stepped out of the cab looking particularly bulky in her parka. She was having some difficulty managing the knapsack and other indiscernible bundles that filled her arms, but with the firm crunch of snow under her feet she hurried up to Alex. As Diana got closer it became apparent that one of her bundles was moving, not just moving but actually capable of self-propelled motion. Alex's face quickly transitioned from curiosity, to realization, straight through to horror and finally ended with disbelief. Squinting against the glare of the street lights and the cold wind she stared at Diana's coat, or rather what was peering out of it, until realization set in.

Fixating on Night-Night, Alex accusingly asked, "Oh, no. You didn't, did you?"

Diana was nonchalant about the whole thing. "Of course I brought her, and hello to you too, Alex!" Diana stroked Night-Nights little head with her furry woolen mitten.

"You are not ready for this, are you?" Diana continued more gently, trying to break the tension and be empathetic at the same time.

"No, no," Alex took a deep breath, "I'm ready. I mean, who wouldn't be?" Then she sputtered, "Here I have a chance to freeze my butt off, stage a pagan fest, possibly get arrested or blown up, throw my career down the drain, fulfill an ancient prophecy that no one has ever heard of and save the world all with the aid of a cat! A black cat for that matter! Who wouldn't be ready . . . and that cat is really starting to freak me out, Diana!" She looked at Night-Night, whose green eyes had become almost luminescent.

As another trail of headlights broke their focus and the next cab pulled to the curb both women were surprised to see that it was not a small round woman getting out. The long dark figure that did emerge looked around and headed toward them carrying a briefcase and flashlight. Diana was confused and Alex was a little taken aback and worried that it might be Richard.

"Who the hell is this?" Diana asked just as Alex recognized him.

"Nathan?" She walked toward him to intercept, "what are you doing here?"

"Nathan?" Diana asked Night-Night, *Who is he and what is he doing here? Hope he's not from the city?*

"Alex?" Nathan laughed a bit. "What a nice surprise. I'm here to meet Moira. I didn't realize you were involved in this, good evening!" He approached the two women. "How nice to see you again."

Alex quickly introduced Nathan and Diana. Alex hadn't planned for Nathan to show up, *what will I tell him,* her mind raced, *please Diana, keep the cat in your jacket!*

"Moira should be here soon," Diana said, "but why are you meeting her here tonight?"

"Well," Nathan said, turning up the collar of his coat. "She asked me to go D.C. and procure an ancient artifact, which was very difficult to do last minute. I was just about to have dinner when she called and asked me to meet her here. I barely made the last flight back into Boston." Nathan said turning on his smile.

"Where is Moira anyway?"

She was actually coming around the other corner behind them. Her cab driver spoke very little English and did not know the detours. He took a wrong turn around the north end and ended up on the same rotary twice. They finally pulled up to the back side of the construction site. At a distance Moira could see the three figures standing near the chamber's entrance in a faint circular glow of light. She paid for the cab but refused to give him a tip after it taking so long to get her there. Pulling her scarf up over her face she moved hurriedly toward the small group. Her sixty something body felt light and free in spite of the cold and despite the touch of arthritis in her knees, she spryly made her way around the construction debris to the entrance. All three were relieved to see her coming, or rather all four.

"Hi, I'm sorry I'm late. Nathan do you have it?" Moira was all business. In response to his nod she added, "Thank you, thank you." Moira embraced them all at once in an awkward group hug with her arms barely reaching around anyone's shoulders. Moira too had brought provisions and had a heavy leather satchel. Nathan opened his brief case and removed a tightly wrapped object.

Handing it over to Moira he said, "I hope you know what you are doing." To the others he added, "My friend at the Smithsonian says that it is a very provocative piece."

Moira took the package and replied, "Nathan have you ever seen the chamber?" She chuckled, remembering how Nathan hated to get dirty. "Come! Let's go."

"But wait, what about Yana?" Diana said looking at Nathan and wondering how much Moira had told him.

"I'll tell the guard to let her through, if she makes it." Alex responded already leading the way.

Four up-rights and one cozy cat descended into the chamber. The cold wind swirled around the opening of the passageway but as they started to make their descent down the tunnel it seemed warmer the farther in they went. Guided only by their flashlights and a few dangling overhead beacons, the passageway took on the feel of an ancient labyrinth. The smell of the dark earth permeated the air around them as their footsteps echoed in the dark with their shadows bouncing off the cavernous walls. Alex and Diana walked in front while Moira and Nathan walked behind at a slower pace, chatting nervously. Night-Night on the other hand was perfectly relaxed and confident, still tucked inside Diana's coat. They had not gone very far when they heard a faint, "OOOOOOOOO."

"What was that? Did you hear it?" Diana asked turning around and looking past Nathan and Moira in the direction of the sound.

"Sounds like an echo," Nathan responded turning around in affirmation.

"Elloooooooo," the noise repeated itself.

"Oh heavens," Diana said as she recognized what it was. Without taking the time to explain she started running back toward the tunnel's opening.

"Helloooooo."

Then Diana was heard shouting in response, "Hello, hello!"

As Diana stumbled toward the surface she saw the silhouette of a solitary figure standing about twenty meters into the opening of the passageway.

"Diana is that you?" it cried out, confirming her identity.

"Oh, I was hoping that was you! I was afraid you weren't going to make it."

"Well I almost didn't," a European accent responded.

Diana and Yana shared a quick embrace and quickly pulled away from each other as Diana said, "I'm glad you are here. I think we all need the help of a gypsy tonight."

"Well, I can never resist a good mystery," Yana replied as Diana led her down the earth's hallway to join the others.

Alex and Moira were having a hard time accepting the bartender's participation, but also realized that with the exception of Diana none of them had ever engaged in any ritual work.

"Are you a witch too?" Moira asked.

"No, not yet anyway," Yana said smiling and placing her left hand on her hip, "I'm a gypsy! But I think the only difference is culture, so I guess tonight I am a witch!"

"So does that make me your token warlock?" Nathan asked lightheartedly. He was quite out of his element and the joke put everyone at ease. Diana quickly replied in her typical offbeat humor, "no, Nathan you are the male sacrifice!"

The four women giggled and Nathan smirked sheepishly.

Moira replied, "I couldn't agree more, Diana!" She winked to Nathan and then commanded the group, "let's walk..."

Together, all six resumed their descent.

* * * * *

As they walked, Alex at first grew more and more worried about their safety. With each step deeper into the belly of the earth her mind recalled the fear she associated with this place. Every strange episode that had happened to her this week had shown her a different side of reality. What had happened to her was actually real. That had been the hardest thing for her to remember when she was on the surface. Down here, it was obvious. The cross-generational memory, the inter-spacial telepathy, the out of body experience, the spirit guide, even being connected in such a way as to be given access to this site, individually were fodder for lunacy. Collectively these pieces of the puzzle started to add up to a kind of treasure map and progressing further and further toward the site that seemed to be the source and magnet for this magic, her fear turned bit by bit to acceptance. As they neared the chamber she became able to exhale one at a time, tiny thin layers of rational protocol and social convention. She started to realize that she was truly glad that she was here, in the now, and wouldn't want to be anywhere else.

The passage bent to the left as the beams of light scanned the earthen floor. Hearts were racing but footsteps were the only audible pulse. The chamber waited silently. Flashlights caressed the opening of the small doorway and four women, one man and a cat came to a dead stop.

No one moved. Breathing was happening but no one moved. After a moment Night-Night started to squirm. She bent her hind legs up against Diana's chest and pushed off, leaping over the threshold. She landed squarely on all four feet inside the chamber, "Meow!"

Diana followed through the crumbled opening, shining her flashlight against the carved walls and bulbous floor. Night-Night walked around familiarly, pausing to flick her tail at the convex altar in the center of the circle. Her tail pointed high in the air as she slowly and deliberately walked the basin's circumference.

Nathan ducked as he entered and was immediately struck by the warmth. The space was like a life-sized cauldron, simmering radiant creative powers; Nathan had never been inside such a place and yet it seemed rather familiar.

So this is what they mean by 'the hollows of the earth', Nathan thought to himself.

As if reading his mind Moira announced, "It is the Earth's womb," while she crossed into the room.

Nathan had a flash of understanding and the further importance of the Ring of Baubo became clear. "Moira, this is amazing," he said in a hushed, church voice. Moira's eyes shone knowingly back at him.

Alex pragmatically relieved her shoulder's burden by placing the bag of supplies and turned to the others, "ok, so now what?" Getting no response, she slapped her hands down to her sides and looked for a place to sit. She needed to focus her mind and release the last few layers of fear and anxiety that they might get interrupted or blown up by Richard. She was still learning that her own thoughts were contagious and it is important to keep a positive vision. She selected one of the small mounds beside her, slid up against it and began to remove various objects from her bag. She lit the candles and placed them on the floor around the chamber.

Moira also set down her sack and the first thing she unpacked was the package brought by Nathan. She unwrapped the ancient stone donut and touched it with the light tips of her fingers. Stone usually feels quite cool. Moira expected this one to feel charged or energized but she never imagined it would actually be warm to the touch. *Who knew that pure potentiality could be so active and powerful, and yet so stable?*

"It is real," Moira said out loud, surprising herself at the sound of her own voice echoing in the small underground chamber, resonating with history.

"Of course, it's real," Diana replied, startling everyone with the force of conviction in her voice. "I have been trying to tell you, it is not just a myth!!! It is a movement!!!!"

"Oh," Moira exclaimed spinning around towards Diana, "you are precisely right! I've known about the myth but it is not just a myth. This Ring is the proof. This is the link." Bending her knees and assuming goddess pose, Moira held the Ring of Baubo high in front of her for her companions to see. As everyone gathered around her, Moira proclaimed the real meaning of the myth:

"According to the legend, this ring is the connection between sentient beings and The All. It is the astral womb, both the gateway and the wheel. Centuries ago this ring was used to charge this and other underground holy sites and to establish a cosmological portal to the center of existence and the cosmic void of potentiality. Our foremothers and ancestors knew and predicted that in the times to come there would be great destruction to the earth and its inhabitants. So in order to ensure the preservation of life and the return of the goddess they charged sites like this one with their great regenerative magic, all around the world. The myth is meant to inspire an evolution of our consciousness and the magic of the chamber is meant to evoke an evolution and great healing of our planet.

"Centuries ago women just like us came to this place to ensure that the world would always have a new beginning. This ring is the original cauldron, predating the so-called "holy grail" by many centuries, the entrance to the womb of the great Mother Earth; the portable cosmic cervix. It has been passed from Babylon to Egypt to Greece and beyond, from temple site to temple site and from culture to culture, from past to present. Each temple it visited was charged by the high priestesses through the contagion of rejuvenation and compassion that is amplified through the power of this ring. Like the wheel of fortune this ring has tracked the rotations of life and the livings' relationship to it. It holds great magic within it and inspires it from without!"

"And that is what we are doing here tonight," Yana added, "fulfilling the prophecy, healing the planet, turning the wheel of the spiral, invoking the re-birth and re-turn of the great Mother-Goddess!"

Alex lifted her head from her thoughts and asked Moira, "You mean this symbolically, right?"

Moira passed her the ring saying, "don't underestimate the power of the myth, Alex."

As Alex examined and scrutinized the ring for its magical powers which were not yet visible, Diana prepared the altar. She rearranged some of the candles and placed numerous objects around the center altar's basin. Nathan and Yana unpacked the rest of the supplies and opened the bottle of Brandy, passing it around without the specially stowed glasses.

"Here, look these over," Diana said handing everyone small packets of stapled pages. "This is the basic structure for ritual work that I have used over the years. It is quite adaptable and compiled from numerous traditions. It begins with the creation of a protective space, which might be particularly important tonight. Moira, I meshed the ritual details your research uncovered from the mystery traditions with some nuanced adjustments I have honed through my own practice. And in case you have since come across a particular chant or practice or meditation or something, I have left places where they can be integrated... Like the Ring of Baubo. The same thing goes to you Yana, if you know what your grandmother would do at any point in this ritual, by all means, speak up. This should be intuitive, so nobody hold back, understand?" Yana winked, while the other faces were blank. "...It's my field, you know, my contribution. Form does matter."

"And going with the flow," added Yana.

Moira glanced at the center, bowl shaped altar and laughed to herself. Richard had suggested it was a receptacle for the high priests' sacred discharge. She caught Nathan staring at it also, but the look on his face was more an expression of concern than amusement.

"Think you can handle it?" she teased. Nathan blushed but there was nothing heinous or hedonistic in the ritual that Diana structured, no references to "male sacrifice" or "group masturbation." He took another swig of Brandy.

The room started buzzing, not audibly but in frequency. Each of them felt it. The spinning and weaving of thousands of centuries of knowledge was about to be released, and the pain of humanity's oppression was about to be alleviated and healed, set back in jointure, a-toned in right relation.

The peculiar pagan party took a moment to read Diana's ritual and prepare for their respective roles.

"Moira," Diana instructed, "why don't you stand in the north, Alex you should take the east, Yana, the west, and I'll be the south." Alex had a small amount of experience with Diana's earth based spirituality and ritual work from their days as roommates. And since entering the chamber this time she had increased feelings of comfort and inspiration, warm fuzzies even. She willingly moved to assume her corner, but anxiously realized, "...which corner is in the east? I'm disoriented down here. I mean, the tunnel turned, didn't it? But it felt like we kept walking straight..."

Diana playfully pretended to be critical replying, "Alex, do you think our ancestors would have been so unaware of which direction the sun rises? It would have been primal knowledge for them!" Then Diana mocked her own scolding by admitting, "...But I did bring a compass. East is there," she smiled as she pointed to a mound. Alex moved her bag over and noticed that it was particularly breezy in this corner.

Nathan and Moira were leaning over the stone ring, obviously discussing it, and very intently. Nathan kept turning it over in his hands, they were comparing the surfaces. One side was just the smooth but richly textured stone and the other had markings.

Yana interrupted them, "Hey!" and she pointed to the Ring of Baubo. "It looks like one of those pendants women and men wear around their necks as jewelry. I have seen them made from all kinds of materials, bone and jade with a cord or chain looped through it. Who would have thought..."

"Well, me for one," said Moira. "People have no idea what they are wearing around their necks or why, and I think some might even be shocked to think that their fashion indulgences are actually political statements." Moira's cynicism was part of her nature. It never left her, even when she was about to channel universal love and healing directly from the cosmos.

"Well, it's a cute joke," Yana said in acknowledgment of the irony.

* * * *

Night-Night did not find it very funny. *Truth leaks out in any way it can*, she thought, *through art, religion, science, literature, comedy and tragedy. Ok, so in this case one of the most powerful symbols of female power, of gynergy, has become cosmetic but nevertheless the symbol is elemental enough to get the job done. It is the orbit, the circle, the cauldron, the womb, the wheel, the "o", the beginning of "om!" It should be everywhere. Truth may go underground for a while, but it will never be tainted.* She sauntered up to Nathan and Moira who were still examining the Ring.

"Meow," she said rubbing her tail up against Moira, stepping closer to Nathan. Night-Night wanted to see the ring. *It has been so very long.* Night-Night could cry from joy, if not for the fact that she was a cat. She blinked and scrutinized it. She hadn't seen it in centuries. It hadn't changed but everything else had. She remembered how the women came together with nature to work and pray and to preserve and inspire life. Night-Night missed the solidarity of purpose from in those days of old and she had been painfully aware that this particular era was severely unbalanced.

Watching Diana orchestrate the ritual Night-Night wished she had hands. *All they have to do,* Night-Night thought, *is simultaneously identify their inner source of love, their connection or channel to divinity, and put the ring in the spot and the rest will take care of itself. Life creates life. Life loves life. It is meant to be self-creating, self-maintaining, self-regulating, self-rejuvenating, contagious! ...just as long as humans can remember to put things back where they find them. Just put the ring back in its spot!* She again walked to the center of the chamber and strutted along the altar's circumference. *Ok, time to get started.*

* * * *

"Ok, time to get started!" Diana announced. She glanced at Nathan and saw that she had left him out of the script and circle.

"Nathan, you are also welcome to join the circle. You can be the ring bearer." Nathan smiled. Alex smiled too.

Joy is contagious. It got past around and Moira wanted to giggle. Diana's aura became a little clearer. With Nathan, Night-Night, Alex, Yana and Diana all around the chamber's inner circle six of the eight mounds were occupied.

Sensing a tingling begin to surge up her spine, Diana deduced that the energy in the chamber was starting to lighten.

Thank Goddess! Night-Night thought as she felt the energy build and noticed that everyone else's auras seemed to be clearing. In instinctive team spirit fashion, Moira, Diana, Yana, Alex and Nathan all grabbed hands and simultaneously accepted presence.

* * * *

A loud crack rumbled through the atmosphere.

* * * *

Richard certainly heard it and it shook him to the core. He had been pacing back and forth impatiently, kicking at a shadowy clump of ice for entertainment. He was waiting for Doherty on a dark corner outside South Station, and the entrance to the chamber. He didn't like being in the dark and he couldn't help but think that the sound might have been the underground explosion that Doherty was supposed to lay. Pangs of guilt mixed with bitter flashes of relief as he tried to decipher whether the sound came from above or below.

Just before the bellowing sound ruptured he was thinking, *what if Doherty didn't get my message, what if he already laid the explosives?*

As it was, his curiosity was getting the best of him. He was dumbfounded when he pulled up only to find that Alex and Diana appeared to be waiting for Nathan. To make matters worse Moira joined the scene and after they passed through the gate another figure hurried down behind them. At least he was sure it was another female.

What the hell are they all doing down there, he thought. He wanted to follow them to see what they were up to. He didn't want to presume the worst, but each of them now posed problems for him and Richard was boiling with rage at Alex's betrayal that seemed self-evident and unquestionable. He couldn't accept risking Alex's life, but he wasn't going to risk his own exposure or failure either.

How could she turn on me and go to her? After everything I have done!

He decided it best to go and see for himself what was happening in that chamber. He left a note with the gate guard to give to Doherty if he came back around, and then he started his descent into the long dark passageway.

* * * *

The four whale scouts, after their long swim, had finally made it to Boston and now dogpaddled in liquid suspense just adjacent to the world trade center. They quite organically began, as if on cue, to excrete deep bellowing sounds from their bellies. As they did so, they began to feel the buzz. Whales everywhere started feeling the high again. While the scouts performed their chant, singing their motives and messages, they blinked wisely at one another to acknowledge the sensation and say, "hey guys I think it's working!"

The feeling kept growing and surprisingly seemed to be coming from underneath the city. They sang on, …Ooooohhhh hawoooooh….

* * * *

When Marino finally got home and collapsed into his oversized lounge chair, he fell into a deep comatose sleep. The exhaustion overtook him and without control he was barreled over with an oversized dose of the sand man's most powerful powder.

It didn't seem like a dream to Marino. His head was clear. He had fallen asleep in the living room's bed sized lounge chair and at some point his wife Peggy appeared to him. She walked into the room as if coming from her study. She came toward him. He noticed the motion of her hips as she walked. She sat down beside him, placing one hand gingerly upon his chest and leaned in toward his face. She kissed him softly on his cheek.

"Ssh," she begged and looked into his eyes with the look of insight and compassion that he had always found so attractive in her. Her eyes spoke volumes.

"I ...have missed you," he said and they held each other in the kind of embrace that stops time. Eternities like this come and go in an instant.

She whispered into his ear.

* * * *

They are present, Night-Night thought proudly. She could sense that the five uprights were ready and regally assumed her place by stepping into the center of the altar.

Let the ritual begin! The people stood in a circle around her. She began breathing a distinctive rhythm from inside the center of the circle. Incense swirled through the air and strong feelings of trust moved amongst them all.

Breathing in and breathing out, inhaling and exhaling, Night-Night seemed to doze a bit from the repetitive motion. Her breath was hypnotic, almost snoring. Everyone's eyes closed, breathing with her. Their breath was gentle and effortlessly grew slower and slower still, following Night-Night's feral lead. Without effort they adopted her rhythm, breathing in and out in unison, in cat snore, in feline bliss, while subtle and strong waves of energy began to fill the room. Breathing energy.

Without warning, and at the same time, they extended arms upward into the moist air, their hands still clasped. Breath by breath, hand by hand, piece by peace they forged a complete unified circle of breath, hands, minds, and hearts. Love filled the room and washed over them. Their auras expanded and contracted with the undulation in their lungs. As their bodies gushed and hands gripped, the silence was pierced with light as the stone mounds began to glow again like orbs. They emitted a pinkish hue only this time radiating a much stronger light. Warm beams of fuscia stretched up the smooth arc of the walls, meeting at the center of the dome above them. It was all encompassing. Their auras blended together in the pervasive light.

The circle is cast, Night-Night thought.

Diana also proclaimed, "The ritual has begun!" In recognition she released her hold to lift up a large white candle and in a voice that seemed to come from both above and below she chanted: "By Magick made, By Magick changed!"

The others followed suit and said in sequence, "Powers of the East! We ask the Air for Inspiration to truly see what Is." Alex, being positioned in the east, lifted her candle. It sparked a flame and burned bright.

The sequence continued as Diana said, "Powers of the South! We ask the Fires to enliven us with compassion and justice." And Yana in the west said, "Powers of the West! We ask the waters for sensitivity and truthfulness." With each direction the candles burned.

"Powers of the North!" Moira added, "We ask the earth to ground us in strength and wisdom."

Diana poured some wine onto the ground as a libation offering and pulled from the chest a loaf of bread. She broke the bread and then put it back into a basket and from the basket, into the chest. She passed it for the others to repeat.

"Grain to bread, grape to wine, magic happens all the time!" They shouted in unison. "Life is the mystery!"

A flooding feeling spilled over all of them. The energy intensified. They rejoined hands and closed their eyelids for the meditation and rising of power as directed in the ritual, but Alex tensed.

She began to feel a convulsion of consciousness coming on. Standing still in the midst of all of this energy had been so stimulating it was also disconcerting. Her perception was off. It was supposed to be on but she still clung to the illusion of control. The swirling of the lights on the wall carvings and the smoke from the incense made the air look iridescent. She thought that it was hot in the chamber but it didn't make sense that it could be. Yet she knew she was perspiring and her head was spinning, or maybe the walls were spinning. *Oh no, not again*, she thought struggling against her own consciousness. This was how she felt before passing out the first time she came to visit the chamber. She looked around, searching for her bearings. Her vision was blurry, but what she could make out was that Moira looked ecstatically happy, Diana was literally glowing, Yana was reciting her people's oral heritage and Nathan looked like he was floating.

The orbs were pulsating, increasing in speed and intensity. They were definitely creating heat. Night-Night was purring, the universe was purring. *Am I losing my mind*, Alex wondered, weakening the glow of her orb as she questioned herself. She glanced to Diana for reassurance, some strand of ground to hold on to. Diana didn't seem to notice, she was watching Yana.

Alex's thoughts were interrupted by another voice which whispered, *just let go Alex. You are not going to pass out, just step between the worlds.*

Sometimes we don't act strong because we are strong and sometimes we are only strong because we act. Alex raised her hands over her head and spread her palms up-ward as if to receive grace. She let go and suddenly proclaimed in a heroic voice, "The law is love and my love is poured upon the earth."[1] She repeated it, "the law is love and my love is poured upon the earth, the law is love and my love is poured upon the earth…" she kept chanting it again and again and as she did so, a circulating light of golden energy running through her compelled them all to sing and dance her chant.

The chanting became infectious and took over all of them. *The law is love and my love is poured upon the earth…* Nathan, Yana, Moira and Diana were pulled into its rhythm and the words pulsated across their tongues. Night-Night's tail jaunted back and forth with the tempo. Illumination beamed directly upward, slid down the rounded walls and puddled on the ground. The source of the light was utterly untenable and in any other context the vibrations caused from its intensity would be unbearable.

They weren't sure whether to stop chanting. They rode its wave.

A warm wind blew around the floor of the chamber and the candles began to flicker. Moira noticed the images carved into the stone wall and floor. They seemed to be breathing with the pulse of the room, almost vibrating. Like sheets of lightning inside their grooves, they burned with the appearance of hot embers and finally actually leapt from the stone.

The spiral peeled out of its etching and spun orange in the air. A circle dropped slowly from the center of the dome and bended with its new found dimension. It twisted and as it did so it could be seen at different angles. Stretched across the dimension of time, the circle forms the spiral; stretched across the realm of consciousness, the spiral becomes the double helix. The double helix expanded and contracted in a multi-dimensional dance and became a circle again. The sacred symbols burned with life.

We should do the next part of the ritual, Diana thought to herself. Diana stopped –referencing the written packet she had prepared and simply proceeded intuitively. Yana had become quiet. Yana was smiling inwardly to herself and her eyes were shut. She had floated somewhere into the beyond though remained a serene conduit. Diana assessed the others. Nathan remained steady; eyes open, mesmerized by the organic shapes twisting in front of him. Moira was particularly alert and exchanged a glance and nod of communication to Diana.

Also acting upon her intuition, Moira stepped forward out of the circle, carefully reconnecting Yana's hand, in the west, with Nathan's who took over in the north as Moira proceeded. She ceremoniously took the ring from Nathan's hand and turned again to the center of the altar.

Night-Night encouraged Moira with a "Meow," but thought to herself, *finally!* Her sleek feline body was pure grace and liquidity as she rose up on her haunches. *Do this right,* she warned her human companions through her thoughts. Night-Night took a final swagger around the altar's circumference to direct Moira's attention to its center.

Moira approached with the stone ring enshrined in both of her hands as though she was protecting it. She came up to where Night-Night stood waiting. The spiral carving on the inside of the basin remained fixed in the stone surface. The spiral's center ended with the image of the Baubo, whose pregnant belly housed a round indentation the same size and shape as the ring. Night-Night quietly retreated to the circle's edge as everyone watched. No one was breathing.

Turning and adjusting the ring in the air to see how it should fit, like in a child's game, Moira said out loud, "It has to be placed just so." She looked back to Night-Night now standing in her place in the circle. She was happy and smiled back to her.

Moira's fingertips searched the etched surface of the stone, feeling as though she was living out a far distant memory. She found the sacred symbols for earth, air, fire and water scripted in ancient imagery on the ring's underside. Crouching down to the floor, she turned it until it fit perfectly around the belly of the wild goddess, signifying that we all come from within her, reminding priestesses throughout the centuries that we are thoroughly connected to this earth, and to each other. We are all siblings. She aligned the ring and slowly dropped it into its space.

As contact was made, the orbs turned to a brilliant ultra-violet glare and a final ring of white light blasted forth from the center of the altar. The power of the ring of Baubo flashed a luminous shockwave that shot out from that one tiny point on the planet and in a brief instant cloaked the entire globe, and then everything in the chamber came to a dead stop. Nothing seemed to happen. Except for the candles, everything was dark.

But the earth was remembering. The ground shook as the spark of parthenogenesis traveled down the Earth's core, igniting the elements and reorienting molecular structures. Electrons not only leaped, but danced into their new orbits. Microcosm to macrocosm, life's DNA exploded in a blinding pulse of light. The ring of Baubo, the portable cosmic cervix spun in its cradle as the portal of life opened. Rebirth. Planetary healing could now begin.

The flow of love and trust continued to surge through everyone in the room. Moira stepped lightly back to her place in the circle. Hearts beating, everyone waited. Six hearts beat as one, rhythms conjoined. The chamber walls started to pulse again and acquired the same beat, creating a harmony. The floor also started to move in a kind of breathing fashion, in and out like the lungs of the earth. Next, the mounds rekindled a pinkish light but transitioned to a rich kaleidoscope of plum and dusty rose. Now it was no longer just their own hearts beating, but the rhythm of the cosmic pulse surged around them.

Bah-boom, bah-boom, bah-boom!

The lights ebbed and flowed in harmony, engulfing the whole chamber in its stimulating reddish glow. The symbols and carvings on the walls resumed their vibrations and again shook themselves free from their station, lifting and rising and turning themselves in the air. The chamber became a living hologram spinning and orbiting around them. The two dimensional drawings of spirals and mountains and moons floated in three dimensional space transforming themselves into miniature universes and galaxies of swirling hurling double helixes, life's DNA, microcosms to macrocosms. Alex, Diana, Moira, Nathan and Yana stood transfixed as the universe danced its most creative dance.

Night-Night chanted, *good, good, good, good vibrations.*

Energies, images and elementals swirled around in the center of the space, creating a vortex as another kind of slow rumbling rose from the earthy floor. Diana felt this cosmic groan in the balls of her feet before she started to hear it. She could tell that the others felt it too. Still holding hands they started to feel this vibration rising, coming up through their heels and ankles, calves and shins. Their knees started trembling just a little bit as the sound moved up their thighs, pelvis, solar plexus, heart, throat, third eye, and before erupting through the crown of their heads the universe stopped to give them a little tickle at the back of their necks and then blasted out, OHHHHHHHHMMMMMMM!

Diana smiled. The sound mirrored the ancient Sanskrit word "OM." When properly chanted with the right breath and tonal quality the word was said to take on the sacred sound of the creation of the universe.

OHHHHHHHHMMMMMMMM! The earth bellowed again. *Of course*, Diana thought to herself and smiled, *the breath that blasts!*

OHHHHMMMMM…, for the third time. The plum lights throbbed in tempo with the resonating …mmm…

The ground rumbled and shook. A loud explosive sound rang out from somewhere above Nathan's head. It was different from the other noises. It wasn't a cosmic crash of lightning or a spontaneous combustion of energy. This sound did not involve a quantum leap of consciousness. It was simply the sound of instability, operating on the frequency of linear, single minded physics and gravity.

"What was that? Did you hear that?" Nathan shouted with mortal concern over the still throbbing astral concert. Gravel started raining down from the ceiling. Alex's eyes opened slowly, Moira and Diana exchanged glances.

"I did," Yana replied with a concerned tone in her voice.

A rift appeared in the wall behind Alex and like an hour glass, sand spilled out of it. Yana shouted a warning, "Look, there's a crack!"

It splintered across the smooth stone surface like an egg shell. Growing larger as they watched, each line split and extended long lanky fingers of frailty in the membrane that supported the city above them.

"It's time to go, now!" Alex broke her grip in the circle, scooped up Night-Night and led the way, "come on!" The sound of falling rocks could be heard outside the chamber door. There wasn't much time to get out of there.

Diana took her cue from Night-Night who looked, for the first time, perfectly content at being swept away in Alex's arms. Diana grabbed her sack and the most precious of her ritual tools. Nathan and Yana didn't hesitate either. Still holding hands, they followed right behind Diana. While they ducked and climbed through the passageway, no one noticed Moira carefully remove the Ring of Baubo and stowed it in her pocket. She also grabbed her notes and files but the gravel was pouring down around her and the sounds of mountains moving burned in her ears.

The group heard the echo of a familiar voice in the hallway scream, "No!!! Aaah!"

"Richard?" they all realized in horror, in unison.

A large boulder crashed to the ground, barely skimming Moira's left ankle.

"Moira!" Yana cried, looking behind her at the sound. But Moira was already moving and making her way through the passageway.

"The Ring!" Nathan suddenly gasped in recollection, "Moira, you have to grab the Ring! Can you reach it?" He didn't know that she already rescued it and she wasn't sure that she wanted him to know, she still needed it. *It is supposed to happen this way*, she argued to herself, realizing that this was part of the transformation.

She looked him square in the eyes as she stooped through the low stone opening, the earth shifting all around them. Nathan moved to re-enter the chamber, but Moira blocked him and Yana grabbed his arm. His heart pounded and his entire body flexed.

"It isn't safe," Yana pleaded, "Come on, let's go!" The echo was not as intense as it was in the chamber but the earth was still howling. There was no way to know whether the chamber, the tunnel or the entire underground was going to cave in at any moment.

More rocks were heard crashing inside the mysterious domed chamber behind them. A secret, Nathan feared, would be lost forever. Reluctantly, he complied and they ran after Alex, Diana and Night-Night, who were looking for signs of Richard as they headed back toward the surface.

Running up ahead through the tunnel, Alex had stopped abruptly. She saw a pile of rubble and boulders and recognized the broken figure beneath the weight as Richard, crushed like a paper tiger. She cried out and wanted to be sick.

Oh God, she thought, as Diana grabbed her arm.

"Alex, there's nothing we can do, we have to go!"

"We can't just leave him," Alex heard herself say in a state of shock and horror.

Nathan, Moira and Yana came up behind them and at first didn't fully register what they were seeing. Nathan bent down next to the mangled body.

"Richard," he whispered, scraping away the nasty debris to feel for a pulse as the world changed all around them.

"What has he done?" Yana gasped.

"He finally destroyed himself," Moira replied.

Night-Night squirmed her way out of Alex's arms, leaping with a soft meow, onto the still shifting ground and resumed her ascent.

"We have to get out of here Alex, we can't move him," Nathan persuaded, "we'll call for help."

"I can't just leave him!" Alex stood transfixed. She couldn't move, she couldn't leave him, but with the next rumblings and the tunnel collapsing behind her, she realized that her life was in danger.

The earth shook again with the roar of Mother Nature reclaiming her underground. The deafening sound engulfed them. Lights far down the tunnel sparked and flashed and shorted out as a wall of water invaded the hollowed space. The guttural gushing was instantly recognizable; the tunnels were flooding. She knew at least that she wanted to live. They had to keep moving, and fast, up towards the light.

Alex caught up with Diana and Nathan, completely out of breath, just outside the mouth of the tunnel. The chain link catwalk that takes them back to the entrance and the security gate, was the highest structure built above the massive crater that had been dug out to serve as the staging area for the Big Dig. The water was rising up around them, slowly, but only because the basin was so wide. The catwalk shook from the force of the water's torrent as Alex took a wearied glanced back to see the entrance submerged… along with Richard.

* * * *

All throughout the night emergency management workers stacked sand bags against steel girders and tried to construct a stronghold to fend off the flooding in the Big Dig tunnels, but the ocean ultimately won out and settled quite naturally into her new territory. Cars would never pass through here, to be sure. And meanwhile, strange noises identified as whale songs were reported throughout the greater Boston area from Cape Cod as far north as Portsmouth. Nature kept vigil and high in the night sky Orion kept count of the orbits while the earth took a moment to adjust Herself.

[1] WINIFRED MILIUS LUBELL, THE METAMORPHOSIS OF BAUBO; MYTHS OF WOMAN'S SEXUAL ENERGY 11 (Vanderbilt University Press 1994).

[1] Doreen Valiente, "The Charge of the Goddess," *in* THE SPIRAL DANCE: A REBIRTH OF THE ANCIENT RELIGION OF THE GREAT GODDESS 90 (Starhawk, 10th Anniversary ed., Harper and Row, 1989).

Chapter Eight
THE ARCHAIC FUTURE

A subtle change in rhythm is all it takes. In the beginning there was desire, but men did not know how to control it. So they organized themselves into militant bands of "true believers" and made war on the body, on the impulses of life, on nature, on women, on other men, and on anything else they desired. But do we not all desire growth? Desire in its highest and purest form is lust for life. After all, what do plants lust after but sun, soil and rain? Is that evil? Lust is biophilia.

An evolutionary spark was set in motion by the harried ritual that occurred that last night and nearby heart chakras were opening. But just like the flash that erupts spontaneously to propel photosynthesis, parthenogenesis, and quantum leaping, it was almost imperceptible and hadn't yet begun to manifest collectively. Happy were those who slumbered, for they shared a dream, although few discussed it. It was a universal, archetypal dream; a living myth illustrating the way this new rhythm could set a new paradigm, tempo, choices, habits, and health ~ the Ayurvedics know this best, as did Night-Night.

The first greatest lesson to learn is that energy is contagious. This is a primary principle to learn from, and for, magic. Cycles of oppression lead to more oppressive cycles. Violence begets violence. Fear creates fear. But those who are pure of heart need only to step aside, to withdraw the power of their energy from such harmful cycles, to avoid its destructive wrath. We must also put new causes in motion, because joy generates joy and laughter is contagious. It is a subtle and obvious mystery indeed, and fit for a goddess! A subtle change in rhythm is all it takes.

* * * *

"Give me the beat, boys, and free my soul, I wanna get lost in your rock and roll..." Yana had been up all night, still surging from the sensations released in the ritual. She was plugged in, singing and dancing in the semi-privacy of her third story apartment in Boston's North End. Her building was equipped with paper thin walls and, unfortunately, this gypsy couldn't carry a tune. But she could keep a beat, even if that beat echoed from centuries past.

The earth has spoken, she thought to herself knowing full well that it was time again to move on. The first card of the tarot deck lay face up on her nightstand, displaying the number zero; the number of the jester, the fool, the fool's journey, an adventurous quest, laughing in the face of reason.

It is not by wrath that one kills, but by laughter. Come, let us kill the spirit of gravity! Remembering the quote from Nietzsche, Yana winced at the unintended irony, given Richard's demise.

Ah, but nature has yet to show her full power, Yana continued, knowing that Richard's passing was a moral play in the dance of life. Anyway, Yana quickly shook the thought, embracing instead the levity of the chamber's opening. The flooding did stop after all just as it crested the top of the crater. It never reached street level. It seemed disaster had been averted; her work was done here.

"Yeah, I believe in a goddess who dances... now a goddess dances through me!" She knew she was going south, but she didn't know where nor did she care. The tarot actually told her very little of the journey itself. It had to be done again and again, as her grandmother foretold. The revolutions of the past are carried forward in every woman and Yana knew that it was her role to help usher in this new creative consciousness. *There will be another opening in the Earth, another rupture, another opportunity for planetary healing. It will happen quickly, but where?*

She wondered to herself. *Which continent, which country? Where, oh where will the goddess be?*

As she zipped up her bag and glanced around the shabby makings of her apartment, she knew she could easily walk away and leave everything. Like her ancestors before her, she would quite literally follow the stars. The gypsy in her was in the groove and on the move. Her body tingled with desire for life. She shut the door behind her as she set out on her way.

"Hoping that the train is on time sweet Mary,
Hoping that the train is on time…"
Trotty, trot to Boston,
Trotty trot, to Lynn,
Careful little pagans that you don't fall in!

Moira looked out over grey undulating surface of the Charles River as a taxi cab sped her towards Logan airport.

At first she was quite shaken over Richard and the collapse of the chamber, but she, like Diana, had assumed that Richard was there to destroy the chamber and believed karmic justice was at play. Either way she was once again finding herself propelled by ancient knowledge.

Clutching her knapsack she was only a little worried about customs, given that she would be traveling with a thousand year old scroll and an older stone artifact, but knew that the ancient prophecy must be fulfilled. The ring of Baubo had to be returned to Eleusis. This destructive cycle had to close.

The return of the goddess is coming; and she'll turn Plato's reversals upside down! Moira chuckled to herself and imagined herself growing wheat.

* * * *

"I don't know how I am going to explain all this to Sebastian," Nathan responded to Paul over the telephone. Then he noticed that a note had been tucked under his apartment door. No telling when it was put there. He hadn't gotten in from his grueling evening until well past the sunrise.

"Ah, Nathan," Paul said, sounding more relieved than concerned. "Do not worry about Sebastian. He will understand; I'll make sure of that. If it's gone there's nothing you can do about it. You did say the ring was destroyed for certain, didn't you? ...And the chamber as well?"

"In another few hours everyone can read about it in the morning paper." Nathan responded while struggling to rip open the fancy envelope, "The whole Big Dig flooded ...it was all very surreal. But yes, it's gone... the ring, the chamber, Richard..."

Nathan gasped when he read the note. In long sweeping letters Moira had written to him:

Nathan, I have the ring. I will protect it and return as soon as I can. Trust no one at Harvard. ~ Courage, M.

Then he cleared his throat, "Ahhm, excuse me." His heart was pounding loudly in his chest, but he knew to remain quiet.

"Well, at least you got out alive. It is regrettable about Richard, but things do have a way of working themselves out, don't you agree?" Paul asked rhetorically. "Harvard will take care of everything."

* * * *

When the mayor took his Sunday morning stroll through the Boston Commons, the sky was a deep beautiful blue and the geese congregating near the decorative fountain were peaceful. But he had disasters on his mind. The city almost flooded, the Big Dig sunk and he mourned the loss of his closest friend.

What was Richard doing down there if it was so unstable? According to Doherty, Boston experienced some kind of seismic activity that radiated all the way to Springfield. Similar shock waves resonated throughout various locations across the country. But the proximity to the eastern seaboard allowed for ocean seepage that none of the engineers could have predicted, or so they said. Miraculously, nothing on the surface was damaged.

As it turned out, the only bit of earth that actually seemed to move in Boston was one relatively tiny area, just over one hundred feet underneath the heart of the city: the chamber. Richard was there when it happened. The earth seemed to just swallow it up, as if in the mayor's world, the earth had foreclosed upon the Big Dig.

He sat down onto a bench to say a little prayer for his lost friend. Before continuing on his way toward city hall, he rubbed his cold face with his gloved hands, trying to understand the constantly spinning wheel of fortune that was his life.

Cold air stung the back of his throat. He was still alive. *Life persists,* he thought as if the bittersweet message had been whispered to him, and he slowly stood to go. As he did so, a nearby goose lifted his head from a downy slumber and yawned, turning an eye toward Marino. Their eyes met and they exchanged a moment of consciousness.

I think I'll add a green campaign to the city's agenda, Marino thought and as he turned to leave, would forever swear that this particular feathered creature gave him a little wink.

* * * *

Alex, like Nathan, was still awake after the previous night's drama. She eventually went home to *try* to sleep and insisted on being alone. Looking out over the city from her balcony windows in the silence of a new dawn, she thought it was anti-climactic for everything to still look the same.

It was not the same, of course. Cosmological and subterranean forces had shifted, frequencies had been altered. The earth traveled in a new orbit and was turning to a new rhythm. What Alex felt was the opening of her heart chakra and she wondered why she didn't notice the beauty of it all before now. *Has it always been this way?* She felt grateful to be alive. *...oh, Richard,* she sighed, shaking her head.

Her phone rang from the bedroom and she left her tea steeping on the edge of the railing, hurrying off to answer it in hopes that it was Diana. *Who else would call this early?* She picked up the phone and heard Diana's voice say: "Hey, I knew you'd be up. Hey, I am so sorry about Richard, I know you've always loved him. Are you doing any better?"

"Oh, I don't know... yes, I suppose so. I guess I never really knew him that well, did I? I am just glad that the rest of us made it out in one piece. Are you okay?"

"Well, I just got the strangest phone message from Moira. You have to hear it..."

"What does she say?" Then she realized better and said, "No, just hold on. I don't want to be alone any longer, I'll be right over." She left the tea. She had sensed this morning that she was still waiting for something else to happen, and intuited that this could be it. She threw on her coat, grabbed her scarf and some cash for another ride down Washington Street.

* * * *

Meanwhile, tectonic plates and geo-planes were starting to shift under the earth's surface. It could be like any other cold February morning in Boston, but it was not. The predicted storm had blown off course and instead headed out to sea, where it slowly petered out like an old rocking chair. There was less threat of fear in the streets today and a feeling of abundance everywhere. Of course these differences, though perceptible, would only impact one's internal reality as much as a person was willing to let it change their thinking. For this contingency, the earth had developed a backup plan.

As if preparing a new space, layers of dirt, rock, sea and sand, expanded and contracted, hollowing out an ancient ventricle. The earth was breathing a sigh of relief. The air was lighter, the sky was bluer, and pods of whales were seen leaving the Boston Harbor, singing a joyful chorus just off the coastline of North America.

Of the few who were beginning to notice the difference, two women and a cat sat acutely aware of the change as they shared some coffee in a brick Victorian row house.

Staring at a transcribed phone message Alex asked, "What does it mean?"

Diana responded, "I'm not sure."

Of course not! Thought Night-Night, *it's never just one step, two step. It's three, four, five, six, seven, eight… nine lives. Nine beats! The circle is never finished. Life goes on and on. As the wheel turns, we are all coming awake. The goddess is coming awake!*

"Play it again." Alex suggested, hoping they had missed some other clue.

Diana hit the button on her phone and they heard the voice say: "Diana, this is Moira, I have to go. This is not over… actually, it's under! Ha, ha!! It is just the beginning. Night-Night knows the way. Follow the Signs!"

Night-Night flicked her tail and thought, *Cat-e-gorically speaking, the earth will have the last Word. In the meantime, keep dancing….and laugh!*

The Goddess is coming, blessed be!

---

* This re-telling of the Goddess myth is an adaptation of the re-telling told to us by Alexander Mulherin in 2008, emphasis ours.

¹ Many male scholars to this day still dispute that the Goddess artifacts painstakingly uncovered and documented by Gimbutas and many others, constitutes proof of the existence of matriarchal cultures. See, for instance users of Wikipedia quoting the *Encyclopaedia Britannica*

that matriarchy is merely a hypothetical social system,
http://en.wikipedia.org/wiki/Matriarchy .

[1] This meditative technique is named "The Crystal Countdown" in LAURIE CABOT WITH TOM COWAN, POWER OF THE WITCH: THE EARTH, THE MOON, AND THE MAGICAL PATH TO ENLIGHTENMENT 183-187 (Delacorte Press 1989).

[1] BARBARA G. WALKER, THE WOMAN'S DICTIONARY OF SYMBOLS AND SACRED OBJECTS (Harper San Francisco 1988).

[1] *Id.*, 347.

[1] *See* http://geo.org/qa.htm

[1] Mary Daly calls for "Hopping Hope;" hope which is not latent and passive, but active verb-bound hope that inspires difference through its inherent quantum conjuring of action into the Now. *See* MARY DALY, PURE LUST; ELEMENTAL FEMINIST PHILOSOPHY 308, 311-312 (HarperSanFrancisco 1984).

[1] WINIFRED MILIUS LUBELL, THE METAMORPHOSIS OF BAUBO; MYTHS OF WOMAN'S SEXUAL ENERGY 11 (Vanderbilt University Press 1994).

[1] Doreen Valiente, "The Charge of the Goddess," *in* THE SPIRAL DANCE: A REBIRTH OF THE ANCIENT RELIGION OF THE GREAT GODDESS 90 (Starhawk, 10th Anniversary ed., Harper and Row, 1989).

Acknowledgments

Undine Pawlowski: Start with one massive public works project, stir in a heaping cup of waste and corruption. Add a handful of frustrated commuters and blend briskly with Boston's blistery winter blizzards. Finish with a bottle or two of red wine and serve at a large round kitchen table.

These were the makings of Her Underground, born from humorous discussions around a kitchen table, with friends and family, all fellow victims of the "Big Dig". The conjuring and cajoling that we had on the topic, by fellow students and professors from a variety of fields, spread the gamut from changing road patterns to the history of religious and racial oppression in Boston, from the origins of our American legal system, to the socio-psychological impacts of grid locked government, from ancient philosophy and goddess mythology to epistemology, academia and quantum physics. We found reprieve and creative relief in the manuscript from the constant, with a lurking feeling that something else was going to happen, or perhaps spring forth from the Earth herself, all because of the "Big Dig".

Of course the story is fiction, but the myth is real. And myth is created by a collective thus a truly representative list of those deserving of my own deep and eternal grateful thanks in seeing that this book was completed.

That said, and without minimizing the gratitude, I extend special acknowledgment to those in Boston, Washington, D.C. and St. Augustine Beach who read, reviewed and critiqued. My sincere apologies to those who read the manuscript prematurely, I'm sure you know who you are.

Of course, an acknowledgment is not complete without recognizing the hard work of our agent, Emerantia, at Gilbert Literary Agency, and her staff, and everyone in our corner at Solstice! In close, I would like to acknowledge the contributions of my co-author Donna Giancola. Thank you for the broad strokes and support of this living vision. The early morning brain storming sessions were some of our many cherished times. People ask me, "how did you write a novel with another person?" While they go on to ask details about the technical methodology, who did what research or wrote which scenes, my first response is simply, "it was a lot of fun." In truth we both did a lot of work, but had tons of fun doing it!

* * * *

Dr. Donna M. Giancola is an associate professor of Philosophy and director of Religious Studies at Suffolk University in Boston. In addition to Her Underground, she has co-authored a book on World Ethics (Wadsworth) and has written numerous articles on comparative religion and philosophy, feminism and eco-feminism. She has lectured extensively in national and international forums from Boston and Hawaii to Oxford, England and India, and most recently, Bangkok, Thailand. In spite of her sunny disposition and attempts at being inspirational, she has been known to have an irreverent word or two to say. Currently, she divides her time between teaching in Boston and writing in St. Augustine Beach FL. Other projects she is conjuring include a Goddess Ritual Book and new novel. Lately, she has gotten her days and nights confused, insists that there is no road to hell, and that the earth is already in Heaven. Her sheepdog is asking for suggestions.

Oh where, oh where would we be without our literary agent! First and foremost, we would like to give our sincere gratitude to Emerantia Antonia Parnall-Gilbert from the Gilbert Literary Agency. Thank you Emerantia for believing in our project, for your clear vision, determination and enduring care. We are so grateful to the universe for you!

Of course, this book would not have been possible to write without the love and support of family and friends, psychics and astrologers, dogs and cats, alike. Hugs and salutations to the following people: To Sue Strobel who had the dubious honor of reading and editing our first, second, and every single subsequent draft. Thank you, Sue, for your encouragement, patience and invaluable insights. You are a good woman! Special thanks, to friends in the hood Barbara Coffey, Barbara Cook, Janice Ronan and all who laughed and shared the hope, Most especially, thanks, to Baubo, the resident sheepdog who along with being furry/fuzzy, soft and round is also a goddess in disguise.

To Suffolk University, colleagues, students and friends, the Philosophy department in particular and my chair, Greg Fried, for their constant and continued support of my creative endeavors. (We all pursue the truth in our way.) Thanks to my research assistant Katrina Cook for her competence, patience and support. To Mary Daly and Maureen Fennessey for having the courage to stand in the light. (Miss you both).

Finally, to the city of Boston. Cheers!!! Dg

Other Solstice Books that might be of

interest

THE SCALES OF SIX

Rosean Mile

On assignment collecting relics in Indonesia, independent curator Gail Weaver learns that an ephemeral plant sprouting prolifically on Sumatra can transform all hair types into gorgeous locks. Seizing an opportunity to make a fortune in the cosmetic market, Gail smuggles plant clippings into the US and sways her apprehensive sister Fran to help seek financing for a shampoo she's made with the Indonesian plant. But dreams of impending wealth are quelled by the shocking revelation of the shampoo's horrifying side effects.

Against a backdrop of career and money problems, shady competitors, legal challenges and romance, Fran, Gail and an exotic Indonesian scientist must race against biological, corporate and media forces to save Fran's boss, and a legion of young women whose quest for beauty is transforming them in ways they never imagined.

Testing human greed against forces of nature, *The Scales of Six* blends suspense, intrigue, and surreal circumstance to weave a new story about an old myth coming to life in the contemporary world.

BLOOM FOREVERMORE

E.B. Sullivan

A romantic mystery. Psychology professor Dr. Sonia Wyland seeks a change from her stale routine by vacationing in California. While shopping at a secondhand store, she acquires a diary written by a woman named Margaret. This journal leads Sonia to believe Margaret is in a dangerous liaison with a man who calls himself Alexander.

Detouring from her plans, Sonia attempts to rescue Margaret.

In this quest, Sonia discovers an intriguing man and quickly loses her heart.

AT WHAT PRICE?

P.A. Estelle

Katherine Gardner is awakened at 6:30 in the morning with a call from a strange woman who claims to have her granddaughter, Rio. This woman is calling the police if Katherine doesn't make arrangements for somebody to pick this little girl up.

Katherine is fifty-six years old woman and all alone, since her husband died over three years ago. Her life takes a dramatic turn when six-year old Rio comes to stay with her. Rio is a scared little girl whose life is filled with uncertainty and fear.

In her grandmother, Rio finds a safe haven and an unconditional love that she has never known in her six short years and Katherine has found a love to fill the void that has been absent for way too long. Unfortunately Katherine's daughter, who deserted Rio, has other ideas.

SCRAPS

Rosemary O'Brien

Angela has been trying to reunite her feuding grandmother and older sister all of her adult life. When Angela's 19-year-old unmarried sister Lisa announced she was pregnant, a stormy argument ensued between Lisa and their traditional Italian grandmother who had raised the two girls ever since their parents died tragically six years earlier. The rift lasted between them for over twenty years. To help mend the family she loves, Angela creates a scrapbook to be presented to her grandmother on her 85th birthday. Will it work?

It may only be a scrapbook, but it's a scrapbook of memories enjoyed, memories missed and the woman determined to piece the scraps together into a family.

DOWN A TUSCAN ALLEY

Laura Graham

A long relationship ends. At 48, house taken by the bank, Lorri has little money. What can she do? And where can she go? Gathering her meager savings and her two beloved cats, she escapes England for a new life in a remote Italian village, never imagining the intrigue, passion and adventure she will find.

Unable to speak Italian, she survives by letting her bedroom to English tourists. She sleeps in the sitting room; it's stifling on the floor, but earning €50 a night makes every flea-bitten moment worth it. When she meets Ronaldo, seven years younger than her, she embarks on a tempestuous love affair. But, having been raised in an institution with the priests since the age of three, nothing is easy for him and he is unaccustomed to love.

Meanwhile, a Quasimodo-like character is watching Lorri in the alleyway; anonymous letters arrive; there's a young rival for Ronaldo's affection; and Sherif, a mysterious man in a black suit, constantly follows her… And hovering in the background is Lionello, the undisputed "wise man", giving advice while enjoying the wonderful theater Lorri brings to his village.

Then disruptive friends arrive and create havoc: Maudie has given up sex and drink and become spiritual; Julian, a Glaswegian hairdresser with dreams of becoming an actor, brings Lorri face-to-face with her ex. A final choice has to be made.

IN THE NAME OF JOANNA

Jean Valli

A mystery about love, friendship and loyalty
Samantha was happy enough with her life in
Dublin. Now working in the manor house of Glendora -
where a woman named Joanna died a year before - she
finds herself torn between her romantic feelings for a man
who people around her seem to believe is a murderer and
her loyalties to those who have befriended her.

As she struggles to break the enigma that is Damon
Bartholomew, temptingly close but hidden beneath the
surface, something she can't quite perceive, shifts and
changes as a shocking discovery begins to emerge.

Her dilemmas and choices are forever changing as
secrets are discovered, and Samantha must play a waiting
game...as each, in their turn reveal their true natures.

The underlying questions are: Was Joanna
murdered? And can a woman, who has been conditioned to
love men who are bad for her, go so far as to knowingly fall
in love with a cold-blooded murderer? *It seems she can.*

As a determined wraith begins to slip back through
the cracks between this world and the next...one must
wonder, can the spirit avenge murder?

Is death really the final straw?

Samantha has always thought so...until now...but...
she has second thoughts

WHATEVER'S LEFT

Nikki Archer

Summer knows that her relationship with Chris is over—she's in her first year of college, and he's touring with his band. Ten years of friendship, and barely twelve hours of romance are gone. Forgotten.

Right.

The more Summer tries to move on, the more she's reminded of Chris. And she'd give just about anything to be the forgetful, instead of the forget-*ee*. Because Chris had no problem taking off without so much as a backwards glance.

As it turns out, one-night stands do an okay job of pushing away unwanted memories. But each new conquest makes her feel cheaper. Each 'improvement' takes her farther away from who she used to be.

Then she hears it; Chris's apology to her, verse after painful verse, playing on every radio station. His words bring everything back, and make her take a long, critical look at the life she's disappeared into. But is he still the same Chris who wrote the song for her? And even if he is, can she find her way back to being the girl he loved?

———————————————